Scout's Honor

Joanne Salemink

ISBN-13: 978-1983597916

ISBN-10: 1983597910

Cover design by Robyn Hepker, Benson-Hepker Designs

DEDICATION

For all the strong women I've learned from:
Mom, Eloise, my grandmothers,
Mrs. Bensmiller, Dean-o, and more.
Thank you.

CONTENTS

ACKNOWLEDGMENTS

Some days it took a village to write this book. I am grateful to the many people who let me bounce ideas off them, gave me advice, or let me know I wasn't as crazy as I thought. A huge amount of thanks go to Scott, Gabby, Max, and all my family and friends for their support, patience, understanding and tolerance.

Thank you to everyone who answered my unending questions and speculations about motorcycles, bars, music, pianos, band names, and much more. All the mistakes here are my own. Sometimes I had to fudge the facts to make the story work – after all, this is fiction, not a how-to manual.

I'm sure I'll forget someone, but here goes . . . this book would not have been possible without the help of: Kendra, Stacy, Karen, Elmer, Sharon, Tony, Shari, Jon, Jim, Lynn, Vicki, Scott, Mark, Rick, Michelle, Kim, Amy, Mike, Adam, the GRIT Gym Tribe, and many, many more.

Special thanks to The National Motorcycle Museum in Anamosa, Iowa, where I found inspiration among the hundreds of motorcycles on display – including a beautiful, black and white 1941 Indian Sport Scout.

1

The best part of being early for a lunch date is enjoying a drink by yourself in the restaurant lounge.

Pour yourself a cocktail at home alone before lunch and your friends stage an intervention. Order a cocktail while waiting for a lunch date at a restaurant and your friends split the two-for-one drink special with you.

I don't have much experience enjoying pre-lunch cocktails because I am almost never – make that *never* never – on time, let alone early. If it is unusual for me to be early, it is unheard of for Vanessa, my lunch companion, to be late. I was worried about her running behind, but I was not going to let her live this down.

Our roles were well established after 45 years of friendship. I run late, she is early. I'm flighty, she's organized. I think outside the box, she designed the box. But lately things were off a bit, and I didn't know what to do. Truth was, lately everything in my life seemed to be off a bit. I was in desperate need of a "Girls' Lunch" to set things right. Or to justify some day drinking.

While I waited for Vanessa, I enjoyed a glass of wine and the company of Billy, the handsome young bartender at Glen View Grille. We met when he did an internship for me in the public relations office at Pleasant Glen College, the creatively-named private, liberal arts college here in Pleasant Glen, Iowa.

"A glass of the house red, my good man. The cheaper the better." I settled in at the end of the bar where I could see the front door, while remaining partially hidden by an immense faux ficus.

"You don't mean that, Ms. Dubs. Let me upgrade you to our cheapest name brand, at least." Billy thought "Mrs. Westbrook" was "too stuffy" for me, and "Mrs. Double-you" was too awkward. Since "Julie" was too familiar, he settled for calling me "Ms. Dubs." He was charming, smart, and had a wicked sense of humor.

"I've worked very hard to cultivate my unsophisticated palate. I'd hate to ruin it now," I said. "You know, I can actually tell the red wines and the white wines apart just by looking at them."

Billy stopped studying the bottles lining the shelves behind the bar and turned to me, his mouth open in mock surprise.

"Oh, really?" His sarcasm was not lost on me. "I'm not sure it matters, anyway." He put a hand over his eyes and picked a bottle at random. "I think management refills all the fancy bottles with the same cheap, box stuff. It started right after Brad hooked up with that new business professor at PGC."

'PGC' was the shorthand most locals used to refer to the college. When they were being polite, that is.

"*This*. This right here is what I miss most about PGC. I am so out of the loop!" Actually, I wasn't surprised that the restaurant manager was dating Professor Anna Anderson. She had set her sights on him at the last faculty dinner I organized.

That was also the last dinner the school hosted. Anna said the events were not cost-effective and recommended eliminating them in a long list of budget-saving measures. The school's board of directors were so grateful that they created a new administrative position just for her – Director of

Strategic Vision. In a move I thought was neither strategic nor visionary, the board cut the lone public relations position and transferred those duties to the new department. Then they used the cost savings to pay Anna more than twice the salary of the part-time Public Relations Director they let go.

Which would be me.

Not that I was bitter.

"Ms. K running late today?" Billy's question caught me mid-sip. I nodded and swallowed, grimacing.

"This one's a little fruit forward and ashy, for my taste." I had no idea what that meant, but it made Billy smile.

"Nice try. It's the same one you ladies always have." Billy rearranged a few bottles while we talked. "It's not like Ms. K to be late."

Vanessa and I had developed a little routine, meeting for lunch every Thursday to solve the world's problems. Getting a handle on our own, middle-aged lives was proving to be difficult. It was much easier to think on a global scale.

Losing my job was only the tip of the iceberg for me. I had just turned my unemployment lemons into lemonade – imagining I'd have more free time to spend with my daughter – when she announced that she would be spending the summer in Chicago after finishing her first year at Northwestern University.

And lately my husband had been treating me like the hired help. But not the fun kind.

That left Vanessa as the only constant in my life. She was the one person I counted on to talk me down off the ledge of insanity. But lately she'd been acting distracted too, and I found myself staring into that great abyss alone.

"Have you checked your messages?" Billy asked.

"Pfft, of course I . . . ." Billy raised one eyebrow. I checked my messages. "Damn. How'd I miss that?" Vanessa had texted to let me know that she was running late.

"Is your ringer on?"

"Pfft, of course my . . . ." There went that eyebrow again. I must have forgotten to turn the ringer back on after I stopped at the art museum. When I lost my job, I doubled down on my volunteer work, including event coordination at the museum. I was supposed to have had a mid-morning meeting with the museum director, but he'd ditched me because I was running late – as usual, his secretary pointed out.

To be fair, Vanessa had troubles of her own. Her husband, a business professor at the state university just up the road in River City, had abruptly left on an extended "sabbatical" which had all the town – except for Vanessa – talking.

Vanessa's text also asked me to let Billy pick the wine for us. Actually it said "*Dear God, PLEASE DON'T pick anything on your own.*"

"Vanessa says I'm supposed to pick out a lively, fresh varietal for us. Maybe a Pinot Merlot," I told Billy.

He snorted at this. "Yeah, right. I got you covered, Ms. Dubs. By the way, I'm putting in an appetizer order for you. You should never drink cheap wine on an empty stomach. You taught me that when you hired me to tend bar at those faculty dinners. I owe you one. I'm fairly certain my ability to mix a White Russian helped me pass German last semester."

"Yet another educational opportunity that the PGC students of tomorrow will miss out on, thanks to Ms. Anderson's keen eye for savings," I said.

On the upside, my unemployment and canceled meeting made me early for lunch and here I was enjoying a drink and the company of a charming young man.

"Uh-oh. Brooms incoming." Billy muttered under his breath. He rushed to the other end of the bar and busied himself at the blender.

"Why Julie Westbrook, what a surprise to see you here! Enjoying the wine and the . . . scenery?" Muffy Smith asked. Her voice dripped with innuendo.

The worst part of being early for a lunch date is getting caught by two of the town's most vicious gossips while you are enjoying a drink and the company of a young man in the restaurant lounge.

Muffy and her shadow and co-conspirator Bunny Jones stood on either side of me, smiling sweetly and insincerely. Muffy and Bunny weren't their real names, of course, but they had renamed themselves during a particularly virulent Preppy phase in the early 1980s, and the names had stuck. Apparently Mephistopheles and Beelzebub were deemed inappropriate for use in a public school. Once the mean girls of Pleasant Glen High School, now they were the mean girls of Pleasant Glen Ladies Auxiliary. Graduation from one lead almost inevitably to membership in the other.

"Hi girls. I'm just waiting for Vanessa." I wasn't sure they heard me. They were both openly leering at Billy. Really? He was young enough to be either woman's son. Or mine, for that matter.

"Oh yes. Poor, dear Vanessa," Bunny said. Her eyes never left Billy's backside.

Come to think of it, Billy was much younger than two of Bunny's sons! She and her husband Larry had welcomed a 10-pound "premie" eight months after they eloped on the eve of our high school graduation. Or nine months after our Senior Prom. However you wanted to count it.

"How is dear Vanessa holding up? How long has her husband been away now? Five months? Six?" Muffy asked. When Billy showed no signs of ripping off his shirt, she reluctantly turned her attention to me.

I didn't give a rat's ass about the timing of the baby's arrival. It was the hypocrisy that drove me crazy. Muffy and Bunny had systematically destroyed the reputation of every girl at PGHS who stepped outside their narrow view of acceptable social norms. Vanessa and I had both been targets of their mudslinging several times. Vanessa had learned to sling back with pinpoint accuracy. My mother taught me to diffuse conflict with humor and a smile.

"I just don't know what I would do if my dear Jeff was gone so long on a business trip," Muffy said, making air quotes at the word "business."

What Vanessa would have said: "I bet Jeff would like to give you the opportunity to find out."

What I said: "Oh, I imagine she's doing the usual home alone stuff. Ben & Jerry's straight out of the carton. Binge-watching Netflix. Not shaving her legs."

Muffy's eyes lit up. "So she's gained a lot of weight?"

"Really let herself go?" Bunny chimed in, smiling broadly.

Unfortunately, sarcasm *was* lost on these two.

"No! No, I was just kidding! She's the same impeccably-dressed, bean pole she's always been." Both women crossed their arms over their chest, frowned and slouched in disappointment, like spoiled toddlers.

"In fact, they call, email, text and Skype every night. Just like newlyweds," I added. I had no idea when Vanessa last talked to her husband because, unfortunately, it was none of my business. It certainly wasn't Muffy's or Bunny's business, either. Of course, that just made all of us more curious. I knew Vanessa would tell me if anything was wrong. Probably.

"And what about your dear Gary? He travels overnight quite a bit, doesn't he?" Muffy asked, probing for another weak spot.

That's the problem with Pleasant Glen. You know everyone's business. And they know yours. Sometimes even before you do.

"Oh, not as often as some," I said. Bunny glared at me, and I remembered hearing that her husband didn't spend many nights at home whether he was traveling or not. I certainly didn't blame him.

I wasn't used to fighting back, and my unintentional counterattack left me feeling guilty rather than gleeful. I tried to steer the conversation to a neutral topic.

"I'm sure Michael will be back for the Auxiliary Gala." That God-awful snooze fest was the Auxiliary's big to-do for the year, and raised funds for various worthy projects. It gave the community's movers and shakers an excuse to buy new dress-up clothes, dust off their company manners, and to see and be seen. Vanessa and I had been trying to breath new life into the Gala for many years and had finally been named committee chairwomen. I suspected it was a ploy to punish us for questioning the status quo, rather than to reward us for our creativity.

Last year Larry and Jeff – Bunny and Muffy's husbands – had both gotten so drunk at the Gala that they propositioned a couple of female lounge singers. Unfortunately those singers were the town's extremely heterosexual mayor and a state representative, performing in drag. Still more unfortunately – depending on your point of view – no punches were thrown and no charges were pressed.

Now both women looked mad enough to spit.

This? This is why I preferred to nod and smile while Vanessa delivered the verbal attacks.

Billy returned carrying two jumbo margaritas in fish-bowl sized glasses before the women could decide if I was being a bitch or if I was just clueless. "The usual, ladies?" he said.

Bunny and Muffy exchanged a guilty look. These were some seriously big-ass, two-handed glasses. I picked up my dainty wine glass and took a genteel sip. Like I said, Billy had a wicked sense of humor. And impeccable timing.

Before I could make another inadvertently cutting comment a waitress arrived to usher the women to their table.

"Thank you, Billy. I owe you one," I said as he topped off my wine glass from a bottle he pulled out from below the bar.

"The good stuff." Billy gave me a wink. "Or at least the better stuff. Don't thank me. I'd back a tanker-truck of margaritas up next to their table if I thought it would keep them away from me. They make me feel like I have a price tag on my forehead."

"I don't think it was your forehead they were looking at," I said, wiggling my eyebrows suggestively.

"Ms. Dubs! I am appalled!" Billy tried to act shocked, but laughed. He turned away, then looked at me over his shoulder. "Do these pants make my butt look big?"

I shook my head and drank my wine. Vanessa had better get here soon, or I would fall off my bar stool. That would certainly give Muffy and Bunny something to talk about.

Of course, I could just quit drinking.

Pfft. They were going to make up whatever they wanted to about me anyway. I might as well enjoy myself.

2

Billy brought me a glass of ice water along with a spinach and artichoke dip appetizer. I smiled brightly and held up my empty wine glass, but he shook his head.

"Wait till Ms. K gets here," he said. I gave him my best pouty face, sticking my bottom lip out and opening my brown eyes wide. I even added the eyelash flutter. Billy finally relented, after switching to the smallest wine glass he could find.

"This is for appearances only. We don't want anyone thinking I've cut you off. Although, if Ms. K doesn't get here quick, I'm calling you a cab. Then I'm gonna kick her ass. Who does she think she is, standing you up, welching on a date . . . ."

"I'm fairly certain that phrase is politically incorrect, and not being used in the proper context." Billy silenced me with a glare.

He pointed at the appetizer. "Eat. Now." Then he smiled and rolled his eyes.

While I continued to wait, a few people I knew stuck their head around the ficus to see if it was safe for them to sneak an early-afternoon drink, or to gather ammunition for the local rumor mill. I smiled and waved, but no one stopped to chat long. I meet a lot of people through clubs and volunteering, but I'm too shy to make friends easily. My family moved to Pleasant Glen when I started kindergarten and the insiders – those who were born in PG – still treated me like an outsider. The outsiders assumed I was an insider and avoided me.

Pleasant Glen has big city aspirations, with small town charm and mindset. The population hovers around 9,000, depending on which manufacturers the city government lures in with tax incentives. The college provides a semi-stable source of jobs and a seasonal influx of students. As the county seat, Pleasant Glen draws in customers and workers from the smaller, surrounding towns.

In turn, we are a bedroom community for River City, the state's fifth-largest city. Less than an hour away, "The City" offers employment and shopping opportunities that fled PG when the state highway bypassed the quaint, but now nearly deserted, downtown.

I had finished the appetizer and was rationing my wine when my phone buzzed. Vanessa's text said she would be there in 10 minutes. She repeated her earlier request to let Billy handle the wine selection.

"Vanessa says she's on her way and you should let me have more wine," I said, holding up my phone as evidence. I put it away before Billy had time to read the text.

"A) She'd better be, and B) I doubt it, but I will anyway. The wicked witches just ordered their third Gargantu-rita. I'll probably have to call their husbands to come get them again. Maybe another glass of wine will make you too mellow to start a fight. No offense, Ms. Dubs, but you have an uncanny way of setting them off."

"No offense taken, Billy, as long as your apology includes a glass of wine."

Billy sighed, but poured me another miniature glass of wine.

"Good God, please tell me you didn't let her pick that!" Vanessa had finally arrived, later than our original time, but earlier than her 10-minute warning. Only she could manage to be early even when she was late.

"You know me better than that, Ms. K.," Billy said, pouring my friend a full, regular-sized glass of wine."You would have been proud. Ms. Dubs shot down Muffy and Bunny all by herself!"

"And she's been drinking wine without me this whole time, I'm sure," Vanessa said. "But she hasn't fallen off her bar stool yet! My little girl is growing up so fast!"

"OK you two, I'm right here and I'm not as think as you drunk I am," I said.

"Really Jules, this is a big day. Let us enjoy it," Vanessa said, lifting her glass to salute Billy.

Maybe it was the wine talking, but I felt proud of myself, too. The last six-months had been rough, and my self-esteem was at an all-time low. I would claim whatever little victories I could.

After Billy had taken our food orders and refilled Vanessa's wine glass – I was strictly ice water now – Vanessa and I settled in at the booth nearest the bar.

"So, what crisis du jour has you running late?" I asked.

Vanessa dismissed the topic with a wave of her hand.

"The usual late-spring crazies. Ass-kissing lawyers with urgent paperwork. Lawyers with urgent paperwork who can kiss my ass. Yadda, yadda, yadda." Vanessa answered without actually answering. She would have made a great lawyer herself.

In fact, she had been on her way to becoming a lawyer herself when she married Michael Kolkwitz, one of her grad teachers at State U. Bewitched by the power suits we saw on *LA Law* when we were undergrads at PGC, she decided to turn her business degree into a law degree. It only took me a year to lose interest in upgrading my BA to a Master's in public relations. Vanessa slogged through another semester before she dropped out.

We all thought she was crazy, quitting when she did. Her parents nearly disowned her. She wouldn't discuss it, and eventually we gave up trying. To this day she refuses to watch *Legally Blonde*. For a while she worked as a paralegal at a local law firm. Then she took an office job at the county hospital here in Pleasant Glen, hoping the lower stress level would help her efforts to become pregnant. It didn't.

———Her job description at the hospital changed so frequently it was hard for me to keep track of exactly what she did. Lately she had mentioned lawyers several times, which was new. Still, with more government regulations popping up daily, I didn't press for details and she didn't offer any.

Muffy and Bunny weaved their way past our table toward the door.

"Helllllloooo Vanessadarling," Muffy slurred, stopping momentarily. "How's darling *Michel* doing?" Using her limited, high-school French skills, she pronounced his name 'Mee-shell.' Muffy worked the Lancome counter at a department store one summer, and she still thinks she's *tres* cosmopolitan.

"He's doing just fine, thanks for asking. Seen darling Jeffrey lately?" Vanessa replied. "I'm in charge of entertainment for the Gala, and I want to get his opinion of a couple singers."

Muffy's face turned bright red. Bunny giggled but stopped abruptly when Muffy glared at her. Muffy stuck her nose in the air, grabbed Bunny's elbow and pulled her out of the restaurant.

"See you at the banquet," Vanessa called after them. She turned to me and shrugged. "I couldn't let you have all the fun."

After the waitress brought us our lunches, Vanessa got right down to business.

"With your new-found cojones, how can anything possibly be bothering you?" Vanessa took a long drink of wine and rolled it around her mouth while giving me the once over.

"How do you know anything is bothering me?" I picked at my "Garden Bonanza" salad, lusting after the pile of fries that accompanied Vanessa's jumbo "Bessie's Revenge" hamburger.

"Because you texted me at least 10 times yesterday to confirm this lunch."

"Well, there's that . . . ." Vanessa's exchange with Muffy and Bunny had been a little more sharp than usual. I decided to use my new-found cojones to ask Vanessa what was bothering her.

"Eh, we'll get there," I said. "How about you? Everything OK?"

"Eh." She shrugged and took another big drink of wine, then raised her nearly empty glass to signal Bill for a refill.

"'Eh' as in 'I'm lovin' life and farting rainbows,' or 'Eh' as in 'I'm finally ready to talk about what's bothering me'?" I asked.

"Tuck those cojones away there, Hot Stuff, or they'll be hanging from my trailer hitch."

"I am so not hearing this conversation," Billy said, setting a fresh glass of wine in front of Vanessa. Then he shielded his man parts with the serving tray and walked backwards to the bar. Vanessa and I both laughed.

"OK," I said. "I'll go first this time, but . . . well, you know you can talk to me about anything, right?"

"Just like you can talk to me about anything?" She sat back in the booth and arched an eyebrow. We had reached an impasse.

Best friends realize that there are some things even best friends don't tell each other. At least, not right away. We were close enough not to be hurt by that. At least, not much.

13

We both knew there are some secrets that are too painful to talk about. Secrets we don't even tell ourselves, because we don't want to believe them. I had been carrying around one of those secrets for a while now, and I decided it was time to share it with the only person I trusted not to judge me, not to dismiss my fears, not to try and sugar coat it.

I took a deep breath. "I think Gary is having an affair."

Vanessa crossed her arms over her chest and looked at me. I rushed ahead, babbling.

"Another affair. Maybe concurrent affairs. Is there a word for that? What's the plural of affair? Affair-I? Affair-E?"

Vanessa shook her head. "Jules, you know I love you, but this is crazy talk."

"No! I've had suspicions before, but this time it's different."

"Different how? Different as in you have proof?"

"Well, not like a signed confession, or an 8x10 glossy or anything."

"Listen to me, Julie. You need to snap out of it." She leaned her elbows on the table. "Gary. Loves. You. He's crazy about you. Why would he ever cheat on you?"

So much for not judging and not dismissing my fears. At least she didn't sugar coat it.

"But . . . the long hours . . . the special projects . . . " I said.

Vanessa continued to shake her head. "I introduced you two. Gary asked me to introduce you."

"He's *changed*, Vanessa. He acts like I . . . like I'm not even there."

"Whatever, Jules." She rolled her eyes and sat back.

There were other things, of course, but I was afraid talking about them would make them real.

"Let's look at this as a practical matter," she said. "What would Gary

14

do without you? Good God, the man can't even do his own laundry, can he?"

I snorted. That much was true. I wasn't sure he knew where the laundry room was.

Vanessa massaged her forehead with her finger tips, then rested her chin in her hands. "I"m sorry, Jules. It's all the lawyers and crap. I'm just so . . . tired." I wasn't sure I was buying her excuse, but it did explain her behavior. Sort of.

"Gary's not a bad guy, Jules. You know that." I smiled and nodded. No sense beating a dead horse. "What's this really all about? Have you been reading those women's magazines again?"

"No, well, yeah, there was one *Cosmo* quiz." Damn, she knew me well. I sighed. "It's just, these past six moths have been such crap. I miss my job at the college. Then there's the whole situation with Emily. I was looking forward to spending time with her."

Gary and I were thrilled when Emily decided to go to Northwestern. Gary was a proud alumnus, it was a great school, and it was close enough for an occasional weekend visit. Emily seemed excited when we were there for Homecoming last fall.

Then she started making excuses for not coming home, and said she was too busy to have us come visit her. Now she would be staying in Chicago for the summer, working with disadvantaged youth. It's hard to argue with something like that.

But I wanted to.

Vanessa reached across the table and put her hand over mine. "You know I love my goddaughter dearly and I would do anything in the world for her, but she's a teenager. It's in their nature to rebel."

"But . . . . "

"You can't take it personally, Jules."

I shook my head, unconvinced.

"And sometimes Emily can be a little shit," Vanessa said. She held her hand up to stop my protest. "I love her, but I can still call a shit a shit, when I need to. I'm sorry to be so blunt, honey. But really? Maybe you need to find a temp job just so you quit obsessing over these little things." Her phone buzzed. She checked the message and scowled.

"Or maybe . . . ." she said as she turned back to me, "maybe you're spread too thin, Little Miss Super Volunteer. You're not the only civic-minded person in town. Let someone else step up. Not me, of course, but . . . ." Her phone buzzed again. She ignored it. "You shouldn't have to do it all. The Gala, the art museum, and I know damn well you're still helping whatshername at the college with those happy horseshit 'Town and Gown' events."

The warm feeling from the wine was fading. Vanessa's abrasive attitude had sobered me up quickly.

"Speaking of happy horseshit . . . I don't suppose you'd like to go to a book reading at the college tonight?" I asked, although I already knew the answer. "Gary's working late, and I don't feel like sitting home alone." And I had promised Anna Anderson I'd help. I hoped to prove the college still needed me.

"I'm sorry honey. You know there's nothing I like more than a good root canal . . . I mean book reading at PGC. It's tempting, but I have a lot of paperwork to catch up on."

"Meet for drinks after?"

"I'm not sure your liver could handle that," she said, pointing at my water glass. "Mine either." She finished her wine with one big gulp, then grimaced. "But you should go, Jules. It sounds like you need a night out."

Vanessa's phone buzzed again. She pushed a few buttons angrily then tossed the phone into her purse. "I'm sorry hon, I have to bail. It's work. Things are crazy-nuts right now." She slipped a twenty under her plate and started to leave.

I shrugged and tried to look pitiful. It wasn't hard to do.

Vanessa sighed and sat down next to me in the booth.

"It will be OK Jules, I promise," she said softly. "Somehow. We'll get through this somehow." She looked me in the eye and held my gaze. "Right?"

That didn't sound like a rhetorical question. I wasn't sure if she was trying to comfort me, or to reassure herself. I decided to suck it up and be strong for the both of us.

"We always do, don't we?" I bumped her with my shoulder. When she didn't answer, I bumped her a little harder, nearly pushing her off the bench. She finally laughed and pushed me back.

"OK, then. It's settled. You go to your little dork-fest. Live it up. I'll think of you at what, seven O'boring?"

"Hmph. That's *nerd*-fest. And it starts at seven O'thirty boring, if you change your mind. These things can get pretty wild sometimes," I lied. "Who knows, maybe I'll pick up some gorgeous intellectual and we'll make hot-nerd, monkey love. "

Vanessa snorted at this, then became serious. "Just don't do anything you'll regret, Jules. I know Gary still loves you. He just . . . needs a reminder." I wished I was as sure as she was. "Either way, give me a call so I know you didn't die of boredom. Or too much hot-nerd, monkey love. *As if.*" Vanessa walked to the doorway, then peered back at me through the ficus and made a high-pitched "*eep-eep*" monkey noise.

After assuring Billy – several times – that I was sober enough to drive,

I headed home to sulk, lick my wounds and get ready for the nerd-fest. I mean, book reading.

There was a slight chance the program would be more exciting than most. *The Honey War: Taxes, Trees and the Iowa Territory* had been written by a PGC alumn, so there would be a packed house. Maybe.

Who was I kidding? These book readings were attended by a crowd of over 70-year-olds there for the free cookies, bespectacled academics there for the networking, and me there for . . . what was I there for? Enlightenment? A good time?

The cookies. Definitely.

Damn my sweet tooth.

3

A high-stakes euchre tournament at the Senior Center cut the book reading attendance in half. Even the author, who looked as if she may have been a witness to the 1839 land dispute, ducked out early to play a few hands.

The small turnout was a bad news/good news situation.

It was bad news because it meant the audience ran heavily to the intellectual and academic side. The atmosphere in the college's small auditorium was thick with the musk of inflated egos, tinged with the acrid smoke of name-dropping. Occasional drafts of tenure posturing stirred up an underlying *Eau de Desperation* exuded by junior faculty seeking crumbs of attention.

The good news was the small crowd meant less competition for refreshments. And the author had brought a gourmet cake with mousse filling. Still, I missed the senior citizens. You didn't want to get between them and the refreshment table, but they were entertaining . . . sometimes more so than the authors.

PGC Strategic Visionary – and Underhanded Job Stealer – Anna Anderson had inherited my event coordination duties along with all my other responsibilities. I was willing to chalk up this scheduling snafu to her inexperience. And her inability to read a community calendar. Really? Who schedules anything opposite a euchre tournament in Iowa?

Still, I could forgive her for that. Serving caffeinated coffee at seven p.m., on the other hand, was completely inexcusable.

I suspected she was trying to sabotage these popular, but not cost-effective events. The book readings were my baby. I had worked hard to promote and schedule them when I worked at PGC. I'd be damned if I'd let her throw them out with the budget-balancing bath water.

That evening's reading was insightful and entertaining. The book was well-researched and detailed.

Oh, who was I trying to fool? "Insightful and detailed"? Those were code words I used in place of "ungodly dull and boring" when I wrote press releases.

One of the English professors nodded off. The biology prof was correcting papers. And the head of the music department was illegally downloading *Pitch Perfect* using the school's wifi. The only person who managed to look even mildly interested was the adjunct history professor. And that was probably because the author was his mother.

Anna seemed to be scheduling the most boring books available. Well! The joke would be on her at the next reading! Anna told me she hadn't read *Twin Gables: Sisters at Heart*, but that it was the "insightful and detailed story of the restoration of two of Pleasant Glen's oldest and most beautiful homes."

That was true, but the book also included details about the lives of the homes' original owners. During the extensive renovations, workers found diaries, scrapbooks and business ledgers in a hidden tunnel connecting the houses. The identical twin spinsters who built the homes were regarded as pillars of the community in 1860. The long-lost archives revealed them to be shrewd businesswomen who operated competing bordellos. They were also more than a little kinky. Even by today's standards.

The authors, distant relatives of the women, had given me an advance copy of the book after I helped them organize a post-restoration, joint open house. Their book reading was going to be standing room only. If it didn't get shut down for breaking obscenity laws.

Although I was no longer working for the college, I was still welcome to play hostess at these events . . . at least those hostess parts Anna thought were beneath her. I was willing to grovel and do whatever menial tasks it took to keep me on the PGC radar for re-hiring. Pride be damned.

My duties that night were to keep coffee cups filled, cake slices plated and napkins at the ready. As I gathered trash and cleaned coffee spills, I smiled and told all my former colleagues how much I was enjoying my new-found spare time. They listened and returned my smile, reassured that I wasn't about to go postal. Then they scuttled away to congratulate themselves on surviving the latest round of cuts. It hadn't been that long since I did the same.

Everyone seemed to believe I was content with my lot, especially those who knew Gary and couldn't understand why I wanted to work in the first place.

Everyone except for the head of the nursing department, that is. She took one look at me holding several half-eaten slices of cake – waste heading for the trash – and shook her head disapprovingly. I swear that woman has not an ounce of body fat and a mustache to rival Tom Selleck's at the height of his *Magnum P.I.* days. Before she left, she made a show of slipping me the pamphlet "10 Warning Signs of Suicidal Depression" tucked discretely inside the pamphlet "STDs and YOU: 10 Warning Signs for Today's Senior Citizens." I wasn't quite sure what to make of that. From our previous run-ins, I didn't think she had a sense of humor. I still wasn't sure.

After the reading everyone else went for drinks to counteract the caffeine, leaving me behind like Cinderella to clean up. But while all Cinderella got was a pair of ill-fitting but adorable glass slippers, I took home nearly a quarter sheet of gourmet cake.

I sat in the driveway wondering if my Prince Not-So-Charming was home. His Escalade was in the garage but the house was dark, except for a dim light I'd left on in the kitchen. It was only 9:30. I had drunk a couple cups of coffee at the reading to be sociable. I had sampled a piece – or two – of cake on the way home. The caffeine and sugar had me buzzing and I really didn't want to be sitting home alone. With or without Gary.

My mother would have said it was too late for a phone call. But she passed away before the advent of cell phones, 24-7 contact, and texting. I decided to risk disturbing her eternal rest and sent Vanessa a text.

Having fun! Wish you were here! Eeep-eeep! Tarzan is a naughty, naughty *boy!*

At least that would let her know I didn't die of boredom. If she replied I could see if she had changed her mind about a nightcap. And gloat about the cake.

I entered the kitchen through the garage door. The pendant light over the center island was glowing softly. A local artisan had made the blown-glass light shade for me after I arranged the opening for his show at the art gallery. It was almost the same beautiful blue-grey color as his eyes. He was talented and handsome and had flirted with me – *eeep-eeep*. As a married woman, I had ignored his advances. Still, I accepted the shade. I was married, not dead, after all.

I was so lost in my thoughts about the shade and the artist and the artist's eyes that it took me a moment to notice the empty wine bottle centered in the pendant's spotlight. It was the same merlot Vanessa and I favored for our impromptu "Wine and Whine" sessions. But we hadn't done that in months.

Gary scoffed at our modestly-priced taste in wine. A prudent, yet image-conscious financial adviser, Gary bought wine by the price tag. He impressed potential clients with his ability to spend money – and by extension to make money – as much he did with his good taste or the taste of the wine. He was all about image. Leaving an empty bottle of peoples-brand wine lying around the house was not part of that image.

Still, if he had brought a client home – a client he wasn't too concerned with impressing – he may have tried to pass this off as a better quality vintage. Knowing Gary, he probably tried to class it up by serving the wine from our antique, cut glass decanter. There were no dirty glasses on the table or in the sink. Then again, he would have left those for the help – that would be me – to pick up later.

I didn't really feel like more clean-up duty, so I turned off the kitchen light and made my way through the darkened formal living room to the foyer. I paused at the top of the stairs leading to the basement, or "lower level," as Gary insisted on calling it.

Typically the only light in the house at this time of night would be the weak glow of the TV in the family room downstairs. By now, Gary would be asleep in his recliner in front of the TV, snoring loud enough to wake the neighbors . . . two towns over.

But tonight there was no light. There was no snoring.

I listened closer and heard a rhythmic, muffled thumping. But it was coming from upstairs, where our bedroom was, not from the family room.

It took me a moment to process "rhythmic," "thumping" and "bedroom," because it had been so long since I had heard – or made – any sort of noise like that. But there it was, the unmistakable sound of a headboard hitting the wall.

It was one thing for me to suspect Gary of cheating at some flea-bag, rent-by-the-hour, no-tell mo-tel. It was quite another to find he had brought his floozy-of-the-month home.

This shit ends now, I thought, filling with righteous indignation. I did my best to stomp up the steps. *He's gone too far, damn it!*

But no matter how hard I stomped, the luxurious loop and pile carpet muffled my warning steps. I'd had a hell of a time picking out a style that wouldn't show wear and would look elegant on the exposed staircase, impressing potential clients. Damn. That was beside the point now.

I've never been able to sustain righteous indignation. It was completely counter-intuitive to my mother's mantra of forgive and forget. For all the times I told Vanessa I thought Gary might be cheating, I never really, 100 percent believed he was capable of such a thing. Even as I climbed the stairs, I thought the odds were more like, say 60/40. It was just the overactive imagination of a bored housewife who watched too much Lifetime TV.

Maybe he was doing jumping jacks. Clumsily.

But no.

Standing in the hall, I had no doubt what was happening on the other side of the bedroom door.

I wondered if this was the best time for a confrontation.

Then I heard Gary's breathing grow quicker and I realized the opportunity for catching him in flagrante delicto – or to call for an ambulance, because he was getting a little wheezy – was coming to a rapid end.

He was having sex.

With another woman.

In our bed.

Under the adorable duvet I risked life and limb – and may or may not have sucker punched a woman in cheap Jimmy Choo knock offs – to secure during the last semi-annual Macy's White Sale.

Focus!

My hand closed over the doorknob and I turned it slowly. The latch clicked free of the strike plate just as the random thoughts in my head clicked into place.

I hesitated, then eased the door open. A shaft of light fell across the bed.

Fell across Gary's sweaty face, eyes closed in concentration.

Fell across the familiar red waves of Vanessa's hair, spilling over my pillow.

She needs to take care of those split ends, I thought.

"Well, fuck." The words slipped out.

Then the irony of that statement hit me and I giggled.

"Literally. *Fuck.*"

What would my mother suggest I do in this situation? Shoot them? Serve them refreshments? Join the fun?

I took two steps into the room, stopping by the intertwined couple's shoulders.

"You were right, Van. Total dork-fest. But I brought home cake from PeeGee's Bakery."

I had no idea why I bothered to whisper. Vanessa's eyes had popped open the moment I entered the room. Gary was off in his happy place. I always wondered where he went – who he was with – in those moments. I didn't think it was me.

I liked to imagine he was . . . well, that didn't matter, did it?

"A . . . little . . . busy . . . here . . . Jules?" Vanessa's whispers were synchronized with Gary's thrusts. I watched the color drain from her face. She looked as if she would rather be anywhere than where she was at the moment.

I'd been there. Gary had that effect.

"Pffft. This won't take long. I'll wait."

I'll wait? What the hell was I thinking? What the hell was I doing?

Part of me wanted to scream and throw things. Part of me wished I could remember the combination to the gun safe.

Part of me was glad I *couldn't* remember the combination.

Part of me wanted to storm out of the room, slam the door, jump in my car, drive away and never look back.

Part of me wanted to collapse in a heap on the floor.

How could this be happening?

Instead, I walked to the foot of the bed, moved a pile of laundry off the exercise bike and sat down. I pedaled absentmindedly, staring blindly out through the window.

How was I supposed to react? Why couldn't I think? Why couldn't I breath?

Even when Gary treated me more like a casual acquaintance than a wife I never wanted to believe he was having an affair. I knew the truth would crush me.

This couldn't be happening.

To believe that Vanessa was involved? That would break my heart.

I couldn't believe it.

I noticed a shadowy reflection flickering on the window. The lumpy duvet was heaving faster.

I wouldn't believe it.

"*Oh,*" I whispered quietly.

"OH," he shouted loudly.

"*My*," whispered.

"MY," shouted.

"*god*."

"GOD!"

The thumping stopped.

I didn't believe it.

I knew from the rustling of the sheets and faded memories that Gary had nailed the dismount and would be leaning over to give Vanessa a quick kiss that would land somewhere in the general vicinity of her face.

"*Oh baby, you're the best*," I whispered.

"Oh baby, you're the . . . *greatest*," Gary said. I thought I detected a little irritation in in his voice. Maybe my whisper wasn't quite as whispery as I thought.

More rustling sheets as he rolled over. Then the deep, heavy, slow breathing of a man slipping into a coma.

"Gary," Vanessa hissed urgently. Coitus interruptus urgently.

"You're my best friend, but I'm not going to loan you my vibrator," I said out loud. I didn't bother to keep the bitterness out of my voice.

"Gary!" Vanessa said, not whispering this time. More rustling as she tried to shake him awake. Or to reclaim her rightful share of the blankets. Gary was a blanket pig. And a sprawler. Sleeping with him was a no-win situation.

"Forget it, Van. He'll be unconscious until at least two o'clock. Then he'll stumble to the bathroom, leave the door open while he pees, stumble back, steal the covers, squeeze your boobs and fall back asleep before you even realize your motor's turned over."

Gary snorted in his sleep then sprawled, throwing an arm over Vanessa. I suspected he was faking it. A lot of that happened in this bed. I'd deal with him later.

Kill them with kindness. I pressed forward the only way I knew how.

"You know what always hits the spot? Cake," I said.

"Jesus, Jules! *Enough with the fucking cake!* Bigger issues!" Apparently Gary's performance had left her unsatisfied *and* cranky.

"Well, it's not really *fucking* cake. It's more of a '*substitute for fucking*' cake." At least in my situation. "*Fucking* cake would just be a colossal waste of cake. Not to mention messy and ultimately, I have to think, unsatisfying in all possible ways."

Vanessa sighed.

"The peasants are starving," I whispered. "The proletariat are revolting."

Vanessa squeezed her eyes shut even tighter.

"Let them eat over-priced, gourmet cake," I whispered.

"Fine," Vanessa said. "Cake." She was grinding her teeth so hard it made my teeth hurt. I almost felt bad for her.

Almost.

"Maybe a shower first? A cold one?" I suggested helpfully.

"Whatever." She sighed again. "Just. . . just. . . ." I could sense her resolve was draining away. *Excellent.* I would twirl my mustache if I had one.

"Don't eat all the frosting and leave me with dry cake." She rallied, shoving Gary's arm off her.

Damn. She was tougher than I thought.

"Scout's honor," I said, heading for the door. I paused. "Any chance you brought more wine?"

"In my bag, by the table." She covered her face with her hands, rolled onto her side facing away from me and curled up in a tight little ball.

"And don't . . . drink out of the . . . bottle . . . ," she said between little gasps. Her breath caught in her throat. Her voice was muffled by the pillow.

"You know me better than that."

Her shoulders shook, but she was silent.

Drink out of the bottle? Heck, I was gonna lick it.

This couldn't be happening.

Joanne Salemink

4

By the time Vanessa finished her cold shower I had eaten another piece of cake. Served her right, bitch. Wasn't she listening when I complained about Gary's performance?

I had also eaten the frosting and filling from two more, large pieces. The crumb-filled plate of destruction sat on the table in front of me. I hid the rest of the cake in the oven. Vanessa had already had her cake in bed. She didn't get to eat the frosting too.

And I had drank nearly half the wine, straight from the bottle, back washing freely. My husband was sleeping with my best friend. I thought a little wallowing was in order.

I felt hurt. I felt betrayed. I felt . . . more than a little sick from eating all that frosting.

Or was that passive-aggressive bitch reflux?

Something about the whole situation felt wrong – besides the obvious, I mean. Something felt wrong in the "my Spidey sense is tingling" way. Gary had never even flirted with Vanessa before. The clerk down at the mini-mart? Sure. Vanessa? No.

And Vanessa was disgustingly, Olivia Newton-John in *Grease*-level, "Hopelessly Devoted" to Michael. We had gotten into a huge argument a few weeks earlier when I criticized Michael for being gone for so long. Vanessa didn't talk to me at all for three whole days after that. I apologized, and neither of us mentioned it again.

That didn't make me any less angry.

"Hey Jules," Vanessa called softly from the kitchen doorway.

"Vanessa." I continued to scrape traces of frosting off the plate. As long as there was sugar on my fork, I wouldn't throw it at her.

"Remember back in college when you walked in on Jimmy Valetti and me? Remember what he said?" Vanessa hadn't moved. Smart girl. She knew I couldn't accurately throw anything that far. And she'd always been a fast sprinter. Over a long distance I could probably run her down, but then what?

" 'A little busy, Jules.' Yeah, I recognized the line, *roomie*." Our dorm room was dark, there was a party raging down the hall, Van Halen was playing loudly. "But you two weren't fucking in my bed. I wasn't dating Jimmy. I sure as hell wasn't married to him! I didn't even like Jimmy." Much.

"Remember how horrible I felt?" Her voice was barely above a whisper.

"Well, you did drink half a bottle of Southern Comfort."

"No. Well, yeah." She sighed. "I mean, remember how bad I felt about you finding us like that? I knew you'd be disappointed." I didn't respond.

"But that's nothing compared to . . . ." Her voice was tight, the pitch rising. She swallowed and sniffed. "Besides, you drank the other half." Ah, that's why my memories were so sketchy.

"You couldn't have put a sock on the doorknob?"

"Jimmy didn't wear socks," she shrugged. "Very *Miami Vice*."

"And you didn't wear underpants. Very slutty."

Vanessa winced. But I wasn't backing down.

"Gary wears socks, Van. I know, because I'm his wife. I wash his fucking socks. I put them in the dryer, I match them up, I fold them and I put them in the goddam dresser for him. He wears. Socks."

I turned back to the table and let the silence between us grow uncomfortable before speaking again.

"I hate that."

"Doing his laundry?"

"No, that no-socks look for guys. Creeps me out. Guys ankles are just . . . eww." That caught Vanessa off guard. She eased onto the seat across from me, keeping an eye on my fork hand.

"You could have done so much better," I said quietly.

"Than Jimmy?"

"Than Gary."

"Jules . . . ."

"Or Jimmy." I interrupted her. "Or Michael." She shook her head at the mention of her absentee husband.

"You've always thought I was a good person. You always think I deserve better. But I'm not. I don't." She was starting to tear up now.

"You are. You do. I know. We've been best friends since . . . forever. We're like sisters. No, we *are* sisters. After my folks died, well . . . you're all the family I have, Van." Crap. Any other time that observation would have made me cry. Now it pissed me off.

Vanessa sniffed. She was a pretty crier. Always had been. That was another reason why I hated her almost as much as I loved her. Pretty criers get hugs and silken handkerchiefs. Ugly criers get odd looks and used, wadded up tissues. I, of course, am an ugly crier.

I pushed the basket of napkins closer to her and changed the subject.

"Jimmy was a putz."

Vanessa dabbed at her nose. To her credit, she didn't use her pretty crying as a weapon. She didn't cry often at all. When she did cry, the tears blossomed on the outside edges of her eyes in perfectly formed, glistening drops. They slipped to the chiseled edge of her impossibly high cheekbones and simply disappeared, carried off by little cherubs.

My face got all blotchy whenever I even *thought* about crying. Great buckets of tears gushed from my eyes and soaked the front of my shirt. My nose ran like a fire hydrant. A delicate sniff kept Vanessa's perky little nose from dripping.

She sniffed again now.

"What ever happened to him?" I asked.

"He married Suzy Carson. They had a passel of kids. He's a stay-at-home dad. I Facebook stalked him." She slid the cake plate in front of her and picked up a fork.

"I meant Michael," I said gently.

She poked her fork at the cake crumbs, searching for a trace of frosting.

"I guess I deserve this," she said, scooping up a chunk of plain, white cake. She chewed it thoughtfully, then reached for a wine glass and the bottle of wine. She paused and looked me directly in the eyes.

"You licked it, didn't you" she said, pointing the neck of the bottle at me.

"Yup."

She shrugged, lifted the bottle to her lips and took a big swig. She didn't even shudder at the floaters. "I guess the whole hot-nerd, monkey love thing didn't pan out?"

"Not so much." She was avoiding my question. She had been avoiding my questions about Michael for months now. Ever since the story about him collaborating with a researcher at another university began to wear thin.

34

"Then again, the new calc professor might have been winking at me. Or having a seizure. Hard to tell."

"I'm sorry, Jules," she said, staring at her cake.

"Eh. He wasn't that hot. And I'm not sure he speaks English. Which may have been kinda sexy in a 'You're better looking when you're not talking' kinda way."

"I meant about Gary." She still didn't look up.

"No you're not. You planned the whole thing. That's why you've been avoiding me. That's why you were late for lunch. That's why you wouldn't go to the book reading . . . well, no, I understood that one. But the wine bottle on the counter? The underwear in the glove box?"

"Yes, I am! Sorry, I mean. But no. I didn't plan anything. I'm not the planner. You are! I'm the doer!"

"HA! You sure as hell are!"

"No! Not like . . . oh shit!" Vanessa rubbed her temples, a sure sign she was agitated. "I was late for lunch because I'm busy! I have a job! Remember what that's like?"

I cringed. That one hurt.

"The book reading? Well, duh! Just shoot me and get it over with for Christ's sake! I forgot the wine bottle because I *wasn't planning* on sleeping with Gary. The underwear?" She looked confused. "What underwear?"

"Never mind." Let her wonder. I sure as hell did. And besides, I was still pissed about that job comment.

"I didn't plan any of this, Jules, really. I'm sorry. It just . . . ."

I glared at her. If she said 'it just happened,' I would launch myself across the table at her. She knew this.

We sat in silence. She picked at the quickly drying cake. I calculated the amount of calories in all the frosting I had eaten, and wondered how many miles it would take to run them off.

"Jesus, Van," I sighed. "What were you thinking? Why Gary?"

"He's not a bad guy, Jules."

"He *fucks* around. He *fucked* my best friend. That does not make him a *good* guy, Van."

"Well, when you put it that way . . . ."

"What way, Vanessa? *What way?* There is no other way. Unless . . . ." I smacked my forehead in an 'oh duh' move. "Unless we say my *best friend* fucked my husband. That *almost* clears him . . . ."

Vanessa twirled her fork. A blush spread across her cheeks. Was she about to cry ugly? Why didn't that make me feel any better?

"You are not the first woman he has cheated on me with." I leaned in over the table, poking it with my finger for emphasis. "You will not be the last. He is a cheating cheater. He is a cheating, lying, son-of-a-bitch." I collapsed back in my chair.

Vanessa's lower lip started to tremble.

"But you are my best friend and I can't help but think somehow he's taking advantage of you. Arrgh!" I grabbed my head with both hands. "Do you have any idea how close my head is to exploding?"

Her shoulders shook as she gasped for air in a classic ugly cry move. She was getting splotchy. Where was my camera when I needed it? I reached over and patted her hand.

"You really screwed the pooch this time, sweetie," I said, as kindly as I could. "What were you thinking?"

"I didn't mean for it to happen." Her voice wavered.

"Bullshit." I sat back in my chair and crossed my arms over my chest. Playing good cop and bad cop was exhausting. I wondered if all this back and forth counted as ab work.

"No, really! You're always going on about how you *think* he's cheating
. . . you have this *feeling* . . . like you're some kind of 'Midwest Medium,'
without the big hair or the nails. Why would he do that? I mean, you're
beautiful, you cook for him, you clean up after him. You do his laundry,
apparently. You can be charming . . . when you want to be. Sometimes
times I wish *I* was married to you."

"He's got me, why would he want any more drama in his life?"

"Then there was that."

More silence.

"He's my *husband*, Van."

"I . . . I didn't mean to hurt you. I didn't mean to sleep with him."

"It just happened."

"Yeah. It just happened." She winced, realizing what she had said.

That was my cue to go full-on, bat-shit crazy.

Instead I got quiet-crazy. Much more dangerous.

"Fuck that," I said in a whisper more ominous than any shout.

"No, really," Vanessa answered vehemently. "You *thought* he was
cheating on you."

"Again."

"Again. I wanted to confront him. You're *my* best friend too, you
know. I wanted to protect you. I left work early. I left piles of paperwork
and a ton of overtime pay for you, and I went to his office. I told him how
upset you were. I told him that he was pushing you away. That you thought
he was cheating."

I nodded.

"I told him he needed to get his shit straight, or you were going to
leave him."

I stopped nodding. She told him I'd *what?*

"I told him you'd leave him, and I'd help you."

She'd *what*?

"I told him I'd personally castrate him." Vanessa paused. "Now that I think of it, that might have affected his performance."

"You said you'd WHAT?"

"Well, it seemed like the thing to say at the time."

"At the time."

"Yeah, well. Like I said, I didn't *plan* on sleeping with . . . ."

"Fucking."

"Fucking him. Whatever. But then he asked . . . ."

"He asked how I could ever think he would cheat on me?"

"Well, not exactly." Vanessa squirmed in her chair.

"What exactly *did* he ask?"

"He asked me about Michael."

"He *what*?"

"He asked me about Michael. And today was . . . ." Giant, perfectly formed teardrops gathered at the edges of her eyes. She shook her head, but the teardrops stayed put. "That threw me for a loop. So I . . . ."

"You what?"

"I started crying."

"Of course." I rolled my eyes.

"Gary gave me his pocket square. I mean, Michael never even gave me an old, wadded up tissue."

"That's because you never need one, pretty crier."

"Of course I do. What are you talking about? I think I made Gary uncomfortable, because he suggested a drink might calm me down. We went to O'Hallorhans, that new brew pub by the mall? We had drinks – the crostini is to die for! I talked and he listened. Well, you know."

"No. I *don't* know. The only time he listens to me is when I tell him dinner is ready."

"See? That's the kind of thing you always say. But he *was* listening. Then I started thinking, well, maybe you were . . . imagining things. Maybe you were just . . . taking it all out on Gary."

This. This right here is why I ate all the frosting. Gary never took me to O'Hallorhans. He told me he hated crostini.

"So you slept with him because he listened to you."

"No. Well, yeah. But I mean, no. Not right then." Vanessa sighed.

"Go ahead. I'm *listening*, for Christ's sake. But I'm not gonna fuck you. Not *right now* anyway."

"Damn it, Jules, I . . . ."

"How many times have I asked you about Michael? Huh? *Huh*? And every time you'd change the subject. And I let you, because I figured you weren't ready to talk. I figured that since we were *best friends* you'd eventually open up to me. All I had to do was give you time, make sure you knew you could talk to me about anything. That I'd always be there to . . . what's that word? Oh yeah, *listen.* "

Vanessa started to tear up again.

"Because you know you can, right? Talk to me. About anything." I sighed, trying to calm down.

Vanessa closed her eyes and swallowed. Two perfect teardrops receded back into her eyelashes.

"Right now I'm listening to you explain how my husband's sleeping around doesn't make him a bad guy. I think I can handle whatever happened between you and Michael." She shook her head. Fine. More time.

"My beautiful duvet!" I had a stomach-churning flashback to the scene upstairs. "I'm gonna have to burn it! Damn it, Van, you know I've been banned from Macy's White Sales for a year."

Vanessa was unmoved. She didn't share my love of fine bed linens.

"What Gary and I did was wrong. And I'm sorry. I'm so . . . I'm so . . . ." She stopped talking as sob after sob ripped through her and she started to hyperventilate.

If we were in a movie, this would be when I slapped some sense into her. In fact, I had just raised my hand in eager anticipation, when she gave me a horrified look. She took a deep, calming breath, closed her eyes, pursed her lips and blew it out slowly, finding her center. Damn yoga classes. She found her bliss, but I was pretty sure I had missed an opportunity to find mine. Slapping her seemed like a much better way to release tension than five minutes of downward dog.

Vanessa squared her shoulders. When she opened her eyes they were still filled with tears, but there was a vacant, hard edge to them as well. She had conquered whatever caused her hysteria, but I could see it took all her effort to keep it contained.

"I'm so, *so* sorry about Gary." Her voice was quiet and even. "I don't know if you can ever forgive me. I don't know if you should. I promise I will do everything humanly possible to make it up to you. Somehow. But . . . ." Her control started to slip. One cleansing breath not only put it back in place, but made it stronger.

"I can't talk to you about Michael yet. Not tonight. You'll make excuses for me. That's not what I need. It's not that simple. I'll pay for the dry cleaning."

"You slept with my husband because Michael left you a dry cleaning bill?"

"What?" Vanessa tilted her head and squinted at me. "Your duvet. I'll have your stupid duvet dry cleaned. Crazy-ass bitch. And they were real

Jimmy Choos. The seller on eBay said so."

I tilted my head and squinted right back at her. "*Who's* the crazy-ass bitch, crazy-ass bitch? Like anyone would sell real Jimmy Choos for less than a hundred bucks."

The silences were getting less awkward. I wasn't sure I liked that, but I was tired of fighting.

"Tell me it was the first time," I said.

Vanessa sighed and rolled her eyes. "You know it was. You helped me set up my eBay account."

"Tell me tonight was the first time. You. Fucked. Gary."

"It was." She spoke softly, looking directly into my eyes.

"Tell me it will be the last time."

She narrowed her eyes and set her mouth in a hard line, but did not reply. I tried again.

"You wanted to prove that he wasn't cheating on me, and instead you ended up proving that he was."

"I didn't mean for that to happen."

"So. End. It."

Her nostrils flared. She continued to stare at me as she replied. "I can't explain. You wouldn't understand."

"No. You *won't* explain it, so I *can't* understand. Do you love him, Van? Because he doesn't love you. Gary doesn't love anyone except Gary."

"Do *you* love him, Jules?"

"No."

I didn't hesitate. I'm not sure which one of us was more surprised. I had stopped loving him a long time ago, but I hadn't realized it until that moment.

What I did love was being *Mrs.* Gary Westbrook. I loved being *married.*

Who would I be if I wasn't Mrs. Gary Westbrook anymore?

"Then what do you care who he sleeps with? He could be out screwing the whole town. What difference would it make?"

"He *has* been out screwing the whole town, Van. That's what I've been trying to tell you. *That's* why I *don't* love him.

"I'm tired of it, Van. I'm tired of the stray earrings, the perfume, the hang-up calls, the 'working late.' The god damn underwear in the god damn glove box . . . it's all so cliché! It's like he was following a script. And I was the biggest cliché of them all: the long-suffering wife. The wife who was too stupid to see what was going on under her own duvet.

"But he's *my* husband, Van. *My*. Husband." I sat up straight.

"And possession is nine-tenths of the law," Vanessa sneered.

"Something like that. *You wouldn't understand*," I threw her words back at her.

"You're right. And I bet you *can't explain it* right now, can you?"

Should have seen that one coming.

"No, I can't. And I won't."

The silence grew uncomfortable again.

"I think we're done discussing this for the night. You should go."

Vanessa looked at me like there was something more she wanted to say, then thought better of it and turned away. I stayed in my chair while she gathered her bag and headed for the back door. Where had she parked? How had I missed seeing her car?

She slipped her shoes on – a tasteful pair of authentic Sperry boat shoes. I had destroyed the Jimmy "Woos." She threw one more glance over her shoulder at me. Then she slowly turned the doorknob.

"I'll call you tomorrow," she said.

"Don't bother."

Her shoulders slumped.

The enormity of the situation sank in. I was loosing my best friend and my husband. My best friend was loosing *her* best friend and *her* husband too, apparently. And I was certain she was being used. Even when I won, I lost. What had she gotten herself in to this time?

"Wait until Monday," I said.

She sniffed, nodded, and walked out into the night.

Joanne Salemink

5

The next morning I was up early.

I suppose it would be more accurate to say I was *still* up, as I hadn't slept at all.

After Vanessa left, I sat on the couch in the downstairs family room. I was afraid I'd kill Gary if I went up to bed, and I just don't look good in orange. I don't care if it is the new black. I tried to sleep, but my mind was racing and my stomach was churning. I should know better than to eat cake late at night. Or to walk in on my husband screwing my best friend.

I was mad as hell, but after the initial shock wore off I reverted to my default mode of pacifist-martyr. I wondered if somehow this was all *my* fault. Had I pushed Gary away? Was I too clingy?

I needed my best friend to help me sort through my problems, or to help me sustain my anger.

My best friend was part of the problem. I would have to make my own decisions.

Most of the time, I avoid making decisions. I float through life, deferring to other people's wishes. I like to think that I'm flexible, but the truth is I don't want to disappoint anyone.

Gary, on the other hand, is an expert decision maker. He is logical and rational. He considers his options carefully. He is confident, without being arrogant.

I thought it was kinda sexy, really. At least at first. That was one of the things that fascinated me when we met. He seemed so buttoned-down, so stolid, so predictable. So unlike the other boys I had dated.

So unlike me.

"Make a list of the pros and cons, Jules." Gary would sigh and shake his head, while I dithered over another inconsequential decision. "Off White" or "Eggshell" paint in the living room?

Forgive Gary or kick his ass to the curb? Not quite the same, but I figured making a list couldn't hurt.

Gary's good points:

1. He doesn't kick puppies.

The end.

Ok, so maybe I was being a little hard on him.

2. He is a wonderful father. He dotes on Emily, but never shied away from correcting her. He went to countless ballgames, band and chorus concerts, and dance recitals, and he volunteered regularly in the school's concession stand.

3. He is good at his job and works hard. He puts in the extra effort, goes the extra mile.

4. He is a good provider. He never denied Emily or me anything we really needed, and went along with most of our "wants," too.

5. He is still a handsome man. I wish I wasn't so shallow, but there it is. Six feet two, and trim from regular workouts. His blond hair is graying evenly, adding to his air of trustworthiness. His startling blue eyes can still take my breath away.

No wonder Vanessa slept with him.

6. He keeps his word. To his clients and Emily anyway. And yet, this was the only time I was *certain* Gary had cheated on me.

Was that a good point or bad point?

Was that a reason to throw away twenty-five years of marriage? It may be old fashioned, but marriage means something to me. You marry someone, you stay married. Period. Richer, poorer, sickness, health, we'd been through all that. The rest? Well, nobody's perfect.

Stupid list.

I hate lists.

I hate making decisions that way. I hate logic.

Just throw a dart at a board, already! Take a chance!

What happened to spontaneity? What happened to passion, intensity and emotion? How long had it been since I felt those things? How long had it been since I felt . . . *anything*?

Fucking list.

Fucking logic.

Fucking tears.

BANG!

I jumped as the morning newspaper hit the glass storm door, startling me out of my funk. I willed my heart rate to slow, while listening to the delivery van splutter away. The muffler almost drowned out the Whitesnake playing on the tinny sounding car stereo.

Fucking 80's hair bands.

I had loved David Coverdale back then. Or maybe I just loved his hair. I bet Tawny Kitaen never found him in bed with another woman. Then again, I bet she knew exactly what to do if she did.

I realized my list-making was getting me nowhere. Gary would be up soon and I needed to be on top of my game. I needed coffee, and lots of it.

I went up to the kitchen to wait and to caffeinate. I brewed myself the last of the Jamaica Me Crazy coffee, the only flavor we both liked. Taking the last of the coffee – of anything – was something I never had done before.

Just for good measure, I hid the remaining single-serve pods of caffeinated coffee and made Gary a cup of decaf. It would be a hollow victory, because he usually stopped at Starbucks, despite being under doctor's orders to limit caffeine.

I knew this because I sometimes retreated to Starbucks myself, hoping to find inspiration far from my "Eggshell" drab home office.

Gary's morning routine was as predictable as everything else about him. At Starbucks, he would flirt with the sweet, young, attractive barista at the counter. She would bat her eyes at him and convince him to buy a pastry to go along with his Venti Carmel Soy-Milk Latte.

Meanwhile, the surly barista who was actually doing the work would roll her eyes and over-extract the shot, making his latte scalding hot and bitter. Then she would butcher the pronunciation of his name, which the sweet young thing had intentionally misspelled on the cup.

I know they do this to everybody, but *really*? The man's name is Gary. G. A. R. Y. Gah. Ree. It's not rocket science, people.

Ten dollars later – fifteen after tip if the server was particularly young and sweet – Gary would take a big drink and burn his mouth. He would sputter and spit, trying to maintain a facade of cool insouciance while lisping through what he thought was a witty pick up line. Inevitably she would smile demurely, and run through a list of obviously fake excuses.

I knew they were lies because I often saw the two barista chicks sitting almost on top of each other on a couch, sharing a coffee and licking frosting off each others' fingers during their break. Good for them! I hope Gary's tips bought them several bottles of cheap wine and quiet liaisons.

Gary had much better luck flirting with the women back at the office who hoped a good word from him would help them get a promotion. Then there were the wives of the men at the office, who hoped their charms could convince Gary to put in a good word for their husbands' promotions.

At least I had thought it was just flirting.

What woman wants to believe that she can't hold onto her husband? What woman wants to think that she's not enough for her husband? That she's not smart enough, pretty enough, young enough, sexy enough?

When you don't want to believe something, it's easy to pretend it doesn't exist.

Sure, over the years I'd found the occasional odd earring in his coat pocket or under the couch in his office. But I'd lost too many earrings myself – under perfectly innocent conditions – to believe anything untoward was going on.

As for the perfume on his jacket? I was highly sensitive to smells, couldn't stand to shop at those dark, aggressively trendy, teen stores in the mall. Working late? Gary had earned his key to the executive washroom the old fashioned way – by outworking, out schmoozing the competition.

Still, the lacy underwear in the glove box rattled me.

That was six months ago.

That was the same time our daughter Emily cut short her trip home for the holidays, made other plans for Spring Break, and decided to stay in Chicago for the summer.

The same time my part-time job at the college was cut.

The same time Gary's corporate retreat was moved to Minnesota, and spouses were not invited.

The first time the retreat was held at a secluded, Minnesota, lake-side lodge with a five-star restaurant, but no fishing charters. An exclusive retreat for a select group of movers and shakers. So select that only two representatives from Gary's office were attending. A retreat which required several after-hours, intensive, strategy sessions with his very attractive, very feminine, very ambitious protege, who was rocketing up the corporate ladder. Strategy sessions at some of the finer dining establishments in River City. Dining establishments that were all located in upscale hotels.

Gary brushed off my concerns.

He rolled his eyes when I asked how any strategy session, regardless of intensity and importance, required a bottle of champagne, charged to a personal credit card rather than an expense account. And all this for a meeting in Minnesota, for Christ's sake.

Once I began to consider the possibility that "we got trouble right here in River City" – with a capital "T" and that rhymes with "G" and that stands for lying, cheating, son of a bitch – things seemed to escalate, until my nerves rattled like a box of unmatched earrings.

I blamed myself, like the good little repressed, depressed, insecure, Midwestern, Catholic girl I am. After all, handsome Gary Westbrook – captain of the PGHS football team, successful businessman, and all-around-charmer – had swooped in like a knight in shining armor and swept-ish me off my feet when I was a broken-hearted, sniveling wreck.

There was always an explanation. I was imagining things. Gary was working hard to please me, to provide a comfortable lifestyle for us. Those 800-thread count Egyptian cotton sheets came at a price.

When I found the matching, lacy bralet, I didn't bother to ask Gary about it. Instead I made a lunch date with Vanessa. And then I found her with Gary.

It was my fault Vanessa met with Gary in the first place. I knew she was upset about Michael, but instead of asking about her problems, I burdened her with mine. She was worried about me. She said Gary would never cheat on me.

She wanted to prove me wrong.

Instead, she proved me right.

I reheated Gary's coffee in the microwave as he finally came downstairs, looking well-rested, refreshed, and freshly-fucked. The bastard.

"Gary, I think we need to talk about last night," I said, before he could take refuge behind the morning paper.

He folded the paper so he could read the story at the top of page three. The headline said something about a brawl at the local senior center over substandard snacks. He sighed wearily, and sat back in his chair. He took a long drink of his coffee and shook his head.

"Wha ith there tho dithcuth?" he said, lisping and wiping scalding coffee from his chin. "A moment of indiscretion, a lack of judgment, a loss of self-control. You should probably apologize to Vanessa as well." He flicked the paper up. End of discussion.

I was so shocked I couldn't even stutter.

"I thought your handling of the situation was extremely juvenile," Gary continued, when I didn't reply. "Walking in on us like that, sock or no sock . . . and then the play by play commentary? Vulgar and distracting. I think it really affected her performance."

Gary had never talked to me like this before. Then again, we never talked to each other in the morning until we had each had at least two cups of coffee. But that was because neither of us could form complete sentences without caffeine, not because we were harsh or hurtful.

"I should *what?*" I spluttered, trying to decide just which part of his statement offended me the most. "Did it ever occur to you that perhaps Vanessa wasn't 'responsive' because she didn't have enough time at bat?"

"I've never had any complaints before." He lowered the paper enough to give me a questioning look. I never complained because I was afraid it was my fault.

"Before? So, you're admitting that this is not your first affair?" I tried to regain control of the situation.

"And you're admitting that you've known?"

So much for having control.

"What makes this any different?" He asked, reaching for his coffee.

"Vanessa is my *best friend!*"

Gary shrugged. "So your problem is *who* I slept with."

"NO! My problem is *that* you slept with anyone, you lying . . . ."

"When did I lie?"

Technically he had never lied to me, because I had never asked him if he was having an affair.

"Cheating . . . ."

"Cheated how? Cheating implies lying, which we've dismissed." Gary sighed as if impatient with my inability to understand. "I am a man. Men have a biological need for sexual gratification. Throughout history, the measure of a man's success has been quantified by his conquests on the battlefield – or in my case the boardroom – and in the bedroom."

"But . . . ."

"I never lied. You never asked. I never snuck around." Gary said, one step ahead of me. "My father slept with all of his secretaries, and Mother never said a word."

"Your father?"

Well, that was a plot twist.

Richard, Gary's dad, had been a very successful insurance agent. Helen, Gary's mom, had been on the board of every charity in Pleasant Glen and several in River City. She had an entire room filled with

"Volunteer of the Year" awards. After retiring to Florida a couple years ago, they opened up their own real estate agency. Their Midwestern charm and work ethic, along with a relentless attention to detail and uncanny ability to sniff out contractual loopholes, had quickly made them the most successful realtors in Dade County. Their client list switched almost overnight from cash-strapped, corn-belt retirees looking for modest, beach-view condos, to rich New England snowbirds looking for private, beach-front mansions.

"My mother entertained herself with an ever changing retinue of pool boys, tennis instructors, and corporate chairmen in charge of philanthropic development. Discreetly, of course," Gary said.

That explained the cold shoulder I received from some members when Helen lobbied for my inclusion in her favorite clubs. It may have also explained why the director of the art museum kept suggesting dinner meetings.

"So if I had . . . ."

"There was nothing stopping you. As long as you were discreet. I always thought you might find someone at those god-awful book readings you went to."

"No, Gary. I took our marriage vows seriously. I love . . . *loved* you."

"And I love you, Julie," he said matter-of-factly. "I don't see what that has to do with the subject at hand."

"You fail to see the connection between loving someone – being married to someone – and having sex with someone else? What does love mean to you, anyway?" Gary had never been overly romantic, but he could be sweet and attentive.

"I take care of you. I provide for you. I enjoy your company . . . most of the time. In exchange for my financial and emotional support, you provide social and emotional support. It's a win-win situation. Beneficial to both parties."

"Beneficial to both parties? What you have described is a business transaction, Gary, not a marriage."

"I suppose the same concepts apply to any successful joint venture," Gary said, shrugging. I had heard him talk this way to difficult clients and marveled at how he could keep his emotions in check. Now it disgusted me.

"So, continuing with the business analogy, what would you suggest if one of the parties was unable to fulfill the needs of the other party, as stipulated in the contractual agreement?" I tried to sound as detached and cold as Gary. Maybe this was the most effective way to communicate with him.

"I would suggest the aggrieved party seek fulfillment elsewhere, and would recommend the contract be amended to reflect the change of status."

Amended? Change of status? Was he suggesting a divorce? Now wait just a minute, Bub! If anyone was going to suggest a divorce it was going to be me!

"Jesus, Gary. This is our marriage we're talking about, not some contractual infraction. How can you be so cavalier?"

Gary sighed again. "Marriage *is* a social contract, designed to provide for the safety and financial well-being of women and children. I haven't broken any of the stipulations of that contractual agreement."

"What about those other women?"

"I never provided nor promised emotional or financial support for any of them."

"What about Vanessa?"

Gary hesitated, his coffee cup poised in mid-air. I'd like to think he was considering his words carefully. He put his cup back on the table, but never took his eyes off it.

"She's no different than anyone else. She has physical needs. Perhaps more so than others, considering the situation with Michael."

"I don't know what's going on with Michael, but I do know she's vulnerable right now, Gary. You pretended to listen to her, and you took advantage of her."

Now Gary looked up at me. His eyebrows were drawn together as if he were confused.

"I think that's something you'll have to discuss with Vanessa. I assumed she had already talked about this whole situation with . . . *her best friend*. Isn't that what you girls do?"

I couldn't think of a time he had ever said something – on purpose – that he knew would hurt me this bad. There was the occasional comment about "putting on a few pounds there, Jules," but I'd just flip him the bird and then throw the cake away when he wasn't watching.

I turned so he couldn't see how much his comments had hurt.

"This isn't over," I said quietly when I heard his chair scrape as he pushed away from the table.

"Maybe not. But I can't be late for this morning's meeting. I said I'd bring Starbucks. By the way, Charlie is flying in for the meeting and I promised him a home-cooked dinner. He's currently out of favor with the top brass, so I think a pot roast would be good enough."

"Then you'd better hope that's the special down at the diner. And while you're at it, maybe you can get the room next to his at the hotel. Be sure to ask for the weekly rates."

"I don't think you understand, *sweetheart*." Gary's voice was low and even. "This house is in *my* name. So unless *you* can find a hotel room with a nice, new, expensive convection oven like this one right here," he slapped his hand down on the latest addition to our kitchen, but his voice never changed. "I suggest you put on a happy face and Betty Crocker-up one of your delicious, welcoming, happy homemaker meals. You can even pick out the wine. Something not too expensive. Maybe Vanessa can give you some ideas."

Without another word, he turned and walked out the door.

I collapsed into a chair at the table and took a long, deep drink of cold, bitter, coffee-flavored water.

Make a list.

Pot roast.

Potatoes.

Carrots.

Wine.

6

I don't know how long I sat there waiting for the tears to come.

But they didn't.

There was just the awful feeling of emptiness. That black hole inside of me had been growing for the last six months, while my life spiraled out of control. It wasn't depression. OK, so maybe it was. I liked to think of it as resignation. Things change, people change, you learn to deal with it.

This time was different.

I had no idea how to change, because I had no idea who I was anymore.

I didn't have a career to define me. Do you know how many forms and surveys have a blank for "employer"? All of them. Do you know how many well-meaning people ask what you do for a living? All of them. "Volunteer" or "stay-at-home mom" felt like non-answers, and more often than not prompted the follow up question "But what do you *do*?"

For that matter, I wasn't really a SAHM anymore, not with Emily at college. I was proud that she was striking out on her own, but I wished she hadn't severed the apron strings so abruptly. It felt like one day I was "Emily's Mom," a welcome fixture by her side or on the sidelines, and the next day I was just the woman who transferred money to her bank account and occasionally did her laundry.

I wasn't a daughter myself anymore. Of course in Pleasant Glen, I would always be known as Ed and Grace Robberson's only child, despite the fact that they had died when I was 20 years old.

I was still Gary's wife, but I wasn't his *wife*. And I wouldn't be either for much longer. What was the point? Not that I needed a man to complete me – men, fish, bicycle, hear me roar, all that feminist stuff. Being Mrs. Gary Westbrook was just another way of distinguishing my place in Pleasant Glen, another role to play.

Then there was Vanessa. We had been best friends since kindergarten. My parents and I had moved in to the house next to Vanessa's family the weekend before school started. Vanessa, dressed in a plaid jumper and white, ruffled ankle socks, her red hair in braids, had knocked on our door bright and early that first day of school. She cheerfully announced that we were walking to school together and that we were going to be best friends.

And we were.

As each layer of identity had been stripped away, I fell back on what was left, *who* was left. Now there was nothing.

No one to define me, but me.

As I sat there moping, I realized that if there was nothing to define me, there was nothing to limit me, either.

It was frightening.

And exciting.

Mostly frightening.

But I didn't feel like giving up.

If I had been floating through life before, now I was well and truly set adrift. It was time to start paddling. It was time to plot my own course. I didn't have a freaking clue what that might be, but I knew I wouldn't find it sitting at the kitchen table feeling sorry for myself.

I would make a plan. Not a list, but a *plan*.

I needed to find a job and a place to live. No more holding out for just the right thing, or waiting for PGC to realize they made a huge mistake when they let me go.

Who had I been before I was Mrs. Gary Westbrook?

A college student. A waitress at The Bar in downtown Pleasant Glen.

Maybe I could get my old job back. Maybe Bob, the owner, would let me rent the apartment over The Bar for cheap.

And maybe monkeys would fly out of my butt.

I hadn't been in The Bar, or seen Bob, in 25 years. Not since I married Gary. I pretended I couldn't go back there because it didn't fit the image of an upstanding, respectable wife and mother.

That was a lie.

There were too many memories linked to that place. Good memories, for the most part. But sometimes those are the ones that hurt the worst.

I met the first man I really loved at The Bar. Maybe Joe was the only man I ever really loved, now that I thought about it.

The Bar was the last place I ever saw him, too.

Joe left, without a word. I fell apart. Gary and Vanessa put me back together.

I married Gary.

And now Gary had left, without leaving.

This time I would put myself back together.

I hadn't thought about Joe in ages. I suppose it was only natural that I thought of him now. I remembered how empty I felt when Joe left. I worked hard to forget about him, but a part of me had always missed him.

After all these years, I still wondered how he was, what he was doing.

I wondered if he had ever thought about me.

If he still remembered me.

All this wool-gathering sucked the gumption right out of me. I couldn't plan for something as nebulous and frightening as my future with the ghost of a long-gone boyfriend hijacking my thoughts.

I needed to do something. Something that required very little thought.

I needed a physical project to focus on. I needed structure and a tangible outcome. I would start with tonight's dinner, and then move on to taking over the world. If I screwed with Gary's mind in the process, so much the better.

I caught sight of my reflection in the glass-front door of the oven. Correction: I would start with a shower, then grocery shopping, then dinner, then taking over the world.

Priorities.

I showered quickly, and automatically picked out the daily uniform of the Pleasant Glen WASP female – khaki pants, a white shirt, and brown leather, tasseled loafers. As I sat at my dressing table curling my expertly tinted, rich chocolate-brown hair I was struck by the distinct lack of color in my outfit and in my bedroom.

And in my life. I had never been a wild child, but I did once have color in my life.

I griped about how Gary had changed, how he had become wrapped up in his work, but what about me? After we married, I threw myself into being the perfect wife. I set aside my interests and focused on Gary and what would make him happy and successful. I thought that's what you did. That's what our moms had done.

When Emily came along, I threw myself into being the perfect mother and wife. Gary and Emily always came first, then me. Maybe. If there was anything left over.

Somewhere along the way I lost sight of who I was, what I liked.

Our bedroom, like every other room in our house, was elegantly spartan. I scoured House Beautiful, Elle Décor and other magazines for ideas, then scoured the outlets to create a budget-friendly version of the latest trends. Everything blended seamlessly in unified blandness running the gamut of off-white hues: "Almond Milk," "Eggshell," "Oatmeal," "Truffle."

It was supposed to be an oasis of calm, but now the lack of color made it seem sterile and dull. No wonder we rarely had sex. Who gets turned on by blah?

There was slightly more color in my wardrobe. That is, if black and gray count as colors.

I opened the doors to my professionally designed, walk-in closet, complete with special order storage units. The adjustable hanging rods held pencil skirts with hems ranging from just below the knee to just above the knee, tailored slacks, cotton-blend oxford shirts, silk blouses, cardigan sweater sets, and blazers that varied by lapel style. I had four versions of "the little black dress," each with a different sleeve style or neckline.

Twelve pairs of shoes in shades of black and gray, ranging from ballet flats to fuck me pumps, were lined up neatly on the adjustable shelves along with one pair of running shoes. My designer purses were carefully boxed for storage.

The lingerie drawer was filled with perfectly matched bra and panty sets in white, beige and black. Boring and practical, they were only slightly more revealing than granny panties.

The underwear I found in the glove box of Gary's SUV were white and lacy. I thought this was absurd. Who wears white panties – lacy or not – to seduce a married man? I could have told her this kind of detail was lost on Gary.

But maybe it wasn't.

I took another look at the contents of my lingerie drawer. Maybe I could have tried harder.

No wonder Gary had affairs.

Not that I think a person's choice of lingerie justifies promiscuity, but maybe it did in Gary's book. Then again, maybe the fact that it was Tuesday justified an affair in Gary's book.

Project number two: Add some life back into my wardrobe. I would need to call Vanessa to set up a shopping trip.

Shit.

I wasn't talking to Vanessa. Project number two would have to wait.

Or not. Dammit, I was a grown-ass woman. I could shop for myself.

Pleasant Glen has only two women's clothing stores – one for teenagers and one for matrons – and I knew the owners of both stores and most of the clerks. If I suddenly started buying colorful clothes they would think I'd lost my mind, or was having an affair. While that might be a fun rumor to start, I didn't want to let someone else to do it for me.

When I went to the River City Mall by myself, the only stores I shopped at were White House Black Market and Brooks Brothers. Neither of those would provide much punch to my wardrobe.

I was a grown-ass woman, who couldn't shop for herself. Clearly my clothing makeover was going to require baby steps.

And, most likely, forgiving Vanessa.

I pondered my lack of clothing options while I ran to the grocery store and started dinner.

"Nothing too fancy," Gary had said. Forget that. I had a reputation to uphold. I was The Perfect Housewife. At least I had been, and I could be for a little while longer.

Besides, I liked Charlie. I wasn't sure what he had done wrong, but if he was out of favor with Gary, I liked him even more. Maybe we could start our own little club.

While the homemade rolls were rising I prepped the pot roast – just like Gary requested. A little fresh rosemary and thyme would make this roast anything but boring. I would add baby red potatoes and carrots later and steam some asparagus. Nothing fancy. Comfort food, upscaled.

For dessert I decided on lemon meringue pie. I make a four egg-white meringue that is higher than high. And Gary hates lemon. Bonus points.

I put the white wine in the fridge to chill, and left the red wine in the basement where it would stay cool. Both were mid- to lower-price range and would be proudly served in their original bottles.

Complete with "Angry Housewife" label.

While dinner cooked, I put together the sexiest, not-sexy outfit I could manage.

I picked out my shortest skirt, the one that hit just at the top of my knee. Then I turned the hem under and tacked it up another good inch so that it hit me mid-thigh, revealing the curves I ran endless hills to shape.

I found the beautiful, hand-painted silk scarf that I made Gary bid on at the last art gallery fundraiser. I told him it was good for his image to support the arts. His generous winning bid had earned us a photo in the local paper, accompanying a glowing report of the event's success.

I had tucked a copy of the picture away with the scarf. Gary looked dashing in his tuxedo, the scarf added zest to my sleeveless, low-cut, little black dress. We were both smiling, embracing, gazing at each other. We were flanked by the art gallery director and the artist, who both looked directly at the camera, a little dazed, clutching the check between them.

We had been the toast of Pleasant Glen society that night. When the party was over, the director had winked at Gary and slipped me a bottle of champagne from his private reserves. I had planned every aspect of the event. I knew this bottle was well beyond the budget.

We went directly home. I put the champagne on ice and slipped into my satin pajamas.

Gary slipped into his den to figure out how to maximize the donation as a tax write off.

Apparently my slinky pajamas, in the classic, boring, two-piece style, were no match for tax tables.

I had carefully folded the scarf, wrapped it in tissue paper and added it to my stash of potential gift items. Mom taught me to always be prepared for unexpected gift-giving occasions.

Tonight this scarf was a gift to me.

I hoped Gary would remember that night and what it had cost him. His little indiscretion was about to cost him a lot more.

I draped the scarf over a white, silk tank. My highest fuck-me pumps, which were made more for standing than walking, completed the look. I even dabbed on the expensive cologne I received from Gary's mom for Christmas.

Dinner looked and smelled delicious, but I hoped both men would be too distracted by my appearance to notice the food.

Revenge is a dish best served by a smokin' hot hostess.

7

Everything was ready when Gary and Charlie arrived at six that evening. The table was set with my best china, linen, and crystal. Dinner had come together exactly right. "Betty Crocker-up" something not-too-fancy, my ass. Gary wanted a scene of domestic bliss? He'd get it. In spades. Asshat.

Gary seemed anxious when I met them at the front door. I suppose he was expecting more drama after the scene in the kitchen. I had played the perfect wife for so long, the act was second nature to me now.

I ushered the men into the formal living room and poured generous highballs using a nice, *expensive* Irish whiskey I had picked up at the store. I served them a plate of prosciutto-wrapped feta and basil bites and a spicy pretzel pub mix to "help them unwind," while I finished in the kitchen. The only last minute prep I had to do was to open another bottle of wine, having drank nearly the entire bottle of white wine doing the real preparation.

Gary, keeping up his side of the charade, came in to ask if I needed help.

I slinked over to him, ran my hands up his arms seductively and loosened his tie. Then I licked my lips, leaned in even closer and abruptly tightened the knot on his tie like a noose.

"You could go fuck yourself," I said sweetly.

"Ah . . . ." Gary took a step back, coughing and loosening his tie. "I see you're still angry."

I leaned back against the counter and crossed my arms, pushing my boobs up to their almost full "B" cup glory. I didn't answer. But I didn't toss my wine in his face, either. That would be a waste of good-ish wine.

"Well, dinner smells wonderful, and you look . . . amazing." He sounded sincere, and for a moment I almost felt bad. He couldn't seem to decide whether to focus on my long stretch of bare legs or my boobs. When was the last time I had gone all out for him? Maybe if I had . . . .

"Listen, I understand how . . . I know you would rather be serving my ass on a platter. But I really appreciate this. Dinner tonight, this meeting, it's . . . it's not what I . . . Charlie's not the . . . ." Gary sighed, and leaned towards me. I stiffened. He took my wine glass from the counter behind me and downed it in one gulp.

"I said some things this morning. Things that weren't . . . I just thought if . . . I couldn't let . . . . This is important, Julie. You have no idea how important. I know you're mad at me, but I really need your help. Please. Please?" His tone was gentle, not pleading, but earnest. Just like that, the cock-sure, cruel, asshat from this morning was replaced by Good Guy Gary, the man I had married and stuck with for all these years.

We stood there in silence a moment longer, as I tried to catch up with the Dr. Jekyll and Gary Hyde transformation. Then he reached up to touch my cheek, the way he always did to show his affection. I flinched and he quickly drew back his hand.

"Well. Well, if there's nothing I can do . . . ." His shoulders slumped. "If dinner's ready I'll get Charlie settled in the dining room and then help you with the food."

"Don't bother," I said. My tone was sharper than I meant for it to be. If he was making an attempt to be civil, so could I.

"Jules." He sounded sad. Or worried. I wasn't sure which.

"I mean," I started again, smiling, trying to lighten my tone. "Don't worry, I've got it all handled. You go do that magic, business-y stuff that you do." I made shooing motions with my hands. "Go! Scoot! Charm! Climb that corporate ladder. I've got your back." *I won't stab you in it just yet.*

Gary stopped with his hand on the swinging door and looked back over his shoulder at me. He smiled, but still looked worried.

"Thank you, Jules." He took a deep breath, squared his shoulders, exhaled, and walked through the door.

I wasn't sure what was going on, but I didn't think Gary was faking his concern. Something was up. Something not good. I was still mad at him, but that was beside the point. Gary seemed genuinely worried about this business meeting. Gary never worried about business meetings. He was the king of business meetings. I had been there to help and support him in those meetings since before we married.

I could put our personal issues aside for a few more hours.

Dinner went off without a hitch. I actually like Charlie. He's probably 15 years older than Gary, prime retirement age, affable and charismatic. He never seemed to me to be as polished or savvy as Gary. Then again, I suppose a good wife would be prejudiced.

I thought of Charlie as a "brown suit" in the business world. Gary was a "dark suit" kind of guy, a little sharper edged than Charlie, but not quite a "pinstripe suit" yet. Gary longed to be a pinstripe. Everything he did was geared towards becoming a pinstripe. It wasn't his only focus – Gary honestly cared about his clients – but he expected to be rewarded for his hard work. He seemed to be headed toward that reward.

At least I had assumed so.

Dinner was a success. Gary was charming. I was adoring. The meal was delicious. Charlie was appreciative. By the time I served the pie, I had almost convinced myself that Gary and I were a happily married couple. Of course, I was chugging a glass of wine every time I passed through the kitchen, so my judgment was a little cloudy.

As I gathered the last of the dishes off the table, I mentally congratulated myself on my Oscar-worthy portrayal of "The Little Housewife Who Could."

"Thank you so much for letting me spend the night here, Julie," Charlie said. "You wouldn't believe the budget restraints corporate is implementing."

Say what?

"It's our pleasure, Charlie," Gary said, quickly. "With Emily off at college, we have plenty of room. Besides, with our early morning meeting, it just seems silly to shuttle you back and forth to the hotel."

Plenty of *rooms*, but not plenty of *beds*, I thought. Emily had taken the twin-size bed from the guest room to college with her. That meant the full-size bed in her room was the only extra one in the house, and I had planned on sleeping there myself tonight.

Gary took the dishes out of my hands before I could throw them. I hadn't realized how tight my grip was until Gary tugged, and I noticed my knuckles had turned white.

"Just give me a minute to help Jules with the dishes. Then you and I can go over the last of the reports. Please, make yourself at home. The whiskey's on the bar."

I waited until Charlie was safely on his way towards the living room before giving Gary the Death Stare. As soon as the swinging door shut behind us in the kitchen I spun around to face him.

"What. The. Fuck. Gary." I hissed.

"Jules, it just made sense. We have a conference call at the office at

7:30 in the morning, and we still have a lot to go over to get ready. It was a last minute decision, I swear. I'm sorry to spring it on you, but . . . it just made sense."

"With Charlie in the only spare bed, where am I supposed to sleep?"

"Um . . . our bed?" Thank you, Captain Clueless, for that unacceptable option.

"After you and Vanessa . . . ? Are you crazy?"

"Now Jules, don't you think maybe you're over reacting a bit? I changed the sheets this morning. What's the big deal?"

"This morning? I thought inviting Charlie to stay here was 'a last minute decision'."

"It was. I just thought . . . I mean . . . I knew how upset you were, and I was trying to . . . to make things right."

"You thought changing the sheets was going to 'make things right'? Are you kidding me?"

"Jules, I can't change what happened."

"No. No Gary, you can't change what happened. You can't change the fact that you fucked my best friend and who knows how many other women, while we were married." My anger was sobering me up. Who knows what I might do in a kitchen filled with knives if that happened. I took a big swig of wine, and followed it up with a wine chaser.

"Fuck you, Gary. Fuck you and your pinstripe aspirations. I'll sleep on the couch." I finished my glass and slammed it down on the counter.

"Um, that's not going to work, Jules." Gary carefully put the dishes in the sink. "We need to go over some reports in the living room to prepare for tomorrow morning's meeting. And the couch in the family room, well, Charlie will have to walk through there to get to Emily's room. That would be a little awkward."

69

"Fine. I'll think of something. I played the loving, supportive wife tonight, but I'll be damned if I'm going to sleep in the same bed with you ever again, you asshat."

"Jules, this is really, *really* important. I have to make a good impression on Charlie. You don't understand what's at stake here."

"Fine. Fine! Emily's room is ready. I straightened it over the weekend, hoping that she'd change her mind about coming home. There are clean towels in her bathroom, too. Just fluff the pillow, give the comforter a shake, and set a bottle of water on the nightstand. Hell, put a mint on the pillow, for all I care."

"Thanks, Jules! You're the best!" Gary leaned in as if he was going to kiss me. I put up my hand to stop him.

"Touch me and I'll cut you." It was an empty threat, but I'd had just enough wine to make it sound real. The momentary look of fear on Gary's face made it worthwhile.

I opened another bottle of wine and set to washing the china and crystal. The warm water and soap suds, as well as the wine, helped calm me down. These were my mom's dishes, not the china I'd registered for when Gary and I had married. Using them reminded me of her.

Which was ridiculous, because she hated these dishes. They were delicate and fragile. And yet . . . despite the gold leaf around the edges, there was something strong and enduring about them.

I finished up the dishes, turned off the kitchen light, and snuck upstairs. I changed into my manly, satin pajamas and wrapped my champagne-colored, satin robe around me. I curled up in the overstuffed chair in my office with half a bottle of wine to pout and contemplate the future.

I pretended to be asleep when Gary and covered me with a blanket. I remember thinking he wasn't such a bad guy after all.

I was too tired to sleep well, especially in a lumpy chair. And I was too drunk to care when I realized I had gone back to my – our – bed. Gary gently wrapped his arm around me, pulling me close. He sighed as I settled in, spooning cozily against his warm body. His deep, even breathing hypnotized me and I finally relaxed, slipping in and out of consciousness. The lines between dream and reality blurred.

When was the last time he held me like this?

When was the last time I felt that tingle of anticipation as his hand slowly slid over my waist and down my belly? The last time that heat spread as he caressed the hollow at my hip bone? The last time he slipped his hand between my legs?

When was the last time Gary rolled me over onto my back and knelt between my legs? The last time I wrapped my legs around him? When was the last time we made love, my red hair spilling over the pillow . . . .

Holy Crap!

That wasn't me. It was Vanessa!

My dream had become a nightmare!

Everything that had happened came rushing back. I threw off the covers and jumped out of bed. I swayed unevenly, trying to recover from the eroticism and the shock.

Then the hangover hit me. My pulse beat in my head.

"Come back to bed, Jules," Gary mumbled, more asleep than not.

I ran to the bathroom and retched. When I came out, Gary was sitting on the edge of the bed, rubbing the sleep from his eyes.

"Lie down, Jules. Charlie and I need to leave for our meeting soon. That's assuming he's feeling better than you do. He drank almost as much as you did. Go back to bed. I'll bring you up some juice and toast. And coffee."

I wanted to protest. But my head was throbbing.

"Thank you," I said, slipping back under the covers.

"I'm not such a bad guy, Jules." He rubbed my shoulder. "I'll get you some aspirin."

I closed my eyes and tried to make the bed stop spinning. When Gary sat next to me, the world tilted and it felt like we both might tumble onto the floor. I moaned at the movement and he chuckled a little. Then he handed me a glass of water and two aspirin and waited until I swallowed them.

"Charlie and I are going to grab coffee and bagels on the way to the office. I'll bring you up something before we leave. Try to rest."

I nodded and closed my eyes.

"Thank you. Again," I said quietly.

Gary brushed the hair off my forehead, and sat beside me a moment longer. I kept my eyes closed and willed myself not to cry.

He could be tender. He could be compassionate. What had happened the other night? Yesterday morning? What about the last 6 months, the last 5 years? This was the Gary I married. The Gary I used to know.

The Gary I missed.

8

I tried to relax, but I was afraid to fall asleep in case that dream was still waiting for me. Worrying about it only made things worse, of course. It's hard to forget something when you're obsessing over it. I listened to the ordinary morning sounds: Gary showering, shaving, brushing his teeth, humming to himself as he dressed. The white-noise finally lulled me into a dreamless sleep. When I woke again, peacefully this time, there was a tray on my nightstand.

True to his word – Gary's good point number six – Gary had brought me lightly buttered toast, a glass of orange juice and a travel mug of coffee. He had also brought me a can of Coke in a koozie and a handful of Dove chocolates. If he thought his sudden kindness was going to get him off my shit list, he had another think coming. It did make me less inclined to kill him, though.

The petty side of me wanted to point out that I had told him a million times that chocolate relieves PMS, but greasy foods are the best way to treat a hangover. Did he think I was a bitchy, lightweight drunk because I was having my period? Typical man. I decided to give him the benefit of the doubt. Chocolate mellows me out that way. Besides, greasy food doesn't travel well, and it would have congealed.

It was almost 10 a.m., and Pleasant Glen State Bank closes at 11 on Saturdays. There was no way I'd have time to make myself presentable, get my thoughts organized, and get to the bank before then.

I realized that I had no idea what our financial status was, or even where and how our money was deposited, other than our checking account at PGSB. I assumed Gary had most of our money invested with his company. But I had no idea who held the mortgage to our house, or if my name was on the deed or not, as Gary had said. His folks had helped us get a loan when we built our new house five years ago, but I had been preoccupied with Emily, house plans and volunteer work. I hadn't paid much attention to the financial aspects.

Gary tried to keep me in the loop. When we were first married we had monthly budget meetings. But that kind of minutia alternately confused and bored me. And Gary grew frustrated trying to explain all the ins and outs to me. Repeatedly. It was just easier and more conducive to marital bliss to let him handle it.

A quick mental inventory of my own assets left me with one undeniable fact: I was well and truly screwed.

I had nowhere to go. No family or close friends – besides Vanessa – to take me in, and limited financial resources of my own. I could get a hotel room in River City – tongues would wag if I checked in at a local hotel – but with my volunteer commitments the commute would be a pain. Even I knew that was a weak excuse.

Besides, I would need to use a credit card to reserve a room. A credit card that was, technically, in Gary's name. I was mad, but I could hardly ask Gary to finance my leaving him. *By the way, could I have an advance on my allowance so I can run away from home?*

I was too proud to take anything from him anyway. I know, "marriage is a partnership," blah, blah, blah. Still, it just didn't feel right to me.

I did have a checking account of my own. Gary's mom had insisted I keep one to establish my credit profile. "Just in case, God forbid, anything should happen to Gary," she had said. I used it to pay for gifts for Gary – using his credit card to pay for *his* gifts just seemed wrong – and frivolous things that didn't fit in my household budget.

I put part of my paycheck in this account every month, but most went in our joint account. The partial salary of a part-time job at a private, financially-strapped college didn't add up very quickly. I mentally calculated the cost of first and last months' rent on a small apartment, a damage deposit, utility hook ups, groceries, insurance, car insurance, gas, and incidentals. I could probably be out on my own for about . . . three months. If I was lucky.

I wasn't big on making decisions – stay with Gary or go it alone – but I was big on making plans. Then again, maybe making big plans was my way to avoid making small decisions. I still wasn't sure how I could go it alone, and I was afraid to rush into anything. We had peacefully cohabitated without much interaction, sexual or otherwise, for nearly a year, this morning's near-disaster notwithstanding. We could probably share the same house for a couple more days without bloodshed.

Probably.

These cheerful thoughts put me right back into wallowing mode.

A quick shower made me feel almost human again. A nice, greasy, fried egg and bacon sandwich along with a Coke on ice completed the transformation. It also left a nice, greasy mess on my stove top. I cleaned that up, and as so often happens when I start cleaning to avoid what's really bothering me, the next thing I knew I had cleaned the entire house. I threw the duvet in the washer – it was too lovely to destroy – while I dusted and vacuumed and washed and mopped and straightened. As I worked, I imagined I was scouring a crime scene. A particularly gruesome murder scene. Involving an unfaithful husband.

I was considering taking a toothbrush to that spot where the toilet base meets the floor – I was going to use Gary's toothbrush and then return it to the holder – when I decided it was time to take a break. Maybe all those toxic cleanser fumes were getting to me.

But first I changed the bedding in Emily's room. I wasn't going to risk trying to sleep upstairs again. Apparently my subconscious mind was a vicious traitor. If Charlie was going to stay over tonight, we'd just have to share this bed.

As long as I was downstairs I decided to go through some of my old scrapbooks to see if I could find a hint of who I used to be. Who, once upon a time, I wanted to be when I grew up.

All my pre-marriage, pre-Gary life had been distilled down and stowed away in three large, plastic totes stacked on shelves in the back corner of my very well-organized basement storage room. I hadn't opened these boxes since we moved into the house. Who knows how long it had been before then.

The first tote held childhood memories: my ragged teddy bear, family photos, Mom's miniature spoon collection, and Dad's favorite pipe. I closed my eyes and breathed in the lingering sweet and woodsy scent of his tobacco. At the bottom of the box was an envelope filled with sympathy cards from my parents' funerals, and two dried and crumbling flowers from their casket sprays.

The second tote was half empty. The quilt Mom gave me should have been in here. I was sure I packed it with my favorite college sweatshirt, and a Spudz MacKenzie stuffed doll from the state fair. Some drunk ISU guy gave the dog to me and Vanessa after we promised to meet him at a party down by the cattle barns. She got the frat-boy, but I got the dog – and the better deal, she said.

One scrapbook was filled with "first day of school" photos of Vanessa and me. Every year the two of us had posed in new, back-to-school outfits, while our parents took our picture in front of the ever shrinking white lilac bush that grew between our houses.

Every year.

The picture from that *first*, first day of school had sat on top of the bookshelf at my folks' house until they died and I had taken it home to sit on the top of my bookshelf. The shelves had changed over the years, but the essence of the picture stayed the same. One little, outgoing, redhead staring straight into the camera, oozing confidence; one little, shy, towhead, chin tucked to her chest, looking out from under her bangs uncertainly at the camera.

That friendship, decreed with such certainty our first day of school, never wavered.

In first grade, when Timmy Smock dumped paint on my head during art time, Vanessa "accidentally" tripped him during second recess.

In sixth grade, when Vanessa started her period at school – while wearing white pants, naturally – I convinced the other girls in our class to change into their gym shorts. Muffy and Bunny refused, of course. This show of solidarity was strictly against school dress code and earned me a trip to the office. Vanessa had stood outside the principal's window making funny faces at me while I received a stern lecture about the dangers rabble-rousers posed to society.

In high school, when Russ Knight – PGHS's very own All-American Asshat – broke up with Vanessa at our Senior Prom, I told my asthmatic, near-sighted, date from the chess club that I had a 10 p.m. curfew and made him call his mom to come pick us up. Then Vanessa and I sat at the Country Kitchen until dawn, making the most of their "Endless Stack of

Pancakes" offer. The restaurant closed for good later that month.

When we were in college, and both my parents died within a year, Vanessa Morris took me home with her and announced to her parents that they were *our* parents and I was her sister.

Betty and Walter Morris could do little but sigh, shake their heads, hug me and ask "So, what is new?"

And now I was just supposed to throw all that away?

How could I possibly do that?

How could Vanessa?

I didn't believe she would.

I took the lid off the third container. I wasn't much interested in my search anymore, but I was too tired to get up.

This tote was a jumble of college stuff: football programs, a pom-pom on a stick, a dried Homecoming mum – why did anyone keep dead flowers? – plastic beer mugs from the West Side bar, a bunch of cassette tapes and my old Sony Walkman.

Emily would laugh at my outdated technology. I could hear her now: "Just your speed, Mom. One button."

I still pestered her with questions about my iPod, even though she was away at school. Truth was, I could figure it out myself if I had to. It was just another excuse to talk to her. These days we only communicated by text and the occasional email. Sometimes I still called, just to hear her voice mail greeting.

She tried to get me up to speed on insta-twitster-picto-chat. I'd call, she'd reply by Snapchat. I'd fumble the Snapchat and have to text her. She'd eventually text back.

I missed her now. Missed her voice. Missed her "MomMomMom" texts.

How long had it been since I had heard from her? Even a text?

I decided to Snapchat her a picture of me with my museum-quality tech. She wouldn't be able to resist replying in some form. I slipped an unlabeled cassette into the player and grabbed the headphones. Then I headed upstairs to search for some fresh batteries.

I was holding the Walkman up by my face with one hand, and trying to figure out where the camera on my cell phone was pointing when I nearly dropped the phone. Taking selfies requires much more coordination than I have. As I grabbed for the phone with one hand, I fumbled the tape player with the other and somehow managed to hit PLAY.

"Hey, Julie."

The man's voice was silky smooth and gentle. For a moment I thought he was there beside me, whispering in my ear. His words wrapped around me in a warm caress.

Startled, I jumped and jerked the headphones out of the jack. The player stopped.

What the hell?

EJECT.

The tape had my name written on it in black Sharpie. Someone must have made a mix for me, but who? It was probably from Gary, giving me crap about keeping this old piece of junk.

Still, it hadn't sounded like Gary. And he wasn't one to make mix tapes. I rewound the tape and listened again.

"Hey, Julie."

Holy shit.

It was Joe.

I drew in a deep, ragged breath. *Calm down. It's just one of those weird things. It's just a coincidence.*

Except that I don't believe in coincidences.

REWIND.

PLAY.

My hand was shaking now.

"Hey, Julie."

His voice sent a shiver down my spine. An arpeggio played on a piano.

"I know it's been . . . crazy lately . . . ." Joe spoke in fractured sentences, the phrases punctuated by chord progressions and snippets of songs, as he worked through his thoughts on the keyboard.

"We haven't had much . . . time alone to talk . . . or to . . . ." He chuckled softly, suggestively. "I just found out . . . we're leaving tonight right after the show, so . . . .

"I wanted to make sure you knew . . . .

"I won't be gone long . . . but it will feel like . . . forever.

"You're . . . you have all my heart, Julie.

"Promise you'll . . . save a little part of yours for me.

"This is . . . it isn't finished, but . . . ."

The words trailed off as the random musical notes became a simple melody with the sweet charm of a song playing on a music-box.

The melody repeated, but this time a rich harmony was added. The music was more complex, full, and achingly tender.

A third repeat. Joe's warm tenor joined the piano. He sang in bits and pieces. The lyrics weren't complete yet, just disconnected phrases as he put into words the feelings he expressed through the music.

"Never doubt my love for you
They can't keep us apart
Save a little place for me
Sheltered in the shadow of your heart."

The piano carried the melody again, slowing wistfully. The final chord sustained, faded into nothingness.

"I love you, Julie," Joe whispered.

The tape turned to white-static.

I drew in a breath. I sobbed as it caught in my throat. My face was wet with tears.

Joe Davenport loved me.

Or he *had* loved me. A long time ago.

He never told me.

For a man who wrote such heart-felt songs, Joe had trouble expressing his emotions outright. He let his music speak for him.

I mean, I knew I loved him. And I thought the feeling was mutual, but . . . .

Did I ever tell him?

We were so young. We were what, 22? 23? We thought we had our whole lives ahead of us.

His career was just picking up. In fact, when he left that night, that was the start of everything for him. He was a rocket shooting up . . . and away. Away from Pleasant Glen, away from River City, away from Iowa.

Away from me.

We never had a chance to say goodbye.

There was a huge crowd at The Bar that night. I was swamped waiting tables. It was the last local appearance by The Average Joes. They had outgrown small, bar venues. This was their goodbye, and the kickoff to a tour of mid-sized college auditoriums.

It was the end of the summer, the last hurrah before school started. Vanessa and I would be starting grad school at State U. She and Gary and a bunch of our friends from PGHS were at The Bar. Everybody was drunk.

Gary had just finished his MBA and was staying with his buddy, Tom, who lived in the apartment across the hall from Van and me.

As soon as the last set was over, I ducked out to drive them home. Joe was mobbed by fans and friends. I caught his attention over the crowd and blew him a kiss. I pointed at my watch to let him know I'd be right back. He smiled, winked and gave me a thumbs up.

It took me so much longer than I expected. Gary and Tom tried to help me carry Van up the stairs, but it was like herding cats. Tom passed out as soon as we got him in his apartment. Gary was a mess. His fiance had broken up with him earlier that summer and he still hadn't recovered. Vanessa may be a pretty crier, but she's helpless when drunk.

By the time I got them all settled in and made it back to The Bar, Bob was just locking up.

Joe and the band had already left.

A promoter had caught their show in River City. He had scheduled an audition for them in Chicago, but it was changed to New York City at the last moment.

Joe tried to get them to wait as long as he could, Bob said. But the promoter pushed them to get going.

Joe promised to call as soon as he could, Bob said.

But he never did.

I tried to get a message to him, but they were on the road. There were no cell phones back then. Their plans changed, the tour changed, the band changed.

I gave up. I didn't want to hold him back, and I didn't want to be a pathetic groupie. I figured he didn't care.

I never knew.

He loved me.

What had happened between the time Joe made this tape and the time he left Pleasant Glen? Where had this tape come from? How did I get it? Why hadn't I found it before?

What if I had known? What if I had tried harder? What if he had? How different would things be if . . . .

I wondered where Joe was now.

Joanne Salemink

9

All that nostalgia – and cleaning – made me hungry. I decided it was time to take a break. My first instinct was to call Vanessa and see if she wanted to order a pizza.

My trip down memory lane had made me soft. Or maybe it was impossible to forget a life-long friendship overnight. I didn't know why Vanessa did what she did or how she could have acted that way.

But I blamed Michael.

I wasn't one of those moms who thought my child could do no wrong, but I did reserve judgment until all the facts were in. I was willing to give the benefit of the doubt to the people I loved, whether it was my daughter, or my best friend.

Regardless, I was on my own for dinner. I picked up a Viva Vegetarian pizza from Munchy's and a six-pack of Bud Light cans. I had learned not to mix melancholy with merlot. Or chardonnay. Gary considered vegetarian pizza a waste of time and never ordered from Munchy's because it was rumored they sold marijuana out the back door. He only drank micro-brews and imports, and only from the proper glassware, properly chilled.

I celebrated my independence holed up in the family room with cold pizza, warm beer and YouTube links. It wasn't much, but I was happy. That is, until I started bawling about half-way through my third "What Happens Next Will Amaze You" video.

Gary still wasn't home – with or without Charlie – but I decided to play it safe and sleep in my sweat pants and a t-shirt. I fished my old tape player out of my lingerie drawer, where I had hidden it, and took it with me to Emily's room.

I fell asleep listening to Joe's voice, and imagining his hands dancing over the keyboard. Soon I was dreaming about those hands dancing over my body. Joe was holding me close, his arms wrapped around my waist, kissing that spot on my neck just below my ear like he used to.

It was the Best. Dream. Ever.

He was whispering something in my ear. I drew back to ask him what he was saying, but when I did, he slipped out of my arms.

"Wait! Wait for me," I called.

Joe smiled, winked, and disappeared.

I woke to the sound of the tape clicking at the end of the reel, and the loneliness of empty arms in an empty bed in an empty house.

Then I heard a thud.

I sat up and listened.

Nothing.

I figured it was the house settling. Or an axe murderer.

Or?

Our bedroom was two floors above me and at the opposite end of the house. I didn't think I could possibly hear Gary and Vanessa from that distance. Unless they were, well, I didn't want to think about the "unless."

I had just relaxed when there was another thud. Louder this time.

Closer.

I recognized it as the thud of bodies hitting the wall as they careened down the hallway.

Really? Were Gary and Vanessa going to try out all the beds in the house?

At least, I hoped it was Gary and Vanessa.

Kind of. I mean, what if it was Charlie? Sure I had joked earlier about sharing this bed with Charlie, but I wasn't serious!

Whoever it was seemed to have stopped right outside the room. The door rattled in its frame and I heard quiet mumbling.

I didn't care who it was. I was tired, cranky, and apparently the only person in my house who wasn't getting lucky. I jumped out of bed, took a deep breath and pulled open the door.

". . . you're a really nice girl and I like you, but I think we should wai-hey-HEY!"

"What the . . HEY!" I shouted.

"What the . . . HEY? MOM?" Emily shouted.

"Mom?" a boy I did not know said. He and Emily had retreated to the far side of the hallway when I opened the door, startling them both and possibly interrupting my daughter's assault on his virtue. We stood staring at each other for a moment, our expressions shifting from surprised to confused. Then Emily and I both started talking at the same time.

"Mom! What are you doing in my room?"

"Emily! What are you doing home?

We both turned to the boy.

"I had no idea . . . I swear! This isn't . . . ." Emily said.

"Of course this isn't . . . ." I turned to Emily. "Wait a minute. What *is* going on here?"

Emily assumed the classic put-upon teenager pose, crossing her arms, sticking out a hip, slouching, and rolling her eyes.

"Mo-om. We weren't . . . . We were just . . . ." She snuck a glance at the boy. "It was a long drive from Chicago. I told Allen he could stay over and drive home tomorrow. I know I should have called first. But it was late."

I wasn't sure that was the whole truth, but they both were blushing now, and I was fairly certain I had ruined what ever "wasn't" going on between them.

"Of course, honey. No problem. Nice to meet you Allen," I said. He stuck his hand out and greeted me, then we were back to standing around awkwardly. "Oh! Well, yes. I'm sure you're both tired. I'll just let you get to bed . . . or rather, Allen can and . . . I'll wait for *you* out on the couch, Em."

After a few more apologies and much shuffling, Allen settled in for the night. Emily and I curled up on opposite ends of the couch and observed each other silently.

I searched for a topic to break the ice. "Well, this is a nice surprise," I said.

Worst. Line. Ever.

Emily did a slow blink and looked at me like I had lost my mind.

"I mean, you coming home. Surprise! I mean, I thought you were spending the summer in Chicago, with Bobby. Your boyfriend." *Who was not Allen.*

"Why were you sleeping in my room, Mom? Where's Dad?" Emily cut right to the chase.

"He had an important business meeting today. It ran late and . . . ." Emily raised an eyebrow and frowned. She wasn't buying it. "Well, I thought it would be best if I slept down here tonight."

Emily sighed and crossed her arms over her chest. "What did he do, Mom?"

Emily was a Daddy's Girl. I didn't want to say anything to upset her, and I certainly didn't want to listen to her blame me for what had happened.

"Oh, it's nothing," I said. "Don't worry. We'll work through it." *When hell freezes over.*

"Mom, I love Dad . . . ." here it comes. "But he can be a real asshat sometimes." Whoa. I did *not* see that coming. "Just tell me what he did. Please?" She uncrossed her arms and her shoulders slumped. She had a sad, worried look on her face.

"He, well, honey . . . he has a girlfriend."

"I should have guessed. I always hated it when my friends' moms used to flirt with him. And he'd flirt right back, of course. And with you right there, Mom! I couldn't understand how you put up with that crap."

"I . . . didn't think you noticed," I said softly. I tried to smile, and shrugged. "Besides, that was just your dad being his usual charming self." I hated to defend him, but I would not bad mouth him to his daughter.

Emily looked skeptical. "I don't know, Mom. That's what I used to think too, but . . . . Did you know they called him 'Hot Dad'? They didn't even bother to learn his real name."

"That's hardly his fault, honey. He couldn't do anything about *their* bad behavior."

"Would it have killed him to wear glasses? To forget to shave?"

That wouldn't have worked. His sex appeal went off the charts when he let a little stubble grow.

"Pfft. There were way hotter dads," I said. "Like . . . well, never mind." Someday she'd learn that bleacher moms talk about everything, and everybody. "Your dad is just a very friendly guy." *And I just happened to catch him being very, very friendly with your Aunt Vanessa.* "He can't help it, honey. Women are . . . drawn to him."

Besides, concession sales were always higher when Gary volunteered.

He was the master of the up-sell. No one ever walked away with just one item when Gary was behind the counter.

"He ate it up. He led them on." Emily was angry now. "If a woman behaved that way she'd be called a 'cock tease.' He was a . . . ."

"Yes, dear, I know," I interrupted her before she could say something I'd regret.

"*Whatever*," she said, complete with eye roll. "It was embarrassing, Mom."

Emily paused for a moment and started picking at her fingernails. "And then, when you guys came up for homecoming, I'm pretty sure he hit on one of my sorority sisters."

"Ohhh," I blew out my breath and sank back into the couch. That creep! I suppose I shouldn't have been surprised. After all, Emily and her friends were about the same age as the coffee shop girl.

"Yeah, well." Emily shrugged, pretending it was no big deal. "She's beautiful. All the dads hit on her. I don't think she even noticed. If he *hadn't* hit on her . . . *that* she would have noticed.

"Anyway, I just decided I'd had enough. That's why I told you guys I was too busy for you to come visit. That's why I decided not to come home this summer. I thought maybe with a little time away, I could . . . forgive him, I guess."

"Oh, honey, I'm so sorry. I didn't know. I thought I had done something."

"Well, yeah, I mean, the whole Queen of Oblivion thing was annoying. All those years . . . I didn't know how you could ignore it. You never said or did anything."

Seeing the disappointment on my little girl's face hurt much worse than walking in on Gary and Vanessa. What kind of example had I set for her?

She looked down at her hands again. "Then I found out Bobby had slept with half of my sorority sisters. Maybe half of sorority row."

She looked up at me, silent tears streaming down her face. "And I didn't know, Mom. I didn't have a clue."

"Oh, honey . . . ." The knife just kept twisting. I was about to find out what she had learned from me, and I wasn't sure I was going to like it.

"We were celebrating after the last finals, and everyone was laughing and bragging about who they had . . . . Anyway, someone mentioned Bobby, and then another and another. And I just felt so . . . tired. And empty.

"He told me I was special, Mom. He made me *feel* special. But I realized, all of a sudden, I wasn't.'"

"Oh, honey, you are special! Just because that . . . ."

Emily waved me off and swallowed her tears. "Yeah, yeah, I know. I've heard all the self-esteem lectures. We get "*O*" magazine at the house. I aced my psych class. And I've had five-hours in the car to calm down."

"You should have called me."

"No offense Mom, but you're about the last person I wanted to get relationship advice from."

"I would have told you to dump his ass!" That bastard hurt my little girl. I'd kill him. Heck, Gary would kill him. Gary would kill him, and the irony would be lost on him.

Emily gave a little snort and rolled her eyes. Evidently she didn't believe me.

"OK Mom, whatever you say. I sent Bobby a break-up text just after we passed Joliet. I turned off my phone after the first six 'You don't understand' texts and the Snapchat videos of him crying." Now *her* bottom lip trembled and *her* eyes filled with tears. "What I really need right now is a hug."

We both scooched to the center of the couch and I wrapped my arms around her. She wasn't my 19-year-old, independent, head-strong, college freshman. She was my little girl.

"I've missed you, Mom," Emily said quietly.

"Me too, honey." I gave her another squeeze and kissed the top of her head. We sat snuggled together for a little while longer, longer than I expected. Then she pulled away.

"So. About Dad," she said.

"Eh. Enough about Dad," I waved my hand, wishing I could shoo away that topic as easily as you shoo away a fly. "How did your finals go? How was second semester? How is the sorority? How's Chicago? Who's Allen?"

"Eh," Emily said, waving her hand in a perfect copy of my response. "School was good. I'm brilliant . . . ."

"I knew that, but verification is nice," I interrupted.

"The sorority was fun until, well, you know. Chicago is great. We're just friends."

I raised an eyebrow. They were not acting like "just friends" in the hallway. Then again, maybe the definition of "just friends" had changed since I was in college.

Emily blushed. "He *is* kinda cute. And sweet." She was quiet for a moment, and looked like she was trying to decide what else to tell me.

"We stopped at Munchy's and I saw that old bumper sticker about 'gas, grass or ass', and I thought maybe . . . I thought maybe I should just . . . . It just seems like everybody else does . . . ."

"Emily!"

"But then I realized that would put me on Bobby's level, and I didn't want to sink that low. Nothing happened, Mom." She rolled her eyes, shrugged and "tsked" me, a combination that made it clear I was straining our newly-restored Mother-Daughter bond. Neither of us mentioned my role in "nothing" happening.

"Well . . . ." I reached out and patted her knee. "I'm just glad you're home. And safe." That would have to do it for the intensive "mom-ing" for now.

Almost.

"But . . . where's your car? Why didn't you drive?" I asked.

"I was so upset when I found out about Bobby . . . I just wanted to get away from there as fast as I could. I figured it would be safer to ride with Allen than to drive myself."

"Well, you did the right thing, smart girl."

"So what about you, Mom. Are you a smart girl? Are you going to do the right thing?"

"It's not that easy, honey," I said. Now it was my turn to look at my hands. "I'm not sure what the right thing is."

"Have you talked with Aunt Vanessa yet?" Emily asked. "Probably not, otherwise Dad would be dead and Aunt V would be in jail. Ohmygod! That's what happened, isn't it? You're sleeping in my room because your bedroom is a crime scene and Aunt V is on the lamb."

"Not exactly." I admired my daughter's imagination.

She nodded her head slowly as if she understood. "Aunt V shanked the 'ho Dad slept with . . . ."

"Really? How many "Law and Order" spin-offs do you girls watch when you should be studying?"

"All-night marathons on Netflix. Only after our homework is done, I swear," she said. "But really. What did Aunt V say?"

"Well, the thing is . . . ." This was going to be tough. Vanessa was like Emily's second mom.

"That doesn't sound good, Mom."

I closed my eyes and tried to stop the tears. I couldn't talk. I shook my head.

"No, Mom. Aunt V would never. There's been a mistake. . . ." Emily's voice rose a pitch, the way it always did when she was upset.

I didn't open my eyes. I couldn't stand to see Emily's face when I told her the truth.

"I found them in bed," I whispered.

"Yeah, but . . . ."

That was my girl. The Princess of de-Nile. I had taught her well.

I swallowed hard, opened my eyes and took her hands in mine.

"No, honey. I found them in bed together . . . while they were . . . ."

I couldn't take it anymore. Silent sobs shook my body. Tears streamed down my face. I had joked about it. I had rationalized, analyzed and denied it. I had tried to make excuses and explain it away. I had felt angry, guilty and sorry for myself.

But I hadn't felt sad. Until now.

"Oh, Mommy," Emily said quietly. She pulled me into a hug, nestling my head on her shoulder, stroking my hair. She held me while I cried, the way I had held her when she was a child.

"Thank you, honey," I said, when I sniffed back the last of the tears. "You have no idea how much that meant to me."

"Yeah, well," she rolled her eyes. "You raised a wonderful daughter, what can I say?" *We* raised a wonderful daughter, I thought, but didn't correct her.

"Seriously, Mom, what are you going to do?"

"Seriously? I have no idea. But I'll come up with something."

"You always do," she said, smiling at last.

"Maybe I'll spend a couple days in Chicago after I take you back for the summer."

"Yeah, well, about that." Emily folded her hands on her lap and chewed the inside of her cheek. "It's kind of a funny story, really." She turned to me and smiled brightly. "Sometimes things do work out for the best."

"I'm listening."

"The job in Chicago fell through. But Claire and I got jobs up in Monticello at that camp for people with disabilities, instead. So the good news is I'll be closer to home. The bad news is I won't have much free time. But you could visit, or maybe do some volunteering there, too!"

"Oh, honey, that's wonderful!" I wasn't thrilled that she hadn't told me about the switch in jobs, but at least she had a plan. At least one of us did.

"I would love to visit the camp, and to spend time with you, but I'm pretty busy already."

"That's what I figured." Emily shrugged. "But I do have a little more bad news." She chewed on her lip again, and gave me her best "forgive me" smile. "Orientation starts tomorrow afternoon. Claire's driving my car back from school. She'll pick me up in the morning and we'll head on up."

"Oh." I tried to keep the sadness out of my voice, but I failed. I just got my daughter back, and now she was leaving again.

"I promise I'll call every night. Well, maybe not every night, but I promise I'll do better. I was just so mad at Dad."

"You know, he's not a bad guy." I must have winced when I said that because Emily laughed. "No, I mean it. He really loves you."

She shrugged. Gary was going to have to work hard to get back in her good graces.

"I have to admit I'm glad it's him you're mad at and not me."

Emily rolled her eyes. "Well, you *are* my mom. I mean, I'm supposed to have issues with you. But would you please, please stop trying to Snapchat me? I really don't need any more shots of your left nostril. At least I hope that's what that was. And for God's sake, learn how to use your iPod. What's up with that dinosaur you were listening to?"

"Ah, well . . . it's just something I found in a box of old stuff." She didn't need to know the whole story. Not yet, anyway.

10

Emily and I talked until the wee hours of the morning. I was exhausted after the last two nights, but I didn't want to miss a single moment of our reunion. We had already wasted too much time.

In spite of all the excitement, or maybe because of it, I didn't hear Gary come home. There was a note on the refrigerator saying he was heading to Des Moines to prepare for a Monday morning meeting with some corporate honchos. I figured things must be serious. Gary had told me long ago that the wheels of business turn slowly, but when they get started, nothing can stop them.

The note was signed "Love, G."

I hoped for the best.

For his sake.

After a breakfast of cold pizza, Allen left for home. I may have eavesdropped a little, peeking through the living room curtains, while he and Emily said their goodbye. They shared a kiss that was a little more than what I would call "just friends," but about right for "let's be more than just friends."

Claire arrived soon after that. I helped Emily unload her dirty laundry and school supplies. While she was re-packing for camp, she set aside her teddy bear and my "lost" quilt.

"I was afraid I'd get homesick at school, so I took this with me," she said, smiling sheepishly. "Whenever I missed you, I'd wrap up in this and pretend you were hugging me. I'll still miss you, but I think you need it more than I do right now."

We hugged for real, then she wrapped the quilt around my shoulders and gave me another hug. My pride in her maturity outweighed the tug of apron strings, allowing me to watch them drive away without crying.

Much.

As I stood in the driveway waving, I knew the time had come for me to do something – anything – about my situation. I had worried about how Emily would react to my leaving her dad. Now I worried about how Emily would react, and what lesson she might learn, if I didn't leave him.

All I needed was to find somewhere I could get a good night sleep. Somewhere I wouldn't be distracted by my own hormones or whoever might end up in my bed. Somewhere I could stay while I figured out my long range plan.

Right now Vanessa was my only option. She and Michael had a big, old house, with plenty of extra bedrooms – and beds. And her job at the hospital gave her a direct line to all the gossip that passed for news in Pleasant Glen. If there was an unadvertised job opening or apartment available, she would know about it.

She was also a computer genius with questionable morals and enough knowledge of the law to keep me from being arrested for stalking. I hoped. Part two of my plan to get on with my life involved finding out what had happened to Joe Davenport. Vanessa was just the woman to help me track him down.

Vanessa and Michael had bought and restored the 1920's foursquare house her grandparents had lived in. All the homes in her quiet neighborhood had comfortably-sized yards, set at uniform intervals, around uniformly square blocks, bisected by uniformly well-kept alleyways. I drove slowly around her block searching for an out of the way parking spot. I didn't want to be seen going into my husband's mistress' house, just in case something went wrong. I wasn't completely sure yet that I didn't want to kill Vanessa, or at least slash her tires. Or kill her *and* slash her tires.

Sunday morning in Pleasant Glen meant that most people were either at church, going out to brunch after church, or still in bed, sleeping off a hangover. I decided that if I *did* kill Gary or Vanessa, I would do it on a Saturday night. The deserted Sunday morning streets would make it easier to dispose of the body.

I parked down the street and around the corner, between two, white, four-door, sensible, mom cars, just like mine. Or just like the one I gave to Emily. Now my chili red Mini Cooper with checkered roof stuck out like a . . . chili red Mini Cooper with a checkered roof. I bought the car from the head of the PGC theater department, using money from my personal checking account. I thought it would be perfect for Emily, but we decided the automatic-transmission mom-mobile was better for Chicago traffic.

Gary called the Mini Cooper my mid-life crisis car. I called it an economical, fuel efficient alternative to Gary's Escalade. Talk about a mid-life crisis car.

I adjusted my oversized sunglasses and pulled the collar of my trench coat up around my neck before getting out of my car. I headed up the alley to Vanessa's house, jogging from one garage to the next, in case anyone happened to be looking out their windows.

My cover was blown by Vanessa's next-door neighbors who had gathered on the deck to watch Dad fire up the grill, but seemed to find my zigzagging through back yards more entertaining. I waved politely, then turned down an invitation to stay for brats and a corn hole tournament.

This. This right here is one of the things that drives me nuts about Iowans. Why does everything in Iowa have to have an agriculture reference? Why not just call it bag toss or yard bean bags or whatever the rest of the nation calls it? Why border on the obscene?

I knocked on Vanessa's back door.

"Can I help you, stranger?" Vanessa asked, opening the door just enough to peer out at me.

"Let me in," I hissed, looking around furtively. The neighbors waved again.

"Nope."

"What? *What?* Let me in, damnit."

"Nope. I don't open my door to strangers, and they don't get any stranger than you . . . stranger."

"Damnit, Vanessa," I hissed again, "it's me, Julie," I said, pulling down my sunglasses to glare at her. The sunglasses were more to hide the bags under my eyes than to hide my identity.

"Nope. Sorry. You don't look like any Julie I know. The Julie I know, my *best friend* Julie, would never skulk around knocking over people's garbage cans. Also *that* Julie swore she would never talk to me again. Or at least not until Monday."

"Open the fucking door, Vanessa," I said, louder than I intended. The neighbors froze mid-wave, a collective look of shock on their faces. I would have to get rid of a lot of witnesses if this went badly.

"Fine. Get in here 007, before you scare the Olsons to death. They finally started talking to me again after you hung those ornaments on my yard deer last Christmas."

"Fun haters. 'Blue Balls' are hilarious." And totally different than "corn hole."

I hung my trench coat over the back of a kitchen chair. There were two glasses and a bottle of wine on the table. I casually peered into the dining room, checking to see if there were more witnesses.

"Expecting company?" I wondered if Gary had lied about the meeting in Des Moines. Maybe I could kill two birds with one stone. Literally.

"Just you, Agent 99. My neighbor across the alley, Aldrich Powers, wants to know if you're wearing anything under that trench coat, and said you could 'de-brief' him whenever you want. Really Jules? I have to live with these people."

"I was trying to be inconspicuous. Just because I'm here doesn't mean I've forgiven you."

"The best way to be inconspicuous is to act normal," Vanessa said quietly, sitting down at the table. "Go about your business and no one will suspect a thing." Was that what *she* was doing? What had happened between her and Michael?

I sat down and studied her, searching for clues. What was she hiding? She looked as bad as I felt.

"You look like shit," I said.

"Hello Pot, my name is Kettle."

"Yeah, well, I walked in on my husband fucking my best friend. And then my daughter and her potential new boyfriend tried to share the bed I was sleeping in. What's your excuse?"

"Oh, Jules. I'm so . . . Wait! Emily's back? When did she get home? And since when is she allowed to have a boy in her room?"

"Since she went away to college, last night, and she's already gone. She's working as a camp counselor this summer. And she promised to text me. She's mad at Gary, not me. But all that's beside the point."

I took a deep breath and prepared myself to eat a little crow.

"I need your help."

Vanessa crossed her arms and squinted at me. I'd seen that look often enough to know she was thinking of how she could hold this over my head for a return favor. I'd done the same to her many times.

"OK."

"That's it? OK? No 'this is gonna cost you'? No gloating?"

Vanessa smiled a crooked smile. "I figure I owe you. A bunch. I've missed you. I hate it when you're mad at me."

"I'm leaving Gary," I said.

Vanessa squirmed in her chair. She opened and closed her mouth a couple of times, like she was searching for the right thing to say.

"Oh! Honey, don't you think that's a little . . . sudden? Maybe you should take a few days to think it over."

"I've *been* thinking it over. And waffling. But when I talked to Emily, I realized staying with Gary after all that has happened might set a bad example for her."

"Yeah, but, what happened was a mistake. A *huge* mistake. There's no reason for Emily to ever know anything about it."

"OK. Let's think about this a minute. A) You're the one who told Gary that if you found out he was cheating on me you'd help me move out." I paused. "FYI, he was. Or did." Vanessa blushed.

"And B) Emily already knows. And she's crushed." Vanessa doted on Emily. She would do anything to get back on her good side. I wasn't above using this to my advantage. "Emily even invited me to stay with her for a couple nights." Sort of. "Which brings me back to the reason I'm here."

"To kill me?"

"No, to ask if I could move in with you."

"Maybe you could just kill me now and get it over with."

"Tempting, Van. Then I could go to jail, and voila, a place to live!" Vanessa didn't see the humor in that solution. "I know it's weird and all, but you're my best friend, and well, I don't have any other options."

She squirmed some more, but I didn't think she seem surprised by my request.

"So, anyway, about that . . . ." Vanessa chuckled a little, the way people do when they're trying to soften you up for some bad news.

"Not exactly the way I had hoped your response would begin. I'm sensing a 'sorry but' coming soon."

"I'm sorry, Jules. But, Gary called me Friday and we kinda talked about this."

"Kinda talked about it how?" I asked. That rat bastard, he'd cut me off at the knees. He knew I didn't have any where else to go. But why would he care?

"Well, we agreed it would look . . . bad. I don't think Pleasant Glen is quite ready for *Sister Wives*. And then there's Michael. Or the absence of Michael. You know how people talk, and Gary doesn't want this to get more Jerry Springer-esque."

"Oh, honey, the only way this could get more Jerry Springer-esque is if I became the surrogate mother for your love child. And the answer is no, by the way."

"That is not on my 'to-do' list. But, can you understand his concerns?"

So, "Mr. Image is Everything" had concerns. Unfortunately, I *could* see his point.

"What if you moved in with Gary, and I camped out here until Michael gets back?"

"I really don't think that's . . . I mean, there's no need to rush into . . . "

103

"You rushed into Gary's bed while he was still married."

"And look where that got me."

No, look where that got me, I thought. I tried using the silent treatment to pressure her into giving up.

Hmpf.

At least 10 seconds of silence and no signs of cracking.

From her.

I could feel the sweat beading up on my forehead.

Time to change strategies.

"So, are you and Gary going to, um, pursue a relationship?"

"Are you kidding me? Why would I date a guy who cheats on his wife?"

Cue the rimshot.

She raised an eyebrow. "Too soon for levity?"

"Just a little." It *was* a pretty good comeback. I snickered in spite of myself.

"Sorry honey."

"But I thought, I mean, that night when I asked you if you would break it off . . . . "

"Told. You *told* me not to see him again. You know how I over react when someone tells me what to do, or what *not* to do. Besides, honey, you need to give Gary a second chance. I think you two can talk this out."

I rolled my eyes.

"Really. If you can forgive me, you can forgive him too, can't you?"

"I *haven't* forgiven you. I just need your help. I'm desperate."

"You wouldn't *need* my help, you wouldn't *be* desperate, if you would just talk to Gary." Vanessa was practically pleading now.

This was getting me nowhere. It wasn't like I was asking her to donate a lung or something. I just needed a place to stay for a little while.

"It's not the same thing, Van. You and I have always been there for each other. Gary . . . Gary's changed. Or maybe he hasn't, but I just never noticed it before. Emily said he hit on one of her sorority sisters. He flirts with Muffy and Bunny for heaven's sake. I can't take it any more."

Vanessa shook her head. I could tell she still wasn't convinced. He *slept* with *her*, for Christ's sake. How much more evidence did she need?

"He's a friendly guy, Jules. I think you're over reacting." Vanessa seemed to be retreating into her calm, happy place, far away from reality. That pissed me off even more.

"Yeah, the two of you were real friendly under my duvet the other night. What makes you think you're the only one?" I was talking extremely loud now. Not shouting, but almost.

"Jules, calm down. I . . . I don't know why we did what we did. Maybe I had too much wine. All I know is nothing like that ever happened before. And Gary, he didn't seem all that . . . comfortable with the way things went. I think if he was some kind of Lothario, he would be a little more . . . skillful, or something."

"And maybe he finally grew a conscious and decided shtupping his wife's best friend was going a little too far. Just because he was momentarily overwhelmed by guilt doesn't mean he hasn't slept with other women. Sometimes practice doesn't make perfect, it just makes, *practice*."

It had taken me two long days to come somewhere near not blaming Vanessa for what had happened Thursday night, and now she was willingly taking responsibility? Defending Gary? Maybe it was a form of Stockholm syndrome. I changed tactics again.

"You said that when you confronted him about cheating he changed the topic, right? Instead of confessing or denying anything, he changed the topic? He asked you about Michael? And when you started crying he took you out for drinks? That sounds like manipulation to me" Vanessa's forehead wrinkled. She seemed to be thinking about this. I pressed on. "Honey, can't you see? Gary took advantage of you."

She gave me a cold stare.

"Of course," she said, her voice just barely above a whisper, but with a cutting edge. "He only had sex with me because it was convenient. After all, I am such a hideous, emasculating bitch, that no man could ever actually *want* to have sex with me."

I enjoy jumping to erroneous conclusions as much as anyone, but Vanessa had just taken it to the next level.

"No, honey, that's not what I meant! I'm *trying* not to *blame* you. Think about it from my perspective. My husband *left* me for my best friend. "

"No. Your husband *fucked* your best friend. He's still your husband." Vanessa sat up and her voice became louder. "Look around you Julie." She waved her hands broadly. "*My* husband *left* me. LEFT me!"

Vanessa's eyes grew big and she clamped her hands over her mouth. It was too late. Her secret was out.

She crumpled in her seat, shoulders sagging, head bowed. Tears started forming in her eyes.

"He left me Jules." She covered her eyes with her hands and started rocking back and forth. "He left me for . . . ." She was crying in earnest now. Great sobs wracked her body.

Michael had *left* her, left her. Not just left for a semester-long sabbatical.

And I had done nothing to help her. Instead of pressing to find out what was bothering her, I had let her suffer alone. What kind of a crap friend does that?

"Who is she?" I may have dropped the ball before, but I could make up for it now. Maybe I could channel all my pent up anger at this new woman. After all, if she hadn't slept with Michael, Vanessa wouldn't have slept with Gary. Maybe.

"Who is she, honey, tell me."

Then again, I never really thought Michael was good enough for Vanessa. He was a nice guy and all, but I always felt like there was something missing. I never said anything – much – because she loved him and he seemed to make her happy. But still. Was I really sorry that Michael was gone?

"Who is she? I'll kill her." Or buy her a bouquet of flowers.

"I'll dance at her funeral." Or take her to the bar.

"I'll spit on her grave." Or we'll do tequila shooters.

Vanessa finally sat up and took her hands away from her face. Her eyes were red, but all traces of tears had been carried away by the pretty-cry fairies. Damn them.

She took a deep breath and let it out slowly. She closed her eyes and ran her hands through her hair. When she spoke, her voice was tired and filled with resignation.

"*He*, Jules. He."

"Yes, honey. I know. *He* left you."

"No, Jules. You should be asking 'Who is *he*."

I cocked my head to one side as I let that sink in.

"Michael left me for a man." Vanessa sighed and reached for the wine bottle and a glass. "Try to keep up."

Well. That changed things.

Joanne Salemink

11

"My husband left me for a man," Vanessa repeated quietly.

How does one respond to that? Poorly, in my case.

"OK, fine. Who is *he*? I'll kill him, I'll dance at his funeral, yadda, yadda, yadda." By the time I got to the third yadda, I realized the whole thing was taking on a hate crime tinge. I lost what little enthusiasm I had for revenge in the first place.

Vanessa poured a splash of wine into a glass and pushed it across the table towards me. Then she put the bottle to her lips and upended it, drinking nearly half in one long draw.

"Van . . . ."

She wiped her mouth with the back of her hand and shook her head. "No! Don't say anything. There is nothing you *can* say. There is nothing *to* say. Nothing."

Pfft. Like that ever stopped me.

"I'm so sorry."

Vanessa snorted.

"I didn't know."

Vanessa shrugged.

"Because you wouldn't tell me."

Vanessa glared at me. "What part of '*nothing you could say*' did you not understand?"

"Oh, I understood it. I just didn't believe it."

Vanessa rolled her eyes and took another drink. A smaller one this time. The bottle was nearly empty.

"Honey, you know it's not your fault," I said.

"Thank you, Dr. Ruth, for pointing out that I did not, in fact, *turn* my husband gay. I feel so much better."

I watched the wine climb the sides of my glass as I swirled it. "That's not what I meant," I said quietly. "And you know it. It's not your fault he *left*."

Vanessa's sigh sounded tired. Or maybe it was the way her face sagged and her shoulders slouched as she sighed.

"No, but it's my fault he stayed married to me for so long." The tears that had been gathering in her eyes started to overflow.

"He tried, Jules. He tried so hard." Vanessa looked at me intently, as if her sincerity itself could convince me. "He *tried* to be a good husband. He was sweet, and kind, and thoughtful. He was affectionate. Tender. He just wasn't . . . physical." The tears began to fall, flowing single file down her face. I realized my cheeks were wet, too.

"I thought we were normal. I mean, all the girls in the Auxiliary joked about how they couldn't keep up with their husbands before the wedding, and their husbands couldn't keep it up after the wedding. We just skipped directly to that second part."

Vanessa upturned the bottle one last time, then took it to the sink, rinsed it out and added it to the recycling bin. She took another bottle out of the cabinet. She uncorked the wine automatically, looking out through the kitchen window while she talked.

"He was a virgin when we married. I wasn't all that experienced, despite what Bunny and Muffy said. It was . . . awkward. I figured it would get better. Then when we – I guess *I* – tried to get pregnant, I thought maybe I was putting too much pressure on him."

She sat back down at the table and poured a glass of wine for each of us.

"We were happy, Jules. Really. In our own way. We were comfortable. Content. I thought maybe that was enough. Maybe we didn't need to have sex." She smiled for a moment. Then her chin started quivering and the smile dissolved into a grimace.

"But I knew better. We both knew. Something was missing. There was always an emptiness that I didn't know how to fill. Eventually it grew too big to ignore. But not so big that we could talk about it.

"He loved me, he just didn't *love* me. But he tried. He tried *so hard* to make me happy. Sometimes it made *me* tired." She closed her eyes and shook her head. "Do you have any idea how it feels when someone has to *try* to love you? When you know it's a conscious effort?"

I didn't know what to say. And for once in my life, I didn't say it.

"I always felt like I was failing him. That it was my fault."

"No, honey." I reached for her hand, but she drew it away.

"I know. It wasn't my fault that he didn't find me *desirable*," she said bitterly. "But it was my fault that he had to live a lie."

"No. It was his *choice* to live that way."

"He didn't see it as a choice. He said he didn't want to disappoint his family. He didn't want to be homosexual."

"That wasn't his choice either."

"I know. *You* know. It just took him a little longer. Until he met . . . someone special. And he realized how happy he *could* be. How unhappy he was."

This was a lot to take in. And Vanessa tried to do it all by herself.

"So. How long have you know this?" I tried to be as gentle as I could, but I was still hurt that Vanessa hadn't told me. I was angry with myself for whatever I may have done to make her not trust me enough to talk.

Vanessa sighed and refilled her glass.

"Six months." So about the time I started whining about my world falling apart, and became too busy to see that her world was falling apart, too.

"Michael really did leave on sabbatical. But I knew he wouldn't be coming back to me. The night before he left, we sat right here and he told me everything. He had already started divorce proceedings. All the paper work was ready for me to sign, all our finances, insurance, the mortgage, everything.

"He said he was trying to be kind. That he didn't want to drag things out. But I thought it just showed how miserable he must have been. How could I have not seen that?"

"Oh, honey. You don't see what you're not looking for," I said. Or what you don't want to see, I thought.

"I guess not." She shrugged and took another drink of wine.

"Why didn't you tell me?" I asked. "I . . . we both have friends who are homosexual. You know that I don't care who you're sleeping with, as long as it's not my husband." Vanessa winced. "Present company excepted for the moment."

"What good would it have done? To tell you. You couldn't have changed anything."

"I could have listened." I didn't even add that I wouldn't have tried to sleep with her like Gary did. "I could have brought you ice cream. And pizza. And wine. And Brat Pack movies on DVD. That's what friends are for."

"You had problems of your own. Problems you *could* solve. Problems you can *still* solve. Gary *still* loves you, Jules. He *needs* you. The two of you can work things out."

Now it was my turn to shake my head.

"I don't think so, Van. Not any more."

She took a deep breath, then looked at me as if she were trying to make up her mind about something.

"There's more," she said. She sounded determined to get it all out in the open.

More? I wondered how there could be more? What could be worse? Unless – Ohmygod – she was dying and her husband had left her!

"His name is Steve." She looked like she was waiting for a response.

"That's the *more*?"

"Not Steven, not Stephen. Steve."

"Honey, I . . . ."

"Steve Austen."

For some reason that name rang a bell. Had we gone to school with him? Had we met him at The Bar? Steve . . . Austen . . . . Why did that sound familiar?

"Oh. My. God!" I slapped my hand over my mouth as I remembered the number one "must see" TV show of my youth!

Vanessa closed her eyes and put a stranglehold on the stem of her wine glass.

We talked over each other.

"Don't . . . ."

"Like the . . ."

"Say . . ."

"'Six Million' . . . ."

"It! Don't say it! Don'tsayit!" She gulped her wine.

I felt sorry for her. Really, I did. But this was just too good to pass up.

"We can rebuild him?" I had to sneak something in there.

"Fuck you." She was only half-serious, I could tell. She was trying not to laugh, too.

"Does that make Michael . . . ."

"NO! Nononono!"

"'The Bionic Woman'?" Even I thought I might have gone too far with that one.

"Bitch! This! This is why I couldn't tell you! I couldn't tell you part of it – I knew you wouldn't care that Michael was gay. I knew that sooner or later I'd let it slip that Michael ran off with Steve Austen, and then, *this*. This would happen!"

"I'm sorry honey, but, really? Can you blame me?" I had to stop talking because I was laughing too hard. Vanessa was back to drinking straight out of the bottle. Luckily I knew were her stash was. "Are you seriously telling me that you didn't make even one 'Six Million Dollar Man' reference when Michael told you?"

"Of course I did." Vanessa slouched in her chair and let her head droop to one side. "He was soooo pissed. I don't think Michael made the connection until I pointed it out. I think that pissed him off the most."

I could see that.

"So, what happens now," I asked.

"What time is it?

"It's 12:30. Should we get lunch?"

"Pfft. I'm having grapes for lunch." Vanessa refilled her glass. "But, by now Michael and Steve are happily married. And waiting to board a flight from Des Moines International Airport to Cancun. The wedding was this morning. Michael's family was all going. Which was good, because otherwise I was going to have to kick their asses."

"Wow! That was fast!"

"I met Michael and Steve at the lawyer's Thursday morning to sign the final papers. That's why I was late for lunch. I gave them a shish kabob maker and told them mazel tov. Then I stopped at City Park and cried for half an hour. The ducks by the pond didn't give a rat's ass. They were mad because I forgot to bring bread crusts."

But she had looked so good when she got to the restaurant. Damn her pretty crying! Ducks my ass. She was probably flocked by swans, begging to do her bidding.

Wait a minute. Thursday? Thursday!

"So that's why you went to talk to Gary." I was starting to connect the dots.

She nodded sleepily. Like I said – she's a pretty crier, but helpless when drunk.

"That's why I refused to believe Gary would cheat on you. Because I wanted to believe that one of us had a marriage based on honesty. I always thought you were the perfect couple. I mean, obviously you had sex! Emily is proof of that!

"I've always envied you two. Gary loves you, Jules. He still does. The way he looks at you when you wear that low-cut, little black dress? The way he looks at you in those sweater sets? You! The 'Boobless Wonder,' still rockin' the cardigans."

Ouch. The girls were offended. Just a little. Because, well, truth does hurt.

This was taking a strange, drunken turn. Time to get her back on course and find out what really happened.

"So, you confronted Gary, you told him I'd leave him, and then . . . ."

"I thought welllll, hey! At least Gary's attracted to *women*! And then I thought, 'Hey! *I'm* a woman!' And Gary *noticed* that I'm a woman. And then he *acted* like I was a woman. An attractive woman. An *attractive* woman that he was *attracted* to." Vanessa was swaying as she talked. I wasn't sure how much longer I had until she passed out.

She leaned across the table and motioned for me to lean in too, like she was going to tell me a drunken secret.

"Attracted in a *sexual* way." She winked at me, as if she wasn't sure I understood what "sexual way" meant. I wasn't sure I wanted to hear the rest of this, but I couldn't stop now.

"So, you're saying he . . . ."

"He. I. I'm not sure who made the first move. There was a lot of wine involved." That seemed to be a theme lately. I hoped Gary's investment portfolio included vineyards.

"The next thing I knew we were back at your house, there was more wine, and we . . . ." She seemed to finally realize who she was talking to and began to self-edit. "I think we both knew we should stop. We both knew it was wrong. But neither of us could, could . . . ."

I watched her eyes fill up with tears. Uh oh. Drunk Crying trumps Pretty Crying every single time. I jumped up and grabbed the roll of paper towels off the counter.

"Thank you." Vanessa unrolled a couple, blew her nose mightily, and then continued. "I'm so sorry Jules. I should have stopped it. But, I . . . I just couldn't. It had been so long. I imagined Gary was Michael and that he wanted me. *Wanted* me! Then I imagined I was you, and that Gary wanted me. I mean you. I mean. Idunno it got kinda weird there for a moment.

"And then you were there! And all I felt was . . . sick." She had that same glassy-eyed look that I had seen Thursday night.

I found myself reliving that moment, too. I had been so shocked, so hurt, to find them together. I didn't know how to react then. I still didn't.

"That's how you looked Thursday night, too, Jules. So sad. So confused." Vanessa reached out and put her hand on mine. "I felt so bad, Jules. So bad. I just wanted to, Idunno. I didn't know how to react. I still don't." At least I wasn't alone.

"Then *we* fought, and I felt worse, and you got all 'don't let this happen again' – like I planned it in the first place? – and I flipped out and got all defensive, and you kicked me out. And I just wanted to die. And you haven't answered my calls or my texts or my emails. And then Gary called and we both said it was a mistake and he said 'but how would it look' if you moved in with me and I agreed. And I thought 'you bastard, you cheated on my best friend, you don't deserve her, I'll do anything I can to help her right now', even though I think you two were meant to be together but maybe some time apart will do you both some good . . . ."

OK, now she was just drunk rambling. *This?* This is why I hated waitressing at The Bar. Too much drunk rambling.

"And that's why after Mass this morning, when I heard Miss Irene was looking for someone to move in with her for a little while, or more like her kids thought she needed someone to move in with her for a little while, I thought, 'HEY! I know just the woman!' And she said 'Oh, yes, I know Julie Westbrook,' and well, you know Miss Irene, don't you?"

I shook my head, uncertain. The name sounded familiar, but I couldn't quite place her.

"She's that little old lady from the bank," Vanessa explained. "Kind of snarky. Funny as hell." I still wasn't making a connection, but Vanessa had already moved on.

"Anyway, then I said 'Great!' And she said 'Please have her stop by at two o'clock. The boys will have started by then.' And I have no idea what she was talking about, but it sounded good and it was boyzzzzz plural, so I figured . . . ."

"I don't know, honey, I mean, I'm not a nurse or anything. If she needs special care . . . ."

"Oh, good god, no. The woman has more energy that the two of us combined. She slipped and fell, not a scratch on her, but her kids think she's a danger to herself. They probably want to take her motorcycle away from her, too."

Motorcycle. Snarky. Rich. Funny. I remembered Gary's mom talking about someone that fit that description.

"But anyway. I told her you'd be there at two, and it's past one now, and you're drunk so we've got to get you cleaned up and over there, because I don't think she'll take very well to you being late for an interview, and this could be the start of something great!"

"It's OK, honey." I lead Vanessa into the living room and sat her down on the couch. "You're the one who's drunk, not me. Why don't you lay down here and rest. I'll get cleaned up and head over to see Miss Irene."

I would be cutting it pretty close if I had to go all the way back home. Vanessa lived about half-way between my house and where she said Miss Irene lived.

"Would it be OK if I borrowed some clothes and cleaned up here?" Vanessa was already asleep. I assumed her snoring counted as a "yes." Van and I were about the same size. I was a little taller, but she wore heels while I wore flats, so pants-length shouldn't be a problem.

I found a familiar pair of khakis and a white shirt and took a quick shower. I opted to wear my own bra and underwear, because A) Vanessa has way bigger boobs than me, and B) Eww!

I let my hair dry naturally, planning to pull it back in a low ponytail with a pretty barrette later, and within twenty five minutes I was on my way to Miss Irene's house.

Vanessa thought this could be the start of something great. I hoped she was right.

Joanne Salemink

12

Irene Truman's address was in one of the oldest parts of Pleasant Glen, jut a few blocks north of the town square. After establishing the commercial center, the early businessmen built their homes here, within walking distance of their shops. The grand Victorian homes showcased their wealth and inspired confidence in their business abilities.

Eventually the need for newer, bigger and more stores moved the center of commerce out to the edge of town. Newer, bigger and more homes followed along. The downtown area was deserted and storefronts sat empty. Many of these big houses were neglected too, or divided into cheap apartments.

When businesses on the edge of town left for River City, the Pleasant Glen Chamber of Commerce turned its attention to revitalizing the quaint downtown, capitalizing on the historic charm. These grand old homes caught the attention of renovation enthusiasts and historic preservationists. Some had already been restored to their former glory, some were works in progress.

I thought about our house and the other McMansions going up in developments on the edges of town. The new construction seemed cold and imposing, with prominent garages overshadowing entryways, and spare, effortless landscaping.

These homes were stately and refined, with wide front porches, gingerbread details, and graceful columns framing colorful, welcoming front doors. Sprawling, mature trees shaded elaborate flower beds and luscious green lawns. Garages were tucked away in back yards.

I was sure Miss Irene's house had been in the family for generations, and had always been well maintained. While my mind was otherwise occupied in the shower, I had been able to connect the dots. I did know Miss Irene. Sort of. At least in that way that everyone in some communities knows everyone else. And I was certain Gary's mom knew her. I wasn't sure if that would work in my favor or not.

While we had never served on any committees together, we did belong to several of the same clubs. Miss Irene was a Volunteer Emeritus – a group of older ladies who had paid their dues, both literally and figuratively – in various social organizations. Having done all the grunt work in their younger years, these ladies were content to sit back and watch as a new generation provided the slave labor required for community service. In other words, to sit back and complain about any changes that were made.

Miss Irene was a bit of an odd duck, more progressive and open to change, and frequently at odds with the other veteran volunteers. She seldom came to Auxiliary meetings, but always had a reserved table in a place of honor at the Gala and at other community fundraising events.

Her monetary donations, while never discussed outright, were significant enough that her eccentricities were tolerated. Rumor had it she was the one who suggested hiring Chippendale dancers for the Gala each year – an idea Van and I always supported.

I was reminded of that detail as I walked up the path to Miss Irene's house. A group of five young men were clustered around the base of a ladder, which leaned against the roof of the front porch. A small, white-haired lady made her way up the rungs.

"Excuse me, I'm looking for Irene Truman." I spoke cautiously, not wanting to startle the climber. She leaned back, holding the ladder with one hand and pivoting on one foot, swinging around to face me. All the boys – none of them looked to be older than their mid-20s – moved to defensive positions. Some steadied the ladder, while others stretched out their arms to catch her. She seemed oblivious to the fuss.

"You found her!" The woman smiled and waved down at me with her free hand. The boys all swayed expectantly, as the ladder shook. "You must be Julie. Give me a minute here to finish up, and I'll greet you properly." She resumed her climb and started rooting around in the gutter. The boys relaxed their stances, but remained alert, looking nervously at one another.

"Is that safe? Should she be . . . ?" I quietly asked the boy still holding the ladder. He appeared to be a little younger than the others, but they all looked to him for directions. "Trey" was embroidered near the right shoulder of his t-shirt. On the opposite side was the logo of a local motorcycle shop, Pleasant Glen Cycles and Motors. The other boys wore matching shirts, but without their names.

Trey sighed and shook his head. "No. It's not. She shouldn't be," he said. Then he looked up at her and added loudly, "But that doesn't stop her."

"Boys, what's my number one rule?" Miss Irene leaned even farther away from the ladder and continued her search as she talked.

"Never judge someone's abilities by their appearances." The boys answered in a well-practiced chorus.

"Yeah, but Big George will kill us if he finds out about this," Trey said. He kept a firm grip on the ladder and a nervous eye on Miss Irene, who was now leaning over the opposite side of the ladder. The boys had shifted accordingly.

"So we best make sure he never finds out," she called down. "A little discretion goes a long way, isn't that right Julie?" She turned her head and fixed me with a meaningful look. How much did she know, and how did she know already? I didn't have time to ask, because just then she found what she had been searching for.

"A-ha!" she shouted as she pulled a leopard-print bra out of the gutter and held it aloft. She leaned back again in her exuberance, waving her frilly pennant above our heads. We all returned to our catcher stances. All except for Trey, who just tightened his grip on the ladder. He seemed to be used to her theatrics.

"Geez, Miss Irene! What was that about discretion?" He asked. The other boys blushed and quickly looked away as the woman made her way down the ladder, bra dangling from one arm.

"You'd be surprised how much zing the elastic in these things has," she said, shaking the bra at me. She gave me an exaggerated wink and laughed. Then she turned to Trey. "Tell your grandpa 'mission accomplished'."

The other boys started to snicker, but one look from Trey and they scattered, busying themselves with yard work.

"Now then," Miss Irene said, wiping her hand on her pants leg before reaching out to shake mine. "I'm Irene Truman. Nice to meet you." If her firm handshake was any indication, we shouldn't have worried about her grip on the ladder.

"Julie Westbrook. Nice to meet you too, Mrs. Truman."

"Oh, please, call me Miss Irene. Everybody does. This is George Herbert Monroe the Third."

"Trey, for 'Third'," the young man said, reaching out to shake my hand. He smiled and twin dimples appeared on his cheeks. He had short, dark hair and big, brown eyes. I guessed he was probably 17 or 18 years old, but he shook my hand and greeted me with confidence and maturity.

"And this is my . . . what's that word, Trey? . . . 'posse'," Miss Irene said. She chuckled, and waved her hands around at the other young men. "Boys! Where are your manners? Say 'Hi' to Julie, here."

All the young men stopped what they were doing to smile at me and wave. "Hi Miss Julie," "Good afternoon, Ma'am," they called. Despite the dirty, sweaty work they were doing, their t-shirts and shorts were clean and neat. And a little on the snug side.

Miss Irene took me by my elbow and led me up the stairs to the front porch. She was a compact woman, about a foot shorter than me, and slender. I figured she had to be in her late-80s, but she had the energy of a much younger person. Her clear blue eyes had a keen look to them, and I doubted that she missed much from behind those stylish, wire-rimmed glasses.

She certainly did not look like she needed a live-in maid or nurse to look after her, but maybe she was just lonely. Then again, with all these young men around – and the racy bra – I wasn't sure loneliness was the issue, either.

"Go ahead, sit down, make yourself comfortable." Miss Irene waved me over towards a wooden rocking chair. She sat nearby on a large, cushioned porch swing. "The view is pretty good from over here," she gave me a little smile and a wink, nodding at the workers.

"You might as well settle in too, Trey, since you're acting as your grandpa's proxy this afternoon." He started to protest, but she cut him off. "Oh, please. I know he sent you over here to keep an eye on me as much as the crew." Trey took a seat on the porch railing where he could watch us and the yard crew.

"I'm a little confused," I said, settling in to the chair. "I was told you needed someone to . . . help out around the house. You seem to have things pretty well under control."

"Oh, hiring a babysitter is my kids' idea," she said, sighing. "My children, bless their hearts, think I'm too old and feeble to be living alone, but they can't be bothered to take care of me themselves.

"Half of them took after their father and grew old before their time. The other half took after me and are still too busy raising hell to be saddled with an old lady. In the meantime, I'm too busy raising hell to grow old. Confounds both groups to no end."

"Now, you know there's more to it than that, Miss Irene," Trey said.

"Yes, it's all that damn, nosy nurse's fault."

Trey rolled his eyes.

"Well it was. Watch your manners, Trey," Miss Irene warned. She turned to me and started to explain. "About a month ago I slipped and fell. Trey's grandpa, Big George, was here when it happened. He tried to help me up, but I got to laughing so hard I couldn't move. Damn near ended up pulling him down on top of me. Wouldn't that have been scandalous!" She waggled her eyebrows at me. Trey shook his head and made a point of looking out over the yard. "Well, he was afraid I'd broken something, and then when I couldn't stop laughing he thought maybe I'd hit my head, so he called the ambulance.

"When we got to the hospital, the nurse asked if I could remember how I fell. I told her I was practicing my pole dancing and I slipped. Because that *was* what happened.

"She couldn't imagine such a thing. She was sure I had a concussion and was delusional. The doctor checked me out and realized nothing was hurt – besides my ego and my backside – but Nurse Ratchet raised a fuss, said it must be some sort of dementia.

"That's the problem with young people today. They think once a person hits retirement age they lose all interest in sex." Miss Irene sat back in the swing, pushing off the floor forcefully in her anger. The swing picked up speed. "You lose interest in sex when sex becomes boring. After fifty-some years you have to work a little harder to keep things interesting, is all. Even after my little detour to the ER, Big George appreciated the effort.

"Awww geeze, Miss Irene," Trey buried his face in his hands.

"Ha! Teenagers! You think you invented sex! Let me tell you, your grandpa and I have forgotten more about sex than you'll ever know!"

"Isn't there someplace else I need to be?" Trey asked her. "Something else I need to be doing? Please?"

"Julie's not blushing," Miss Irene said. "Well, not much. That's a good sign, anyway. Why don't you take her out to the apartment. Fill her in on anything you think I've missed. I'll be along in a little while, then you can tell me your story, dear."

Trey jumped up from his seat and headed toward the stairs. He seemed anxious to get moving before Miss Irene could launch into another embarrassing story.

"I don't know why you and Grandpa don't just get married or at least move in together."

"We've both been down that road," Miss Irene said shaking her head. "I love your Grandpa, but I don't need a man around the house, leaving the toilet seat up and getting in my business. I'm just too set in my ways. And so is he. You of all people should know that. Go on now, go. We don't have all day."

Trey led me around the side of the house and across the back yard to the garage. From the size of it, I guessed it had been originally built as a carriage house. Doors for three car stalls, with room to spare, opened on to a basketball-court sized parking area next to the alley. A flight of stairs ran up the building's near end.

"Do you really think she needs someone to live with her?" I looked up at the door and started to feel hopeful for the first time in a long time.

Trey shrugged. "I don't know. I'm not sure I completely believe her story about the . . . well, her dancing. But we were all pretty shook up, seeing her in the hospital.

"Dad and I live with Grandpa, but he spends most of his time here. They've been . . . I guess you'd call it dating, since before I was born. After Miss Irene fell, her kids freaked out, and demanded she get someone to watch after her. We thought she and Grandpa would finally get married. But she just dug her heels in deeper. She must like you."

"How can you tell?" I didn't think I'd said enough to make an impression yet.

"You're the first one she's shown the apartment to." Trey smiled. "She turned a couple people away before they even got out of their cars. And a few others didn't make it past the pole-dancing story. She's right, you don't scare easy."

"Well, after what's happened to me lately, it's going to take more than the thought of an elderly stripper to shock me."

"Wow," Trey said. I thought I could see a new respect in the way he looked at me. "That bad, huh?"

"You wouldn't believe me."

"Noooo, that's OK," Trey said putting up his hands in a signal to stop. "No need to tell me any more. Listening to Miss Irene is one thing, but . . . ."

I laughed. "Don't worry. I'm not quite that . . . open."

"Yeah, Miss Irene's a wonderful lady. But she is kinda . . . ." Trey hesitated.

"Blunt?" I suggested. "Straightforward?"

"Headstrong. But please don't tell her I said that."

We both laughed, then stood at the base of the stairs chatting idly as we waited for Miss Irene. Trey told me he was finishing his junior year at PGHS. I wondered if he and Emily had ever crossed paths. It's a small enough school that most students at least recognize everyone, but big enough that they might not know each other well.

"What's the deal with the yard crew?" I asked. "And how does the motorcycle shop figure in?"

"Dad calls this Miss Irene's Finishing School. A couple of these guys are my friends from PGHS, the rest either work at the shop or are doing an internship there. Grandpa owns Pleasant Glen Cycle and Motors. Well, he and Miss Irene are co-owners."

I raised an eyebrow questioningly.

"Way back, when Dad was little, Miss Irene got sideways with the owner of the repair shop where Grandpa worked. I guess this guy treated her like she was just some dumb woman, no offense, and didn't take her seriously as a customer. Grandpa had done some work for Miss Irene, and she knew he was honest and respectful, so she offered to set him up in business for himself.

"Her one stipulation was that anyone who worked for Grandpa had to treat every customer who came through the door with courtesy and respect. She said a woman's money spent just the same as a man's, and it didn't matter what she was spending it on." Trey shrugged. "Seems like a no-brainer to me, but Dad says there are still some cycle shops that ignore women customers. And he's had to fire a few guys who didn't measure up to Miss Irene's expectations."

I was impressed – with Miss Irene, Big George and Trey's dad. And Trey.

"Over the years Grandpa, and now Dad, have organized work crews to help out around here as a way to test the guys' manners. Miss Irene keeps an eye on us, makes sure we're always behaving the way she thinks we ought to, and makes sure we're good representatives of the shop. Sometimes friends or customers have asked Dad to take their sons on, just to help polish off the rough edges. Trust me, if there's one thing Miss Irene knows how to do, it's polish off the rough edges."

"Ahhh, that's just because I have a few rough edges myself," Miss Irene said, joining us. "Trey, why don't you go on and finish your work. I'll show Julie around. I think your tender little ears have probably heard enough for one day." Miss Irene reached out and gave Trey's ear a tweak as he tried to duck around her. "Dinner's at six, so plan your time accordingly."

"Yes, Ma'am. It was nice to meet you, Miss Julie," Trey said before leaving to join the rest of the work crew.

"So, what do you think of Trey," Miss Irene asked me as the boy disappeared around the side of the house.

"He seems awfully nice," I said truthfully. "He sure thinks the world of you." Miss Irene stood a little straighter and smiled proudly.

As much as I was looking forward to seeing the apartment, I didn't want to get my hopes up too high. I wanted to find out as much about the situation as I could, without offending Miss Irene. Although after the bra and the pole-dancing story, I thought it would take a lot to offend her.

"I'm still not sure why you're looking for someone to move in," I said.

"My kids can be terribly stubborn. Not sure where they got that from." She rolled her eyes and laughed at herself. "And they have Big George and the boys on their side this time. I'm outnumbered. So, I agreed to find a roommate, at least until I can prove that I'm not a danger to myself.

"You are a little more . . . female than I had hoped for, but Big George was very clear on that point. He insists on being my only male overnight guest. Silly old man." She blushed like a school girl. "As if I'd have eyes for anyone else after all these years."

"Then why don't you two . . . ."

"Nope! That's enough about me for now." Miss Irene dismissed my comment with a wave and turned to climb the stairs. "The sooner I show you the apartment, the sooner you can start moving in."

"But don't you want to get to know me a little first?" I asked.

"Well, of course, dear. I just thought that if I found my husband in bed with my best friend I'd want to get the heck out of Dodge as quickly as possible," she said.

I stopped where I was, too surprised to go any further. CNN is no match for the Pleasant Glen grapevine.

Joanne Salemink

13

I was still standing there, trying to figure out how or why Miss Irene knew about my situation, when Trey came jogging back.

"Big George called. He asked if you want him to take a look at The Scout before dinner." Trey said this without blushing, so I didn't think "The Scout" was code for anything kinky that I didn't want to know about. Probably.

Miss Irene scowled. "Making me get a babysitter is one thing, letting The Scout go is another." Trey shifted his weight from foot to foot and chewed on his lip.

"Oh calm down, boy!" she snapped. This only made Trey more anxious. Miss Irene sighed and softened her tone. "I'm sorry, hon, you know – and your granddad knows – that's a sore subject with me. I want to hold on to her a little longer. I don't think she's done with me yet."

I was dying to know who – or what – The Scout was and how she fit in with this strange family dynamic, but I didn't want to appear too nosy.

"Is this something you need to discuss in private?" I asked.

Miss Irene studied me a moment, tapping her finger on her chin, as if seeing me for the first time. Maybe that nurse was right, I thought. Maybe she did have a concussion.

"You could be the answer to more than one problem, Julie. And The Scout could be the answer to yours!" Miss Irene's face lit up with a bright smile.

"Trey, tell your granddad there may be a change in plans. Then you can pull The Scout out and dust her off." Miss Irene looked me over again. "We'd better find out what Julie thinks of her before I get too carried away. I'll show Julie the apartment, then you can show her The Scout."

Trey looked at me and grinned. "You're gonna love her! Trust me!" He fiddled with his cell phone, then he turned and hurried away, talking excitedly.

"He's a good boy," Irene said, watching Trey make his way back to the house. "Of course Big George and J.J. wouldn't have raised him any other way."

"J.J.?" I asked.

"Trey's dad, George Junior. Big George's son." Miss Irene explained. "My youngest ones used to stumble over 'George Junior.' It came out 'Juh-juh Juh-nya.' We took to calling him J.J. so they wouldn't develop a stutter. If I'm feeling real ornery I call them Big, Medium and Small.

"Trey's mom passed away when he wasn't much more than two. Poor little squab." Miss Irene shook her head sadly. "J.J. and Trey moved in with Big George, and I helped raise Trey just like I helped raise his dad. But that's another story for another time.

"Now then. What about you? Do you think you could handle traipsing up these stairs on a regular basis?" She bounded up the steps and stood on the landing waiting for me. I continued my slow climb, struggling to organize my thoughts.

"This will be your own little refuge. It's not much, but it's private. You'll be out of my hair, I'll be out of yours. You can have your man friends over, I can have mine."

"Well, sure, but I . . . uh, I'm not expecting any . . . company." Miss

Irene had apparently heard about Gary and Vanessa, but I wondered what other rumors were circulating. No one in Pleasant Glen ever let the truth stand in the way of a good story. I mean, I *had* been talking to Billy at the restaurant, and then Charlie stayed over. Either encounter could easily have been blown out of proportion.

"I'm not sure what you may have heard, but it's not like . . . . I mean, how do you know about . . . ?"

"Please," Miss Irene gave a little flap of her hand. "This is Pleasant Glen. There's no such thing as a secret among certain circles. Sometimes it's a blessing. Although most of the time it's just a pain in the ass."

I wasn't buying it. Miss Irene and I didn't run in the same "circles." My skepticism made me frown.

"Helen, Gary's mom, called me," Miss Irene said.

"Gary's mom," I repeated dully. How did our story get all the way to Florida so quickly? I leaned my back against the garage. "But how did she. . . ."

"Shirley, Muffy's mom. That woman is such a gossip. The acorn didn't fall far from the tree. They're both a couple of nuts." I smiled weakly at Miss Irene's joke, waiting for the rest of the story.

"Helen knew I was looking for help. My oldest daughter lives in Florida – she's one of my 'old before their time' kids. She talked to Gary's folks about finding a little condo for me. Not too close to her, of course. Helen knew I'd never leave Pleasant Glen and told her so. Still, when Shirley called Helen with the news from Muffy, Helen thought about me. Helen's just madder than a wet hen about what Gary did, by the way. And she thinks you two can still work things out. I told her we're not all as saintly as she is. That will probably get me kicked off the Christmas card list."

This was all too much for me to process. I must have looked a little queasy, because Miss Irene asked if I needed to sit down for a moment. I slid my back down the side of the garage, coming to rest on a step. Miss Irene sat on the edge of the landing, a couple of steps above me.

"Honey, I heard enough about your situation to know you need a little time to sort through things. I've been there. I know it's rough. I won't press you for details, but if there's anything you want to talk about, I'll listen. There's nothing you could say that would shock me."

I snorted, thinking about the bra in the gutter and the pole dancing.

Miss Irene chuckled, too. "Well, yes. I suppose that much is obvious."

"I just don't know where to start. So much has happened so fast." I shook my head and stared blindly out over the back yard.

"It's not as bad as you think, honey."

"My husband slept with my *best friend*. And my in-laws – in *Florida* – know, for goodness sake. *You* knew about it!"

"Well, like most people, I make it my business to know everyone else's business." Miss Irene smiled a little. "And everyone else thinks they know my business. But we're talking about a very small circle, made up of very small minds, here."

She leaned against a railing post and sighed. "I'm old enough now not to be of much interest, but there was a time right after my husband Frank's motorcycle incident, when he wasn't with us anymore . . . . Well, scandal just seemed to be my middle name.

"This was long before your time. But I remember feeling like I was living under a microscope. After a while I realized most people were too busy stuffing their own skeletons back into their closets to worry much about me and mine. Eventually they moved on to the next drama. They always do.

"Of course these days I'm a little better at keeping my business *my* business. Surprising what a few well-placed donations – with the promise of more to come if discretion is observed – will do." Miss Irene gave me a mischievous grin.

I sighed. The chances of me making a "well-placed donation" were slim. Part of me knew that most people in Pleasant Glen didn't know, or care, about what went on in my bedroom. But right now it was hard to ignore the gossips who did.

Which was worse? That Gary had cheated on me, or that so many people knew about it?

"What I mean is, I'll respect your privacy. Unless there's something you really want to talk about. Then I'm ready to listen to whatever you have to say."

What was it I had told Vanessa? "You can tell me anything"? What if she had told me about Michael? Would she still have slept with Gary? I hadn't told anyone *all* my fears – not even Vanessa. What if I ended up sleeping with the first man who offered to listen to me?

I told Miss Irene everything, from my suspicions about Gary, to losing my job, to my uncertain financial situation. She listened quietly, never interrupting.

"So, what are you going to do next?" she asked when I was finished.

This again. Somehow I had hoped it would be different.

I sat up straight, squared my shoulders and faked a smile.

"Oh, I don't know, but I'm sure it will all work out." I spoke with a confidence I didn't feel.

Miss Irene didn't say anything. She cocked her head and watched me. I felt my smile begin to slip and my shoulders begin to sag. The job, the apartment, it had all seemed to be falling into place, but now I wasn't sure.

"Is that how you really feel?" Miss Irene asked.

I took in a deep breath to fortify myself for the next lie, but instead the truth came tumbling out.

"Hell no. I'm scared to death. I have no clue what I'm going to do next. But no one wants to hear that. Or maybe they do, but I'm not going to give them the satisfaction."

Miss Irene leaned forward and patted me on the shoulder.

"It's OK to be scared, you know. In fact, I was a little worried when you said that you weren't. But you seem tough. You just need a few breaks to go your way. Maybe I can help. Maybe The Scout can help."

"So, about 'The Scout'. Who, what . . . ?"

Miss Irene grinned and that ornery glint returned to her eyes. "All in good time, my dear. I love to build up the suspense. The Scout deserves a little drama. First, let's take a look at the apartment." I pulled myself up off the step and joined her as she opened the door.

"After Frank bought the farm and I went back to work full time at Daddy's bank, I turned this into an apartment for the nanny," Miss Irene said. "There's furniture hidden under the boxes. Use anything you like. I'll have J.J. and Trey carry the rest downstairs. You can earn your keep by helping me sort and get rid of some things."

The gambrel roof, which gave the garage a barn-like appearance outside, created a high ceiling inside. Bumped-out dormers, three-windows wide, were centered on both long-side walls, flooding the space with light. A kitchenette and an enclosed bathroom were located on the far end, opposite the entry.

I knew a fresh coat of bright white paint – not "Off-White" – and a few colorful accent pieces would enhance the open, airy feel. The 1950's-style kitchen table with chrome legs was retro-cool, if a little dusty. New, floral cushions would liven up the white, wicker love seat, and the open-metalwork bed was perfect for my patchwork quilt. There would be nothing blah about this space when I was done with it.

"What do you think?" Miss Irene asked.

"Definite possibilities," I said, smiling. I was looking forward to decorating to suit my tastes, not to impress anyone else, or to try and reproduce the latest fashion.

"Good! You kids can start to move these boxes downstairs tonight after dinner – get you out of the house while I break the news to Big George. I'm guessing you'll want to move in as soon as possible?" she asked.

"Sooner," I said wearily. My new-found optimism flagged as I thought of the work it would take to get this space cleaned up.

"I have more than enough guest rooms for you to use while you get this sorted out," Miss Irene said. "I'll put you down at the other end of the hall so your snoring doesn't bother me. You shouldn't be able to hear the bed springs creaking from there."

My head snapped up in shock.

"Relax, sweetie. I'm just kidding." But, as she turned away, I swear she added "As far as you know."

There was a low rumbling as one of the garage doors below us was opened.

"That would be Trey and The Scout. What do you think? Are you ready to meet her?"

"Ready as I'll ever be, I guess." And curious.

Miss Irene and I walked downstairs just as Trey was pushing the most beautiful motorcycle I had ever seen into the driveway.

I was used to squat, burly Harley Davidsons, lumbering down the road like shoulder-heavy bears.

I was used to wasp-waisted crotch rockets, ridden by testosterone-fueled boys.

I was used to hard-used and home-patched Honda mini bikes, ridden by farm kids too young for a driver's license.

But this.

This was different.

The Scout was low slung and unmistakably powerful, yet graceful.

White accents and chrome trim highlighted a collection of sensual curves subtly masked by luxurious black paint. Instinctively, I reached out and brushed my fingertips down the gas tank and across the warm leather seat. I held my breath. My pulse quicken. My hands ached with the desire to caress that sinuous body.

"Amazing," I whispered. I was falling in lust.

"It's the skirted fenders," Miss Irene said.

The white side panels of the fender skirts swept over the spoked wheels, giving the bike a sleek look. A thin line of chrome accented the contrast between the white panels and the black arched top of the fender, reminding me of a pair of classy spectator pumps. The tail of the fender flipped up slightly in a coy, flirtatious wink. A sassy touch. Tiny details bridged the gap between masculine and feminine, elevating the Scout from machine to a work of art.

While Miss Irene and I stood quietly admiring the motorcycle, Trey bounced on the balls of his feet, unable to contain his excitement.

"If you think she looks good, just wait until you hear her sing," he said. "Can I start her up, Miss Irene?"

Miss Irene nodded and smiled. Trey quickly threw his leg over the seat and abruptly yanked the bike upright.

"Remember what Big George told you," she cautioned. "You need to take it slow with us older gals." She turned to me and rolled her eyes. "Typical man. He doesn't understand the value of foreplay. Always in a rush to get to the main attraction."

Trey took a deep breath and slowly blew it out, calming himself. Leaning deeply over the gas tank to set the choke, he stood with his head just inches away from the engine, holding the bike securely between his thighs. His head was turned away from me, but it seemed like he was whispering to the motorcycle.

I caught his eye as he stood and gave him a questioning look.

Trey shrugged and grinned. "Cold starts are always tough. I know it sounds silly, but she likes it when you talk to her," he said. His left hand cupped the Rubenesque tank tenderly. "Sometimes she gets in a mood and needs a little sweet talk."

Trey glanced at Miss Irene, then leaned towards me, "Big George taught me that, too," he said in a stage whisper.

Miss Irene chuckled. "He's a smart man, your grandfather. I've almost got him trained up into husband material."

Trey's eyes opened wide.

"I said *almost*. Well, what are you waiting for? Start her up. There's another lesson for you, son. When a girl's ready to go, *she's ready to go*."

"Yes ma'am," Trey said. He turned the key and raised up out of the seat to kick start the bike.

The Scout had some very feminine attributes, but it was still a good sized motorcycle. I prepared myself for a deep, throaty, ground-shaking rumble, or a discordant pop-pop-pop.

But Trey was right.

She did sing.

Her voice was honey-smooth, and as seductive as her curves. She crooned a slow, sultry torch song. She sang of heart break – and of confident resilience. Trey goosed the throttle gently and The Scout responded with subtle, soaring vibrato before settling back into her dramatic, earthy, contralto purr.

"Big George says everyone hears something different . . . hears what they need," Miss Irene said. "That's her gift. All I know is she sounds different to me now than she used to. That was Big George's gift." She smiled and a misty, far-away look crossed her face. "Maybe I *should* marry the old goat, after all."

With a turn of the key, The Scout's engine stopped just as smoothly as it had started.

The magical spell was broken.

"Eh, no sense rushing into anything." Miss Irene turned to me. "Do you ride?"

"I used to. I took a class, got my license, bought a little Honda. Then things . . . changed." My parents died, I met the man of my dreams and lost him, I gave up on dreaming and lived a decidedly practical life until I found my husband fucking my best friend. I kept those thoughts to myself.

Miss Irene cocked her head to one side and looked at me like she was still waiting for an answer.

"I'd . . . like to," I said. I hadn't even considered riding a motorcycle in years. Not since Gary and Emily and the Auxiliary. Not since I grew up and became dull.

"I'd really like to ride again," I said with a smile.

"Trey, when your grandad gets here, tell him we're going to need The Scout in top condition. On second thought, never mind. I'll tell him after supper. He's always easier to deal with after a good meal. Maybe he has me

142

trained, too."

Joanne Salemink

14

"So, what did you think of The Scout?" Miss Irene asked, as we walked back to the house.

"She's beautiful. There's something about her that defies explanation. Are you sure she's not enchanted?" I was only half kidding.

Miss Irene laughed. "When it comes to The Scout, I wouldn't rule anything out. She seems to have that effect on some people. I still ride her, just not as far or as often as I'd like. Big George thinks the old girl needs a rest. I think she needs a new challenge."

We sat in a pair of vintage, turquoise, metal lawn chairs, tucked in the shade of a big oak tree. Miss Irene looked at me and smiled, but there was something almost pleading now in her tone of voice, and the sad set to her eyes.

"Maybe you can understand why I'm not ready to give her up yet." She shook her head. "My kids, on the other hand . . . . They've always tolerated her, but none of them ever felt the pull she has on me. Frank, he . . . well, with Frank it was complicated." I thought she sounded a little wistful when she talked about her husband. I wondered why she had kept the motorcycle after what had happened to him.

"Big George has done a wonderful job with The Scout, you'd never know she had been in an accident," I said.

Miss Irene tilted her head to one side and looked at me questioningly.

"I mean . . . you mentioned Frank's motorcycle accident, and that he was, well, 'not with you' after that. I figured The Scout must have been pretty damaged . . . ."

She tilted her head to the other side and looked even more confused.

Maybe she did have dementia, but it came and went, I thought. Maybe she had learned to compensate.

"Ohhh." Miss Irene nodded slowly as if she were replaying our conversation in her mind. "No, honey, there was a motorcycle *incident*, not an *accident*. Frank didn't die, but he was banged up pretty good. I guess I didn't make that clear."

"But, you said Frank 'bought the farm'."

"Yes, honey. He did. After we divorced, he bought a small, hobby farm, half-way between here and River City." Miss Irene giggled. "Maybe my phrasing was off a bit." She was full-on laughing now, doubled over, slapping her knee. I could see why Big George hadn't been able to get her up off the floor when she fell during her pole dance.

"Oh, honey, no. Frank took his mistress out for a spin on The Scout, and then she ran him over. He broke a few bones, but he didn't die. Oh, goodness no.

"All his fast living and loose women did catch up with him, though. He's in a nursing home up in River City. I visit him once or twice a month. I'll tell you the whole story while we're making dinner."

I helped Miss Irene get the roast in the oven, then went home to pack a few necessities. I planned on picking up the rest of my stuff when I moved into the apartment. The first things to go in my bag were my tape player and Joe's tape.

Gary wasn't home from Des Moines, but the message light on the home phone was flashing. I liked the permanence of a landline, and the validation of having my name listed in the phone book. Gary said I was the only person who ever used that number, along with the millions of telemarketers who ignored the "Do Not Call" list.

I checked the message anyway.

It was from Gary.

He had tried to call my cell phone, but the mailbox was full, he said. I didn't doubt it. I had turned the ringer off after Vanessa's sixth apology call.

Things in Des Moines were complicated, but promising, he said. The successful dinner with Charlie was proving to be more helpful than I could imagine, he said. He wouldn't be home until Tuesday at the earliest, Thursday at the latest, he said.

I could live with that.

He loved me, he said.

I wasn't sure I could live with that.

I stopped at Vanessa's on my way back to Miss Irene's. Vanessa was lying on the couch, nursing the mother of all afternoon hangovers. She had a package of soda crackers and a large cola with ice on the table next to her. She gave me a bottle of wine to take to Miss Irene as a thank you gift. She toasted me with her soda, wished me well on my new endeavor, and vowed that she would never drink again. Or at least not until Tuesday.

She apologized again for sleeping with Gary.

I took another bottle of wine.

I thanked her again for setting me up with Miss Irene.

She handed me a third bottle, a folding waiter's corkscrew, and a plastic wine glass and told me to hide them in my overnight bag. She told me she had heard that Miss Irene and Big George were "rambunctious and noisy," and asked if I had earplugs.

She also said that if they *were* "rambunctious and noisy" she wanted details.

After settling in to one of Miss Irene's extra bedrooms, I joined her in the kitchen to finish making dinner. Miss Irene told me that she and the three Georges made a special effort to have dinner together at least once a week. I felt honored to be included in their plans.

I couldn't remember the last time Gary and I sat down together for a meal. One of us was always working late or at a meeting. We had tried harder when Emily was home, but she was busy, too. Lately, on those rare occasions we were both home, the TV or newspaper seemed to be a preferable dinner companion.

I shuddered as I arranged some frozen dinner rolls on a baking sheet, but there wasn't time to make anything from scratch. While dinner finished cooking we opened a bottle of Vanessa's wine, and Miss Irene told me the story of her husband's motorcycle "incident."

Miss Irene's Story

I met Frank Truman soon after I graduated from secretarial school. I was only 19, but I was sure I had the world, and my place in it, figured out.

Father was the president of Pleasant Glen Savings and Loan back then. I worked as a teller during the day, and took as many business classes as I could at the college. After work, Father taught me all the things about running a bank that you can't learn in school. Pleasant Glen was quite conservative in 1945, but Father could see a day coming when women would be allowed to hold management positions. He wanted me to be ready when that time came.

One day Frank came in to set up an account. He had taken a sales job with ReadyGrow Hybrids and planned to make Pleasant Glen his home base. Oh! Frank was a natural born salesman. Father used to say "Any salesman worth his salt could sell ice cubes to the Eskimos. Frank could sell a humidifier to an Iowan in August."

Frank was so handsome, with those lake-blue eyes and his blonde hair swept back just so. I could never decide if he looked more like Gary Cooper or William Holden. He was a real man's man, but there was a gentleness in his eyes that kept him from being too masculine.

And it wasn't just his looks. He was so charming! That was the secret to his success. He listened to you with such gravity, that you found yourself telling him secrets you didn't even know you had. And when he gave you advice, whether it was which shoes to wear or which seed corn to buy, you took that advice without thinking twice.

I'm doing a horrible job here. I'm making him sound shallow and calculating. He wasn't. He was honest and sincere. He was a hard worker and generous to a fault. He used to get into so much trouble for extending credit to dirt-poor farmers. But you know, those farmers always came through, even if he did have to carry them for a month or so.

Frank believed in people. And when he believed in you, you started believing in yourself. I earned straight A's in my classes after we married, even though I didn't have much time left over for studying late at night!

No, Frank's downfall was his wandering eye. But that's not right either. That was just a symptom. It was his restlessness that got him in trouble.

He fought that restlessness as best he could. Early on he could distract himself with some sort of project or a new job. He was always working his way up through the sales ranks, then jumping ship to a new company and starting all over again.

Frank was a good father, a good husband, a good provider . . . for as long as he could be. I suppose I always knew it would only be a matter of time before he grew restless with being married.

The ladies were drawn to him like bees to honey. At first the attention itself was enough. He enjoyed being adored. But I could tell he was starting to get bored even with that.

Then he told me about this motorcycle he found tucked away in some farmer's barn. I thought maybe he had found a way to scratch that itch for adventure.

It was a beaut, he said. A 1941 Indian Sport Scout. A little dusty and neglected, but low mileage and in great condition, considering. The farmer's son had bought it just before shipping out for service in the War. When the boy came home – and thank God he did come home – he had changed. He'd seen enough action and wanted a quieter life. Still, his father kept the motorcycle, hoping his son's innocence would return some day, too. The boy moved to California and the motorcycle stayed in the barn, untouched, where his father had stored it.

Frank was selling farm equipment by then and had just convinced the farmer to upgrade to a new, bigger tractor. The farmer needed more storage space, and decided that it was time to sell The Scout.

Maybe I should have seen some sort of omen in the farmer's story, but all I knew was Frank was more excited about this motorcycle than he had been about anything in a long time. Business was going well, but it was getting routine. He needed some excitement in his life.

Six children under the age of ten was about all the excitement I could handle. I was just plain worn out! So that part of our marriage wasn't keeping his attention either. I hoped this motorcycle would give him the thrill he needed.

Without telling Frank, I contacted the farmer and made him a fair offer on the motorcycle. He hadn't even started it up in nearly a decade, so I knew it was going to need attention. I asked around, and everyone said George – Big George – was the best mechanic in town.

George was working at a little auto shop downtown, fixing whatever came in the door, making the owner a mint of money. George has always had a way with engines. I swear he can talk to them.

I was there when The Scout was dropped off at the shop. Big George quietly inspected the motorcycle, poking and prodding, admiring the workmanship. He looked up and nodded, dismissing me and the shop owner, and set right to work.

His boss gave me an estimate for new tires, seals, hoses, and who knows what else, anticipating a fat paycheck. He said they'd contact me in a couple of weeks when the work was done.

He called me three days later.

He could have called me sooner than that, but he was hoping George would find something else to fix, something else to bill me for. The Scout was a new challenge for George and he threw himself into his work. Personally, I think George has always had a crush on The Scout and vice versa. She just blossomed under his care.

I can still remember the look on Frank's face when he came home and saw that motorcycle, all shined up and sitting in the garage. I was sure I'd found the cure for what ailed him. And I was surprised we didn't add to the family that night!

Frank took meticulous care of The Scout. He called George about every little pop, ping, or oil drip. George told Frank to leave the maintenance to him.

That's how Frank met George's wife, Doris.

I never knew Doris personally, although I saw her around town a couple times. She was a lively thing, quite a bit younger than George. They seemed like an odd match, but he was totally smitten with her and she seemed to dote on him. And they had a new baby – little George Junior.

I don't know if it was postpartum depression – we didn't talk about those things back then – or if she and Frank shared the same sort of restlessness. Doesn't matter anyway. Frank and Doris started meeting while George was at the shop and Frank was supposed to be out making sales calls. They were discreet. Isn't that the word they all use?

George and Doris lived over in a new development on Levitt Street – small, modest homes at modest prices, Pleasant Glenn's first brush with suburbia. Frank used to leave The Scout at their place for George to look after whenever she was acting up.

Frank cut such a dashing figure on The Scout, Doris was always begging him to take her for a ride. One fine, sunny day he gave in and took her to the Tasty Freeze on the edge of town. Big George was out on a service call, saw The Scout in the parking lot and stopped in to check on her.

Frank and Doris were taking full advantage of the secluded picnic area at the far edge of the parking lot. They couldn't be seen from the Frosty Freeze, and didn't notice the bright red Chevy flatbed idling in the driveway. But George noticed them.

He waited for Frank and Doris to unclench and compose themselves. Doris headed over to the ice cream shack, leaving Frank standing by the white rail fence bordering the lot. George pulled up close, hemming him in.

George was standing by the front bumper talking to Frank when Doris returned. She saw Frank pinned up against the fence and assumed the worst. She should have known George couldn't harm a fly, but her guilt made her panic. She jumped into the truck to move it and free Frank.

Only problem was, she barely knew how to drive, much less how to drive a manual transmission. She turned the key without engaging the clutch and the truck lurched forward.

Frank had relaxed and leaned back against the fence once he realized George wasn't going to kill him right then and there. His relaxed posture may have saved him from more serious injuries. As it was, he took the impact like a rag doll, flopping forward over the hood of the truck as it hit him.

Doris' screams turned hysterical when she saw Frank crumple onto the hood and then slide down out of sight as the fence gave way behind him. The fence had been erected more for quaint decoration than for serious traffic control. This also worked in Frank's favor.

Big George sprang to action. He threw open the door, pulled Doris out of the cab and set the parking brake, saving Frank from further injury.

Alerted by Doris' histrionics, the owners of the Frosty Freeze ran out to the parking lot. From their vantage point it appeared as if Doris had intentionally run over Frank. And that was what they told the police and the ambulance crew.

Statements were taken, with both men trying to convince the authorities that Doris had not acted out of malice or fury. It wasn't until Frank declined to press charges that the police begrudgingly ruled it an accident.

Frank was transported to Pleasant Glen Hospital. He had broken bones in both legs just below his knees, a dislocated hip, a cracked pelvis, and a doozy of a bump on the back of his head, but nothing worse.

George stopped by our house a couple days later to apologize. He said Doris had run off to Tulsa to live with some distant relations, leaving Junior with him.

I told him Frank was already on the mend, but that it would be a while before he could ride the Scout again, if he ever could.

George told me he could find a buyer for The Scout if I wanted him to. He said I could easily make money off the deal.

"She's a beautiful machine," he said. "She deserves someone who will appreciate her."

Something about how he personalized that hunk of metal struck a chord in me. I'll admit, I was furious when I found out what had happened. I blamed Doris, I blamed The Scout, I blamed myself. I blamed everyone except Frank.

But now Doris was gone and Frank was in the hospital.

I looked at The Scout, sitting there in the back of George's truck. It would have been so easy to push her off, watch her crash onto the brick street. But then the setting sun reflected like a flare off that chrome headlight, and painted a blush on those white fender skirts.

I looked George straight in the eye.

"Can you teach me how to ride her?" I asked.

George didn't hesitate. "Yes, Ma'am."

I don't know why I kept her. At first I think I wanted to remind Frank of what he'd done. But he had a hitch in his get-along that reminded him everyday. Maybe I kept her to remind me of what he'd done. Well, you know what that's like.

In the end I guess it didn't matter. Whatever thread of domestication Frank had spun for himself unraveled. When I walked in on a nurse giving him a blow job in his hospital bed, I knew he was beyond remorse.

I waited until he was able to get around on his own to start divorce proceedings. It was all quiet and professionally handled. Frank didn't put up any fuss. He moved out to the farm, but stayed involved in our children's lives. They blamed me at first, but after an ever-changing array of girlfriends and a couple of step-moms, they came around.

Father arranged for me to work from home until the scandal blew over. I was already taking care of my own brood, so I convinced Big George to let George Junior join the party. That man, wonderful as he is with machines, had no idea how to deal with a toddler.

True to his word, Big George taught me how to ride The Scout and how to take care of her. Some nights I'd leave the older kids in charge after dinner and go for a short ride around town. I needed a little escape now and again. After a while, George talked me into adding a side-car so I could use the Scout for running errands or take the kids along. Heck, sometimes I took the dog.

I kept The Scout as a reminder of all I'd been through, the good and the bad. There was plenty of bad. And plenty of good. The Scout brought me the adventure and excitement Frank and the farmer's son had missed.

She also restored my confidence in myself. By the time Father retired from the bank, I was Vice President of Operations. Let me tell you, not everyone was happy about a woman VP!

Of course The Scout and Big George turned out to be a package deal. I wasn't sure I needed a man in my life after Frank, but having your own personal mechanic does come in handy. We made quite a team, the three of us. Sometimes I think The Scout's the only reason Big George has put up with me for so long. Then I remind him of the fringe benefits that come with being a personal mechanic.

And that's why we need to make dinner extra special tonight. Big George will be taking your measure. He thinks, and my kids think, it's time for me to sell The Scout. If we can't convince Big George you're up to the task, well . . . . I've had several offers on The Scout already. I'm just not sure what I'd do without the old girl. So for goodness sake, don't let the roast dry out!

15

At 7 p.m., precisely, I heard the deep rumble of men's voices and laughter from the backyard. There was a polite, quick knock on the back door before Trey opened it and walked in to the kitchen.

Trey was followed by a slightly shorter version of Trey, with a liberal sprinkling of gray in his dark brown hair. And *he* was followed by still another, slightly shorter yet, version of Trey, with snow-white hair.

Lined up in a row there in Miss Irene's kitchen, Trey, J.J. and Big George looked like a set of nesting dolls. I looked at them and blinked hard, not trusting my vision. When I looked again, all three men were staring at me. Each had the same look of concern on his face. They looked at each other, sharing some silent communication. This only made the similarities more obvious.

I turned to Miss Irene, my jaw hanging open, and blinked again. My astonishment must have been plain, or else she was used to this reaction.

"They don't see it," she said, shrugging her shoulders.

She held out a stack of plates for Trey to take to the dinning room. "Here you go, son. Make yourself useful."

"Good evening Miss Irene," he said, taking the plates from her and giving her a peck on the cheek. "Hi, Miss Julie." I noticed he was much more relaxed and boyish without the yard crew around.

"And for you," Miss Irene said, holding a pitcher of ice water out for

J.J.

"Yes, ma'am. Good evening, ma'am." J.J. gave Miss Irene a slightly mocking, short bow before kissing her cheek. He smiled and winked at me. "Nice to meet you, Julie. Duty calls." He raised the pitcher high and then dipped his head again to Miss Irene as he back through the swinging door, following his son.

"Watch your manners, boy!" Miss Irene and Big George called out in unison. Then they looked at each other, grinned and chuckled. The electricity between them made the hair on my arms stand up.

I noticed the way Miss Irene blushed and looked at Big George, her chin tilted down so she peered up at him coyly. The way he stood a little straighter and puffed out his chest just a bit. I thought about the bra, and the pole dancing.

I was charmed by them.

I was jealous of them.

I wished I'd followed Van's advice and packed a pair of earplugs for later.

"Pleasure to meet you, Julie," Big George said. He took my hand in his. Despite his age and the callouses from years of handling wrenches, his hand felt warm and soft as it enveloped mine. He smiled at me, and I saw that his gentle, brown eyes had the same ornery glint as Miss Irene's.

He brought his other hand up around the back of mine, giving it a quick squeeze. I'm a sucker for the two-handed handshake. I was completely charmed and went a little weak at the knees.

"All right you two," Miss Irene said, interrupting the moment. She held a bottle of Vanessa's wine and a corkscrew out for Big George, and tilted her head toward the door. "There's still work to be done. Send Medium and Small back for the food."

Big George gave me another smile before turning to Miss Irene. "Yes, Ma'am," he said, then added a husky "Good evening, Dear." His soft, sexy tone and the tender, lingering kiss they shared made my heart skip a beat.

Miss Irene and I both watched as he strutted – there was no other word for it – out of the room. My eyes caught the cocky tilt to his head. I'm certain Miss Irene's eyes were directed lower. We both sighed.

"That one's *mine*," Miss Irene said, giggling like a drunken teenager at the prom.

I thought he would be a much bigger man. I mean, a name like *Big George* creates certain expectations. And the way Miss Irene and Trey talked about him with such gravity and awe, deferring to him even in his absence, I pictured a giant, barrel-chested man, who was loud and boisterous.

Big George wasn't much taller than Miss Irene. He was at least three or four inches shorter than me, maybe 5'5" on a good day. He was spare, but solid, with a wiry build. His close-cropped white hair showed the eventual progression of J.J.'s and Trey's hairlines, receding at the temples until there was just a little peninsula of hair left on the top of his head.

There was a kindness about Big George, a restrained power. He was a listener, a quiet and thoughtful man. Big George's presence drew you closer, while Miss Irene's reached out and knocked you over. They complimented each other perfectly.

Dinner at Miss Irene's was like a scene from a 1950's sitcom. Big George said a brief, non-denominational grace before we began eating. The conversation was lively, gentle teasing was frequent, and polite manners were always observed. They were so warm and welcoming that I almost forgot I was there to win Big George's approval.

After we finished eating, Miss Irene asked J.J. and Trey to help her clear the table and get dessert. Big George and I were left alone in the dining room to get better acquainted.

I was prepared for an intense interrogation rivaling the Spanish Inquisition. But Big George was a gentleman. We talked about life in Pleasant Glen, people we knew in common, how the town had changed. Typical Iowa small talk. He inquired politely about Emily and about my volunteer work in the community, but avoided mentioning Gary. I suspected Miss Irene had already filled him in on all that.

Still, there was something about the way he listened, the way he watched me, that gave me the impression he was gathering more information than my answers provided. I had just begun to relax and enjoy the conversation – Big George was telling me about the time Muffy demanded they use only *extra* virgin oil in her BMW – when Miss Irene, J.J. and Trey returned with the pie and decaf coffee.

Miss Irene fussed over Big George, serving him a large slice of apple pie, garnished with cheddar cheese. She also gave him a generous scoop of ice cream in a separate bowl. The rest of us had our ice cream nestled up next to the still-warm, cheese-less pie. Big George raised an eyebrow and gave me a little smirk. It was clear to me that he knew Miss Irene was buttering him up, but he didn't try to stop her.

After doing everything she could to make sure Big George was satisfied, short of feeding him his pie herself, she sat down to her own dessert.

"So, what do you think of our girl?" Miss Irene gave Big George an innocent look, but I was sure she had been listening at the door to our entire conversation.

Big George looked from Miss Irene to Trey, then rolled his eyes.

"You two have already made up your minds," he said. "I'm not sure what my opinion has to do with anything. Julie here is a fine girl. I think she'll fit right in." The three of us shared a smile of relief.

"Besides, Trey says she hardly flinched at all when you told her about your dance lessons."

"Oh, Dad!" J.J. looked at the ceiling and shook his head.

"Which is more than I can say for you, son," Big George said, causing J.J. to blush. "I only ask that you try not to be a bad influence." I looked at Big George in surprise. Miss Irene snickered.

"I meant you, Irene," he added.

Now it was my turn to laugh. Miss Irene gave Big George a playful swat on the arm and a look of adoration.

Big George's approval of me was all well and good, but there was another issue at hand.

"What about The Scout?" Trey asked.

Miss Irene inhaled sharply and her eyes grew big. Apparently she thought this topic required more finesse than the subject of me living there.

"Well, now, George, I think what Trey is trying to say is, although I wouldn't have put it quite so bluntly as that," she gave Trey a sharp look. "What I was thinking was, given Julie's situation, and what with my present, albeit temporary restrictions, I was thinking that The Scout could use a little exercise, and Julie could use a little of The Scout's special therapy, and . . . ."

Big George chuckled. "Really, Irene? You think I don't know what's going on here?" He crossed his arms over his chest and sat back in his chair. Miss Irene remained perched on the edge of her seat, clasping and unclasping her hands anxiously.

"If I can trust Julie with one of my girls, I ought to be able to trust her with both of them, don't you think?" He reached over and took her hand in his. "And besides, my dear, I trust your judgment."

Miss Irene beamed, and I was certain that someone was going to get lucky that night. I think J.J. had the same thought, because he shook his head again and rubbed a hand over his eyes.

"You *will* take a class from a certified instructor and get your license." Big George returned his attention to me, but continued to hold Miss Irene's hand.

"As luck would have it, a new class session starts tomorrow night," J.J. said. "Registration is full, but someone always drops out at the last minute. Worst case scenario, I may have to bring in a retired instructor to help me." He grinned at Big George, who nodded in consent. "I'll call you tomorrow with the details, Julie. Ladies, I know you had planned on having me and Trey help move some boxes down from the apartment, but it's getting late and tomorrow is a school day."

"Aww, Dad. It's the last week of school. It's not like I'm going to miss anything importa . . . ."

J.J., Big George, and Miss Irene each gave Trey a disapproving look. He didn't stand a chance.

J.J. turned to me. "The first class is all bookwork and videos, Julie. We have some smaller bikes that you'll use when we start riding. I'll have my top mechanic" J.J. looked at Big George, "check over The Scout so she'll be ready to go when . . . *if* you pass the class."

"Oh, she'll pass, Dad. No worries," Trey said.

I wished I felt as confident as he did.

I was a little disappointed about the delay for my apartment, but I was also exhausted and looking forward to what I hoped would be an uninterrupted night of sleep. Miss Irene really had set me up in a guest room at the opposite end of the house. Still, I was on edge from the previous three nights' misadventures, and I jumped at every creak and groan – especially the groans – that the old house made.

My thoughts were still racing, so I opened the wine Vanessa had tucked into my overnight bag and logged on to Facebook for some mind-numbing scrolling. Nothing caught my eye. It was a Sunday night, and the rest of the world had better things to do than post funny cat memes.

I heard the low sound of voices filtering up from the kitchen through the duct work. I thought about Miss Irene and Big George, and about Emily and Allen, Vanessa and Gary, and Michael and Steve. It seemed like everyone else had someone to hold – even if it was just for one night.

I wondered who Joe was holding. If he was holding anyone.

I typed his name in the Facebook search bar and hovered the arrow over the magnifying glass icon.

Did I really want to know?

Yes.

Maybe.

Definitely.

Click.

There are a lot more people named Joe Davenport on Facebook than you might think.

I ignored the empty, blue-shadow profile pictures, as well as the pictures of cats, dogs, half-naked women and old men. That still left an absurdly high number of possible Joe Davenports.

There are also a lot more bands named The Average Joes than you might think.

But there was only one Joe Davenport Fan Page.

It was pretty basic. Most of the posts were shout-outs recalling concerts from long ago. Some included grainy, faded photos of Joe and the band in silhouette, backlit by starbursts of stage lights. There were a couple posts about him working with some new, up-and-coming artists I had never heard of.

The "About" tab included a link to his web page. Why hadn't I thought of that? Why hadn't I searched for him sooner? The Internet made stalking so much easier!

On the other hand, I had been *a little busy* lately. I shuddered at the sudden flashback to Gary and Vanessa. And before that, I had thought that Joe made his feelings for me perfectly clear by leaving so abruptly.

But now.

I pondered all this as I looked over his official web page.

The main photo was of Joe at the height of his popularity, only a year or two after I had last seen him. He was sitting at the piano, smiling, just the way I remembered. He looked a little tired, I thought, but he hadn't shot to the top without working hard. It wasn't that I *hadn't* followed the news about him at all back then, I just tried to limit my exposure. It had been a case of self-preservation.

I cried for a week – unfortunately I'm not exaggerating – after he left. Vanessa and Gary had propped me up, forced me to eat, and kept me going. Eventually I was down to just crying myself to sleep every night. Then every other night. Then only once in a while.

When Joe's songs slipped into regular rotation on Top 40 radio I started listening exclusively to NPR. When *they* did a story on him I quit listening to radio all together. At first I would hyperventilate whenever one of his songs played in public – at the mall, in a restaurant, walking across campus. Eventually I learned to block them out. For the most part.

It was like hearing "your song" after breaking up with your high school steady, only much, *much* worse, because it wasn't just one song. He had a string of hits that first year. Each of them was a knife to my heart.

Then Gary suggested we start dating. I liked him. He had done so much for me. He was sweet and nice and organized. He was not Joe.

How could I say no?

The lack of personal information on Joe's web page frustrated me. There wasn't much more here than had been on Facebook. Photos from old concerts. Album covers and publicity stills. I studied the pictures of the up-and-comers. I didn't recognize any of them. I hadn't really kept up with modern music, aside from whichever boy-band-of-the-month Emily listened to.

These musicians all had that edgy-hipster, Adam Levine stubble-beard look to them. The only one who stuck out was the old guy in the back. I looked through them again. Skinny jeans, saggy jeans, old guy. Tight T-shirt, tighter T-shirt, old guy. Leather jacket, pork pie hat, old guy.

After a while, the "old guys" all started to look alike. I clicked on a photo to enlarge it. The old guy kind of looked familiar. He kind of reminded me of . . .

Joe!

I enlarged another photo, then another.

Holy shit! Joe *was* the old guy.

When did that happen?

I sat back, and ran my hands through my hair, trying to make sense of this. I mean, he didn't look bad. From what I could see. He was partially hidden behind a piano in each picture.

He just looked . . . *old*. His hair was graying, his face a little fuller, his eyes a little more weary.

But that smile. That was *definitely* his smile.

I sat up and leaned over so I could see my reflection in the mirror.

I needed to get my roots touched up. I didn't just have bags under my eyes, I had steamer trunks. I hadn't gone for a run since Thursday morning. I could feel the cellulite colonizing my thighs. Pretty soon they'd be using my ass for the screen at the drive-in theater. They could probably show a double feature back there.

I looked old.

Maybe I should cut Joe some slack. I had been looking for the boy I knew 25 years ago. I had been looking for a 24-year-old with thick, dark hair, and a slim, rangy build.

Joe wasn't 24 anymore. Then again, neither was I.

I opened a video link in another window, but the focus was on the newcomers. I thought I could hear Joe's touch in the richness of the harmonies, the way the melody progressed throughout the song. I thought there was something definitely "Joe" about the arrangement.

Of course, that was what I wanted to hear.

Back on Joe's web site, I took a quick look at the "Biography" page. Some of it I already knew, but this helped me catch up on Joe's recent activity and filled in some details I had forgotten. I was surprised by how much celebrity gossip and rumor I remembered that wasn't part of his official biography.

The night they left Pleasant Glen, The Average Joes' audition had been moved to New York because of an emergency with another band the agent represented. The lead guitarist and the drummer of that band had gotten into a brawl during a rehearsal and all the members ended up either in the hospital or jail. The Average Joes, ready and available, took their spot as the opening act.

This sudden transition took its toll on some of the band members who weren't expecting to be so far from home in such a big spotlight so soon. Discontent and homesickness soon threatened to tear them apart.

Meanwhile, the keyboard player for The RayBands, another group represented by the same agent, found himself facing tax evasion questions from Canadian authorities. By mutual agreement and with no hard feelings, Joe was tapped to replace him, while the rest of the Average Joes returned happily to Iowa.

When the lead singer of the RayBands left to start a commune – with a dozen underage girls – Joe was ready to give up and return to Iowa. But his new bandmates, impressed with his musical abilities and easygoing personality, named him as their frontman and keyboardist and became "Joe Davenport and Above Average."

In just over a month, Joe had gone from being a regional hit to attracting nation-wide attention. It was an unlikely chain of events, a once-in-a-lifetime occurrence, made possible by being in the right place at the right time, with a tremendous skill set – as well an appreciation for the absurdities of life, and good sense of humor.

As I reviewed his biography, I thought about how each serendipitous stroke of good fortune took Joe closer to stardom, but further from me.

After this meteoric rise to fame, Joe's career seemed to plateau. The record company pushed Joe to stick to a formula. Joe wanted to explore new sounds. Grunge and alternative rock took over the airwaves. Joe faded from public view.

I didn't know that he had continued to write music, and to mentor other musicians. According to the website, he had his own recording studio "in the heartland" and was working on a variety of projects. It glossed over the information I really wanted. Where was he now? Was he married?

The "Contact" page listed an email address for a booking agent, Sophia LeClaire. I was instantly jealous. Who exactly was this Sophia, anyway? What was she to Joe? I felt awkward emailing her with inquiries about an old flame. What could I say that didn't sound desperate?

The "Upcoming Tour Dates" page was much more interesting.

Big, bold letters announced: "New Eastern Iowa Performance Dates Coming Soon!"

That was not the exciting part.

The exciting part was the small, italic letters that indicated the page had been updated a week earlier.

16

The rest of the night passed quietly without any dramatic interruptions, but much too fast. Miss Irene knocked on my door at seven the next morning to let me know there had been a change in plans. J.J. was bringing over a small crew to help move everything out of the apartment. They would be there in an hour.

I showered, dressed quickly and was enjoying my third cup of Miss Irene's excellent coffee when they arrived. I've always thought coffee tastes better when someone else makes it, and apparently I wasn't the only one. Big George, J.J., and the men they brought with them eagerly accepted Miss Irene's offer of coffee as well.

"I don't know how she does it," J.J. said, blowing the steam from his cup. "But Miss Irene makes the best coffee in town."

Miss Irene beamed, and Big George gave her a wink.

"It's the percolator," she said, returning the wink. "Big things always perk up when the going gets hot."

The other men seemed to have missed the exchanged of winks, but J.J. pinched the bridge of his nose, like he was trying to push away a headache – or clear away a mental image. He leaned toward me to speak confidentially.

"That's one of the reasons I organized this work crew. I'm not sure what time he got home last night, but Dad was singing at breakfast. I know from experience that can only mean one thing." He shook his head. "I figured I'd better get you out of this house and into that apartment before they corrupt you. Or set you up for years of psychotherapy."

"I think it's kind of sweet," I said. I looked over at Miss Irene and Big George, their heads close together, talking quietly. Big George was gently laughing and Miss Irene was blushing, trying to contain a smile.

"You say that now, but wait until you come home earlier than expected some night and find them . . ." J.J. shuddered. "Well, never mind. I just figured you'd like a little privacy. They spend most of their time together over here, so . . . . Trust me. You'll want a quiet place of your own.

"It doesn't matter how old you are, you never get used to the fact that your parents have a love life. Especially if you don't have one." He swirled the coffee in his cup, watching it without really seeing it. I instinctively put my hand on his arm and smiled at him. I understood exactly how he felt. Seeing the affection those two shared warmed my heart, but it also made me a little melancholy. I wondered if I would ever find a love like that.

"I think most of their flirting is just the result of them being stuck in perpetual adolescence. Although if Trey acted the way Dad does, I'd have shipped him off to an all-boys school long ago." He looked up just as Big George whispered something in Miss Irene's ear, his lips brushing her cheek.

J.J. groaned and closed his eyes. "And sometimes I think they do it just to embarrass me."

Big George winked at me. I was pretty sure J.J. was right. But he was awfully cute when he blushed. He was only, what, nine or ten years older than me? Maybe if things with Joe didn't . . . . No. I wasn't giving up without a fight. Not this time.

"Don't you have something for Julie, son?" Big George said.

"Oh! Yeah, well, about that . . . " J.J. hemmed and hawed before coming to a point. "The good news is there were a couple of cancellations for the motorcycle class, so I got you in, no problem." That was good news!

"The bad news is there's an on-line portion you have to complete before class starts. Tonight." J.J. rushed ahead, like he was trying to convince me this wasn't as bad as it sounded. "That's the real reason we're here. I figured we could help you get all the stuff moved down to the garage in an hour or so and you could have the rest of the day to study."

I flipped through the slim manual he handed me. It looked like there was a lot of information in it. I had taken a similar course the last time I got my motorcycle license, but that was more than 20 years ago. I felt my smile start to slip.

"It's not tough, just a little tedious," J.J. tried to reassure me.

"But I'll be here to help you!" Miss Irene sounded a little too enthusiastic for my comfort. Big George's face went white. J.J. patted my hand.

"You'll do fine," he said. "Call *me* if you have any questions." He leaned close and added quietly, "Miss Irene is an excellent rider, but she has her own way of doing things. Ways that aren't necessarily law-enforcement approved."

Coffee klatch over, we all trooped out to the garage, where Big George gave us our orders. Miss Irene and I were sent upstairs to the apartment. We would go through the boxes, sorting and labeling them as needed. The other two men would carry them down to the garage, where J.J. would arrange them as guided by Big George.

The boxes were already pretty well organized. Miss Irene pointed out which piles to move and when, occasionally squealing with delight or

171

sighing over a particular memory. I did the toting and fetching, setting aside things Miss Irene wanted to take a closer look at.

While we worked, we talked. I knew PG Cycles & Motors was housed in an historic building just off Main Street – everything in downtown Pleasant Glen is housed in an historic building – but that was all I knew. Miss Irene seemed to enjoy telling me about the business, and the men who ran it.

The shop specialized in motorcycle repair and sales, but they also worked on just about anything with an engine, she said. Big George and J.J. ran a tight ship. They set high expectations for their employees, in terms of both work quality and work ethic, as well as behavior, whether they were dealing with customers directly or not.

The yard crew was an internship program, created primarily for younger men with little or no work experience. She giggled a little as she admitted the snug uniforms were her suggestion. She hoped that by emphasizing their appearance, the men would learn not to judge others based on theirs.

"Besides," she said, "I liked to see a well-tuned male body as much as I like hearing a well-tuned motor."

That brought the discussion around to The Scout. I ask her why one of the Georges didn't ride it.

"Big George *can* ride," she said, "he's just never developed a real desire for it. He's more interested in how things work. He rides to get a feel for the performance of the machine, rather than for the enjoyment of riding. He became an instructor so he could teach other people to ride safely and how to take care of their motorcycles.

"J.J. rides some, but he's too busy with the shop and what not to ride just for the sake of riding. It wouldn't hurt him any to cut loose and have a little fun now and then." She grinned at me when she said this. I thought about his dark brown eyes.

"He's a fan of classic British motorcycles – BSA, Triumph, Norton. He's developed quite a reputation for himself and the shop, dealing in and repairing European motorcycles. Big George is very proud of him. And so am I."

"What about Trey," I asked. He had been so excited yesterday to start her up.

"He's your typical teenage boy. He loves anything with an engine, but he's drawn to things that are newer, bigger, faster, louder. He admires The Scout, but he'd rather ride one of those Japanese speed machines – much to his father's chagrin."

Miss Irene pulled a picture frame out of a box, smiled broadly and then hugged it to herself.

"Oh, my heavens! I've been looking for this!" She sighed and handed it to me. It was an old, black and white photo of her sitting astride The Scout, beaming. She looked natty and proud, dressed in an old-style riding suit of dark trousers and short jacket. A scarf was tied jauntily at her neck. The Scout gleamed.

"Big George took that photo after my first long ride with the Motor Maids. A bunch of us Eastern Iowa gals rode out to Omaha to meet some girls from the Nebraska chapter." She sighed. "I had such a wonderful time. It was nice to meet other women who liked to ride. Didn't make me feel like such an outsider. Big George tried, but he just couldn't understand how riding The Scout made me feel. Those gals did. For some of us it was the first time we'd really been in control of our lives. Or been so free."

She ran her fingers gently across the glass and spoke wistfully.

"Over the years I've had a few bigger bikes as the rides grew longer, but none of them ever measured up to The Scout. I suppose everyone has their own style, their own way of doing things. It's just a matter of finding something – someone – who understands. The Scout still has plenty of spunk left in her, she just needs to find the right partner."

Miss Irene sighed, and added the picture to the "save" pile. Then she dug around in the box a little more.

"Big George doesn't think I know about the little modifications he's made for me, but I do." She pulled out the trousers and jacket she had been wearing in the photo. "He's probably right, too. I was always a little more . . . daring than he was comfortable with. At least when it came to The Scout." She held the jacket up in front of her, judging the size. "Maybe I'll take Big George on a little cruise down memory lane tonight." She gave me a wink and I blushed. Maybe J. J. was right about needing a quiet place of my own.

We finished moving the boxes and the furniture that I didn't think I would need and called it a morning. The men were just leaving when a service truck pulled up. Miss Irene had hired a handyman to make sure the plumbing and electrical systems were in order and was having internet service installed in the apartment.

The improvements, as well as my salary, were coming out of a trust fund established specifically for her children's inheritance, Miss Irene said. Originally she had thought their greed would overcome their concerns for her well-being and she would be allowed to continue to stay home alone. Even with what I considered to be a generous salary, this arrangement would cost less than a nursing home.

I was in no position to argue, and I didn't think it would do me any good to try. I was even more grateful when she gave me a check for a partial week's salary in advance, pointing out I would need boots and gloves when the riding portion of the motorcycle class started.

"Speaking of which, we'd better get you started on your reading." Miss Irene shooed me toward the house. "There'll be plenty of time to clean and paint and organize tomorrow. And I promised the handyman I wouldn't hover. Hmmph. Apparently I have a bit of a reputation."

Miss Irene set up a study area for me at the dining room table. J.J. was right. The book-work portion of the class was mostly common sense and I quickly finished the reading.

I may have finished it even more quickly if Miss Irene hadn't been constantly checking up on my progress. She fluttered back and forth between the kitchen and dining room, refilling my coffee, bringing me home made cookies, and fussing about everything from the lights to my posture. I understood why the handyman had insisted she stay away.

Her nervousness rubbed off on me, and I made a few careless errors on the first on-line quiz. Luckily, Big George arrived and offered to take her out to lunch just as I started the second section. We talked a little bit and he calmed me down, while Miss Irene made me a sandwich. She even cut it diagonally, and garnished it with a pickle and chips. I felt like a kid again. It was nice to have someone take care of me for a change.

I suspected Big George was taking Miss Irene out mostly for my benefit, and my suspicions were confirmed when he gave me a knowing nod as they walked out the door.

Then he told her that J.J. wouldn't be home for lunch, and that they would have the house all to themselves. I nearly snorted soda out my nose when I realized the implication. Maybe this wasn't for my benefit.

I finished up the next quiz without any mistakes and rewarded myself by downloading Joe's first album. It had been recorded soon after Joe Davenport and Above Average started their maiden tour. Many of the songs were originals Joe had been working on or performing with The

Average Joes before they left Iowa.

Listening to him sing took me right back to 1990. These were the songs I cried so hard over and tried so hard to ignore. I was still able to remember every word, every key change, every shift in tempo.

After scrolling through the same page over, *and over* again, I realized I couldn't listen to Joe while doing my homework. His voice still hypnotized me.

Even after I had turned the music off, I could hear his voice in my head. I just couldn't shake the image of him in his mid-20s. I imagined him on stage at The Bar, playing and singing, cracking jokes and laughing with The Average Joes.

During my next study break I did a Google search for pictures of Joe. And I set a timer to keep me on task.

As I scrolled through the images, I found myself drawn to the older shots, despite the poor quality. This was the Joe I remembered. Or maybe it was a reflection of how I wanted to remember *me* – young and in love, idealistic and hopeful, with taut skin and perky boobs.

I was still having trouble reconciling the pictures of the young Joe I knew with his more current photos. Clicking back and forth between screens was getting me nowhere. Finally I opened my publisher program and pasted similar photos of young Joe and older Joe side by side so I could compare them more easily.

The hair was startlingly different. When we were young, he wore his bushy hair long enough to curl up at the ends, especially in the back where it hit his shirt collar. Still, it wasn't rock-star long, like the glam metal bands. He looked more like a CPA who had missed a couple hair appointments than a rock star back then.

Now his dark hair was shot through with gray, still just slightly more black than gray, and military-style short. It had also started to recede, revealing the worry lines that creased his forehead.

I considered the standing appointment with my stylist every 10 weeks to have my color enhanced, and decided I really didn't want to start throwing rocks about his hair.

I thought Joe had filled out a little. He may have put on a few pounds – who hasn't? – but it looked good on him. His chest and shoulders seemed broader, and I noticed he was sitting up straighter at the piano now.

His lips were just as full as they had been when we were young. I wondered if they were still as warm and soft. Were they still so firm? Would my skin still feel the same heat as they traced their way down my neck? Lost in these pleasant thoughts, I reached out to touch them. I laughed at my impulsive action, then let my fingers brush the screen.

Reassured that this was "my" Joe, it was easier now to spot the similarities between old and new photos. He still crouched over the keyboard like he was attacking it, playing with such power and passion. At other times he relaxed and let his slender fingers float across the keys in a gentle caress. He still had a habit of singing from one side of his mouth or wrinkling his nose and closing his eyes when he was reaching for certain notes. His face was every bit as expressive as his voice. He still threw his head back when he gave himself over to the music. He did the same thing whenever he was overcome with emotion – whether it was laughter or passion.

His smile was easy to recognize. It wasn't quite a cock-sure as it once was, but I knew some of that had been bravado. He looked more relaxed now, more self-assured. There was a little bit of smirk playing at the edges of his lips, as if he was amused by some private joke.

Then there were his eyes. Those beautiful hazel eyes that could go from green to brown in an instant, depending on his mood. They were the same – big and beautiful, so expressive. So easy to get lost in. Young Joe's eyes seemed wary of the camera, or maybe they were issuing a challenge. There was something more gentle, accepting about older Joe's eyes. The lines around them were new, but surprisingly sexy.

He still had those impossibly long eyelashes God cruelly gives so freely to men, when women have to pay big bucks at the cosmetics counter for them. I could never quite forgive him for those.

I looked at the pages I had created and realized that if anyone ever found them, they would think I was some sort of crazy, stalker-woman. I might as well pin them up to the walls of a closet, light some candles and make a little shrine already.

The timer went off. I still had two more sections to go before class.

I clicked on the red, "close" icon. The program asked if I wanted to save my changes.

My finger hovered over the mouse button.

I hit save and hoped my computer never fell into the wrong hands.

I still had so many unanswered questions.

I still had two units to finish before class tonight.

I still didn't know where Joe was, or if he was married.

All I knew was that part of me was still in love with him.

Or maybe that it would be easy to fall in love with him all over again.

17

I finished the classwork and still had enough time to stop at the farm supply store to look for a pair of boots before class. I found an adorable pair of hard-soled, ankle-high, work boots in a supple suede. They were pink. *And* on clearance! It was like we were destined to be together.

The clerk, a no-nonsense type with steel-gray hair, cat-eye glasses secured with a rhinestone chain, and sensible, black pleather, lace-ups, sneered as she rang up my purchase. I shrugged and grinned sheepishly before slinking to the automatic door – which didn't open automatically. The clerk rolled her eyes as I waved my boots to trigger the sensor so I could leave.

On my way to the college, I thought of all the witty comments I should have come up with five minutes sooner. Distracted, I automatically drove to the lot behind the administration building, where my office had been. It was after 5:00 p.m., and the lot was empty. According to Anna Anderson, overhead lights and ventilation systems after five were not cost-effective. I felt sorry for the ever-shrinking crew of night-shift custodians.

I pulled in to a parking space near the door and inched forward until my bumper tapped the "Reserved for Anna Anderson" sign. I never had a reserved space. I thought about Big George pinning Frank against the fence at the Frosty Freeze. I wondered which would crumple first, my bumper or the sign post. Would replacing the sign be cost effective? What about replacing my bumper? I sighed, backed out, and drove to the other side of campus.

PGC had a small, but beautiful campus, filled with big, old trees and equally big, historic buildings. During the day, waves of students ebbed and flowed along the sidewalks at the top of each hour. By late afternoon, the campus was nearly deserted, especially during finals week. I assumed most of the students were studying. Or, more likely, heading downtown to The Bar for a study break.

Traffic would pick up again as soon as the "non-traditional" students started arriving for night classes. When I had been an undergrad, the "non-trads" had seemed so old. There was always one of them who monopolized class discussion in their eagerness to fit in. Now, I was a non-trad. The campus I was so familiar with suddenly felt lonely and foreign.

I re-parked near the new athletics building and went inside to search for our classroom. I had been in the building just once, last fall, when I helped plan the ribbon cutting and open house. Construction delays and bad weather pushed the event back until after I had been let go. In the meantime, Anna had downsized the food service staff right out of the ability to produce the homemade treats everyone had come to expect at school gatherings. And she placed a strict one-per-person rule on the dry cookies she imported from a mega-box, club-store in River City.

According to Billy, my bartending informant, students used the leftover cookies as street-hockey pucks – until an errant shot broke a car window. The football coach threatened to complain about the refreshments, but didn't want to attract undue attention to his program. He worried that the team's eight-year loosing streak might cast doubts on their cost-effectiveness.

180

I found a small cluster of students waiting outside the classroom. They lounged in silence, heads bowed, eyes glued to their phones. No one looked up as I joined them and stood awkwardly at the edge of the group, phoneless.

"Good to see you all here so early, especially on bottle-buck night," J.J. said, picking his way around the cyber zombies to unlock the door. A couple of the boys bumped fists, although I doubted they were of legal drinking age. That hadn't stopped me and Van, either. Of course, back then the drinking age was lower, and Mondays were quarter-draw night at the bars.

J.J. greeted each of us, taking attendance as we filed past him.

"Don't even think about sitting in the back of the room," he said. The boy leading the herd stopped mid-sit, then sighed, stood up and walked to the front row. Two more boys joined him, two sat behind them, and the two girls sat behind them.

"Hi, Julie! Just got the report for the on-line quizes. Way to go!" The boys in the front row looked up briefly from their phones and shared a knowing look. Great. I was already on my way to being "that" non-trad. I took a seat behind the girls and vowed to keep my mouth shut

The first night was a chance to review and to clarify information from the readings, J.J. explained. I let the kids answer the questions, sticking to my vow to not monopolize the discussion. The longer I kept quiet, the more I began to second guess myself. Then I noticed the girls were letting the boys answer the questions – incorrectly – even after the girls had whispered the right answers.

After a couple of blatant guesses and blank stares, J.J. called on me for an answer. I panicked and hesitated before speaking. One of the boys in the front row looked back at me and smirked.

I thought about the lady at the farm supply store. I thought about Anna Anderson and her reserved parking spot.

Screw them.

I raised an eyebrow, pursed my lips, and leveled my best "Disapproving Mom Face" at the boy in the front row. Then I answered the question. Correctly.

Smirking Boy slouched in his seat. The other boys squirmed and sat up straight. The girls' shoulders shook with silent giggles. One of them looked back at me and gave me a thumbs up.

The atmosphere in the room changed, or at least I thought it did. The girls started contributing more and the boys listened respectfully. J.J. seemed to relax a little. So did I.

When we divided up for small group activities, I tried to stay involved without being too much of a "Mom." Instead, I let myself be distracted by J.J.'s humming. There was something familiar about the tune, but I couldn't quite place it. Something that reminded me of Joe.

Joe had so many musical influences, he could play just about anything and make it sound familiar. He used to joke about filling requests for songs by playing something "reminiscent of a song, but not quite the song." Still, he managed to put his own special spin on everything he played.

"What do you think, Julie?" I had been so busy trying to "Name That Tune" that I hadn't noticed J.J. calling my name. The other students looked at me expectantly. I felt my cheeks getting warmer.

There was a 50-50 chance this was a yes or no question. The girl next to me smiled, then nodded and whispered "yes." The other girl winked and giggled.

"Umm, yes?"

The boys – J.J. included – didn't seem to notice anything.

"He *is* pretty cute, for an old guy," the winker whispered. She was right, and that was a much easier explanation than the truth.

"OK, then. It's settled! We'll start class tomorrow afternoon at two, in the parking lot here. But if I find out anyone skipped a final . . . you're grounded!" J.J. said. The kids laughed, but I thought he looked serious.

While I was day dreaming, the other students had convinced J.J. to rescheduled the riding sessions. Since it was finals week at both the college and the high school, we could get an earlier start on Tuesday and Wednesday, and finish up Thursday morning. I was just looking forward to being done with cleaning and painting the apartment. And class.

We all walked out of the building together, talking to each other instead of our phones. J.J. and I watched as the college kids headed toward their dorms and the high schooler started his car and drove off. Then J.J. followed me to Miss Irene's to "check up on Big George."

Part of me wondered if it was really Big George he was checking up on. Part of me hoped not. I envied the way the three Georges and Miss Irene all looked out for each other. I missed that close-knit, caring aspect of family.

When was the last time Gary or I had called each other just to check in? His current barrage of texts were much more self-preservation oriented than concern oriented. Things between Emily and I were improving, but not there yet. A text is a weak substitute for a call, but it sure beats nothing.

That reminded me of the goosebumps I got from listening to the tape recording Joe had left me. And that reminded me of the tunes J.J. had been humming during class. I took advantage of my insomnia to download more of Joe's music. While I listened, I thought about the first time I met Joe Davenport.

I had worked at The Bar for more than two years and could pick my own hours – as long as I worked Friday and Saturday nights. That was fine with me, because there was live music on weekends. Bob scheduled great bands with loyal fans who knew how the bar scene worked. They bought plenty of drinks, behaved well, and tipped generously, ensuring my gratitude and prompt service.

I kept my distance from the musicians themselves. Mom had warned me that musicians were wild and dangerous, although I was never sure how such a quiet and reserved lady would know anything about "wild and dangerous."

Still, I took her at her word, and let the other girls deal with the talent while I kept the audience happy. This kept the band managers happy, which kept Bob happy, which kept all the servers happy – except for a few heartbroken, would-be groupies.

It was early Wednesday evening, just three days after I graduated from PGC. The crowd was starting to clear out after Happy Hour – which could stretch to two or three hours, depending on Bob's mood. I took care of the tables while Bob talked up the folks at the bar, including Joe. Bob had told me he planned on booking Joe and his band regularly that summer.

"I know it won't last, Julie," Bob had said, shaking his head. "The kid has real talent. Mark my words, he's gonna be big." Bob's son had heard Joe perform at some frat party up at State U. He immediately called Bob and held the phone out the window – these were the days of corded phones – so Bob could listen, too.

After hearing The Average Joes in person, Bob called up a fellow bar owner in River City. They worked out an informal agreement to share the group, Thursdays through Saturdays, for four weeks. Bob was so confident in their potential that he included an option to book them as The Bar's house band for the remainder of the summer. Bob claimed nothing piqued interest in booking a band quite like *not* being able to book a band. He may have been right.

After two weeks, Bob had to fight to get the band even for one night. The Average Joes split their Thursdays between The Bar and The Landing Strip, spending weekends at bigger clubs in the Quad Cities or Des Moines. Soon they were playing increasingly larger auditoriums in St. Louis, Minneapolis, and Peoria.

By the end of the summer . . . well, by then Joe was gone.

But the night we met, Joe sat at the bar working out details of the performance agreement with Bob. Joe was wearing jeans and sneakers with a white button down shirt. His blue and gold striped tie was casually loosened, and his shirt sleeves were pushed up to his elbows. He looked like all the other young business professionals who stopped in after work.

Except for the hair. That's what tipped me off. I kept my distance.

There was something about Joe that both thrilled and frightened me. Some magnetic tug that made me want to linger at the bar whenever I brought up a tray full of empties or picked up an order. I figured this was the "wild and dangerous" part Mom had warned me about.

A few customers were finishing up their last half-price drinks. Melvin Steinhocker was sitting alone at a table at the end of the bar. He was usually harmless. He bussed his own table, tipped well and always ordered the same domestic draft. He routinely left 20 minutes after Happy Hour ended, whenever that was, and helped make sure anyone who shouldn't be driving wasn't.

Regardless, he could still be a pain in the ass when he chose to be.

I was clearing the table next to Melvin's when he reached out and gave me a swat on my butt.

I straightened up and smacked my bar rag down on the table hard, sending up a spray of stale beer and bleach water. Melvin sat back in his chair, aware that he had crossed a line.

Before I had a chance to lay into him, Joe stepped between us. I don't know what he thought he was going to do. Melvin was a good foot taller than Joe and had at least 20 years and 60 pounds on him.

"Sir, I don't think . . . ."

I was in no mood to take any shit from anybody – regular or not, primo tipper or not. And I damn sure didn't need to be rescued by some musician. I pushed past Joe and leaned over Melvin, shaking my finger in his face.

"*You*! You need to keep your hands to yourself, or I'll tell Norma. And we both know that will not end well."

I wheeled around to give my would-be rescuer a piece of my mind.

"And *you*! You . . . ." I was looking directly into his beautiful, hazel eyes, framed by those ridiculously long eyelashes. The tug I had felt when I stood near him at the bar was overwhelming now. It stole my breath away and scrambled my brain.

". . . are kinda cute." He looked scared to death of me, leaning back so far I was afraid he'd fall over. "But don't think I'm going to change my mind about musicians, because I'm not. You can buy me a drink later, though."

I gave Joe a smile, picked up my tray full of empty glasses and took them to the bar.

"Holy shit! Is she always like that?" Joe asked Melvin as I walked away.

"If you're smart, you'll run away now," I heard Melvin say. "If you're smarter, you'll stay."

Joe stayed, nursing his beer until Bob threatened to charge him rent on his bar stool.

186

I wiped and re-wiped the tables, and offered refills as soon as I delivered fresh drinks, looking for any excuse to postpone my break.

Melvin called his wife from the pay phone in the back hallway and told her not to wait dinner. I overheard him say "it's a real life soap opera, or a train wreck waiting to happen." Then he moved to the far end of the bar near the door, where he and Bob whispered furiously. They looked up every now and then to check on Joe and me, or to add another dollar to a growing pile between them on the bar.

There were only a handful of customers, so Bob asked Joe if he'd like to take a look at the piano and check out the acoustics.

"Foul!" cried Melvin. "That's cheating!"

"All's fair, buddy boy," Bob replied, adding another bill to the stack. "Besides, if something don't happen soon, she's gonna wear out the tables, or frighten off the customers."

I wasn't sure what those two were up to, but I figured I should probably be offended.

Joe looked over at me and I found another table to clean. He sighed and ambled to the platform at the back of the room. Bob's cherished, old, upright piano sat center stage. Joe whistled in appreciation as he ran his fingers over its glossy, black shell. He carefully lifted the fallboard covering the keys.

Everyone stopped whatever they were doing – drinking, betting, wiping, breathing – when Joe sat at the keyboard. He twisted the switch on the piano lamp, the click echoing in the nearly empty room. Joe tilted his head slightly, listening to the echo, judging the way the sound carried. He noticed the hush in the room and slowly turned his head to find us all watching, waiting. He raised an eyebrow and turned his attention back to the piano, shaking his head and muttering. I guessed it was something about "crazy people." At least that's what I would have said.

He played a few simple chords and arpeggios, slowly at first, then faster, warming up his fingers and getting a feel for the keyboard. He repeated a rapid succession of notes, testing the action of the keys and the strength of the strings.

"You break a string, you pay for repairs," Bob shouted at Joe. "Damn, the old girl's never sounded so good," he added quietly.

Joe looked over his shoulder and grinned mischievously. Then he launched into a simple, bluesy number, pounding out a syncopated rhythm and testing the dynamics. Satisfied with the lower range, he switched to a classical sounding piece in a higher register – he told me later it was a riff on a Bach Invention – punctuated by short runs and trills.

He segued into snippets of popular songs, playing just enough to tease us before moving on to the next one. He was playing hard and fast and sweating, but didn't show signs of slowing down. He worked in snippets of Billy Joel, Elton John and Joe Jackson along with old standards that had Melvin cheering.

Joe looked up, and catching my eye, moved seamlessly into Van Morrison's "Brown Eyed Girl." He began singing quietly, playing up the wistful tug of the lyrics. Then he added more swing to the rhythm, bringing out the sensuality and playfulness. By the time he got to the "*Sha la la - la la dee dahs*" everyone was singing along.

I was enchanted. No one had ever sang to me before. I gave in and swayed a little, smiling – beaming, really, I suppose – as Joe finished the song. He let the piano's final notes fade away before relaxing and turning to face us. He shrugged humbly.

The small crowd clapped and gathered around him as he walked to the bar. I hung back, letting the others congratulate him. My smile grew each time he craned his head around a well-wisher to catch a glimpse of me.

Finally he managed to break away.

"Don't think I'm going to change my mind about waitresses, because I'm not," he said. "You can buy me a drink, though."

Bob gathered up the pile of ones he and Melvin had stacked up and waved it at us. "Never mind that. First round's on Melvin." Bob looked at the other customers. "And one on the house."

Joe and I sat in a corner booth and talked until closing time. Bob and Melvin did their best to make sure we had some privacy, while still keeping a close eye on us. They even finished the clean up for the night.

By midnight, the last of the customers had gone, and the chairs were all stacked on the tables. Melvin and Bob yawned pointedly. We got the hint. Joe and I had both parked out back in the alley, and we lingered under the security light, leaning against Joe's old farm truck. Joe was staying with friends up in River City for the summer, and had to work the next day, but neither of us wanted to say goodnight.

The police chief – who I knew from church – drove by once, twice, three times, on his nightly rounds. With each pass he drove slower and looped back quicker. The third time by he slowed to a crawl, gave me a disapproving look and tapped his watch.

Joe waited until the patrol car eased around the corner, then pulled me close, tilted my chin up and kissed me. It was a gentle kiss, tender, slow, earth shattering and all too brief. We reluctantly pulled apart, smiling drunkenly, shyly.

"Tomorrow, then?"

"Tomorrow."

I floated home to dream of him.

I dreamed of him again that night.

Joanne Salemink

18

Tuesday morning I had to go back to our house to pick up some information for the Auxiliary Banquet and Gala. It always had a way of sneaking up on me, no matter how many times I had helped organize it. We were six weeks out, and it was past time to get serious.

In many ways the event planned itself, since nothing ever changed much. Verbal agreements were made for the next Gala even before we finished cleanup for the last. Still, we had to go through the motions of reserving the community center, confirming the menu, and making sure our emcee – who had been the host for all 60 years – still had a pulse.

Selecting a charity to benefit from that year's Gala was by far the most contentious and challenging part of the whole process. Each of the ladies had their pet projects, so regardless of which program we selected, someone was sure to complain.

Gary had left several messages on my cell phone saying he wouldn't be back from Des Moines until later that afternoon. Still, I waited until after 9 to leave Miss Irene's, knowing Gary would be at the office by then if he had come home early to surprise me. The house was empty and quiet. It already had that dusty, stale smell houses get when no one is around to stir up the air. I felt like I was walking into a stranger's house. This stranger had very good taste, but it was all just too . . . antiseptic. I missed the warmth and laughter that filled Miss Irene's home.

The message light on the land line was blinking. Two voice mails were from Gary, repeats of the messages he had left on my cell phone. He probably didn't believe that I had actually moved out.

The third message was from Muffy. I didn't even think she had our home number. She and Bunny were vice-chairs for the Gala this year, although they typically did very little besides show up for publicity photos. Muffy usually called my cell phone whenever she was in danger of doing any actual work.

"Julie-darling, there's no good way to put this, so I'm just going to come right out with it. You know it pains me, but, well . . . . The girls have been talking and, given the current state of . . . *affairs*," she was interrupted here by the loud braying of Bunny's laughter.

"We know you must just be beside yourself with . . . all that's going on right now, and we think it would be in everyone's best interest, what with the gossip . . . ." If there was gossip to be heard, she would be the one spreading it. "And we certainly don't expect you to work with . . . that man stealer. So we've decided it would be in everyone's best interest if Bunny and I . . . ." *Beep.*

Muffy's rambling was cut off before I could reach through the phone lines and strangle her. Unless that sentence ended with "jumped off a bridge," and somehow I didn't think it would, I was hoping that would be the end of things. Instead, the answering machine cued up the next message. I could hear Bunny chattering away in the background.

"I'm getting to that," Muffy said to her. She must not have heard the beep starting the recording. "It's not my fault she has a cheap-ass machine with a short . . . Oh! Anyway, Julie-darling, Bunny and I are willing to step in and take the burden of planning the Gala off your shoulders. Although, heaven knows, we have more than enough to do ourselves already. What can I say? Anything for the good of the Auxiliary," Bunny said something in the background again. "Of course, Bunny, that's what I said. Anything to help you, Julie-dear. You can always count on us. It's so important to know who your *real* friends are in times like . . ." *Beep.*

Good god. Would she ever get to the point? I braced myself for the third installment. This time the message started with the sound of Bunny taking a deep, noisy breath before launching into a quick recitation, glossing over the most important information.

"Anyway, we've called for an emergency meeting of the Auxiliary board this morning at 10:30 at The Grille if you can make it and we'll certainly understand if you can't, but at least we've done our duty by calling you and tah see you later dear." I could hear both women cackle in the brief moment before Bunny hung up.

It was already 10 o'clock, and the recording said the calls came in at 9:45. The bitches had been thorough. Not only had they called at the last moment to notify me of the meeting, they had left a message on my home machine, when they no doubt knew I was not staying there. If they had called Vanessa, and I doubted they had, she would have been at work.

I had a momentary pang of guilt – how could I suspect them of being so underhanded? – and checked my cell phone. I had three missed calls from Miss Irene, all within the last five minutes, but no messages from Muffy or Bunny.

This meant war.

It was a hostile takeover. A military coup. A revolution.

Who was I kidding? They weren't that smart.

It was a childish stunt, attempted by two power-hungry, attention seeking pin-heads. Pin-heads who had no idea what was involved in planning an event like this. Pin-heads who would end up ruining a project I had worked hard to maintain and grow over the past seven years.

I thought back to high school, when Vanessa and I had stuffed napkins in chicken wire until our fingers bled, only to have Muffy and Bunny hold the first-place trophy for our class float in their perfectly manicured hands. Or three years ago when Vanessa and I stayed up all night assembling and filling 300 individually wrapped popcorn-box party favors for an Oscars-themed Gala after Muffy and Bunny "forgot" their one and only job!

First it was Anna Anderson and the open house cookie fiasco. Now it was Muffy and Bunny and the Gala.

If they thought I was going to take this lying down, they were out of their narrow little minds.

Not today, damnit.

Maybe last week I would have rolled over and played dead, but not this week. Last week I had nowhere to go and no one to go to. This week I almost had an apartment, almost had my motorcycle license and I almost knew what happened to my ex-boyfriend.

It wasn't much as far as pep-talks go, but it was better than nothing.

This week I had Miss Irene, the Georges and The Scout.

That was better.

I had dressed for the dirty work of cleaning and painting my apartment, but luckily I still had clothes here at the house. I ran upstairs and changed into my Suburban Wonder Woman uniform of khaki pants and white silk shell. I added a little extra power to the outfit by tying my hair back with the red silk scarf and slipping on a pair of semi-sensible "don't fuck with me pumps." These shoes had a lower, thicker heel than the usual fuck me pumps, but would still allow me to tower over the Prep-ermint

Twins.

I was out the door in 10 minutes. On the drive over to The Grille I called and left urgent messages for Vanessa on both her home machine and her cell phone, and let Miss Irene know the jig was up and that I would meet her at the restaurant.

I walked in to The Grille at 10:25 only to find that Muffy and Bunny had started the meeting early. Sneaky bitches. Really? Did they forget that I'm always late for everything anyway? There were just enough members there for a quorum – all hand-picked, I was certain.

Muffy, not surprisingly, seemed surprised to see me. Bunny glanced nervously between Muffy and me. Muffy took one look at my sturdy – yet stylish – ass-kicking heels and my fierce scarf and took a step backwards from the podium.

I pounced on this display of weakness, adopting the superhero stance – feet shoulder-width apart, hands on hips. This may have been a little overkill, although it did make me feel more confident. And, truth be told, my confidence was starting to waver as I looked around at the other Auxiliary members' faces and wondered how many of them knew about Gary/Vanessa/Michael, and how many of them knew about Gary's mother/father.

"Julie, darling, whata . . . whata . . . ," Muffy swallowed, then cleared her throat. "What a nice surprise. So glad you could join us this morning." She didn't even try to conceal the displeasure in her voice. "So brave of you to be out and about, considering . . . ."

Oh, hell no. She was not going to fake pity me in front of all these women.

"Can the crap, Millicent. What are you up to?" *Millicent!* How could I have forgotten that was her given name? At least, I thought it was. She'd been Muffy for so long, I doubted even she knew what her real name was.

"Well, darling, I only had your well-being in mind," she continued with her simpering, batting her mascara-clumped eyelashes at me. "We all thought that you would be too distraught to give the Gala your full attention." She stretched out her hands to indicate the other women in the room, who were now leaning back in their chairs as if to distance themselves from her. Never underestimate the influence of a jaunty red scarf.

Muffy hesitated as she realized her fickle friends were deserting her. She grabbed Bunny by the shoulder and roughly pulled her to her feet. Bunny's face flashed from white to red and she wobbled a bit. For a moment I was afraid she might pass out from the sudden change in blood pressure. I hoped she'd have the good sense to topple in Muffy's direction if she fainted.

"I see." I inhaled deeply through my nose and slowly blew the air out between my pursed lips. This was an attempt to calm my nerves, but it made a satisfying angry sound. Muffy and Bunny exchange a worried look. "Your concern for my . . . well-being . . . is quite touching." And uncharacteristic, I thought, but I couldn't risk offending the other Auxiliary members with snide comments now. This was still a sensitive situation, requiring finesse.

"So, you would like to become more involved with the planning?" I asked. "You have ideas you would like to share with us?" I turned the tables on Muffy, mimicking her gesture to include her former followers. "You have some plans for the venue? The caterer? The *entertainment*?" I advanced on the women while I talked, and now I stood directly in front of them. I drew myself up as tall as I could to look down upon them. There was a good five inch disparity in our heights. They had not planned ahead and were wearing flats instead of power shoes.

Rookie mistake.

Never bring a knife to a gunfight, and never wear ballet flats to an ass-kicking. Of course, you should never wear heels during a zombie apocalypse, but that's a totally different situation.

My point is, I had them on the ropes and they knew it.

And then Vanessa burst in.

"I'm here, I'm here! WhatdidImiss?" She must have run from the far corner of the parking lot, and, having ignored the zombie apocalypse-shoe rule, had managed to break off a heel in her rush. I told her those weren't real Jimmy Choos! She must have pulled them out of the trash after I threw them away.

Everyone's attention shifted. I'm sure they expected me to turn on my former-friend turned husband's-mistress. I had no doubt the phone lines would be buzzing as soon as this meeting adjourned. In fact, a few ladies were already texting updates.

Muffy took advantage of my momentary distraction.

"Hello, Vanessa-darling. Julie-dear was just about to tell us all about the plans you two have made for this year's Gala." She shifted her weight to one foot, rested a fist on her hip and arched her eyebrows, certain she had me by the short hairs.

Because she did.

Despite years of lobbying for a new and improved Gala, Vanessa and I hadn't actually come up with any new and improved ideas. But I'd be damned if I'd let these women know that. Vanessa opened and shut her mouth a few times and blinked rapidly, as if willing inspiration to strike. Finally she shrugged her shoulders and gave me a look that said "take it away."

Some might have thought she was throwing me under the bus, but I could tell from the glint in her eye and the slight smirk to her grin that she had total confidence in my ability to bullshit my way through an explanation. I looked out across the room, took a deep, cleansing breath and hoped that monkeys would fly out of my butt with the biggest, grandest plans for the Pleasant Glen Women's Auxiliary Gala that had ever been hatched in the spur of the moment.

Instead of flying monkeys, something else caught my eye through the windows. Miss Irene had just pulled up on The Scout and was arguing with the manager about parking in the handicapped spot. Miss Irene was waving a blue and white handicapped parking permit card around, and Brad was pointing at The Scout, apparently not convinced that she could be both handicapped and riding a motorcycle.

Slowly but surely the wheels in my head started turning. I thought back to dinner with the Georges. Trey had mentioned something about the high school music department having a crisis. Something about the sprinklers in the auditorium . . . .

"We'd like to try something a little different this year." My mouth started talking before I had finished thinking. Not a completely new situation for me. "We all know how important the fine arts are to our community, and the Auxiliary has been so wonderfully supportive of the Art Gallery." The women smiled and nodded at each other, proud of themselves. Muffy rolled her eyes. Vanessa made a "move it along" gesture with her hand.

"I'm sure you've *all* heard about the crisis at the high school auditorium, and how it has devastated the music department." The women nodded slower as they tried to remember relevant rumors. Those who hadn't heard anything were desperate not to look like they were out of the loop and nodded quicker.

"That's why we would like to suggest that this year's gala benefit the Pleasant Glen High School Music Department." Muffy, whose pet project was park beautification, looked crestfallen. The rest of the women, who had either been in music at PGHS or had children and/or grandchildren in the program, applauded enthusiastically.

"And?" Muffy gave me a bored look. "What's your new and different approach? We're all supportive of the local music department, darling, but we've already donated our time and baked goods, *and* had our cars washed *and* bought endless cheesecakes, nuts, and boxes of fruit. What can you do to freshen things up?" The nodding continued along with whispers of discontent. Mutiny was nigh.

"A concert . . . more like a festival. We'll feature local groups, of course, but we'll bring in a headliner to draw a crowd from outside of town." I knew the ladies were enthusiastic about donating money, but they were even more enthusiastic about donating *other people's* money.

"And this headliner would be?" Muffy was just not giving up.

I looked to the almost-lawyer for backup.

"We are currently in contract negotiations and are not at liberty to discuss names, but suffice it to say, this will be a concert Pleasant Glen will not soon forget." Vanessa did not disappoint.

"All in favor say 'Aye' and meet me in the lounge. First round is on me," said Miss Irene. She had slipped in while I was talking and now made a detour past Bunny and Muffy on her way to the bar. "You ladies might want to check your phone tree. Somehow I didn't get the call about this meeting until it had almost started. Luckily I was on my way to the bank when your mom got a hold of me, Bunny. I would have hated to miss this one!"

Muffy and Bunny slung their purses over their shoulders and stomped out of the restaurant, completely ignoring Miss Irene's offer to buy them a margarita.

"I have no idea what you have in mind, Julie-dear." Miss Irene winked at me as we watched the door close behind them. "But I like where it's headed. And I like the way you put those two in their place. With class. Speaking of class . . . you're soda only, dear. J.J. would never forgive me if you showed up to class tipsy. He is awfully cute when he's angry but you probably shouldn't provoke him until after you get your license."

"You can explain *that* to me later," Vanessa said. "In the meantime, those ladies in the lounge are going to be wanting an explanation of another kind. So unless I'm misinterpreting that look of total clue-lessness on your face . . . . "

"I'd better bail on the booze and start making plans?"

"Something like that. Call me when you and those new cojones of yours are ready to give me orders." Vanessa gave me a quick hug and a big smile. "I'm proud of you, Jules. You done good."

"Now, did someone mention margaritas?" Vanessa linked arms with Miss Irene and the two women headed for the bar, while I headed to Miss Irene's to panic, plan and prepare for class.

19

I was still buzzing from my success at the meeting when I got to class. Everyone seemed energized and eager to start riding. The class motorcycles had moderately sized engines, making them lightweight and maneuverable, and easier for beginning riders to handle. I chose one that had a traditional, upright style. Most of the boys picked the sport style, which would give them a more aggressive riding stance as they leaned over the gas tank.

Those bikes reminded me of the 1980's crotch rocket that seduced me when I was in college. Vanessa and I were young and stupid; the boys we met were cute and *not* from Pleasant Glen. Our flirtation lasted long enough for us to realize the motorcycles were all they had going for them. Long enough for them to realize they weren't going to get in our pants. Long enough for me to decide I wasn't content to sit on the back half of a motorcycle seat. Not that I didn't enjoy wrapping my arms around whatever his name was. After we ditched the boys – or they ditched us, depending on your point of view – I bought a used Honda Rebel, with a gorgeous, candy red paint job. Then life got in the way and I sold it.

After picking up our helmets and motorcycles, my classmates and I stood around awkwardly, looking nervously at each other and the bikes. J.J. sighed and shook his head at us.

"This happens every time. It's like I'm chaperoning a junior high dance. They're not going to bite you. Introduce yourself. Get to know them."

J.J. made us point out each of the controls before giving us the OK to continue. Just that small act of throwing my leg over the seat and straddling the bike made my heart race. We practiced each step slowly and repeatedly until it became second nature. We walked the bikes, we turned them on and off, tested the throttle and the brakes, and even honked the horn. Finally we started the bikes, and rode slowly across the lot in first gear. It took forever, and was over much too soon.

The rest of class progressed in the same way. J.J. was patiently reassuring as we increased our skills. By the end of the day we were confidently upshifting and downshifting as we rode figure eights around the lot. Despite taking frequent breaks, my wrists and ankles started to ache from holding the unaccustomed positions. My legs and butt were numb from the constant vibration of the engine.

I was exhausted by the end of class, and was relieved to see the younger students looked tired, too. Before I left, J.J. told me Miss Irene had been texting him non-stop for progress updates.

I checked my phone and saw that she had been texting me as well. So had Emily.

Call Dad. Driving me crazy.

Gary usually called or texted me once or twice when he was away on business. During this trip he had been texting and calling several times each day. I wasn't sure if he was carrying over this new fetish for communication to our daughter, or if he was texting her because I wasn't answering his calls. I had sent him a few non-committal texts, just to be polite.

Emily and I, on the other hand, had been sending several short texts each day. We were rebuilding our relationship in baby steps, but it was coming along. Apparently she wasn't quite ready yet to forgive her dad.

The chicken in me, the part that avoided making decisions, wanted to send Gary a text.

The newly confident me realized we needed to talk in person.

Gary was standing at the stove making a grilled cheese sandwich when I walked in to our house. The window over the sink was open and the ceiling fan was on, but I could still smell the burning butter. I resisted the urge to make the sandwich for him. Gary was a big boy. He could take care of himself. Or he could learn how.

Gary looked like he had stepped out of an Eddie Bauer catalog. He was wearing a pair of crisp, dark blue jeans – he never wore faded denim – and brown leather penny loafers. The cuffs of his blue, pinstripe oxford were neatly folded back. When the smoke detector started chirping, I wasn't sure if it was his cooking or my lustful admiration that set off the alarm.

I swear, perimenopause was sending more hormones rushing through my body than adolescence ever did. The worst part was I knew exactly what to do with those hormones this time around. I just didn't have a practical outlet for them.

Gary moved the burnt sandwich to a plate while I reset the detector.

"I don't know how you do it, Jules," he said. Was that admiration I heard in his voice? "I hated my mom's grilled cheese – please don't tell her I said that – but yours . . . well, you've always been a great cook. You make even the simple things seem fancy." He looked down at his sandwich and grimaced.

"I suppose we could shake a little cajun seasoning on that and call it a 'blackened' grilled cheese," I said. Gary chuckled. "Or you could throw that sad thing away and I could show you my top-secret, sandwich secrets."

"It's a deal!" Gary ran his hand down my arm and I felt goosebumps ripple in the wake of his touch. He looked me in the eye, and his voice took on a soft tone. "I promise I'll pay attention this time, Jules." The cheese wasn't the only thing that was melting.

Damn him.

Where had this sensitive, caring man been for the last year? Where had he been last week? Oh wait, that's right. This sensitive, caring man had been sensitively caring about getting laid by my best friend last week.

He stood distractingly close to me while I demonstrated the steps to grilled cheese success. He let one hand rest low on my back, reaching around and across me with the other. His chest pressed against my shoulder and his arm brushed mine each time he reached out to assist me. He anticipated my needs – handing me the knife, the butter, the cheese slices. We were working together so well, so comfortably. Part of me didn't want it to end.

When my sandwich had toasted to golden brown perfection, I cut it diagonally and eased the halves apart to expose the gooey, melty goodness that can only be achieved by using name-brand, plastic-wrapped, cheese-like slices, cheap white bread, and real butter. I took a bite, letting the cheese string out tantalizingly between the sandwich and my mouth.

"Now it's your turn. Mmmm-mmm," I moaned, exaggerating. Just a little. Gary's eyes never left my lips. He reached out and gently brushed a crumb off my bottom lip with his thumb. My knees trembled. I turned away before I did something stupid.

"Nope. Dif onef's myhn," I said, taking a big bite and talking with my mouth full.

Gary sighed. I retreated to the relative safety of the other side of the table to watch him assemble and fry his sandwich. I couldn't see how it was browning, but I did have an excellent view of his backside when he turned to use the stove.

Damn him.

I couldn't deny the fact that we did make a good team. Our individual strengths complimented each other. When had the teamwork stopped? When had we stopped trying? It just seemed so much easier to divide the labor. To let Gary handle the finances, to let me handle the housework.

When was the last time he flirted with me like this? When was the last time I flirted with him? Maybe our growing apart wasn't all his fault.

A much easier question: When was the last time he cheated on me?

Gary finished cooking his sandwich, and sat down catty-corner from me at the table. We ate in silence.

"When are you coming home?" Gary asked the question as casually as if he were asking me how my day went.

Never. In my head the answer was simple. But somehow, I couldn't say it.

"I don't know," I finally said. Gary nodded and took another bite of his sandwich.

"When are you going to quit sleeping with other women?" I asked my question in the same casual manner as he had.

Gary quit chewing, but didn't say anything. He swallowed and set his sandwich down on his plate. He did not look at me. I decided to press harder.

"How many, Gary? How many women have you slept with while we were married? I have a right to know. Do you even remember their names?"

"Two. " His voice was quiet. His eyes never left his plate. "Two. Vanessa and Amanda. That's all, Jules."

"But last week you said . . . ."

"Last week I was scared and stupid and mad. I said a lot of things I shouldn't have." He looked at me at last. "I made a mistake, Jules. I made one mistake, and then another and another. Things got out of control." His gaze returned to his plate. He picked at the crust on his sandwich.

I sat back in my chair and crossed my arms over my chest. Sleeping with just two women was obviously better than sleeping with half the town, but it was still two too many. I had a box full of unmatched earrings that hinted at more. I didn't know if I trusted him any longer.

"Let's start with the first mistake," I said.

Gary took a drink of water and carefully set the glass back down exactly on the condensation ring it had left on the table.

"I slept with Amanda at the corporate retreat. I didn't plan it, it just happened."

"You plied her with champagne and caviar before you went on the retreat. That sounds like planning to me."

"She ordered it. I paid." He swirled the ice in his glass while he turned to look me in the eyes. He wasn't groveling. He wasn't weaseling. He was stating facts. Businessman Gary. "We were celebrating. Being asked to that retreat was a big honor. It was a huge step, professionally. We worked hard to get there."

I wanted to point out that I like to celebrate with champagne and caviar too, that I worked hard to support his working hard.

"That retreat introduced us to some very important execs. We went from being nameless drones at a random office out in the sticks, to being on the corporate radar. They started hinting about promotions. And the hints kept getting stronger." He picked at his sandwich again.

"One night after we had all been drinking, Amanda followed me into my room. She said she was tired of being judged for things she hadn't done. She said everyone already thought we were sleeping together, so maybe we should just go ahead and . . . . Then she, well, she got pretty persuasive . . . and imaginative . . . and we . . . ." He leaned his elbows on the table and put his face in his hands.

"I'm a man, Jules. You were so wrapped up in losing your job, and Emily not coming home, and Vanessa's problems. You treated me like I was . . . . "

"The hired help?"

Gary shrugged. "I guess. But not the fun kind. Amanda paid attention to me. She was so caring, so eager, so . . . imaginative. So flexible."

I rolled my eyes. Didn't he understand the concept of "too much information"? I could be imaginative. Maybe. I could be flexible, if I worked at it. Nah. At least one of us would wind up with a pulled muscle if I tried.

"Then she said that she could be an asset to me when it came to promotions . . . or she could make sure I never advanced any farther."

"She threatened you?" Holy shit!

"Well, not the first time. I mean, she emphasized the mutual benefits, but she didn't mention liabilities until later." This was bad on a whole different level.

"*She* came on to *me*, Jules. At the time I didn't think she could really do any harm."

"At the time?"

Gary closed his eyes and massaged the spot at the top of his nose between his eyebrows.

"Turns out they were talking promotion, singular."

"And?"

"And now we are both among the top four candidates."

"Shit." Even as angry as I was, I could see that Gary was well and truly fucked. In more ways than one. Some wives might blame this all on the "other woman." I thought Gary shared responsibility. He had obviously been a willing participant. Repeatedly. Still, I didn't think it was right for Amanda to play him like this.

"I need your help, Julie." Gary looked at me, and I could see the desperation in his eyes. I knew how badly he wanted to climb that corporate ladder. "This promotion is important to me. To us. It's a stepping stone. At this level, things happen much faster. The Des Moines office is a short stop on the path to Chicago and beyond. This is what we've been working for, Jules. But I can't do it without you."

I knew he meant the corporate office would be much more likely to promote a happily married man, as much or more than he meant he needed my love to get him through the long, lonely nights. I knew that he was good at his job, and that he was – would be – an asset to the company. I knew he didn't deserve to get screwed over by a less qualified candidate who thought she could sleep her way to the top.

"I'm sorry Gary. I just . . . . What Amanda is doing . . . it's not right. But I . . . I need to think about it."

"I understand." Gary looked and sounded disappointed, but he didn't pressure me.

"OK," I said. "That was mistake number one. How did that turn into mistake number two? Did Vanessa seduce you, too?"

"No. I knew we could work through the situation with Amanda. Then Vanessa came to my office and issued her ultimatum. She said you thought I'd been cheating. Honestly, Jules, even after what Amanda said, about 'everyone' thinking she and I were sleeping together . . . I never thought you had so little faith in me."

I held up my hand to stop him from making a fool of himself.

"But you *did* sleep with Amanada."

"I mean before that. I didn't pay attention to the rumors, because I wasn't doing anything wrong. I mean, Christ, Jules! You do something nice for a woman – you hold the door, you compliment her – and everyone thinks you're sleeping with her. I was trying to be nice! Then to find out that you . . . ."

"It wasn't just me. Emily noticed, too. That's why she cut us off – she saw you flirting with her sorority sister."

"Her sor . . . Oh, the hot blonde. Really, Jules, even you stared at her." Damn. He was right.

"What about the girl down at Starbucks?"

"Charlie's niece? Or her girlfriend, the surly one? Charlie doesn't care for the girlfriend. I don't think he'll approve of anyone she dates. I stop in every now and then to check up on them."

"Back to Vanessa."

"When Vanessa said you would leave me and that she would help, I panicked. I knew you'd turn to her. I couldn't let that happen. Not with the promotion on the line. I can't do this without you, Jules. I had to make her understand. I asked her what Michael would do if she left him and . . ."

"She started crying."

"Yeah. She was hysterical . . . and kinda hot." I shook my head. Stronger men than Gary have fallen victim to the pretty cry. "I thought a drink might calm her down. But then she started rambling. You know how she gets when she's drunk. One thing led to another . . . ."

"And you thought fucking her was a good idea? After everything she told you?"

Gary gave me a confused look.

"Shit. You weren't listening to her, were you?"

"Well, drunk Vanessa can be hard to follow." Gary shrugged. I told Vanessa he didn't listen!

"Michael left her, Gary. They signed the divorce papers that morning."

"Ohhhh, shit." Gary's eyes grew wide. "I didn't know, Jules. I swear."

That I could believe.

"OK. Fine." I shook my head. "You slept with Amanda because she seduced you. You slept with Vanessa because you panicked. You're quite the victim, aren't you, Gary?"

"I made mistakes, Jules. I'm not perfect. I can't change what happened."

I rubbed my forehead.

"Any other mistakes you want to get off your chest?"

"Mother never had an affair. I shouldn't have said that. I was mad. I lashed out." Gary sighed. "I don't know. I thought maybe you were suspicious of me because you . . . but I knew better."

"Your dad?"

"He's . . . . But Mom's always stood by him, Jules. She knows he loves her. He's just . . . ."

"An asshat?"

"He's my dad, Julie." Gary's eyes flashed with anger. Then he slumped back in his chair. "I never really thought about it, I guess." Gary unfolded and neatly refolded the cuffs on his sleeves.

"That's why they moved to Florida. Mom started spending more time with that art gallery guy – there was nothing going on, she would never let that happen – but Dad couldn't stand it. He thought they could make a clean start in Florida."

All this time I thought the gallery director was hitting on me. He was probably checking on Helen.

"Did it work?"

"I guess so. Mom doesn't say much. I think she misses Pleasant Glen, though. She keeps pretty close tabs on things up here." Gary gave me a half smile, leaned over and took my hands in his. "She's worried about you, Jules. She's worried that Miss Irene will be a bad influence."

I shook my head. Both women were so strong, so smart. And so different.

"Come home, Jules." Gary gave my hands a squeeze. "Come home. Things aren't so bad. We 'll get through this. We're a great team."

Sitting with him here in our kitchen felt so normal, so comfortable. It would be easier to stay, I thought.

"We'll go back to the way we were. You can redecorate the house again." Gary smiled. He was so handsome when he smiled. I melted a little.

"You can give up that silly motorcycle thing. You can quit dressing like a hoodlum."

This? This right here is why I will never get a concealed carry permit.

I was wearing the dark pink, long sleeve t-shirt with a small Pleasant Glen Cycles and Motors logo that Miss Irene gave me. My new boots were poised to kick Gary in his ever-so-tight ass.

I pulled my hands away from Gary's grip and sat up straight.

"No." I had believed the happy home lie before.

Gary stared at his empty hands for a moment and his shoulders slumped. He licked his lips and swallowed. I watched his Adam's apple bob on his graceful neck. I noticed the gray in his end of the day beard stubble, the little wrinkles around his mouth, under his eyes. He looked so vulnerable.

"Just think about it, Jules." His voice was quiet. He didn't look up. "You don't have to make a decision yet."

"I need to go," I said. My throat was tight.

I got up from the table. I walked out of our house.

I drove to Miss Irene's. I climbed into bed.

And then I cried myself to sleep.

20

I woke up feeling frustrated and exhausted. It seemed like I had been stuck in the same dream all night long – a dream in which I was stuck waiting in a line, all night long. I hit the snooze button and pulled the covers over my head, needing a few minutes to clear my thoughts.

I figured the symbolism was obvious – subconsciously, I felt like I was stuck in a hopeless situation. As the alarm went off the second time, I realized Gary had felt that way, too. But instead of trying to fight it, he had given in. I understood his reasoning. I didn't agree with his conclusions, but I understood why he did what he did. Sort of.

I had a choice to make. I could give in – I could go back to sleep and go back to Gary – or I could keep trying.

I decided to go for a run.

Miss Irene and Big George were at the kitchen table when I went downstairs. I must have looked even worse than I felt.

"Oh, dear Lord!" Miss Irene blurted out, when I walked through the door. "I mean, good morning, dear. Are you sure you're feeling up to a run this morning?"

I nodded half-heartedly and poured myself a cup of coffee.

"Trey finished painting the apartment last night. You can move in any time," she said. "Or not. I'm going to miss having you in the house. I hadn't realized how lonely it gets here after George goes home."

"Hmph. She means she needs someone around to fuss after. Some old habits are harder to break than others." George got up from the table, put his cup in the sink and gave Miss Irene a peck on the cheek before leaving for the shop. He patted my shoulder gently as he passed by, then said quietly, "Doesn't mean you shouldn't try, though."

*****

Our house – Gary's house – was on the edge of town. I was used to running on quiet country roads and wooded trails. From Miss Irene's, I was limited to paved residential streets and narrow sidewalks.

I was passing through a little park, slowing my pace to catch my breath, when I noticed a khaki-clad butt sticking out of a hydrangea bush.

A familiar, khaki-clad butt, hunched over familiar, spider vein-lined cankles.

Muffy's cankles.

Members of the Pleasant Glen Floriculture Society, Muffy included, took care of the landscaping in the city parks. I escaped PGFS after killing off the "easy to care for" spider plant my mother-in-law gave me. I tried to warn her. Helen was a plant's version of Snow White. African violets and orchids bloomed as she walked by. Silk flowers wilted in my wake.

"Why Julie Westbrook, you poor dear, how are you doing? I've just been worried sick about you! *Wor. Ied. Sick!*" Muffy emphasized each syllable by shaking the weeds held in her gloved hands like pompons. "You were so . . . aggressive at the meeting yesterday morning. Not at all like yourself. But I suppose with what you've been through that's to be expected."

The woman just crawled out of a hydrangea bush, yet she still looked ready for a Gap commercial. Her khaki walking shorts and white, authentic

Polo, polo shirt were spotless. She was wearing an adorable, broad-brimmed, straw hat that I would kill for. How she managed not to lose that monstrosity in the overgrown shrub was beyond me.

"Uh, yeah. About that . . ." maybe I had been a little harsh. Then again, she had tried to steal my event from me.

"Don't you worry about that, darling. No hard feelings. You are obviously under a lot of stress." She accepted an apology I did not offer, for behavior I thought was justified. That irritated me. And made me feel guilty.

"Bunny was supposed to contact you sooner about the meeting, but she got caught up in a project at the animal shelter." *Like hell*, I thought.

"I know she acted a little rashly, calling for that special meeting, but she was worried. The Gala will be here before you know it, and we – *she* – didn't think you'd be able to give it your full attention. We wanted to ease your burden, unlike some of your other so-called friends." Just like that, she made Bunny the scapegoat and insulted Vanessa.

"In retrospect I can see how you might have misinterpreted our efforts. But isn't the success of the Gala all that really matters?" And she topped it all off by laying a guilt trip on me.

"Bunny thought perhaps the animal shelter and Floriculture could be joint beneficiaries this year. But your suggestion is even better. The school's music program is in dire straights. Bunny and I have such fond memories of our days in the PGHS chorus, and of course our kids did, too." As I recalled, Bunny and Muffy's kids were sent home from the choir trip to Florida for drinking, but now wasn't the time to bring that up.

"I'm sure someone will step in and fund the budget shortfall at the shelter. It's not like the animals need to eat *every* day. And I'm sure they can squeeze a few more litters of kittens in. They're small. They don't take up much space."

The coup de gras: graciousness in defeat with a second order of guilt trip. It worked. I imagined a cardboard box, overflowing with kittens.

"Maybe the Auxiliary can do something specifically for the shelter once the Gala is over," I said.

"You are *such* a sweetheart!" Muffy put one weed-holding hand over her ample bosom, somewhere near where her too-small heart would be if, indeed, she had a heart. "Always willing to help. Always thinking about the good of the community. Bunny was so worried about you and Vanessa being able to work together after . . . well, you know. But then, you two have always shared *everything*, haven't you? It's OK honey, no one blames you a bit for turning to chocolate for comfort. So what if you've gained a few pounds? There's just that much more of you to love!" She smiled and winked at me.

These were the kind of comments I expected from Muffy.

"And obviously crying yourself to sleep, too. Try some cucumber slices on those bags, dear. *Big* slices. It's so good to see you up and about, getting a little sun. You're looking a little wan. Just make sure you don't over do it. Sunscreen doesn't *repair* damage . . . ."

"Um, running makes me blotchy." I wasn't sure why I felt the need to defend my appearance. She just had that affect on me. "I should really keep going . . . . " I started to ease away before Muffy could make me feel any worse. I hadn't been eating that much chocolate, had I? I mean, I was wearing spandex running shorts. They're supposed to be snug.

"It's perfectly OK, honey. You do what's best for you right now." Muffy followed me. "Just know that whenever you're ready to talk, I'm ready to listen. *Whatever* you need to talk about. No matter how dirty or depraved . . . ."

I stuffed my earbuds back in and sprinted down the path.

I hurried back to Miss Irene's, took a quick shower and got ready for the second day of riding class. Miss Irene told me Big George was sending over some men to move the furniture back up to the apartment. I wasn't sure how I could ever repay them for all they had done for me. She suggested I start by bringing home a bottle of wine for dinner and chocolate syrup. I didn't ask what she and Big George had planned for the chocolate syrup. I wasn't sure I wanted to know.

*****

J.J. started class with an exhaustive review. The other students and I were anxious to get back on the bikes. J.J. didn't say anything, but he stood with his arms crossed, frowning as we tried to hurry through the drills. I recognized that look. I had given it to Emily many times when she ignored my advice. I felt like he was just waiting for someone to screw up.

It didn't take long. Several students dumped the clutch, stalling the engine as soon as they started riding. A few shifted gears too early, causing the bike to jerk as the rpms dropped off. Others shifted too late, revving the engine.

I managed to keep it together during all this, which, of course, set me up for a bigger mistake. I became over confident and careless. As I walked my bike around a curve to line up for the next exercise, I turned the handlebar too sharply, upsetting the balance. I felt the weight shift and knew I wouldn't be able to muscle the bike back up straight. Instead I had to let it down slowly, cussing to myself the whole time. For a split second I stood there in disbelief, looking at the bike lying between my feet. Then I leaned over and hit the engine kill switch.

One mistake had led to another, and before I knew it, I was screwed. Why did that sound familiar?

Damn.

I looked up and saw J.J. walking towards me. I hated to disappoint him, almost as much as I hated making such a stupid mistake.

"Are you OK?" J.J.'s brown eyes were warm and filled with concern. It was all I could do to nod and hold back tears of frustration. He put his hand on my arm and gave me an encouraging smile.

"You handled that just right, you know. Sometimes you have to let go. It's OK ."

Knowing he was right didn't make me feel any better. I took a deep breath and nodded.

Now that we were all lined up, J.J. turned my accident into a teachable moment. I explained to the rest of the class how I had let my mind wander, and that the bike slipped away from me.

"You've all had times today when you let yourself get distracted," J.J. said. "The only way to deal with some of these problems is to practice . . . and pay attention. When you're riding in traffic, little problems can become big problems in a hurry. You always have to be aware of what's going on around you. People do stupid things. You have to be ready to ready to react."

We spent the rest of the class practicing defensive riding maneuvers. It was a little nerve-racking, even under slow-speed, controlled conditions, but it was exciting.

It was also exhausting. I knew I looked like hell, all helmet hair and dragging-ass tired, but I had to make good on my promise to Miss Irene to stop at the store. Despite J.J.'s warning about being aware of our surroundings, I let down my guard after loosing another battle with the automatic doors at the market.

Big mistake.

Bunny ambushed me, popping out from behind a pyramid of oranges.

"Why Julie Westbrook, you poor dear, how are you doing?" Bunny's commentary was nearly the same as Muffy's. The only difference was that she blamed everything on Muffy.

Bunny also thanked me for volunteering to organize the animal shelter's adoption day carnival. That was news to me, but I was too tired to argue.

Before I could escape, Bunny expressed her concern for my ruddy complexion and suggested I lay off the vino for a while. Then, noticing the chocolate sauce in my basket, she told me she was glad I was getting my appetite back. She said she thought I was wasting away to nothing and could stand to put on a few pounds.

Bunny also reminded me that she was there whenever I needed a sympathetic ear, no matter how disgusting and humiliating the stories were. The last time Hell had frozen over to the extent that it would need to freeze over for me to talk to either Bunny or Muffy about anything remotely involving Gary or Vanessa, dinosaurs had abruptly stopped roaming the earth.

I added two more bottles of wine and a package of double-stuffed Oreos to my cart. And a carton of cookie dough ice cream.

Miss Irene and Big George could spare a little of that chocolate sauce.

*****

By the time I got to Miss Irene's, she and Big George had fired up the grill and were enjoying cocktails under the tree in the backyard. Sitting with these 80-year-old, X-rated lovers was the sanest part of my day.

Miss Irene and I chatted, enjoying the peaceful, Iowa evening, while Big George manned the grill. They were so comfortable together, anticipating and responding to each others' thoughts and actions, that I wondered – not for the first time – why they hadn't married.

Trey and J.J. still hadn't arrived by the time the steaks were done, but Big George said we should start dinner. Miss Irene poured a glass of wine for each of us, and set a plate with a baked potato and steak in front of Big George and herself.

She handed me a small plate filled with wilted lettuce that was browning at the edges, and a single, withered carrot.

I blinked my eyes and stared at my plate. I thought of the hungry kitties at the shelter. I looked at Miss Irene.

"Helen called me this afternoon. She's worried that you're putting on weight," she said, barely concealing smile.

Big George rolled his eyes.

"Muffy called her mom after seeing you this morning. Then Shirley called Gary's mom to let her know how hard this separation has been on you," Miss Irene said. "According to Muffy, you've gained at least 20 pounds. You're eating Ben & Jerry's straight out of the carton, binge-watching Netflix and not shaving your legs."

"Give the girl some real food. She's too damn skinny," Big George said.

"I told Helen not to worry. I promised I'd take care of you," Miss Irene said, handing me a plate with a steak and potato. "Her heart is in the right place. She knows Gary is far from perfect. That woman has had her share of trials, although I may not have always agreed with the way she handled them."

I wondered if she meant Richard's affairs or Helen's friendship with the art gallery director. J.J. and Trey knocked on the back door just then, so I couldn't ask her. Not that she would necessarily tell me. Miss Irene could be tight-lipped when the mood struck her.

We all enjoyed a nice, relaxing dinner with plenty of motorcycle-related stories. The party finally broke up about nine o'clock. Trey was anxious to meet up with some of his friends, J.J. said he had some things to prepare before tomorrow's class, and Miss Irene made some comment about needing to be in bed by ten o'clock.

I did not want to stick around to find out what she meant. I crossed the back yard, looking forward to spending my first night in my quiet, cozy apartment all by myself.

In my rush to get to the ice cream into Miss Irene's freezer, I had left my cell phone in my car. The phone started ringing just as I opened the car door. I swiped the answer icon in time to hear Vanessa swearing.

"I got yer' horn right here, asshat! Damn brain freeze!" There was a clunk and a thud, which I recognized as the sound of a cell phone bouncing off the dashboard and hitting the floor.

Rather than getting caught in that awkward game of phone tag where we both try to call each other at the same time and both end up getting a busy signal, I decided to wait for her to call me back. I went up to my apartment and checked the texts that I had missed. All of them were from Vanessa.

Call me.

Fine. I'll call you.

You better fucking answer.

Vanessa still hadn't called back yet, so I checked my Voice Mail. More messages from Vanessa.

OK, fine. Have it your way. If you don't call me back in five minutes, I'm coming over there and making a scene. And I don't think Miss Irene will like that. On second thought, maybe she will. Call me back. That woman scares me. (Click)

I'm on my way. I have PeeGee's cake. And ice cream. And wine. Maybe I'll get a shake for the road. Maybe I'll order pizza. If it gets there before I do, I'll pay you back. Oh, and call me. (Click)

Vanessa still hadn't called back when I heard someone pull into the driveway.

"OW! Fucking small cars! No fucking headroom!" A car door slammed. Hard. "My next car's gonna be a Hummer, you piece of shit midget car!"

I figured Vanessa's arrival attracted Miss Irene's attention. She probably applauded Vanessa's outburst. Miss Irene still drove a Lincoln Town Car land barge that Big George kept purring like a kitten.

I opened the apartment door just as Vanessa reached the landing. She had a full grocery bag in each hand and held a to-go cup between her teeth. The cup was missing its lid and a trail of chocolate dripped down the side, ending in a splotch on her shirt. The straw narrowly missed her eye. I reached for the cup, but she growled, thrusting a heavy grocery bag at me instead. She then grabbed the cup with her free hand.

"Where have you been? I've been worried sick about you!" She threw her arm and the drippy cup around my shoulders and pulled me in roughly for a hug. "If only someone would invent a device which we could carry with us to keep us in constant contact with those we love and worry about." I wriggled out of her embrace before she could spill her shake on me. "Oh wait! They have. It's called a cell phone. You have one. Use it! What the fuck, Jules?"

"Sorry, Mom," I said. "I had dinner at Miss Irene's. I didn't realize I needed to check in with you first."

"Don't take that tone with me, Missy," Vanessa said as she walked into the apartment. She set her grocery bag and cup down on the kitchen table, then sighed. Her shoulders slumped. "I was so worried about you. You won't believe what I heard."

"Let me guess. I gained 20 pounds, quit shaving my legs, and I carry around a bottle of cheap wine."

Vanessa looked confused. "No. You lost 20 pounds, exercise all the time, and carry around a bottle of cheap wine."

"So you . . . ."

"So I brought all your favorite comfort foods: cake, ice cream, chips, cookies, and frozen pizza. I was afraid you'd seduce a delivery boy."

"So this is all . . . . " I said, looking through the bags.

"To fatten you up," she said. "Because I *have* gained 20 pounds and I'm not about to be the fat friend."

"You brought wine to a wino."

"No. That's for me."

"There are two bottles."

"I'm in this for the long haul. I'm willing to sacrifice my liver for you. That's just the kind of friend I am."

"You know this is ridiculous, right? I just saw you yesterday. There is no way I could have lost 20 pounds since then. I've lost 190 pounds of lying, cheating husband, but not 20 pounds of Julie."

"I know." Vanessa put the ice cream into the freezer, then held up the frozen pizza and looked at me questioningly.

I shook my head no. "Steak and potatoes."

"Can I come live with Miss Irene, too?" She slid the pizza in on top of the ice cream. "My house is big and scary and lonely."

"You brought all this food for a sleep over?"

"Well, if you insist. My overnight bag is in the car. Along with two more bottles of wine." Vanessa was already at the door, her hand on the knob. "I knew Muffy was just making up rumors. But I still feel bad, Jules.

Honest. I'm so sorry."

I know," I said quietly. "Go. Get your stuff. We'll drink wine, braid each others' hair, and make prank phone calls." She headed out the door. "And if you hear moaning or giggling coming from the back porch – or the back seat of a car – please, for the love of god, do not check it out."

Vanessa squinted her eyes and tilted her head, looking at me questioningly.

"Just trust me on this one."

21

We opened the first bottle of wine while I told Vanessa about my run-ins with Muffy and Bunny. Vanessa was particularly amused by them putting me in charge of the animal shelter fund raiser after deciding I was incompetent to organize the Gala.

Miss Irene had heard Vanessa's driveway tirade and came up to make sure no one was injured.

"You can't beat a big car for safety and comfort," Miss Irene said. "And they're a hell of a lot more fun at a drive-in than a compact." This made Vanessa collapse in a fit of giggles. I don't think she believed the stories about Miss Irene's libido until then.

"Now, what are your plans for the Gala? Bluff and bluster will only get you so far." Miss Irene filled us in on the details behind the music department's emergency. Her network of gossip contacts included the secretaries at the high school and at least one source at the county's emergency dispatch office.

A couple of electronically savvy seniors planned to tap in to the PA system and blare Alice Cooper's "School's Out" throughout the building during graduation practice. The principal found the cheap mp3 player and residential lighting timer the culprits had duct taped together and mistook their improvised electronic device for an IED of a entirely different kind. He grabbed the package and ran from the auditorium's light booth, but neglected to disconnect it from the rack of audio equipment. This set off a domino effect in the overcrowded room. Sound and light boards crashed to the floor, overloading electrical circuits and sending up sparks and smoke, which triggered the sprinkler system.

Any equipment not damaged in the initial crash was ruined by the sprinklers. The insurance company was reluctant to pay, citing human error and a faulty electrical system.

With Miss Irene's help we put together a plan for a wildly revamped Auxiliary Gala, and started the second bottle of wine. For the first time in the Gala's 60 year history, we were going to open the event to the public. Premium tickets would be available to Auxiliary members – at a premium price – giving them an opportunity to maintain an air of exclusivity, and access to a private bar.

We replaced the usual rubber-chicken dinner with barbecue meals by the county beef and pork producers. Living in Iowa does have its benefits, freshly grilled pork loin and steak sandwiches being chief among them.

Our entertainment would showcase performances by the same high school students we were hoping to raise money for, guaranteeing a large crowd of proud parents. In addition, I would contact Bob, my old boss from The Bar, about booking some groups with a regional appeal who might be willing to do a short set for very little pay.

I had someone in mind for the headline act, but I wasn't quite ready to share.

This was one of those times I missed Emily. She and her friends were always going to hear area bands play. I sent her a quick text to ask her opinion and to tell her I loved her. She replied, asking me to give her dad another chance. Apparently they had made up. I decided to ignore that issue for now.

Miss Irene promised to keep an eye on Bunny and Muffy via her web of informants.

"Well, girls, I'd better get back home. I left Big George to ponder a selection of negligees. He may think he's getting the milk for free, but he still has to work for it," Miss Irene said. On her way out the door she turned and gave us an exaggerated wink. "If we get too loud for you girls, just eat your jealous, young hearts out!"

"Is she always like that?" Vanessa asked, after Miss Irene had gone.

I shrugged. "Actually, that was pretty tame for her."

"Do you think she'd adopt me?"

I was sitting on the floor with my back against the love seat. Vanessa eased out of the rocker and sat next to me. A comfortable silence fell over us as we drank our wine, and listened – with a mix of suspense and dread – for Miss Irene and George.

"When you found me and Gary . . . well, you know . . . why didn't you post something nasty about me on Facebook?" Vanessa asked, out of the blue.

"Why would I do a thing like that?"

"I don't know, it just seems like that's what most women do when they find out their husband's been cheating. That, or they rent a big billboard, maybe put an ad in the paper. I think it's supposed to help with closure."

"Sounds more like open-sure to me," I said. "Besides, I try to keep my crazy hidden."

"How's that workin' out for you?"

"About as well as you might suppose."

"So . . . not at all?" Vanessa smiled at me.

"Not even close." I shook my head. "Why would I wave my dirty laundry out in public like that?"

"That's remarkably evolved of you, Jules. I'm proud to be your friend," Vanessa said, raising her empty glass in a salute. Then she waved it around, indicating she was ready for a refill.

"Anyway, why would I humiliate myself like that?" I asked, opening bottle number three.

"I think it's supposed to humiliate Gary and me," Vanessa said.

"Maybe. But I'm caught up in this too." I sighed. "Besides, you're still my best friend. I love you too much to do something like that to you. And Gary, well, he's not worth the effort."

"Did it ever occur to you that you haven't taken this out on Gary because you still love him?" Vanessa stared into her wine glass as she talked.

I studied her. Her husband had left her, and Gary had used her, whether it was just for sex or to get at me. Part of me wanted to hug her, hand her a pint of ice cream and tell her everything would work out.

But part of me wanted to slap her for sleeping with my husband, hand her a gallon of ice cream and wait for her ass to double in size.

It was complicated.

"I've thought about that," I said, finally answering her question. "When you've been married as long as we've been, I don't think your feelings can change over night. I still care about him. I can't believe I'm about to say this, but . . . he's not a bad guy." I took a big drink of wine, trying to wash away the bad taste that phrase left in my mouth. "I don't think we've been *in love* for a long time. If we ever were."

Vanessa unwrapped another piece of chocolate, wadded up the foil wrapper and tossed it onto the pile between us. If anyone could understand how I felt, I figured it was Vanessa.

"Honestly, why do you even have a Facebook page if you're not going to whine or creep on people?" she asked, reaching for another piece of chocolate.

"I use it to brag about my kid, like everyone else does. And to find funny cat videos. Besides, I never said I don't creep on people. I just said I don't like to post too much information about myself." I pulled my laptop off the desk and started it up.

"You are human, after all! I was starting to worry. I thought maybe I'd have to start calling you Saint Julie."

"Hardly," I snorted. "For example, I already looked up a few of the bands I remember playing at The Bar back in the day." I pulled up Joe's Facebook page.

"That's Joe Davenport." Vanessa recognized him right away.

"Um, yeah. You remember him?"

"Let's see . . . incredible singer, amazing piano player . . . swept you off your feet."

I smiled. She did remember.

"Then he dropped you like a bad habit. You cried for weeks. Nearly drove me insane with worry."

My smile fell. She did remember.

"*That* Joe Davenport? Why, yes. As a matter of fact I do remember Joe Davenport. Why?"

I felt my enthusiasm fizzle like a cheap bottle rocket.

"Well, I was thinking, we need a headliner, and . . . ."

"And you thought it would be a good idea to call up the guy who broke your heart?"

"Well, that might be a little over the top." I said.

"I was there Jules, I waded through the mountains of snot-soaked tissues. He broke your heart."

"But . . . ."

"But *what? What* Jules?"

"But nothing. *Nothing.*" I tried to sound unconcerned. Vanessa rolled her eyes. "I mean, we need a headliner. What are the odds we can find someone who can bring in a crowd and that we can afford? We need some kind of hook. And, well, I know . . . I *knew* Joe. I thought maybe he'd be willing to help us out. For old time's sake."

"Bullshit. You're upset and you binge listened to Bruce Springsteen. Now you're goin' all 'Glory Days' on me. But I'm here to remind you, that particular glory day didn't end so well." Vanessa studied the dregs at the bottom of her glass. "I gained 10 pounds over that breakup, too." She looked up at me and shrugged. "I'm a sympathy eater."

"I think you're reading a little too much into this."

Vanessa filled our wine glasses.

"Oh really? Let's recap, shall we? Wife feels neglected," Vanessa pointed at me with her glass. "And rightfully so. Wife needs to restore self-confidence. Wife's knee-jerk reaction is to do something stupid." She pointed at herself this time, then took a big drink. "Wife ends up hurting best friend – or causing best friend to gain ten pounds." She twirled her glass to indicate both of us, then drained it, swallowed and shuddered. "Again."

"This isn't about you and Gary," I said. Vanessa paused mid pour and snorted. "Well, not entirely."

"I just don't want to see you make the same mistake I did, honey. I mean, well, you know." Vanessa shook her head. "Joe could be married. He could have a girlfriend."

"He could be married *and* have a girlfriend," I said, thinking of Gary.

"Or he could have a boyfriend."

That's a conversation stopper, right there.

"Or he could be single," I said, quietly.

"HA! I knew it! Little Miss '*We Need a Headliner*,' my ass. Besides, you said you just came up with this idea, but your browser history shows 'Joe Davenport' hits last Friday." Vanessa had commandeered my laptop and was running a Google search for *Iowa musicians excluding Joe Davenport*. "What's this? A *file* labeled 'Joe Davenport'? You *have* been busy, haven't you?"

"No – wait! Don't open that." I lunged for the computer.

"Holy shit, Jules. You're one lock of hair shy of being a creepy stalker," she said as she scrolled through the images of Joe I had downloaded.

"I just wanted to make sure it was the same guy. He's changed since I last saw him."

"Ya' think?" Vanessa raised an eyebrow. "It *has* been a few years." She scrolled some more. "That's him alright. Not bad. Still looks more like a farmer than a rock star."

"It's worth a try, right? I mean, we *do* need a headliner." I felt my confidence in the whole situation eroding.

"OK, honey, what the hell. You know this is a long shot. Despite your impressive Google-stalking skills, you apparently missed the news that Joe's star is once again on the rise." With a few key-strokes she pulled up a gossip column that hinted Joe might be staging a comeback tour.

"Our little fundraiser might be pretty small potatoes for him," Vanessa said. She reached over and gave my hand a gentle squeeze. "He didn't seem to have too much trouble moving on to bigger and better things the last time. He may not have the same ideas about 'old time's sake' as you do."

"I know. It's just, well, I wish I would have known then, what I know now," I said.

Vanessa leaned over and put her head on my shoulder.

"Believe me, honey, I know what you mean. But that kind of thinking won't get you anywhere." She sat up and gave a dainty little sniff. "I've tried and tried to figure how I could have missed seeing *why* Michael was so miserable. You just have to make the best decisions you can, with the information you have."

"So what do you do when that information changes?"

"You adjust. You accept it." Vanessa managed a half-hearted smile, her eyes brimming with tears. "You buy them a kabobber and move on."

I hesitated.

"One of my biggest regrets when Joe left was that I never got the chance to tell him I loved him. I just assumed he knew." I said.

Vanessa smacked her forehead with her palm. "I can't believe you didn't tell him you loved him, you dork."

"I was going to. I just thought we would have more time. And then . . . . we didn't."

"Men. Can't live with 'em, can't assume they're mind readers. Dork." She punched me in the leg. I probably deserved it.

I took the computer back and opened my music files. I had transferred Joe's recording from the cassette tape to my computer to save wear and tear on the tape.

"But when everything turned to shit last week, I went through some boxes of old stuff and I found this . . . ." I clicked on the play arrow. Vanessa listened without saying word.

She was still speechless when the recording ended. A pale pink blush had spread across her cheeks, and giant, glistening, pretty-crier tear drops trembled on the edges of her eyelashes.

"I know, right? If I had found this back then, I would have never given up on him."

I played the just the part when he said he loved me a second time.

"You mean, when you two were . . ." Vanessa wiggled her eyebrows suggestively, "you never blurted out 'I love you' in the heat of the moment?"

"We never . . . ." I wiggled my eyebrows.

"You're telling me that a couple of 20-somethings dated hot and heavy and exclusively for what, three months, and you never . . . or said 'I love you'? No wonder he dumped your ass. Dork."

I grabbed her hand before she could punch me again.

"Believe me, I wondered if that was the reason he left. Sometimes I felt like I should have . . . . I mean, I wanted to. We came close." I blushed, remembering how close we had come to having sex. Joe had been patient and very creative about finding ways to do everything short of having actual intercourse. Still, even then I knew "almost" making love wasn't the same as making love.

"What about you and Gary?"

"Not until the honeymoon. I told him I had promised my Mom. I think I was just afraid."

"But Gary had a box of condoms in his medicine cabinet – I borrowed a couple. Did you know you can blow those things up to the size of a watermelon?"

I shrugged. "Must have been left over from his ex-fiance, Pamela. Maybe that's why she thought he was sneaking around – she kept count of his condoms! Maybe you're the reason she backed out of their wedding!"

"Nah, this was after you two were . . . but she did come back and . . . . " Vanessa's forehead furrowed in concentration. Then she shook her head and took another drink, as if the effort to think was too much. "That was so long ago."

"Anyway. Not the point. If I had listened to this back then, I would have never stopped trying to get in touch with Joe." All week long I had been torturing myself with this thought. What if I had made one more call? What if I had just jumped in the car and drove to New York, or Chicago, or L.A, or Poughkeepsie? That was part of the problem – Joe traveled so much during those first couple months that I never knew for sure where he was, or when he would be there. I had made a few calls, only to find out the band had already moved on, or the schedule had changed and no one knew where they were headed next.

The flip side of that coin was that Joe hadn't tried to get in touch with me, either. His taped love confession was heartening but it didn't change the fact that he hadn't called. Of course, Vanessa and I had moved to River City two weeks after Joe left, so it would have been almost as difficult for him to track me down.

Unless he didn't want to. Unless he wasn't a mind reader and didn't know that I loved him, too. Unless he was tired of "almost" sex.

"Didn't it seem weird to you that Joe never called me? You know, after he left?" I asked Vanessa. She had a vacant stare on her face. I wasn't sure if she was ready to pass out, or still thinking about watermelon-sized condoms.

"Huh? But he, there was, and then, we thought . . ." Vanessa blushed. She had drank at least twice as much wine as I had, and it seemed to be catching up with her all at once.

There was a time when we were younger when Vanessa and I closed down the bars with alarming frequency. There was a time when we could drink nearly four bottles of wine between us and wake up bright and chipper and eager to start the day at the crack of noon.

Those days were long gone.

I was about to give in and call it a night – or a morning – when I heard Big George singing as he walked to his car.

"Irene goodnight, Irene goodnight

Goodnight Irene, goodnight Irene

I'll see you in my dreams."

Vanessa and I crawled to the open window to peek out. J.J. told me Big George never stayed overnight at Miss Irene's because he didn't want to set a bad example for Trey. He was always back at his house before Trey woke up. He made breakfast for the three of them, then stopped at Miss Irene's for coffee on his way to the shop.

"That is the sweetest thing I have ever heard," Vanessa drunk-whispered.

"Good night Julie, and Julie's friend," Big George called out as he got into his car.

Vanessa looked at me, her eyes and mouth open wide in surprise. She had no idea how loud her drunk whisper was. I'd tried to tell her many times.

"I think I'm in love," she said. "Does he has a younger brother?" We both giggled.

"No, but . . . ." I thought about J.J., and how much he was like his dad. They were both so considerate, so sweet and charming. I wondered what J.J. would have done in Joe's situation. Would he have given up on me so easily?

"I wish someone would sing to me like that," I said.

Vanessa yawned and curled up on her side, resting her head on her arm. One of Vanessa's superpowers as a helpless drunk was her ability to fall into a deep sleep in the blink of an eye. Once she was asleep, there was no waking her. She smiled and stretched, mumbling as she gave in to a contented sleep.

"You mean like Joe did, before Gary made him leave?"

22

Vanessa's other Helpless Drunk Superpower was her inability to remember anything that happened while she was drunk. The next morning she had no idea what I was talking about when I asked her why she said Gary made Joe leave.

She also asked me to quit yelling, turn off the sunshine, and take the dead cat out of her mouth. Then she rolled over, pulled the sheet over her head and went back to sleep. Right after she asked me to call in sick to work for her. She had migrated from the floor to my bed some time during the night. I had forgotten how much I enjoyed sleeping alone.

I was feeling less than perky myself, although I wasn't sure how much of that was hangover and how much was nervous anticipation of the final day of class. Breakfast with Miss Irene and Big George eased my hangover, but only partially calmed my nerves. Miss Irene peppered me with questions she thought might be on the written test, making me more nervous. Big George sighed, and rattled his newspaper at her fussing.

"Have a little faith in the girl, Irene," he said as he headed for the door. "Or at least have some faith in her teacher. You know *he* had a good teacher." Big George winked at me and smiled. "You'll do fine, dear. Don't worry."

Class went much better than I expected. I only missed one on the multiple-choice test, and I passed the riding test with flying colors. It seemed like everyone got their big mistakes out of the way the day before. We all earned our certificates of completion, and we caravaned immediately to the driver's license station at the county courthouse downtown to get our licenses.

Miss Irene, Big George and Trey were waiting in the parking lot when we came out. Trey had ridden The Scout and Miss Irene had brought me balloons and cupcakes for a surprise celebration. I thought my classmates seemed a little envious. I wasn't sure if it was because The Scout was looking particularly beautiful, or because of the way my friends supported me.

After our impromptu party, J.J. met me back at the college to supervise my first ride on The Scout. Miss Irene and Big George had taught me the elaborate ritual required to start her, as well as how to use the hand shift and foot clutch. Big George did everything he could to keep The Scout running smoothly without swapping out the original systems for modern controls.

But I hadn't actually ridden her yet. Big George was a stickler for rules. No matter how much Miss Irene tried to charm him – and I tried not to think about which charms she might have used – he wouldn't let me ride The Scout, or any motorcycle, outside of class before I had my license.

I figured that was OK, as riding the smaller, newer bike in class let me concentrate on fundamentals. The Scout was a whole different set of challenges. She had a bigger motor than I was used to and was heavier, but her low-slung profile gave her a lower center of gravity, so she had great balance.

"Just remember, she's a senior citizen," Big George told me before I left the courthouse. "She can be a little temperamental, and sometimes her joints are little stiff."

"But don't underestimate her!" Miss Irene said. The two of them were standing side by side, and from the way Big George jumped and grinned, I guessed she had goosed him to emphasize her point.

"She's a little more work, but she's worth it." Big George glanced at Miss Irene out of the corner of his eye. Now it was her turn to give a little jump, a smile lighting her face.

As I stood over The Scout, I couldn't stop smiling either. I ran my hands from the voluptuous fullness at the top of her gas tank down to where it narrowed at the seat. I tested the balance of the bike, holding it firmly between my legs, aware of just how powerful she was. Somehow this sexy, strong machine made me feel sexy and strong too.

I thought for a moment about The Scout's story, and about the other people who had stood like this before me. I thought about the farmer's son, his taste for adventure used up in the war. I thought about Frank, how he had found adventure, but it cost him his family. I thought about Miss Irene. Her adventures on The Scout had bought her independence, but at what price? Why hadn't she married Big George?

Big George told her everyone hears what they need in The Scout's song. What had they heard? What would I hear?

I leaned in low to set the choke and rested my cheek on the gas tank for a moment. I whispered to The Scout, like Trey had done.

"Hello, Gorgeous. I'm listening."

When I stood up, I noticed J.J. was watching me and shaking his head.

"I'm surrounded by crazy people," he said. "You realize The Scout is just a machine, right?"

I raised an eyebrow. He grinned.

"But don't tell anyone I said that. They'd disown me."

J.J. watched carefully as I went through the pre-ride check and the process of kick starting her. He knocked on The Scout's rear fender before sending us on our way. I could just barely hear him over the purr of her engine.

"Take good care of her." I wasn't sure which one of us he was talking to.

The first lap was a little rough. The old-style, plunger-type rear suspension made the Scout's ride feel stiff. I was nervous about shifting, and tensed up every time I had to let go of the handlebar to reach for the hand shifter. But as we eased back around to where J.J. waited, pacing slightly and rubbing his hands together, something clicked.

"Don't fight her," Big George had told me. "You're going to have to work together to find common ground." The motions for shifting gears on The Scout felt similar to the manual transmission in my Mini Cooper. I figured out the rhythm for rocking my foot back and forth to disengage the clutch and smoothed out my gear changes.

I fell into synch with the Scout's vibrations and felt myself relax. As I relaxed, the ride became more comfortable. J.J. motioned for me to stop, but I smiled and shook my head, and started on a third lap.

After the fourth lap, J.J. turned me loose to ride around the nearly deserted campus, not that it was much bigger than the parking lot. Still, the stop signs and what little traffic there was made it more challenging. After several loops around the school, I felt my butt beginning to get numb. I reluctantly returned The Scout to J.J., climbed into my car, and headed out to face reality. I still had a Gala to plan, and some old ghosts to face.

*****

The Bar was an Eastern Iowa legend. The current owner, Robert

Fitzgerald Donnelly — Bob — had inherited The Bar from his father, Patrick Robert, who inherited it from his father, Fitzgerald Patrick, who inherited it from his father, Robert Fitzgerald Donnelly.

The original R.F. Donnelly won the drinking establishment in a poker game in 1892. Enamored by the ornate carvings on the oak and mahogany Brunswick triple arch back bar, Donnelly had risked his farm, his house, and — rumor had it — his eldest daughter's hand in marriage on a royal flush, which may or may not have been legitimate. His Irish luck held, the bar's owner didn't question the cards, and his daughter eloped with the bar owner's son anyway. The winning poker hand, now yellowed and faded from age, still hung in a frame in the center arch of the back bar.

R.F.'s wife Elizabeth, of steadfast German stock, was said to have been less than enthused, especially when she found out what had been wagered. His charm won her over, and her homemade sausage and sauerbraten won over the lunch crowd. Not much, other than the menu, had changed about The Bar since then.

Bob bought and annexed the adjoining building — a hardware store that had abandoned the downtown for a strip mall — when he joined his father in the early 1970s. The expansion doubled the capacity, improving The Bar's ability to host bands. Bob could stand at the bar and look through strategically placed, oversized doorways into the new section and have a clear view of the stage, located at the rear of the addition.

All four generations of Donnelly men were sweet voiced, Irish tenors and shared an affinity for live music. Bob and The Bar supported a wide range of musicians, from rock to classical. He drew the line at piano recitals. "We all have our limits," he said.

The centerpiece of The Bar's musical spotlight was a 1925 Steinway upright. Rumor, supported by generations of Donnelly men, was that the piano had been a gift from Al Capone. The Bar's original upright had been critically wounded in a shootout between rival bootleggers over a shipment of Iowa's own Templeton Rye bound for Capone in Chicago.

Theories varied on why the bootleggers detoured through Southeastern Iowa on their way to the Windy City. Some said they were looking for an alternate route that wasn't closely watched by revenuers, other said they sampled the goods and got lost.

The alleged bootleggers – re-purposed Iowa farmhands – were poor shots at best and worse when confined by close quarters. Ducking behind overturned tables, they took turns shooting in the general direction of the other group. This may have gone on until someone was actually hit, had not Fitzgerald P. Donnelly charged out from behind the bar waving a barrel stave, after a shotgun blast tore through the Bellevue Piano Company player piano.

Shooting at, or being shot at, by another overall and fedora wearing bootlegger was one thing. Having a diminutive, angry, red-headed, Irish bartender bearing down on you wielding a barrel stave was quite another. Shooting ceased immediately, apologies were mumbled, and F.P. donated a few bottles of "the good stuff" from a secret stash to seal a peace agreement.

The Capone legend went so far as to claim that a ding in the back bar was the result of a celebration by Capone and his inner circle, enjoying a holiday in February, 1929. Legend also attributed a bullet hole in the ceiling of the upstairs apartment to a celebration between Capone and Mary Ellen Reilly, which was interrupted by Mary Ellen's husband. Muffy and her mother never discussed this family rumor.

*****

There were plenty of parking spots available right out front of The Bar at two o'clock in the afternoon, but I parked a discreet distance down the street. Half the town already thought I was a lush, I didn't want to reinforce that image.

I stepped inside and closed my eyes to adjust to the dim lighting. I breathed in the mix of afternoon smells – the beefy aroma of the lunch special, the warmth of well-waxed wood, the soapy sanitizer in the bar sink, and the stale smoke that continue to leach from the brick walls, despite the state's public smoking ban.

A few stragglers were finishing one last beer and swapping one last story before heading back to work. A dark-haired woman, wearing this year's, fitted Brooks Brother's cream-colored blouse – which I had been lusting after for weeks – sat alone at a table in front of the stage, her back to the door. She had apparently brought her work to lunch with her. A half-eaten salad was pushed to the far side of the table, forgotten as she multi-tasked, talking on her cell phone and typing into a laptop.

Bob was in his usual place behind the bar, washing glasses and talking to a man sitting on a stool in front of him. I walked over to join them.

"What's a girl gotta do to get a drink around here?" I asked, leaning against the bar. Bob laughed and leaned across to give me a quick kiss on the cheek. The other man – I finally recognized him as Melvin Steinhocker – held out his arms for a hug. I hesitated, then gave him a quick squeeze.

"Glad to see you looking so good, Julie," Bob said. "I was getting worried there, what with . . . well, you know."

"Oh god, what did you hear, Bob?"

"Awww, it's really not important. I knew it was all gossip."

"No, I want to know. I've already heard that I lost 20 pounds or gained 20 pounds, that I never leave the house, that I never stay home, and that I carry a bottle of wine wherever I go. Or don't go."

Bob crossed his arms and leaned against the back bar the way he always did when he was getting ready to tell a story.

"Full on Britney Spears," he said, nodding his head slowly. "Someone said they saw you at the Style Shack. Said you shaved your head and got a tattoo. Short skirt, commando, the whole nine yards."

"I got my hair colored the same as I do every month. Maybe a little darker than usual."

"And the tattoo?"

"Are you kidding me? I have trouble committing to a hair color, let alone something more permanent."

"See Melvin, I told you. You owe me 10 bucks."

"You bet on whether or not I got a tattoo?"

"At least I bet that you *didn't* get one." Bob shrugged. "But just for argument's sake, if you did get one . . . where would it be, and what?"

I put my hands on my hips and leaned to one side. "Your name. On my left butt cheek. That way the whole world will know that you've always been a pain in my ass."

"Make it 20, Melvin," Bob laughed. "That's my girl."

"What about the commando part? Don't leave us hanging, Julie," Melvin said.

Lucky for him I was still feeling frisky from riding The Scout. I sat on the neighboring bar stool and slowly crossed and uncrossed my legs, impersonating Sharon Stone in *Basic Instinct*.

"If I told you that, Melvin, you sure as hell wouldn't be *hanging*."

"Jesus H. Christ, Julie! I'm a married man. Norma would kill me." Melvin drew back away from me and took a long drink of his beer. "If you didn't give me a heart attack first." He took another drink, then sat the empty glass down on the bar. "With my luck, first you'd give me a heart attack, then Norma would come in and unplug my life support."

Bob shook his head. "How ya' been, stranger? You haven't been in here since. . . ."

"I know. I just . . . ." I had only been back to The Bar once since the last night Joe played there. Vanessa and I were moving to River City and I still hadn't heard from him. When Bob said he hadn't heard from him either, I burst into tears. Bob had hugged me and Melvin had patted my hand while I cried. Both men did their best to console me.

"Funny you should come in here today, of all days, " Bob said. He shifted his weight and looked at Melvin. Melvin was suddenly very interested in something at the bottom of his empty glass.

"What do you mean?" I asked.

The two men looked at each other, as if expecting the other one to explain.

"Wellll," Bob said, drawing the word out. "It's just that . . . ."

"Damndest coincidence," Melvin added.

"Kinda like a little . . . what would you call it . . . ." Bob looked at Melvin, waiting for him to finish the sentence.

"Well now, I think you could call it a reunion, of sorts, Julie-girl." Melvin rushed to get the words out. He reached out and took my hand, holding it in one of his thin, bony hands and patting it with his other. The gesture felt creepily familiar, and the feeling only got worse as he rambled on. Bob nodded encouragingly at him.

"Now, you know sometimes reunions can be a little awkward but sometimes they can turn out real nice. Well, this one is just *such* a surprise that . . ." Melvin's words trailed off.

"That we all need to keep an open mind and not jump to conclusions." Bob added.

"Or shoot the messengers."

"I think if we all stay calm and such, that . . . ."

"This will be one of them real nice kinda reunions." Melvin finally ran out of words.

"Or a real shit-storm," Bob said under his breath.

"Guys, I know it's been a long time, but . . . ." I hadn't followed a single word they said.

"Holy crap, Bob!" A voice called out from the back hallway. Correction: not a voice, *the* voice. I turned around and watched as Joe Davenport ran up the steps to the stage.

"How long has it been since you cleaned out that storage room?" Joe shouted. He looked towards the bar, holding his hand over his eyes to shield them from the stage lights he had just turned on. "I had a hell of a time tryin' to find the light switch. Glad to see you haven't upgraded the electrical."

I knew he couldn't see us – couldn't see me – with those bright lights between us. Still, I panicked. I hadn't expected to see Joe. Not yet. I figured I'd talk to Bob, see if he knew where Joe was, how to get in touch with him, what he was up to, whether or not he was married. Then I'd formulate a plan, practice what I would say to him, lose 20 pounds for real, assemble a smoking hot outfit, get my hair done, get a manicure . . . .

But there he was. I wasn't sure if I wanted to run away or rush the stage and swoon at his feet, although I was leaning towards throwing up.

"Now, Julie-girl," Melvin said. He was still holding my hand, and he gave it a squeeze. "Let's just relax. Maybe she needs some whiskey, Bob."

"You mean you need a whiskey, you chicken shit." Bob grabbed a bottle of Templeton Rye and three glasses. "Maybe we all do," he said, pouring generously.

"Piano players, 'bunch of bitchy little girls'. Some things never change," Bob shouted towards the stage. "Speaking of which . . . ." His voice dropped off as he looked back at me.

I shook my head. "Not yet," I said quietly.

Joe was sitting at the piano now. He played a few chords gently, tentatively, testing out the play on the worn keyboard.

"When's the last time you had this hunk of junk tuned?" Joe yelled. He broke the chords down into arpeggios, playing them faster and louder, hitting the keys harder and with more confidence.

"You break a string, you pay for repairs," Bob yelled after one particularly loud section. The random scales became a ragtime number, then morphed into a slower, melodic, classical piece.

"Why don't you just let me buy you a new piano, old man," Joe replied. "I'll take this relic off your hands," he spoke and played softer now, his hands caressing the keyboard.

"You've always had a hard-on for my piano. You know you could never find another one with that sound."

Joe shook his head. "Just let me borrow it for a couple days then. Let me take it back to my studio." I thought I recognized a snippet from "Brown Eyed Girl" before Joe returned to playing scales.

Here we were again, after so long. The moment I had been hoping for. And I had no idea what to do.

"It's your play, Julie-girl," Melvin said, giving my hand another squeeze. "I got the Oldsmobile parked right out front. Just say the word and I'll whisk you away."

Bob snorted. "That old rust-bucket's hardly a get-away car. And you're hardly the whisking type. If anyone's whisking Julie away it's gonna be me. " Melvin started to object, but I cut him off.

247

"It's OK fellas. Nobody's doing any whisking." Their bickering had broken the tension I felt building inside me. I didn't know what I was going to do, but I wasn't going to run. "It's just . . . . Why didn't he call me, Bob?"

"What? But he . . . well, I guess that's something the two of you will have to discuss." Bob looked over my shoulder. "He's a good man, Julie. A good man."

23

Without looking, I knew Joe was standing behind me. I knew it from the way Bob suddenly turned to rearrange the bottles on the back bar. From the way Melvin swiveled his bar stool, turning his body away from me while twisting his neck so he could still watch me over his shoulder.

I knew it from the energy that surrounded Joe, or whatever you want to call that magnetic pull some people have. I couldn't breath. The skin on the back of my neck tingled, longing for his touch.

I inhaled, closing my eyes, and felt myself reflexively sway towards him. The tingle spread, racing along my shoulders, down my arms and across my chest. I shivered as it washed down my spine and around my hips, slowing to spread between my thighs and turn my legs to jelly. I was caught in a near orgasm of desire, expectation and memory that intensified until Joe was right behind me and I felt the heat of his body against my back. I exhaled and, whether pushed backward by my breath or pulled by his magnetism, I brushed against him. He gasped. I smiled and straightened slightly, reluctantly breaking the bond.

It didn't last.

Joe put his hand on my right hip and moved even closer to me. He reached around me, resting his other hand against the bar. He leaned forward, pressing gently against me. I could feel his chest on my shoulders, his crotch solid and warm against my ass. His thigh slipped between mine. I took a deep breath and shuddered slightly.

All of this would have gone unnoticed at a crowded bar. Caught up in the crush of people eager to get another drink before the next set started, Joe used to sneak up behind me like this when I was working. He would chuckle suggestively, his breath warm against my ear. It was one of our inside jokes. I complained all the time about drunken couples groping this way and blocking the waitress station. The drunken couples seldom stopped at this covert level of PDA. Occasionally Bob threatened to hose them down with the soda gun. Once he actually carried through on his threat.

There was no crowd this afternoon. The near solitude and our shared history made this seemingly accidental contact feel unmistakably erotic. I had never envied those drunkenly oblivious couples so much, with their desperate pawing and sloppy, face-eating kisses.

Melvin, now effectively blocked from me by Joe's arm, choked on his beer.

"Shit. This is better than cable," he said, looking at Bob in the mirror behind the bar.

"Don't make me use the soda gun." Bob didn't turn around, but he did move two bottles that were blocking his view. His reflection grinned at us. My body shook as I tried to stifle a giggle.

Joe coughed and shifted his weight, pushing my hips away from him slightly. To make up for lessening the pressure from our waists down, I pressed my shoulders against his chest. He sighed, a small puff of air tickling my neck.

"Bartender, two boysenberry kamikazes, please," he said, ordering my favorite drink from so long ago. How often had he teased me about that being a silly drink for a barmaid? He even threatened not to order it for me, saying it emasculated him.

"No one drinks those anymore," I said, smiling and turning to face him. I leaned back to get a better look at him, propping my elbows on the bar.

"Maybe not, but that's what I want." He had both hands on the bar now, trapping me between them.

I didn't see the 50-something entertainer from the YouTube videos. I saw the 20-something piano player I fell in love with. His short, graying hair made the gold flecks in his hazel eyes glow. His face had lost that lean, angular look of youth, but his smile was the same. His full lips tempted me more than ever.

I watched those impossibly long eye lashes flutter as he glanced down to take me in. With my elbows back, the girls were on display front and center. I was glad I had worn a good, supportive bra, and not the boob-smashing sports bra I usually wore under t-shirts. The shirt and faded jeans that I had worn to riding class were just snug enough to give him something to look at.

"Do you always get what you want?" I raised one eyebrow. He was even more sexy than I remembered. Why had I ever let him get away?

"No," he said softly. He pushed off the bar to straighten up and slowly folded his arms across his chest. He cocked his head and looked me over again, more slowly this time. "But I keep trying." He looked me right in the eye. "No matter how long it takes."

"That's good to know." I pushed off the bar now and ran my hands up his arms, from his elbows to his shoulders. He uncrossed his arms and reached for my hips.

"Hi, Joe," I said, stepping into his embrace. I wrapped my arms around his neck.

"Hi, Julie." His hands were warm on the small of my back as he pulled

251

me closer. We still fit together perfectly, I thought, as I nuzzled his neck. Joe whispered something in my ear, or maybe he kissed me, I don't know. I was so lost in the sensation of our various body parts meshing – angles, and curves and straightaways interlocking like puzzle pieces – the rest of the world fell away.

"You still got that soda gun handy? I might need a little cooling down myself," Melvin said to Bob.

"How 'bout a beer on the house instead. Beers all around," Bob said. "Haven't made those candy-ass drinks since 1988," he muttered.

I laughed and took a step backward, sliding my hands down to hold Joe's elbows. He let me slip away just far enough for decency, still keeping his hands on my hips.

"It's good to see you, Joe."

"Good to see you, Julie." He raised a hand to my face and rubbed his thumb along my cheekbone, then cupped his hand around my jaw and pulled me forward to kiss him. The momentum was broken when his arm was tugged away.

"Julie? *Julie*? Surely this is not *the* infamous Julie, is it?" The woman in the Brooks Brothers' shirt appeared at Joe's side, swaying slightly and bracing herself on Joe's arm. Her skinny heeled, black patent calfskin, platform stilettos were drool-worthy gorgeous, and unless my eyes failed me, authentic Christian Louboutin. They were also no match for the ancient, slightly warped wood floors of The Bar.

"I don't think that word means what you think it does, Soph," Joe said, never taking his eyes off me.

"Whatever," she said dismissively. I thought her tone of voice indicated she knew exactly what "infamous" meant, and that it was exactly the word she meant to use. The woman edged herself in front of Joe, establishing a physical barrier between us. I recognized this as a move to mark what she thought of as her territory and wondered why she didn't just pee on him and get it over with.

"I'm Sophia LeClaire, Joe's . . . *manager.*" She giggled exaggeratedly and looked coyly over her shoulder at Joe. His gaze was fixed on me and his smile never wavered, but I noticed his jaw was clenched. Sophia returned her insincere smile to me and extended her hand daintily for me to shake. I resisted the urge to crush it in my grip. I hate limp fish handshakes.

"Joey's told me so much about you."

I knew this wasn't true. I knew he hated being called Joey. I knew this was the first time she had ever called him that, by the way it tumbled, unfamiliarly off her lips. I felt her jealousy radiating off her.

I was wrapped up in my own jealousy. I recognized her from the photos on Joe's web page. They looked happy together in those pictures and I had wondered how much of Joe's life she managed. I comforted myself with the thought that photos can lie, remembering how Gary and I had looked in the news feature from the art gallery fundraiser.

So-FIE-Ah my ass, I thought, bitterly. I doubted the authenticity of her name just as much as I doubted that her perky, extra-large boobs were standard issue. I recognized her intense green eye color from a contact lens display at the optometrist's, and her blue-black hair from the picture on a box of hair-color at the dollar store. But that blouse was magnificent. I wondered if she had a Brooks Card.

I was surprised by the intensity of my jealousy. Or was it just a knee jerk reaction compounded by a fit of shoe lust?

"Wow, I just received your email from the fan site this morning," Sophia said. "I haven't even had time to reply. I was going over Joey's calendar and, I'm afraid he's busy that weekend. As you must know, Joe is very much in demand." She paused chattering long enough to realize that neither of us were paying any attention to her.

"I mean, well, I was so surprised this morning when he told me we were coming out here. I hardly had time to clean up our breakfast dishes, did I Joey?" She giggled again and snaked her arm around his waist. I did not miss her implication that Joe hadn't called her for breakfast, he had simply nudged her.

"I didn't realize anyone even knew Joey was going to be here," she glared at Bob. "We are trying to keep a tight lid on his public appearances ahead of his big announcement."

"Surprised the hell out of me when you two showed up," Bob said to her. He continued to putter behind the bar. Bob had faced down tougher women in more sensible shoes. "Then again, today's just been chock full of surprises."

"Hasn't it just." Sophia rolled her eyes.

"It was a lucky coincidence," I said, trying to redirect her anger.

"Whatever." This time she didn't bother to disguise her disdain.

The sudden drop in temperature must have been felt throughout the room. Bob slowly reached for the soda gun. Melvin slid his beer glass down the bar and leaned away from us.

I wanted to play nice. Really, I did.

Instead I gave Joe my sluttiest look, licked my lips and said "Joe and I were just . . ." I let my voice drop and become more husky, "catching up on old times." I stepped to Joe's side, opposite of Sophia. I trailed my hand suggestively down his arm and squeezed his hand.

"Call me later," I said, breathily, looking up at Joe and trying to contain my giggles. Without missing a beat, Bob tossed Joe a pen. He snagged it just before it hit Sophia in the face and gave it to me. I cradled his hand in mine and wrote my phone number on his palm, just below his thumb, where he always used to write himself notes.

I held his hand to my chest and winked, before turning towards Sophia.

"So nice to meet you, *So-fee*," I said, an insincere smile of my own plastered across my face. I saw Joe's lips twitch in amusement. He tilted his head and gave me a half smile and a raised eyebrow that I took as a mix of amusement and curiosity

"I'll walk you to your car," he said. He cut his eyes back to Sophia, then slipped out of her embrace. He caught up with me at the door, brushing against my shoulder as he reached out to open it. I turned for one last look, taking in a glaring Sophia, arms crossed and nostrils flaring, and a smiling Bob and Melvin toasting their survival with a shot of Templeton Rye.

"I'm sorry, *Joey*," I said, after the door closed behind us. "I couldn't resist."

"That's ok. She'll get over it." Joe shrugged, then glanced back at The Bar. "Or not."

"I really didn't know you'd be there. I didn't mean to cause problems." Manager or more, I figured Sophia could probably make Joe's life miserable if she wanted to. "She seems like a very nice person." The ultimate nice-girl comment, only slightly less insincere than "her heart's in the right place," or "I'm sure she means well".

Joe raised his eyebrows. "No one knew I'd be there. It was a spur of the moment thing. I'm working with a young group that needs . . . the right exposure. I wanted to ask Bob about a gig. As for Soph, she's a good manager. I'm not so sure about the nice person part."

"So, she's your manager?" I hated fishing for answers like this.

255

Especially when I wasn't sure I wanted to know the answer. Was she Joe's girlfriend? Fiance? Wife? Would it make a difference? If I were sensible I would shake his hand now and walk away.

"She's my manager, Julie. End of story." Joe smiled. He seemed to know what I was getting at. "Sometimes she accompanies me on personal appearances. She makes a certain . . . impression, when necessary."

I raised an eyebrow.

Joe leaned over and whispered in my ear. "She has at least one much richer, much more influential boyfriend."

I smiled at Joe's innocence. Rich and influential did not, necessarily, trump a combination of handsome, funny, smart, sweet, sexy – and oh, yes – musically gifted. Sophia obviously considered herself more than "just a manager," I thought. Was Joe too clueless to realize that? Or was he just playing me?

"So how's, um . . . Barry?" I knew Joe knew Gary's name, but I let it slide.

"He's . . . it's complicated," I said.

Joe nodded and looked back towards The Bar.

"We've had some . . . issues. I've moved out."

"I'm sorry to hear that." Was he, I wondered? He crossed his arms and studied me. He didn't say more, but he didn't leave, either.

"Yeah, well . . . ." This was even more awkward than I had expected. "I was going through some boxes the other day, stuff from way back, and I found this." I dug around in my purse and pulled out the cassette. I had been planning to ask Bob about it. I gave it to Joe. "It's from that night. Your last show at The Bar."

Joe turned the tape over in his hands, but didn't look at me.

"It's a beautiful song, Joe. Did you ever . . . think about finishing it?"

"I could never work out the timing," he said, thoughtfully. "I can't believe you could find anything to play it on. Thank God it wasn't an eight-track." He held it out for me to take back. "I suppose I should be . . . ." He tilted his head towards The Bar.

I was loosing him. Again. I could feel it. My heart grew heavier. I reached out for the tape and our fingers touched. The spark that passed between us made me catch my breath. I looked up at Joe an saw the briefest glimmer in his eye. He felt it too, I was sure of it.

What if I had tried harder back then? What if I tried harder now?

"That was the first time I heard it, Joe. Last week." I rushed ahead, impulsively. "I don't know how it ended up in that box, or where it has been, or why it I never saw it, or when you . . . or how . . . ."

I felt my face grow hot, felt the tears building up. My throat tightened and I had to gasp for breath.

"I never heard it until last week, Joe. I never knew."

Joe was still looking at the tape, at our hands.

What else could I say? Maybe I had read too much into his taped message. Maybe too much time had gone by. Maybe the heat, the attraction I had felt when we were in The Bar was just wishful thinking. Maybe I was just desperate to feel that desire. What was it Vanessa had said? Gary had looked at her like she was "an attractive woman he was attracted to"?

"All this time. I always wondered." Joe's voice was quiet.

I closed my eyes and concentrated on holding back the tears.

"I never knew, Joe." I whispered.

An eternity passed.

Overly dramatic, I know, but I couldn't believe that this series of coincidences could end so disappointingly. I don't believe in coincidence. I would have bet the farm – Frank's farm – that things turned out better than this.

This ending, quite honestly, sucked.

I had tried. I sighed one last time, and pulled the tape towards me.

Joe's finger brushed mine, warm and soft and gentle, but he did not let go of the tape. I looked into those beautiful hazel eyes, nearly brown now, framed by those ridiculously long eyelashes. He tilted his head and I watched the tension drain away from his face, saw his jaw unclench.

"Maybe I should take this home with me. Listen to it again. Give it some thought," he said.

"Oh! Um, yeah. That would be, um, great! Good. I mean. You know. Take your time. I burned a copy of it on my computer." I winced. *Could I sound any more desperate?* Joe smirked.

"That's a good idea," he said. "I'll make a copy, then I can return this to you. Maybe we could meet for dinner sometime?"

"I'd like that," I said, all the while thinking *How's tomorrow?*

I wanted to take him back to my apartment right that minute. I wanted to go back to The Bar and catch up over a pitcher of boysenberry kamikazes. But I realized I needed time to sort out my emotions. Seeing Joe again had brought back a lot of old feelings. And created a lot of new ones, too. We weren't kids anymore. Things were different now.

"There are a few more things I need to finish up here," Joe said. "How about if I call you later? If I can get your number again." He held up his hand. The ink had smeared. I programmed his number in my cell phone, then called him so he'd have mine. What if we'd had cell phones 20 years ago?

We stood there, unsure of how to say goodbye, as a few more moments passed. A sleekly sensible family sedan drove past. Peter Gabriel's "In Your Eyes" flowed from the windows. I glanced around us. We were standing in front of Mrs. Kim's antique store, across the street from Stella's Stems and Such. Downtown Pleasant Glen isn't a beehive of activity, so most store owners spent a lot of time watching the world go by their plate glass windows, like fish in a fishbowl.

I could hear the rumors already. "Julie Westbrook was standing on Main Street holding hands with a stranger" would quickly become "Julie Westbrook was going at it in broad daylight in the backseat of her car," regardless of how difficult that would be in the Mini Cooper.

I wasn't quite ready for that yet.

I leaned over and gave Joe a quick peck on the cheek, and hopped in my car before I could get carried away.

He was still standing there when I got to the end of the block and looked in my mirror. I turned the corner and he was gone from my view.

Joanne Salemink

24

I was so giddy after my encounter with Joe, I'm not sure how I managed to drive back to my apartment. I didn't think the day could get any better.

Then I pulled up the alley and saw The Scout parked behind the garage. I parked beside her, got out and slowly walked around her, trailing the back of my hand along her cool metal curves, running my fingertips across her warm, leather saddle. I realized I could ride her right then if I wanted to.

I could ride her back to The Bar and pick up Joe and we could ride off into the sunset together, leaving Sophia in our dust, her fake bosom heaving with sobs.

The day really couldn't get any better.

"There you are, Jules! I was so worried about you!" Gary scooped me up in a bear hug, pulling me away from the Scout, pressing my face to his chest, kissing the top of my head.

The day really couldn't get any worse.

"Gary! What the heck?" I pushed away from him, then instantly regretted it when I saw his eyebrows draw together in hurt and confusion.

"It's just . . . you startled me. I was off in my own little world." I gave his bicep a squeeze to make up for my impulse reaction. The ditzy girl excuse seemed to satisfy him.

And to be fair, it wasn't like it was torture, I mean, Gary has a great body. His classic fit, mesh Polo was 100% cottony-soft, and the black color made those little streaks of gray at his temples go positively silver. Plus there's something about his body chemistry that heightens the "rugged, masculine scent" of classic Polo cologne.

"I was so worried about you," he said, taking my hands in his. "No one seemed to know where you were. Mrs. Truman said she hadn't seen you since lunch . . . and after some of the stories I've heard . . . ."

"I'm fine. I had some things to take care of around town for the Gala." That was more or less the truth.

"Jules, it's just . . . you're not returning my calls, your texts are so brief, you're going off on your own, and God knows what else," he said, nodding toward The Scout. "You're just not yourself. I'm worried. Mom's worried . . . Emily's worried."

He played the daughter card.

"I'm fine, really. It's just that there's so much to do for the Gala, so little time to do it in."

"Then let me help." He took my hand and led me over to the stairs. He sat down and gently tugged my hand until I sat next to him on the narrow stair. It was a tight fit, but he put his arm around me and pulled me even closer. "What do you need? Corporate is big on charity work right now. There are grants, matching funds. I have contacts in Des Moines who could help with the entertainment. You wouldn't have to go begging to that . . . that piano player."

"How did . . . ."

"Vanessa called me this morning. She's worried about you, too. She remembers what it was like when – what *you* were like – when he left the way he did." He gently took my chin in one hand and turned my face to his. "I know you're upset with me honey, but *I'm* here. I made a mistake, but I'm *here*." He drew back slightly, lowered his hand and shook his head. "He treated you like dirt. He led you on and then left you and didn't look back. He didn't deserve you then. Why waste time on him now?"

Gary made a compelling argument. He always did. No wonder he was such an effective salesman.

"He's gone on with his life. How many times has he been married? You know those musicians, groupies backstage every night. Always on the prowl. Maybe he did you a favor, leaving like that. I know I'll never be able to thank him enough." Gary pulled me close again, and kissed my cheek.

I thought about Sophia. I knew Joe had been married at least twice. The press had a field day with his first union. He married a flashy, young rock singer two weeks after she joined his tour. That was soon after Gary and I married. She had been in and out of rehab, then died of an overdose not long after they divorced. A string of increasingly younger girlfriends had followed. His second wife had been nearly half his age. Not that I paid any attention to that kind of gossip. Much.

"When are you coming home, honey? It's been almost a week." It seemed so much longer than that. "The house is lonely without you. *I'm* lonely without you." His breath was warm on my cheek. His lips soft as he nuzzled my ear.

I squirmed away. "Why did Vanessa say you made Joe leave?"

Gary stiffened. He had been rubbing my back, but that abruptly stopped.

"She was drunk?" He smiled and tilted his head toward the recycling bin. Damn. There was at least 60 cents worth of redeemable bottles in there. "At least, I hope she helped you empty those. I'd hate to have to tell Mom the rumors are true." He smiled and reached his arm around my waist again.

"Unless it's the one about you moving back home," he whispered in my ear.

"Huh. I haven't heard that one." I scootched away as far as I could, which wasn't very far.

Gary sighed. I relented.

"I just . . . I can't . . . not yet." I'd gone at least six months without sex, and now I had two gorgeous men whisper in my ear within two hours? What next? Would I wake up to find George Clooney flipping pancakes in my kitchenette? Naked?

"OK. It's ok. I can wait." He kissed my cheek gently, then slowly pulled away. "But . . . how about dinner while I wait? You know I hate to eat alone." *Since when?* I wondered. Gary smiled and looked at me sideways, flashing his adorable dimple. Damn. That was his deal-closing smile. My stomach started to growl.

"But I'm not really dressed to go out, and I'm way too tired to make anything," I said, searching for a graceful escape.

"I think you look wonderful. And I've already taken care of everything." He pointed to a delivery car from Pizza on the Square pulling in behind The Scout. A large Mucho Meaty and a six pack of Moosehead Lager, just like he used to order that fall after Joe left, when the thought of eating sickened me. Gary would flash that dimple and charm me until I gave in and ate a slice of pizza, just like I was doing now.

We went up to my apartment. There was a beautiful bouquet of mixed flowers on the kitchen table. I had locked the door, but Gary knew I always kept a spare key taped to the bottom of a Isabel Bloom sculpture – this time it was a sleeping cat – right outside the front door. The flowers were beautiful, of course, but that petty part of me wondered why he never bought my favorite flowers, daisies. I always suspected he thought they were too common, or that he – or his secretary – couldn't remember I liked them.

As we ate, we talked about inconsequential things. Eventually the topic of his promotion came up again.

"The brass has been asking about you, Jules. I've told them how busy you are with the Gala, but they're anxious to talk to you. They consider themselves a family-centered business. I've . . . we've worked so hard for this. I can't do it without you, Jules. I don't *want* to do it without you. Come home."

"I . . . ." I thought about Vanessa and Amanda, the blonde co-ed, the women' in Gary's office, and all the bleacher moms. I thought about Joe and Sophia.

"I'm not ready yet," I said.

I walked Gary to the door, kissed him on the cheek, then stepped back out of his reach. I watched as he walked down the stairs, turned and waved. I watched as he walked across Miss Irene's backyard, to the street out in front of her house where he had parked. I noticed the lights downstairs in Miss Irene's house turned off and the ones upstairs came on after he pulled away.

It seemed like Gary was putting a lot of effort in to getting back in my good graces. All these sweet gestures, the little reminders of how it used to be. I felt guilty for being suspicious of Gary's motives. But it was just a little too much, a little too late. Where was this concern for me when he was fucking Amanda – or Vanessa? I wanted to believe that was the extent of his wanderings, but I couldn't shake my doubt.

Still, it made me think. About us. About Joe. And I realized I had, once again, left my phone in my car.

I had a text from Joe. *Heading to Des Moines. Back tomorrow with band. Dinner at The Bar?*

I must have typed at least 10 messages, trying to find the perfect balance between excited and casual, without sounding desperate or asking if Sophia would be joining us.

Sounds great! It was lame, but I fumbled the phone and hit send by accident. At least auto correct hadn't messed it up.

Joe replied quickly. *Setting up at 5, dinner for 2 at 7?*

No Sophia. *Yes!* Delete, delete, delete.

Can't wait. Deleeeeeete.

See you then! Send.

I knew I wouldn't be able to sleep with Sophia on the brain, so I decided to do a Google search. Nearly half of the pictures in the results were of her and Joe. Most of these were from the last couple of months, since the rumors of Joe's comeback had started circulating. It seemed like Sophia had her arm around him, or was somehow clinging to him in all of them. Joe's gaze was usually directed at the camera or at the crowd. Her eyes were almost always on him.

Most of the other pictures showed Sophia in the company of one of three distinguished, older-looking gentlemen. The descriptions indicated they were from New York, L.A., and Dallas, respectively, and each was a wealthy businessman and scion of society.

None of them compared to Joe Davenport, as far as I was concerned.

25

Vanessa called early the next morning. Or maybe it wasn't so early, but I had stayed up late surfing the net, and binge watching videos of Joe in concert. This made for some very pleasant dreams. I resisted untangling myself from his imaginary embrace to reach out for the phone. Dragging my brain and verbal skills out of that happy place was next to impossible.

"Hmmpf?" was the best I could manage.

"A little tired this morning?" The last time Vanessa had been this chipper before 10 a.m. was . . . never.

"Meh?" I had one eye open now. Good God. It was 7:30. Something was seriously wrong with this situation.

"Well, we could both use a few more late nights in our lives."

I yawned. Vanessa forged ahead.

"So, I take it things went well yesterday?"

I thought about The Bar and Joe and plans for our not-date. That woke me up.

"Very well! Tonight could be a late night, too!"

"Oh, Jules, that's wonderful! I knew you and Gary could work things out! I'm so happy for you guys!"

Gary? What? How did she . . . oh wait, that's right. She was Gary's little snitch. She was probably behind all his romantic gestures. Damn it.

She's allergic to daisies.

"Well, actually . . . ." How was I going to tell her that Gary had nothing to do with my late night?

"*Another* late night, huh? Please tell me you won't be wearing those granny panties you had on when I stayed over. I mean, I'm sure your fuddy-dunderwear was no match for the passion of the moment last night. But for round two? You're gonna have to put a little effort into this, Jules."

"But. . . ." I wanted to put a stop to this before she got too carried away. On the other hand, she did just say I wore fuddy-dunderwear.

"I smell a shopping trip! With my guidance, of course. Your idea of sexy lingerie is solid color panties. We'll celebrate with lunch at Bottiglia Italiano. I know carbs can make you bloaty, but they're also a good source of energy."

"But . . . ." What was wrong with solid color underwear? I have some lovely beige hipsters. Exactly the type that Sophia LeClaire wouldn't be caught dead in.

"But what? You guys are empty nesters now. You could go at it like bunnies, all day, every day, in every room in your house and not worry about anything besides rug burns!"

"Well, I don't know . . . ."

"Oh, think outside the box springs, Jules!" There was a wistfulness in Vanessa's sigh that made me realize this wasn't just about Gary and I getting back together. This was about Vanessa and the second chance that she could never have with Michael.

"But, don't you have to work today?"

"Pffft. I have a backlog of vacation time coming that accounting is salivating over not paying me for. It's not like anyone's going to be denied treatment or die or anything. Well, actually, it is, but they won't. Not for a couple days, anyway. Come on honey, let me dream a little."

I knew I could really use her help to look my best for my not-date with Joe. And I needed to explain to her why the whole reconciliation thing with Gary was not going to happen. I needed to be strong. I needed to be honest. Even if it disappointed her.

"What time do we leave?"

I could disappoint her after lunch.

*****

Vanessa was a ruthless shopper, dismissing everything I picked out as being too conservative. She made me cut up my White House Black Market Rewards card – right there in the mall.

"Left to your own devices you dress like an 80-year-old museum docent." I thought about Miss Irene. She *was* an 80-year-old museum docent, and she still had racier lingerie than me. "I mean, face it Jules, your clothes are tasteful but boring. That look is fine for your volunteer work, but not for a hot date. What do you guys have planned, anyway?"

I decided strategic truth telling was in order.

"We're taking it slow. Meeting at The Bar for drinks." I could fill in the rest of the truth later.

"Hmmm, casual, with a hint of nostalgia. I can work with that. I'm thinkin' short skirt – show off those long legs of yours – and a low cut blouse to show off . . ." she paused and looked at my size-B-cup-if-we're-being-generous chest. "Did I mention your long legs?"

Vanessa picked out a swingy, crimson skirt that was just short enough to hit me where my thighs slimmed out without drawing attention to my knobby, old-man knees. And it was on sale. In typical Vanessa-style good fortune, she found a blouse that complimented the skirt perfectly – *at a second, completely different, trendy boutique,* no less. Also on sale. I had trouble matching Garanimals on my own. I did manage, however, to pick out a pair of coordinating sandals.

"Hmf. I suppose the ankle strap is sexy enough to offset the lame, kitten heel," Vanessa said. "But I'd go higher."

"You don't have to walk in them." I thought about Sophia lurching across the uneven floor at The Bar. I could barely navigate that floor in tennis shoes. On impulse, I bought a pair of black, glittery, low-top Vans sneakers, too.

Next stop: Lingerie.

As soon as we walked in the door, Vanessa handed me an application for a Victoria's Secret Angel Card.

"By the time you replace all your fuddy-dunderwear, you'll be a platinum member," she said.

"I like my fuddy-dunderwear," I whined. "It's comfortable, it's practical. It covers my ass. What more could I ask for?"

"A little spice? A little action?" Vanessa suggested. "You might like granny panties, but does Gary?"

If the white, lacy panties and bra in his Escalade were any indication, the answer was no. What I really wondered was did Joe like granny panties? I thought about Sophia, and the groupies. Probably not.

"No. No he does not," Vanessa continued. "Gary loves you but he does not understand why you wear undergarments that even the Amish would shun. By the time he fights his way through all that fabric, the thrill is over."

"It's not like I'm . . . ."

"I know, honey. This is not your first rodeo. You two have fallen into that comfortable, married-couple stage of sex." Or a comfortable, married-couple stage of abstinence, I thought. "But now's the time to reignite that spark. Sometimes things need a little . . . push to happen," Vanessa picked up a pretty bra that had more padding in one cup than I have in both boobs combined, and shooed me towards the dressing rooms.

"Don't they have anything a little less . . . pushy?" I asked.

Vanessa sighed and rolled her eyes. "This is Victoria's Secret. It's all push."

I hesitated.

"I can't explain it, honey. The sexy doesn't come from the push, the sexy comes from how the bra makes you feel inside. Yeah, sure, your granny panties are comfy and all. But there's something about putting on pretty undies that makes you feel pretty on the inside, too.

"It's like when you suit up in your boring, office appropriate, business-wear and sensible flats. But underneath it all you're wearing a sexy thong and matching bra, and you're the only one who knows. It's like having a secret identity. And maybe that sexy secret gives you the confidence to tell your boss to stuff the Magruder file up his penny-pinching ass. Or at least it gives you the confidence to think about telling him that, while you nod and smile and accept the fact that you're in a dead end job and your husband . . . . Well, anyway. Trust me. Be open-minded. Think about it from Gary's perspective."

Apparently Vanessa had more issues than I realized. I meekly took the bras she had picked out and closed the dressing room door. I was pleasantly surprised by how well some of them fit, and how they made me feel.

Vanessa was right.

Plus? I don't know who designed those dressing rooms, but I'm pretty sure that combination of lighting, mirrors and paint would make anyone look good in anything. God help us if more retail stores figure out that overhead fluorescent lights and cold tile floors are not conducive to making consumers feel good about themselves or the products.

I felt very good about these products. So good that I had the confidence to buy the lacy red thong Vanessa picked out. I'm sure the helpful salestwig thought that I was a middle-aged woman desperately trying to restore some romance to her life. Because I was.

I bought the thong anyway. I wasn't exactly sure how, or why, you wore this scrap of fabric, but there was no denying that I felt sexy just thinking about wearing it.

Finally it was time for carb-loading and truth-unloading.

"I ran into Joe Davenport yesterday," I said, after we were served our pre-lunch drinks. Like Vanessa said, this was not my first rodeo.

"You what? *The* Joe Davenport? Joe, *who we just frickin' emailed,* Davenport?"

I sipped my white wine. I was trying to be nonchalant but there was this huge boulder in my throat and I wasn't sure if I could swallow or if overpriced chardonnay was about to spurt out of my nose.

"Wait, *ran into* as in he stepped in front of your car and now you need manslaughter-type bail money? *Ran into* as in he caught you trying to break into his house and now you need stalker-type bail money? Or *ran into* as in you both just happened to be in the same place at the same time and where the fuck is that waitress because I need another glass of wine?"

"I went to The Bar yesterday afternoon to talk to Bob about the Gala and Joe was . . . ."

"Wait, you went to The Bar without me? You went to The Bar in the middle of the day? Are there photos? Are you yanking my chain? Because if you are, Jules, so help me God . . . ."

After assuring her that I was not kidding, that I *had* been to The Bar in the middle of the day, and not sparing any details about Sophia, I dropped the bomb that it was Joe, not Gary, who I was meeting for dinner. Vanessa pushed a crouton around her salad plate, unable to get her fork under it or through it.

"Let's think about this rationally. Early, *working* dinner, public place, back-water, townie-bar. Could be innocent enough." She brutally stabbed at the crouton, shattering it, then sat back in the booth and let her salad fork clatter against the glass plate. "Manager-with-benefits conveniently absent? I forbid you to go."

"*What?*" You would have thought I dropped an entire tray of dishes, the way every head in the restaurant turned toward me. In fact, my sudden outburst did cause one bus person to do just that. "You what?" I leaned against the table. "The woman *who slept with my husband* says *what?*"

"OK, poor choice of words." Vanessa put her hands up in a surrendering motion.

I relaxed and sat back as the waitress brought our lasagnas.

"Will that be all?" The fresh-faced co-ed smiled and backed away, but not quickly enough.

"A bottle of white, a bottle of red, perhaps a . . . oh, I don't give a fuck. Get me a bottle of wine and get it here quick. I'm a great tipper, and I'm even better when I'm drunk. Just get it here chop-chop." Vanessa simultaneously chugged the rest of her glass and snapped her fingers. The frightened waitress just stared at her, mouth and eyes both opened wide.

"Chop *fucking chop.*" Vanessa slammed her empty glass down on the table with a ferocity that scared even me. The waitress scurried away. We had barely touched our entrees when the bartender/sommelier approached our table, bearing a bottle of red wine, a supplicant approaching with his humble offering.

"Yeah, yeah, yeah. Just pour the fucking wine. Excessive tips all

273

around. And, for you, a bonus tip." The attractive young man looked anxiously at Vanessa. "Don't fuck your econ prof, no matter how cute he is."

She was taking this better than I thought she would.

We ate in silence, letting the pasta soak up the alcohol.

"So," Vanessa said calmly, "you're having dinner with Joe." It was the scary kind of calm.

"Yep."

"You ever watch that game show, *Let's Make a Deal?*" I nodded yes. "I see Joe as being that mystery grand prize behind door number three. He could be a fantabulous prize package, or he could be a goat."

I nodded. She had a point, after all.

"Gary is all the prizes that you've won so far. Are you sure you're willing to risk all that – 25 years of marriage, an amazing daughter, financial security – on what's behind door three? Gary's a known variable."

"Gary's a known cheat and a liar," I said.

"He's a man who made a mistake . . . ."

"Mistakes, plural," I said. "With a capital M. He fucked at least two other women while we were married, including my best friend."

"He's a man who made mistakes and is sorry and is trying to make amends." A large glob of tomato sauce fell off her fork and landed . . . on her plate. *What the fuck?* My t-shirt had tomato sauce, blue cheese and coffee stains on it already.

That was the final straw. She didn't get to claim pristine moral values *and* a pristine white silk blouse. I leaned on the table, narrowed my eyes and shook my fork at her.

"Since when did you join 'Team Gary"?" I asked. "What happened to *'She's going to leave you and I'm going to help her'?*"

Vanessa put down her fork, folded her hands on her lap and stared at the table.

"Haven't you ever made a mistake – a huge mistake – that you instantly regretted?" She spoke quietly. "You two were the All-American couple – handsome, successful, happy."

"Appearances can be deceiving, Van."

"But you *were*, Jules. Maybe not lately, but there was a time."

I shrugged. We always made a good team, but there was something missing.

"I want everything to go back the way it was. I want you guys to get back together. I want Emily to talk to me, I want . . . ."

"Michael's not coming back, sweetie." I tried to be as gentle as I could.

"I know. I just want him to be happy. I want you all to be happy. That would make *me* happy."

Poor, sweet, delusional Vanessa.

"What if Joe makes me happy?"

She shook her head. "What if Joe breaks your heart? *Again?*"

"But you heard the tape. He said he loved me. Don't you want to know what made him change his mind?"

"That's the only reason I didn't ship you off to the nunnery when you came up with that hair-brained scheme to contact Joe." We both smiled. Her parents used to threaten us with the "nunnery" whenever they thought our skirts were too short.

"Just give me one night," I was pleading with her now. "One night to extract a full confession. Just me, Joe, and the secrets Victoria sold me. I'm pretty sure that thong will make at least one of us happy." I wiggled my eyebrows. Vanessa rolled her eyes and muttered something about unethical interrogation methods.

"OK, but I have one thing for you to keep in mind. Do you remember that last semester I was deluding myself at grad school, when you and Gary were happily planning your wedding?" I nodded.

"Michael and I had been dating a while, but it didn't seem to be going anywhere. Now I understand why, but then? All I knew was that my friends were getting on with their lives and I was spinning my wheels with this sweet, frustratingly chaste man.

"There was this huge, semi-respectable business department reception for alumni donors and visiting grad students. Michael left early. It was a beautiful, Indian Summer day, the football team had won, the whole campus was crazy.

"Anyway, I met this gorgeous guy from Purdue. There was flirting, sparks, drinking, more flirting. Next thing I knew we were down at the old limestone ice skating shelter, nothing between us but the light of the harvest moon."

"Sounds unbelievably romantic," I said.

"Sounds unbelievably stupid," Vanessa said. "And cold. And uncomfortable. We did it on a limestone bench, for Christ's sake."

"Yeah, but . . . ."

"Yeah, but the next day he went back to Indi-fucking-ana. I had all sorts of bruises and bug bites all over my body."

The waitress brought us our check.

"I never heard from him again. Michael proposed over Thanksgiving break. I accepted. I quit school at semester, we married in the spring and that was that. Door number three was a goat, Julie. As young and stupid as I was, I knew that a base-model Pontiac was better than a goat."

Vanessa slipped her credit card in the pleather check binder and the waitress whisked it away.

The afternoon ended in a draw. We rode home in silence, neither of us speaking until Vanessa pulled up outside my apartment.

"Thank you," I said, getting out of the car.

"Jules, think about what I said."

I sat back down. I couldn't leave things so broken between us.

"What if Michael was waiting on the back steps for you when you got home? What if he told you he'd made a mistake and he wanted a second chance?"

Vanessa smiled crookedly and shook her head.

"We haven't made each other happy in a long time. Maybe we never did," she said. I raised one eyebrow and waited for her to make the connection.

"Now, what if you ran into Purdue Pete at the courthouse?"

Vanessa sighed.

"He has tenure at the University of Michigan. I went to a conference there with Michael. He said he looked for me the next day, but someone . . . ." She stopped with a little gasp. "Someone told him I was engaged to Michael. That's why he didn't call."

"At least he had an excuse." I felt my face grow hot and blotchy. I blinked hard to push back tears. That old doubt and hurt crept back into my head, crowding out my confidence and excitement about dinner tonight.

"Why didn't Joe call me?"

"Jules, I . . . I guess that's something the two of you will have to work out." Vanessa gave my hand a squeeze. "That is, if he can form complete sentences after getting a look at you in your new outfit!" I tried to return her smile.

"Let him see what he missed, huh?" I wiped a couple of escaping tears away with my free hand.

"Oh Jules, I remember how Joe looked at you. It was like you were the only woman in the room. You could go in there wearing a feed sack, and he would know what he missed. Although that would be a terrible waste of my shopping mojo. That fun-derwear only works if you wear it."

I smiled for real this time.

"Just . . . just think about what you're doing. And why you're doing it."

I climbed out of the car, shut the door, gave Vanessa a thumbs up, then headed for the stairs. I heard the passenger side window slide down, and she called after me.

"And *don't* do it on a limestone bench!"

26

I still had plenty of time before I was supposed to meet Joe at The Bar. I showered, shaved my legs, and moisturized obsessively. Then I put on my new clothes, checking my progress in the mirror. I smiled to myself as I modeled the thong and matching bra. They were beautiful and made me feel sexy and powerful – the same feeling The Scout gave me.

If I turned my hips, stuck out the girls, and sucked in my tummy, I decided I still looked damn good for 50. If the lights were low and Joe was properly distracted or motivated, maybe he wouldn't notice the stretch marks and cellulite.

And if he did? Well, he would have to deal with it. So what if I didn't have the body of a 20 year old any more? I had plenty more to offer.

My confidence grew as I slipped on my new blouse and skirt. For once my hair curled just the way I wanted it to. I didn't even poke myself in the eye applying eyeliner. I fastened the delicate buckle on my sandals, and stepped to the mirror for the final inspection.

I twirled, watching the skirt flare up a little, flashing a scandalous amount of thigh.

I looked good.

I *felt* good. I felt sexy.

I felt like a fraud.

I wiped off some of the lipstick, eyeshadow and blush. I took off the skirt and heels and pulled on a snug pair of jeans and the black, glittery Vans. I did not touch my hair. One does not tempt the fates of coiffure.

I stepped in front of the mirror again.

This was a Julie that I could recognize. One that Joe could recognize.

This Julie looked happy and comfortable, confident and sexy.

I made a quick detour through the garage on my way to my car. I ran my fingers over The Scout's gas tank and took a moment to appreciate her beauty.

"Wish me luck," I whispered. I patted her leather seat, walked to the door and headed to The Bar.

*****

Joe had texted me more details about our not-date. Dirt Road Party was a young, popular band from the Des Moines area that he had been mentoring. He thought they had potential and was preparing them to take the next step. Their gig at The Bar that night was designed to be low key, with no publicity and early hours, a chance to fine tune their performance in front of a fresh audience.

When I got to The Bar, they were finishing the sound check. The crowd was small, typical for this early on a summer Friday night. The band had a few family members and friends filling up the front tables. Joe waved me over to a booth in the back, near the sound board. It was secluded enough for privacy, and far enough from the speakers that we could talk without shouting. We still had a good view of the band and the crowd.

"You look great," he said. He kissed my cheek, then whispered in my ear. "*Really* great." He kissed me again, on that spot below my ear. The spot that always made me go weak in the knees.

"So do you." I slipped my arms around his waist and stared at his lips, wishing I could give him a real kiss. The way he grinned and drew me closer made me think he felt that way too.

I saw his eyes dart around the room, then he brushed his lips quickly and gently over mine. There's a good chance I moaned. His kisses had that effect on me.

"Wow." Joe's voice was soft and husky. He leaned his forehead against mine. His lips brushed over mine again. Joe pulled his head back, but didn't let go of me.

"There's a few more things I need to check on, then I'll, uh . . . ." He leaned forward to kiss me again, then stopped himself and grinned. "I'll be right back. Stay here. Don't leave." He walked backwards, his eyes never leaving me, until he bumped into a guy carrying a cable. As they walked towards the stage together, Joe looked over his shoulder at me and winked.

I watched him walk, appreciating the way his light blue, chambray shirt clung to his shoulders. His shirt was untucked, but it was short enough not to interfere with my view of how well his Levi's hugged his ass and thighs. His jeans weren't tight enough to make me worried about circulation, but just tight enough to make my hands itch to touch him. Even his worn, brown leather, chukka boots looked sexy in a masculine, comfortable kind of way. I was glad I had toned down my outfit.

When he returned, Joe was carrying styrofoam to-go boxes and two bottles of beer. He had talked Bob's wife, Liz, into making us a couple burgers after the kitchen closed for the night. I doubted there was much Joe couldn't talk Bob or Liz into doing for him. The burgers were warm, the homemade fries crispy, and the beers were frosty. It was the perfect meal for our not-date.

We ate while the band warmed up. Joe was waiting for a signal to start his introduction. Our conversation dwindled. We had exhausted most of the light, small-talk topics we could think of, but didn't have time to start anything more serious.

My phone rang, interrupting what could have become either an uncomfortable silence, or a chance for me to kiss a small smudge of ketchup off Joe's lower lip. I dabbed at it with my napkin, in a very Mom-like, reflexive way, as I checked the caller ID.

It was Vanessa. She knew where I was. She knew what I was doing. I knew she wouldn't call if it wasn't important.

"Please tell me this is not bad news," I said, answering the phone. I gave Joe my best *I'm so sorry look*, all big eyes and fluttering eyelashes.

"I have bad news."

"No, wait, you don't understand. That's not how this game works. When I say 'tell me this is not bad news,' you can *not* say 'I have bad news.' That is the exact opposite of 'not bad news'."

Joe smirked, then slid out of the booth. "I'll be right back," he said.

"I'm sorry to interrupt your date, Jules, and it goes without saying that I want a complete, and I do mean *complete*, rundown tomorrow. But since you answered your phone I'm guessing you're not in bed right now, because if you answer your phone while you're in bed with Joe I'm going to kill you."

"Focus, Van. Focus." Her rambling was getting us nowhere and wasting time on so many levels. I was sure Joe was politely trying to give me privacy for my call.

"Right. Coach won't let us use the stadium for the concert because he's worried about the field." The high school's football field sat in a bowl-shaped depression that made it a natural amphitheater. PG is a football town, so we knew this was a long-shot. Plan B was to set up a stage on the parking lot between the football field and the city park, with seating in the park.

"So I was down at City Hall applying for the park use permit and they told me they're starting a major renovation right after the Fourth of July. We have to move the Gala up before that."

"But that means we only have three weeks to prepare," I said, slumping back in the booth. That would be nearly impossible. Still, we had all the basic arrangements in place. We would have to start our publicity campaign Monday, if not sooner, and fill in band names and schedules as we went.

"I suppose we could scale it back, make do with two or three local groups, and use the show choir as the headliner." It wasn't the best option, but at this point I figured it was our only option.

"The No Talent Slugs have offered to play. Actually, they begged me to play," Vanessa said.

"Are they any good?"

She hesitated.

"They're not . . . bad, exactly. And they're very popular, in a weird sort of way. It could be good for fundraising. Kind of a 'fund the arts so your kids don't wind up like these guys' deal."

The Slugs were formed by some show choir parents who weren't content to let their kids have all the fun. Or who really wanted to embarrass their kids, one or the other. They had developed a sort of cult following. What they lacked in talent, they made up for in enthusiasm.

"It's better than nothing, I guess." I tried to sound more confident than I felt. It could be done. We'd just have to make the most of it.

Joe finished his introduction of Dirt Road Party and made his way back to our table. I promised Vanessa I'd call her in the morning and told her to book the band.

"I hope that wasn't bad news," Joe said. He smiled and slid in close to me. He gave my knee a squeeze, then moved his hand up to mid-thigh. I nearly forgot how to speak.

"Well, it wasn't exactly *not* bad news." I pressed my knee against his and put my hand on his thigh, matching his hand's position.

I filled Joe on the situation, summarizing the Gala, the coup attempt, and our suddenly shortened time frame.

"But Vanessa said she's lined up The No Talent Slugs, so we should be able to piece together enough groups to make an evening of it."

"I love The Slugs!" Joe looked genuinely excited.

"You've heard them? Are they any good?"

"No. They're awful. But their fans are great. They drink. A lot." Joe shrugged. "I know a couple of the members."

"The only thing better than a good bar band is a bad bar band with fans who have loose wallets," Bob said. He had brought us more beer while I was explaining my troubles to Joe. Bob sat down across from us. "And from what I can tell, you're not going to have to 'piece together' anything."

"What do you mean?"

Bob snorted. "Miss Irene's web of informants is just as efficient at spreading news as it is gathering news. She brought her cabal of Auxiliary ladies in for an early happy hour, after your meeting the other day. They had a very loud brainstorming session. I've been fielding calls from groups all week. Everyone wants to know how they can get on the bill."

"You? But . . . ."

"I couldn't very well leave those old biddies in charge of entertainment, now could I? I've worked hard to build a good reputation for music in Pleasant Glen. I'm not about to let them spoil that. Pfft. Like Miss Irene expected any less from me."

"Oh, Bob, I don't know how I can thank you enough." I would have hugged him if there wasn't a table between us.

"You can make sure Miss Irene keeps her clothes on."

"Done! At least, I'll try."

"How about me?" Joe asked. "What can I do?"

Bob had a job now, and he was all business. "Well, for starters, Dirt Road Party is really good. Where've you been hiding them?"

"They're yours. Sign them up."

"But . . . ." I tried to protest.

"No, Julie. I want to help. I don't know why Sophia said I was busy."

Bob looked at me and rolled his eyes. "The boy's clueless."

"Maybe I can sit in with The Slugs . . . ."

"They'd cream themselves," Bob said.

"Or these guys." Joe nodded towards the stage.

"Or you could just man up and do a solo set. What about all those 'come back kid' stories I've been hearing?" Bob played hardball.

"I'm all yours." Joe sat back in the booth and looked at me. "That is, if you want me."

Those eyes, those lips, those hands, that ass? What's not to want, I wondered.

"Of course I want you, Joe." I let a grin slowly ease across my face and gave Joe a smoldering sideways glance. "The Gala could use you too."

"Oh fer Christ's sake. I don't think the soda gun will reach clear over here. I'm trying to run a respectable establishment." Bob heaved himself up and out of the booth. "You two get this crap out of your systems while I go check on Melvin. I left him tending bar. Good thing this is a beer crowd. Fuckin' 'boysenberry kamikazee' bullshit." Bob muttered to himself and shook his head all the way to the bar.

"Joe, you don't have to do this. The missing tape, meeting you tonight, I wasn't trying to use our past to get you to perform. I just . . . ." I started blushing. Joe smiled.

"Go on," he said.

"I was using The Gala as an excuse to see you again."

"You don't need an excuse, Julie. You never did." Joe leaned over and gave me a slow-motion kiss that stopped my heart.

"But why . . . ." I swayed like a drunk when the kiss ended. Why had he ever left me in the first place?

"Enough already! We have a music festival to plan." Bob was back, and he brought a bucket of bottled beers and an order pad with him. "It may have escaped the attention of you two lovebirds, but we have a hit on our hands. Melvin had to deputize a couple helpers. They're running their asses off." Bob collapsed on the bench across from us. "God, I love this bar. I owe you, Joey-boy."

There was not an empty seat in the house, and they were standing two-deep at the bar. This was the magic of the cell-phone era.

"We make an announcement about the Gala at the end of the night, and by tomorrow morning, your Gala is Pleasant Glen's version of the Wadena Rock festival. Minus the mud and the drugs, I hope." Bob positively glowed with excitement.

And to think, all I wanted to do was meet the piano player.

After that, there wasn't much for me to do, besides sit back and enjoy the band and the pressure of Joe's thigh against mine, while the boys – and by boys, I mean Bob – put together a schedule for the festival.

Between answering questions from Bob and from the sound guy, Joe and I started the long process of catching up. I told Joe a little about Gary and a lot about Emily. I explained how I ended up at Miss Irene's, including a summary of the whole Gary/Vanessa/Michael disaster. And I told him about The Scout.

Joe told me he had married, divorced, married and divorced before deciding to enjoy being single – there was no mention of Sophia. He compared his career to a wild thrill ride that had ultimately left him as disillusioned with the music industry as he was with marriage. He walked away from the rock star-life when it became more of a chore than a joy. He continued to write and record, and to perform where and when he liked. He had built a small, but top-quality recording studio on his farm near Des Moines. His collaboration with other artists – writing for them, performing with them, and advising them – had led to his recent "rediscovery."

We both carefully avoided any mention of, or questions about, the last night we had both been at The Bar, when The Average Joes had been the band on stage, the band on the verge of something big.

By the time Dirt Road Party finished their second encore, my infatuation with the young, brash piano player had been replaced with a deepening admiration and affection for the man he had become. Although I still thought he was pure sex on a stick, dipped in chocolate.

We Iowans do love our State Fair foods and know that everything is better on a stick. The chocolate? That was just for fun.

Joanne Salemink

27

We stuck around after the show long enough for Joe to introduce me to the band. They were ready to celebrate and Bob was ready to work out the first of many details for their performance at the Gala. Joe and I were ready to be alone.

Joe had parked in the alley behind The Bar, so we snuck out the back door. As we made our way through the service hallway, we ducked into the storage room to kiss, just like old times. And just like old times, Bob somehow knew what we were doing.

"Move it along back there, you two! I run a respectable place here," he yelled down the hall.

Joe still had the same, blue and white, 1970's Ford F150 pickup. He opened my door for me, shutting it carefully after I was in. How long had it been since anyone had done that for me? I automatically started to buckle my seat belt, then stopped and – just like old times – I slid over next to Joe on the bench seat. He smiled and put his arm around my shoulders as we drove down the block to my car. It was so nice snuggling next to Joe that I considered leaving my car there, but I wasn't quite ready to feed those rumors.

Joe followed me to my apartment and up the stairs. I thought maybe this was just an excuse for him to watch my ass as we climbed them, or at least I hoped it was. I didn't spend all that time running hills for my health. I mean yeah, I did, but, this was a better reason.

I unlocked and opened the door, and switched on the small, table lamp. The moon was shining in through one set of windows, and a streetlight glowed through another, adding to the ambiance.

I turned and smiled at Joe. It had been so easy to talk to him at The Bar. Everything there was familiar and casual. Now I started to feel awkward. Technically I was still a married woman. Joe was, well, I still wasn't sure what his relationship status was. What was I thinking?

What was I *thinking*? I was thinking that I had caught my husband having sex with my best friend. I was thinking that my husband had admitted to having two affairs. I was thinking that my 89-year-old landlady was getting more action than I was.

Joe smiled and put his arms around my waist.

What was I *thinking*? I was thinking that I was on my way to becoming single. I was thinking Joe was incredibly sexy. I was thinking I was incredibly horny.

I leaned forward and kissed Joe, putting my hands on his chest. His lips were warm and soft. Just like old times.

Joe returned my kiss, holding the back of my head in his hand, increasing the pressure. The kiss trailed away, and we relaxed, smiling drunkenly. I sighed as Joe slid his hand down my spine to the small of my back. His touch was strong and gentle. I felt the heat building between us. It was getting hard for me to think straight.

"Would you like a tour?" I meant it as an innocent question, but as I asked it I wrapped my arms around Joe's neck and pressed my chest against his.

Joe raised an eyebrow. I realized that either came across as incredibly dirty or just stupid.

"Of the apartment, I mean." Joe coughed to cover a laugh.

"Obviously." I was making this worse. I stepped away from Joe, took a deep breath and shook my head. "Anyway, let me show you around. My place. My *apartment*." Joe's shoulders were shaking from holding back his laughter.

"Lead on, please," he said, politely.

I dramatically swept my hand from side to side, like a game show hostess presenting the showcase prize.

"Here we have the living area – where I do all my living. Over there is the kitchen, dining room, and bathroom – for kitchening, dining and bathrooming. And that's, um, it." Joe chuckled.

"It looks great. It looks like you," he said. I smiled. This was the first time I had ever lived alone. The first time I had ever decorated a place to suit my own tastes.

Joe pulled me close and whispered in my ear. "It's sweet and cheerful." He gently kissed my jaw bone. "Warm, charming . . . ." He brushed his lips over mine. "Home."

My knees buckled and my train of thought deserted me again.

"Maybe we should, um, sit down," I said, turning towards the wicker loveseat. Miss Irene had tried to talk me out of it when I rescued it from the charity pile.

"That old thing won't stand up to much hanky-panky," she had said. She lobbied hard for an oversized, overstuffed Victorian fainting couch, pointing out how sexy the crushed velvet upholstery and curved lines were. But I wouldn't give in. "Oh well. I guess there's always the bed. And it's only two feet away," she said.

I thought of that now. My head turned automatically to the bedroom area. An adorable, vintage, chintz curtain, only partially drawn, was all that separated the "living room" from the "bedroom". Where my bed was.

Where I wanted, more than anything, to be with Joe.

Now.

Or five minutes ago.

"We could sit here, or . . . ." I tried to speak again.

"Or?" Joe grinned, and tilted his head to the side. It was at the perfect angle for a kiss.

What else could I do?

My hands raced up his arms, coming to rest on his broad shoulders for a moment before gliding along to the back of his neck and pulling his head down to meet mine.

Joe left one hand on my lower back and brought the other up between my shoulder blades, bringing our bodies closer together. I felt the heat of my desire spreading everywhere we touched – and our bodies touched everywhere.

Joe had always kissed with his whole body. Every possible part of us was interlocked – feet, knees, thighs, hips, bellies, chests and lips. Our bodies meshed with certainty and ease, the long years of separation falling away. Our hands stroked shoulders, backs, hips and butts, while our lips traced chins and ears and necks.

He felt so good. *We* felt so good together.

I drew him backwards toward the bed and kicked off my shoes. He paused just long enough to take his shoes off, then crawled onto the bed with me. He hovered over me for a moment, propped up on his elbows, his eyes flitting from my eyes to my lips. He ran his thumb over my lips.

"Julie," he whispered, staring at my lips. His voice gave me goosebumps. I threaded my arms through his and rubbed his back. I pulled him down onto me, as I rose up to meet him.

We kissed and caressed and pressed and explored like a couple of teenagers. Like the horny 20-somethings we had once been. The difference was that back then I would have pulled away to keep things from going "too far."

This time, as I felt my desire growing, felt him growing harder against my thigh, I stoked the fire. I wrapped a leg tightly around his, grinding against him.

"Jesus, Julie," Joe gasped, pulling his head back just far enough so that we could see each other without crossing our eyes. I noted with satisfaction that our hips were still locked in mortal combat. He brushed the hair from my forehead and held my face in his hands. He kissed me lightly on the nose and teasingly brushed my lips with his.

"Did you come to The Bar tonight just to seduce me?" he asked, between kisses.

"No!" I said. But the way I arched against him exposed my lie.

He kissed me just below my ear and chuckled, a low rumbling in his chest that sent vibrations through other parts of his body.

"Really?" he asked, before kissing the same spot again. I gasped with pleasure.

"Yes. No. Maybe. Wait, what was the question again? I could never think straight when you did that," I said. He trailed his electric kisses down my neck to my collarbone.

"I remember," he said. He kissed the hollow at the base of my neck. "I remember a lot of things." He sighed and lifted himself up off me, easing the pressure between my legs. Just a little. "I think this would be a good time to stop before we . . . do something we might regret."

He started to roll off me but I grabbed him by the hips and held him tightly. He had always been so honorable. He had always respected my decision not to have sex. He had always stopped before we got carried away, and he never complained. Still, I couldn't help wondering if that had made it easier for him to leave me.

I wouldn't make that mistake again.

"Things are different, Joe. We're not twenty anymore," I said. I slipped my fingers inside the waistband of his jeans and slowly brought them around to his fly. I unbuttoned and unzipped his jeans and slid my hands inside. Then I reversed course and let my hands find their way back across his hips to grab that great ass.

He sighed again, and drove my head back to the pillow with a firm kiss. I brought a hand around to the front of his shorts, but he pulled my hand away.

"And you're not single anymore," he said.

"But I am. It's over. I've left him." The words tumbled out in a desperate stream.

"You've been gone for what, a week? Two?" Joe asked. He tried to smile, but his eyes were dark and sad. He kissed me lightly. "You're not ready yet."

"Oh, I'm ready, alright!" I said, kissing him deeply and pulling his hips down to meet mine.

"You know what I mean," he said, chuckling, when I finally let him go. At least now the smile reached his eyes.

"You don't understand . . . ."

"I want to understand," Joe interrupted. "I want to understand everything that has happened since that night, Julie. Why you didn't . . . ." He closed his eyes and shook his head. "I missed you so much."

"I never forgot you, Joe Davenport. No matter how hard I tried." I rolled him over onto his back, and straddled his leg again. "I always knew something was missing. *You* were missing."

He didn't resist as I poured all my pent up desire and longing into one deep, passionate kiss. I stopped only when I grew lightheaded. I pressed my forehead against his and struggled to catch my breath.

"What do you want from me, Julie?" Joe's voice was quiet and low.

It was my turn to pull back. I took in his chiseled features, the stubble along his jawbone, the gray hair at his temples. His beautiful eyes had turned to a cool green, hiding the warm gold flecks that usually welcomed me.

What did I want? I wanted answers. How had he left me so easily? What was really going on between him and Sophia? What *did* I want?

"I want you," I finally answered. "Whatever little part of you I can have." I brushed his lips with mine. "For however long I can have it," I whispered.

"Whether that's one kiss . . . ." I kissed him gently.

"Or one night . . . ." Another kiss, deeper and full of meaning.

"Or . . . ." I buried my face in his neck. I wanted to be greedy. I wanted our lost time together back. I wanted to spend our future together.

"You're not a one-night girl, Julie. You've always been so much more than that to me." He held my face in his hands, looking deep into my eyes. Despite what I had told Vanessa, despite how I had lied to myself, I knew that one night with Joe would never be enough. Still, I was willing to take what I could get.

"We have to start somewhere." I slipped my hand around to the front of his boxers and slowly began caressing him.

"Julie, you're killing me." Joe's eyes closed and he shuddered slightly.

"That is *definitely* not the outcome I'm hoping for," I said.

He smoothly rolled me over onto my back, then nuzzled my ear as he ran a hand down across my belly. He undid my jeans in one fluid motion, rubbing the back of his hand against the silky front of my thong. His fingers traced along the lace edge, up to the thin strap on my hip. He rolled back far enough to get a good look at it. He smiled.

OK, so the thong *was* a good idea.

"Nice," he said, raising an eyebrow. "And it matches the bra." His eyes flitted to the edge of the bed, where our shirts had been discarded earlier. "Hmmm. Are you sure you're not trying to seduce me?" He hooked his thumb under the strap of my thong and followed it around my hip, cupping my bare backside in his hand.

"Very nice," he said, grinning.

God bless Victoria and her secret, I thought.

Joe still had one leg strategically placed between mine. No matter how much I wriggled I couldn't move enough to break his hold and wrap both my legs around his hips. And no matter which way I twisted or turned, I couldn't shimmy out of my jeans.

This? This is why Vanessa suggested the swishy, short skirt. Why hadn't I listened?

Joe seemed unconcerned by our overabundance of clothing.

Granted, it had been a long time since Gary and I had sex, but I was fairly sure a little more freedom of movement was required than what Joe and I were currently enjoying. There were certain vitally important parts which were not fully accessible. Maybe Joe had some secret sex technique known only to musicians, I thought, hopefully. Maybe it was all a matter of timing. Maybe I just needed to relax. Maybe I was going to spontaneously combust.

At last he shifted his weight and I made one desperate attempt to push his pants down past that magnificent ass, confident that I had convinced him to give in to our desire. He hesitated, then removed his leg from between mine, only to secure both my legs between his, depriving me of even the delicious pressure of his thigh pressed against my crotch.

This was not the way things needed to fit together in order to do what I had in mind.

He raised up, kneeling above me and removed my hands from his pants, holding my hands in his. He kissed each hand gently, then laid them at my sides.

"Not yet, Julie," he said quietly. Then he gave me the gentlest of kisses, as if he could snuff the raging inferno of my lust with a light breeze.

Wha-huh? My oxytocin-addled brain froze. His gambit worked. Sort of.

"But . . . ."

Joe sighed. "The timing isn't right. You're hurt and angry. Confused."

Did he think I was on the rebound from Gary? If anything, I was still on the rebound from Joe leaving me the first time.

"This isn't about . . . ." I started to protest, but Joe cut me off.

"Maybe we both are."

Both? Had Sophia dumped him? Or did he mean . . . . I had always assumed it had been easy for Joe to walk away from me. What if our breakup had been as hard on him as it had been on me? Vanessa had said Joe wasn't a mind reader, but neither was I, damn it. I needed answers.

"What . . . ."

Joe stopped me with a kiss that was slow and gentle, and yet so passionate it almost – almost – left me feeling as spent as if we had made love. My neurochemical level spiked and my train of thought chugged down the rails. Joe did not fight fair.

"When I saw you at The Bar, it felt like nothing had ever changed. But it has, Julie. We've both changed."

"I still feel the same way about you, Joe. I never stopped . . . ." But maybe he had, I realized. He had left me before, after all. And now Gary had, too. I was such a fool. "Unless you . . . ."

"No! My feelings haven't changed. They will never change. I think that should be obvious." Joe raised an eyebrow and adjusted his hips so that his erection pressed against my crotch again. I closed my eyes and moaned, enjoying the contact. He was so frustratingly close. He shuddered. "You've always been able to drive me crazy. With or without the lacy thong."

"Without . . . now there's an idea!"

Joe chuckled. "Let's file that plan away for another night. We deserve a fresh start. If we rushed into something tonight, it wouldn't be fair. To either of us."

I gave an exaggerated huff of a sigh to express my annoyance, but smiled. Just because he was right, didn't mean I had to like it.

Joe didn't fight fair, but neither did I. I made one last attempt to seduce him. I ran my hands up his chest, bit my bottom lip, and pulled his face down to mine. Despite his defensive position, I was still able to tilt my hips just enough to accommodate his bulge between my thighs. The increased friction caught us both by surprise and we gasped as the fire abruptly reignited.

"It's not too late to change your mind, you know," I said.

"I fell in love with you the moment you almost slugged me," he said. "I've waited this long. I can wait a little longer. There's no rush. I'm not going anywhere."

He grinned and kissed me gently, then rolled us on to our sides so we lay facing each other. He slowly untangled his legs from mine, kissing my neck to distract me. He drew his knees up slightly, distancing his hips from mine.

Damn. Once upon a time I had used that same move on him.

He wrapped his arms around me and slowly pulled me close, kissing my nose, my forehead, the top of my head.

As I snuggled closer, he began humming softly. I pressed my face against his chest, feeling it vibrate beneath my forehead. I breathed in his familiar scent – warmth and soap and music. When I closed my eyes and breathed in Joe, I saw music, I heard music, I felt music. Music was a part of him, and everything about Joe triggered an auditory response in me. I felt myself being carried away by his melody now, floating on his song. I let myself relax and melt into his embrace. I yawned and my eyes drooped. I slipped my knee between his, feeling his still hard erection against my belly. I smiled to myself, sighed, and let his music carry me off to sleep.

"Those years I spent so broken

Cast adrift, no guiding star

Could it be I've found my way back,

To my harbor in the shadow of your heart."

Joanne Salemink

28

Waking up next to Joe was just as wonderful as I remembered. It was also more frustrating this time around. I had changed into a short nighty – nothing too sexy, but better than my man-jamas, Vanessa had conceded – and I convinced Joe he'd be more comfortable without his jeans.

"You're not just trying to take advantage of me, are you?" He grinned, and declined my offer to help him remove his pants.

"Yes. Yes I am." Honesty is the best policy, right?

"Good. I like that about you." Joe kissed my nose as he climbed back into bed, sans jeans. He wrapped his arm around me and rolled me onto my side, curling up close behind me. This strategically secured me beneath his arm, eliminating any chance to let my hands explore his shorts. My only consolation was feeling his hardness pressed against my rear all night, and the way his sleep-breathing – steady and even on my ear – stopped short when I rubbed against him.

I was enjoying the peaceful morning, spooning with Joe, and contemplating my next attack on his chastity when the phone rang.

"I hope I'm interrupting something," Miss Irene said.

"Sadly, no. He's a man of high morals and great restraint." I spoke in a stage whisper. I knew Joe was pretending to sleep from the way he held my hips away from his crotch.

"That's too bad, honey. But since you're up and he's not," Joe coughed and pulled me back against him, letting me know how wrong Miss Irene was, "Big George needs you to run The Scout down to the shop. He wants to make some adjustments for you. Maybe Joe can give you a ride back. Might do him some good to see the way you wrap your legs around . . . ."

"We're on it, Miss Irene. Thanks!" Sometimes she still managed to embarrass me. I wondered which of her tipsters told her about Joe.

*****

I introduced Joe to The Scout, and was pleased by his response. He took the time to look her over, squatting to get a better look at her engine, openly admiring her.

"She's beautiful, just like you, Julie. You never cease to amaze me." He held my helmet out to me, then drew it back. "Now, about you wrapping your legs around something . . . ."

"You'll always be my first choice," I said. I hugged him, then brought one leg up and around him to remind him what he was missing.

After a short delay, we headed off to Pleasant Glen Cycles and Motors. Big George was waiting for us. He looked Joe over from head to toe, and frowned.

"Hmph. The musician," Big George said. Then he turned to me and smiled.

"I've been thinking about the way you ride, Julie. There's a few things I want to try that should help you and The Scout adjust. You can wait in J.J.'s office." He looked at Joe and narrowed his eyes. "Won't take long."

I grabbed Joe's hand and pulled him through the shop.

"What was all that about?" I asked Joe.

"I don't think Big George approves of me courting you."

"And Miss Irene is disappointed you didn't . . . ."

Joe backed me up against J.J.'s desk and nudged my knees aside so he was standing between my legs. He put his hands on my hips and drew me closer.

"I'm going to have a heck of a time trying to please both of them," Joe said as he began kissing my neck.

"Well, you already know how you could please me." I arched my back and ran my fingers through his short hair. Things were getting interesting when we heard voices in the hall. Joe and I jumped apart guiltily, expecting Big George. Joe sat on a sofa made from the backseat of a car, while I leaned against the desk.

"Hey Julie! Dad said you were in here. He's working his secret magic and told me I was getting in the way." J.J. was half way across the room before he noticed Joe. "Joe! I heard you were in town." Joe stood and they shared a brief, back-slapping, man hug.

"Have you met Julie? Julie, this is . . . wait a minute." J.J. looked back and forth between Joe and me, his eyes open wide. "You're *the* Julie? *Joe's* Julie?" Joe grinned. J.J. turned to me. "And you wound up married to Gary Westbrook?" J.J. shook his head. "No wonder I didn't put two and two together. You went from Joe to Gary? That's a . . . huh." He shook his head again and shrugged.

"Wow. Joe finally found his Julie. In my office." J.J. looked at Joe, then at the sofa, and the color drained from is face. "And you were *alone*, together, in my office! For how long? Oh, man! No! Not on my couch! That was the backseat from Debbie VanDenberg's Thunderbird! I know it saw a lot of action when I was in high school, but . . . ."

Joe laughed. "You said Debbie VanDenberg wouldn't give you the time of day, let alone any action. And no. Nothing happened," he waved his hand between me and himself. "The virtue of your furniture is still in tact, as is mine." He winked at me.

"Oh, please!" J.J. said. "Who knows what kind of influence Miss Irene has been on Julie."

I should have been offended, but he did have a point.

"So, I take it you two know each other?" I asked, trying to change the topic.

"I was in an early version of The Average Joes," J.J. said, nodding.

"We enforced the 'Joe' part pretty loosely, and the talent part even more loosely," Joe added.

"Yeah, Dad is still pissed about that. I'm not sure if he was worried you'd try to steal me away from the shop, or if he's mad you didn't."

"So that's why he gave you the death stare," I said to Joe. "I thought it had something to do with me."

"It probably did," J.J. said. "Dad and Miss Irene think of you as one of their own, you know. You're the little sister I never had." He put his arm around my shoulder and gave me a very platonic, sideways hug.

"Let's face it, Joe. You got lucky. She could have had a real man, but this is Iowa, not Arkansas. I'm totally off limits. You realize what this means, right?"

"If I hurt her you'll come after me?"

"No, I'll go after *her*. She's not *really* my sister, you moron. And *you're* definitely not my type. Besides, by the time Miss Irene and Big George get done with you, there won't be anything for me to go after. Especially with what happened the last time."

"I'm not going to let that happen again," Joe said, quietly.

"See that you don't." Big George struck a menacing pose, filling up the doorway where he stood, wiping his hands with a shop rag. He nodded his head for me to join him, then spoke in a gentler tone.

"Julie, I need you to take The Scout for a spin, to see how these adjustments suit you."

"It's nice to see you again, Mr. Monroe," Joe said. For a moment I thought he had been possessed by the spirit of Eddie Haskell, from *Leave it to Beaver*.

"Joseph." Big George finished wiping his hands and put his fists on his hips, looking even more ominous. "I see you still have your father's truck. You've learned the importance of taking care of the things that are important to you."

"Yes, sir. I saw The Scout once, before . . . . " Big George raised one eyebrow and Joe seemed to lose all his composure. "But this time it's . . . ." I thought I saw beads of sweat forming on Joe's forehead. "She's very special. Even more so now . . . ."

"She means a great deal to me, Joseph. And to Miss Irene."

J.J. had his back to Big George, and was making faces at Joe, laughing at his discomfort.

"Don't you have some work to do, son?" Joe grinned as Big George turned his attention to J.J.. "Joseph always was a bad influence on you."

Since I seemed to be the only one who Big George wasn't angry with, I tried to soothe the waters.

"I didn't know J.J. was a musician," J.J. and Joe shared a horrified look, like they were afraid I'd irritate Big George further. "Did he get his talent from you? You did such a lovely job of singing the other night, when Vanessa and I heard you."

Big George's expression softened.

"Thank you, dear. But my talent, and J.J.'s, is in the garage. Joseph is the true musician. Still, there's very little a man won't do for the woman he loves." Big George took my elbow and led me out of the office, looking back over his shoulder once. "Or there shouldn't be."

305

*****

The next few weeks flew by as we finalized plans for The Gala. Everyone pitched in. Miss Irene pulled strings behind the scenes to swing an alcohol permit and to extend the hours for the noise ordinance waiver. Big George and J.J. recruited security and admissions workers. Bunny and Muffy handled advance ticket sales.

Even Gary came through. We used the grant his corporation gave us to rent two mobile bandshells. Groups would alternate between the two stages, allowing one to set up while another group finished performing.

The Gala had grown to an all-afternoon event. Overwhelmed by the response to our call for bands, Bob and Joe narrowed the field to eight groups, in addition to the show choir, No Talent Slugs, Dirt Road Party and The Average Joe's. The program would start at 1 p.m. with the show choir, followed by four high school groups, then the regional acts. The Average Joes would take the stage at 10 p.m.

Joe split his time between Des Moines and Pleasant Glen, helping Bob line up sound and lighting equipment and finishing work on his own projects. We texted, called, and even Skyped when we were apart. Things were different this time around. Technology made it easier to keep in touch, and we were more aware of how precious our time together was. We had so much catching up to do. Sometimes I thought I was learning as much about who I was and what I liked, as I learned about Joe.

We talked about everything.

Everything except what happened the night Joe left Pleasant Glen.

When we were together we perfected ways of not having sex, while coming as close as possible. Joe remained frustratingly adamant about not sleeping together. His second marriage had imploded after his wife had a very public affair. Although I had served Gary with divorce papers, we were still, technically, married. Joe said he wanted us to have a clean start.

"I shouldn't have come on so strong that afternoon at The Bar. I knew you were a married woman," Joe said one night when he called. "I thought I could be casual. But as soon as I held you in my arms – no, even before we touched – it was like we had never been apart.

"Then you told me that you and Barry," I laughed at his intentional mistake, "were not together, and Bob filled me in. I knew I had to find out if you . . . I tried to keep it low key that first night."

"I wasn't very low key, was I?" I said, remembering how aggressive I'd been.

"You have no idea how hard it was not to . . . I wanted you so much. But I couldn't do that to Gary, or to you. I feel like I have to draw the line somewhere. A wise young woman told me that once you have sex with someone, there's no going back." My mom had told me that when I first started dating, and I had used that as an excuse when Joe and I had become serious. I was touched, and a little annoyed, that he remembered.

"What we have now, Julie, is so much more than back then. I won't let anything, or anyone come between us again."

What is it about a noble man with moral standards that makes him so sexy? He had just explained why we should not have sex, and all I could think about was how much I wanted to make him change his mind.

"It's a good thing you're in Des Moines, or I'd be all over you. And this time I wouldn't take no for an answer," I said.

"It's a good thing you're in Pleasant Glen, because I'm not sure I'd be able to say no."

Aside from conversations and messages filled with double entendres, Joe and I kept our relationship as private as possible out of respect for Gary and Emily. That was fine with both of us. We would much rather spend our available time together alone, not sharing each other with anyone else – with the exception of Miss Irene and Bob.

Sometimes I thought we were being too private. Gary continued his blitzkrieg of charm and romance. He seemed to know when Joe was *not* around, and would drop by the apartment with flowers, or quaintly romantic dinner plans. Emily was still firmly Team Gary, but Vanessa's support wavered. I repeatedly told Gary it was over, that I was ready to move on with my life, but he dismissed my protests.

"Jules, honey, we built a life together. We raised a wonderful daughter together. Where's that musician been? He ran out on you the last time, why do you think this time is any different?"

When I was with Joe, it was so easy to believe that we could have a future together. But when I was alone, with Gary playing the devil's advocate and Joe in Des Moines with Sophia or any of the socialites he was so often photographed with, my confidence wavered.

Regardless of what might or might not happen with Joe, I knew I could not stay married to Gary. I cited Gary's infidelity and irreconcilable differences as grounds for the divorce, and asked for a modest settlement – despite objections from my lawyer, Vanessa and Miss Irene. I wasn't out to get Gary, or to break him, I just needed enough to get started on my new life. I had my own insurance and retirement plans for the future, and my job with Miss Irene could keep me afloat until I found a more permanent job.

When he wasn't actively trying to win me back, Gary pleaded for me to wait until the promotion had been settled to divorce. The wheels of business were back to turning slowly, and he thought any hint of marital discord could derail his chances. While Gary never came right out and said anything, I knew he had turned down some plum assignments so that we could stay in Pleasant Glen. I had wanted to put down roots and stay close to what little family we had. Gary had sacrificed so that Emily could stay at PGHS and I could stay at the college.

So I continued to wait, and continued to play the role of supportive wife for his bosses. I was so busy with the Gala that I didn't have to do much other than smile, shake hands, and gush about what a dedicated father and conscientious businessman Gary was. That much, at least, was true.

Joe was a good sport, in part because he had to attend a couple of high profile social events with Sophia and the socialites. Our time apart, pretending to care about other people, made our time together even more special.

Through it all, I made time to ride The Scout. Each time I heard her engine purr, my self-confidence grew. She was perfect for short trips around town, and I felt like a bad ass pulling up to last-minute Gala meetings. When things got too stressful, I'd take her on longer rides. I felt the tension melting away as I cruised past never-ending cornfields.

One day I considered riding her all the way to Des Moines to surprise Joe. In the end, a minor crisis had erupted, and I didn't even get a chance to call him until it was late in the evening.

"Huh, well, I mean, I'm sorry you had such a bad day, and of course I would have loved for you to come out. But it's probably all for the best. I had a pretty hectic day, too. You may have been disappointed," Joe said when I called. He sounded distracted, and – I'll admit – not nearly as upset as I had hoped he would be.

"No, yeah, I understand," I lied. "Dropping in unannounced is probably not a great idea. It's . . . I mean, I . . . well, like you said, it's been a long day, and I probably shouldn't keep you. I just wanted to check in, see how . . . you know."

"Julie," Joe interrupted my rambling. "Look out your window, sweetheart."

There he was, standing next to his truck in my driveway, in the soft glow of the streetlight.

"I had an awful day, Julie, and I knew the only thing that could make me feel better was holding you in my arms. I don't know what I would have done if you weren't here."

It was harder than ever to stick to our plan of celibacy that night.

29

The Saturday morning of The Gala arrived right on schedule. Thanks to everyone's hard work we were ready to go. Friday's early set up made it seem like we knew what we were doing. The heat and humidity were unusually bearable for an Iowa summer day, driving the mosquitoes to Minnesota.

The show choir took the stage promptly at 1 p.m. for the opening ceremony, much to the delight of a larger-than-anticipated crowd. Joe and I snuck away to the back of the audience during a break between two high school groups, The De-Tazzlers and Cow Tippers. We sat close – but not too close – on a park bench under a sprawling oak, taking a moment to relax. I used my official-looking clipboard as a excuse to move closer to Joe, pretending to go over last minute details with him.

"So, I was planning to throw my lingerie on stage later," I said. "Would you prefer a bra or panties?"

"I would prefer taking them off you myself after the show." He bent his head to mine. "Especially if it involves that red thong."

"I guess you'll just have to wait and see." I raised the clipboard to hide a quick kiss.

Joe leaned back and stretched, casually putting his arm on the bench behind my shoulders and crossing his legs so that his ankle was on his knee and his thigh rested on mine. Then he started singing that line from the song "Jack and Diane" about running off behind the shady trees and doing what he pleased. Joe always quoted songs when he was feeling playful. I had missed that.

"You hate John Mellencamp. But that does sound like fun," I said, giving his knee a squeeze.

"Hate's a strong word. Besides, he's pretty nice, once you get to know him."

"Impressive, but how close does Six Degrees of Joe Davenport get me to Billy Joel?" Joe rolled his eyes, then straightened as he noticed we had company. Emily was headed towards us, her stride quick and purposeful.

"Hi, honey! I got your text, but I didn't think you were coming until later!" I jumped up and hugged her tightly. Emily hugged me back, but it felt a little stiff, setting off my Mom-dar. I could sense something was wrong.

"Slow weekend at camp. I left early." This was not like Emily. She gave Joe a weak wave. Then she took my hands in hers and lowered her voice. "Dad called. He's worried about you. *I'm* worried about you."

"Pfft. I'm fine. A little stressed, but fine. Everything's going according to plan here." I looked around the park. Nameless, another high school group, was setting up. The crowd was growing. The beer and food lines were moving smoothly. I looked back at Emily and smiled. "You know how nervous I get when things go according to plan."

Emily laughed and squeezed my hands.

"I'm sure you have everything under control," she said. "Besides, you survived The Great Pony Poop Party. What could be worse than that?" She turned to Joe. "All I wanted for my eighth birthday party was a pony ride. How was I to know I shouldn't feed them buttercream frosting and hot dogs?" Joe chuckled.

"On the up-side, my roses were beautiful that year," I said.

"That's my mom, always making lemonade out of lemons. And that's why I need to talk to you. Alone." She looked at Joe. "You don't mind, do you, sir?"

"No. Not at all. I should go check in with Bob, anyway." Joe stood but I grabbed his arm before he could leave. I had a feeling I'd need him to support me – or to keep me from killing Gary – when I found out what had Emily so worked up.

"No, wait. Please. I mean, really, Em. He knows about the pony poop, what could be worse than that?"

"But Mom!" Emily gave me the same pleading look that once got me to buy her a pair of ridiculously high, sparkly, platform pumps. It wasn't working this time. Emily sighed, and pulled me to secret-sharing range.

"Dad thinks you're having an affair with one of the musicians," she whispered. I started to giggle. Misinterpreting my meaning, Emily stepped back and sighed. "I know it sounds crazy, but he's really upset."

I put my arm around Emily's shoulder and turned her to face Joe. He had stuck his hands in his pockets and was slowly shifting his weight from foot to foot, like a little boy expecting to be scolded.

"Emily, this is Joe Davenport, lead singer for The Average Joes." Emily's eyes grew wide. "We dated a long time ago, before your dad and I got together."

"This guy?" Emily pointed at Joe. "*He's* Joe Davenport? *The* Joe Davenport? *You* know an honest to goodness rock star? You *dated* him? " She turned to Joe. "No offense, Joe – is it OK if I call you Joe? – but you look more like a farmer than a rock star." Joe was wearing faded jeans, scuffed work boots and a PG Cycles and Motors t-shirt. He looked like one of Miss Irene's yard crew.

Joe gave Emily the same half-grin that once graced the cover of Rolling Stone.

"I get that a lot," he said.

"And now we're . . . dating again," I added.

"You're *what?*" Emily looked at me in disbelief.

I probably could have handled that better, and I was just about to fix my mistake when I was interrupted.

"You! I thought I told you to stay away from my wife!"

I had been so focused on Emily that I hadn't noticed Gary approaching.

"She wasn't your wife when you told me that. I'm not sure she was even your girlfriend." Joe's voice was quiet and calm, a contrast to Gary's angry outburst.

"You what? When?" I spun around to face Gary.

"The first time he ran off and left you," Gary said. "I told him to leave you alone."

"I didn't run. You said she didn't want to see me again."

"*What?*" My shout was covered by an extended percussion solo played by Future (F)Harmers of America, a thrash-country group. "When I asked you why Vanessa said you made Joe leave, you denied it! You said she was drunk!"

"Well, she was. And technically I didn't deny it."

"No. You're not going to wiggle your way out with 'technically' this time." I started to move towards Gary, but Joe ran his hand down my arm, redirecting my attention.

"He's not worth it, Julie." Joe knew better than to try and hold me back.

"That was so long ago. What difference does it make? He left. I didn't." Gary didn't know when to stop.

"Ohhhh, Dad," Emily said, shaking her head.

"Honey, maybe you should go now," I said to her.

"The heck! My mom is about to kill my dad, and I just found out she got dumped by a rock star. There's no way I'm leaving!"

"I didn't dump her."

"I'm not going to kill anyone."

"Oh, don't be so melodramatic. Of course you are!" Somewhere in the midst of all that, Miss Irene had joined the party. "And with all these witnesses, it's going to be pretty hard to dodge the charges. In case you haven't noticed, the Gala is a huge success! The church ladies are putting out an emergency call for more bake sale desserts. The Catholics are considering you for sainthood. The Methodists are naming a 100-cup coffee urn in your honor." She shrugged. "Not that there's much difference."

I sighed and looked out over the crowd. So far we hadn't attracted much attention, although I was pretty sure Bunny and Muffy were creeping in our direction. Then again, the entire crowd was closer than before. We expected the parents would leave after the high school groups finished, and that the audience would grow slowly until the finale. Instead everyone seemed to be staying. And coming early.

"OK. Fine. Let's all remain calm, before we wind up as the lead story on the grapevine." I stared down each member of our little group.

"When did you get so bossy?" Gary asked. "That's not a very attractive trait."

I gave him a withering glare. "Would you please explain to me what you two were talking about?"

Joe and Gary looked at each other. It seemed neither of them was willing to speak.

"Joe?"

"I got worried when you didn't return my phone calls . . . ."

"Wait. What calls?"

"I called from The Bar that night, right before we took off," Joe said. "I couldn't leave without saying goodbye. Even if it was to an answering machine."

"I never got any message. There were never . . . ."

Joe frowned and shook his head. "I called from every . . . ."

"It was Van's idea," Gary interrupted.

"Whoa! Wait a minute buster. You're not throwing me under the bus that easy." Vanessa shouldered her way into our cluster. "It was an accident, Jules. You had gone back to The Bar to look for Joe. I saw we had a message and . . . well, after it played, I must have hit erase. I was going to tell you in the morning, but I forgot. You know how I get when I'm drunk."

Joe took my hands in his and held my gaze. His hazel eyes were liquid gold, warm with compassion. "Julie, honey, I left messages from every pay phone at every rest stop and gas station we hit on our way to New York."

"There were never any . . . ." I blinked back tears and struggled to catch my breath.

"This explains so much," Joe said. He pulled me into his arms and kissed my forehead gently.

"I swear, it only happened once," Vanessa said. "I didn't . . . ."

"I did."

Gary's confession punctuated the silence before Roundup Resistant started their set. His voice, strong and confident, led perfectly to their guitar-heavy downbeat. Or that could have been the sound of my brain exploding. Joe caught me as my knees buckled.

"Mom? *Mom?* Let's sit down, Mom." Emily took my elbow and eased me onto the bench. Joe sat on the other side of me, holding my hand. He glared at Gary, his face red with anger.

"Take a deep breath, Mom. Are you feeling faint? Do you need to put your head between your knees? I'm sure there's an explanation. Dad can explain. Right, Dad? Please, Daddy. Please?" Emily's eyes filled with tears. I knew I had to pull myself together. I looked up at Gary.

"Why?"

"He wasn't right for you, Jules. You weren't cut out for his kind of life. You need a home, a family, roots – just like me. Those were the things *I* could give you, not him. I needed a wife who could be my partner, someone like my mom. So I erased his messages and threw away his letters."

"That wasn't your decision to make," I said. I started to shake. Emily squeezed my hand. Joe rubbed his thumb across the back of my other hand.

"Hey, he agreed with me!"

I turned to Joe.

"When I didn't hear from you, I went crazy. The promoter put me on a plane back to Iowa. You and Vanessa had already moved to River City, but Gary was at your old apartment. He told me you didn't want to see me again. He said you deserved a better life than I could provide for you." Joe shook his head. "The band – bands – were breaking up. I figured maybe Gary was right.

"I figured things would settle down in a couple weeks. I wanted to prove myself as a musician, one way or another. I wanted to prove that I could provide the kind of life you deserved." Joe gave me a sad, crooked smile. "Things didn't settle down. By the time I made it back to Iowa again,

Bob said you were engaged to Gary. I figured I missed my chance. I figured you were better off."

"Oh, Joe." I reached up and held the side of his face in my hand, rubbing my thumb across his cheek. "That wasn't your decision to make, either, sweetheart."

"What the hell? You're taking his side? I was just looking out for you!"

"No, Gary, you were looking out for Gary. Joe was looking out for me."

"Po-tay-to, po-tah-to. What's the difference? I needed you then. I need you now. We made – we *make* – a great team! Don't you see, Jules? I need you more than ever. This promotion, you know how sensitive the situation is. The selection committee loves you! All our dreams are within reach. There's nothing stopping us now, honey, nothing."

"That's your dream, Gary, not mine. I'm done. This 'team' was based on a lie. Our whole . . . ." I heard Emily sniffle, and stopped short. She was biting her lip, trying not to cry. None of this was her fault. She didn't deserve to get caught up in our argument.

"You're right. We did make a good team. Nothing can change that," I gave Emily's hand a squeeze, then turned back to Gary. "But I'm done. The selection committee wants you, not me. You're a wonderful businessman. A wonderful father. They'd have to be fools not to see that."

"Jules, please. You know . . . what they're concerned about." Gary looked at Emily, then back at me. Evidently he hadn't mentioned the affair with his co-worker while he was telling Emily about Joe. Figures. "You know how important your support is. Please help me, just this one last time."

"Please, Mom?"

Joe nudged my shoulder with his. "What happened, happened. We can't change the past. We can only make the most of what we have now. It's one day. I'm not going anywhere."

I sighed. Sometimes I hated taking the high road.

"Fine. I'll play nice today, Gary, but that's it."

Emily leaned around me to look at Joe.

"Thank you," she said. He winked in reply, and I think she blushed a little. He was a rock star, after all.

"Well, if the excitement's over, I suppose we should get back to work," Miss Irene said to Vanessa. "Better make sure the food stands are ready before The Rusty Church Keys take the stage. There's something about a bluegrass band that always drives up food sales." The two women had only taken a few steps before Miss Irene turned around.

"By the way, who's the hussy?" she asked, pointing to a woman headed our way.

"And where does she shop?" Vanessa added.

Sophia wobbled across the grass on a pair of bright blue pumps that perfectly matched her bright blue, leather miniskirt. The plunging neckline of her tight, black blouse barely kept her enhancements contained, especially when her heel caught in the soft turf and nearly sent her sprawling – and falling out of her shirt.

Gary rushed to lend her a steadying hand and arrived at her side slightly before a disappointed Charlie – in town with the corporate contingent – did. I watched Sophia's expression change from annoyed to flirtatious as she took in Gary's Rolex, Ralph Lauren slacks and polo, and his handsome face. Mild-mannered Charlie in his slightly frayed Dockers didn't stand a chance.

"Ugh. Hot-Dad to the rescue," Emily said, slouching down on the bench and crossing her arms over her chest. "Honestly Mom, how did you put up with him for so long?"

Joe leaned back, put his arm around me and gently rubbed Emily's shoulder.

"It's not all his fault," Joe said. "Sophia enjoys making a certain impression."

Joe hadn't said much about his manager, except that she disagreed with every aspect of his involvement with the Gala. He finally convinced her she could promote it as an example of his work with young musicians.

Sophia clung to Gary's well-formed bicep for support as he guided her to the bench. She dropped his arm as soon as she saw Joe sitting close to me. Gary blinked with confused. Emily made little retching noises. Joe coughed to cover his laughter. I seethed in silence.

"Joey, you left so early yesterday morning we didn't get a chance to talk!"

"Not the time, Sophia," Joe said.

"But . . . ." Sophia smoothed her skirt, then wiggled a little as she squared her shoulders. I wasn't sure if this was to entertain Gary and Charlie, or if she was buying time while contemplating her next move.

"We need to discuss some important business matters." She gazed up at Gary and batted her eyelashes. "I'm sure these *gentlemen* will understand. Business is business, after all. Won't you please excuse us?"

I couldn't see Emily's face, but I swear I could hear her roll her eyes.

I patted Joe's knee and smiled at him.

"It's only one day. I'm not going anywhere," I said.

"A lot of traffic on the moral high-road today," Joe said quietly as he sat up straight. He started to lean toward me to give me a kiss, but I cut my eyes at Charlie. Instead, Joe winked at me and took Emily's hand and kissed it.

"If you ladies need me, I'll be around. And I'll have my cell phone on. No excuse for missed messages." Joe bumped into Gary as he passed by, giving him a frosty look.

Joanne Salemink

30

As the afternoon progressed, I felt like a pinball. I ricocheted from group to group, welcoming people, answering questions, helping out wherever needed, and eating up enthusiastic support of the Gala and congratulations on a well-run event.

I was exhausted, and my face hurt from smiling. It was worth it because I knew each handshake, each performance, brought things closer to the end. It all brought me closer to going back to my quiet, cozy apartment with Joe.

I was polite to the selection committee members, but kept Emily between Gary and me at all times so that I wouldn't be tempted to strangle him. I invented small emergencies to keep me busy and away from Gary's dog and pony show. Unfortunately these imaginary crises also kept me away from Joe.

Joe and I did managed to steal a few short moments to ourselves here and there, but soon we were limited to a discreet touch while passing, or a smile or wink from across the park. No matter how crowded it got, I instinctually knew where Joe was. Whenever I looked up, I found Joe looking for me, too.

By 8 p.m., when The No Talent Slugs started warming up, the park was bursting at the scenes. We would have had a real Woodstock on our hands, if Bob had not convinced me to double the number of port-opotties. Melvin was at the entrance to the beer garden, checking IDs, and giving impromptu sobriety tests to anyone leaving. Bob had scheduled extra help at the bar prior to and during The Slugs' set. I used my official privilege to sneak in for a drink, but Bob pressed me into service, urging customers to visit the "special guest bartender" and to tip generously.

While the crowd had been supportive and enthusiastic all afternoon, The Slugs were obviously their favorite so far. The crowd loved them and their marginal ability, and the band bantered playfully with the audience.

"Just remember, the drunker you are, the better we sound!" the lead singer – if you could call what he did "singing" – said, causing a couple school board members to frown. When Miss Irene stepped in to update the amount raised on the tally board, the frowns immediately disappeared.

The band radiated a pure joy of music, and seemed to revel in their mediocrity. There was no doubt they were giving it their all and loved every minute of if. The crowd, perhaps encouraged by the lead vocalist's limited range and questionable pitch, sang along.

It was hard to tell who was more excited – the band or the crowd – when Joe joined them. Then again, Joe looked pretty excited himself.

When Joe sat in with The Slugs, and later with Dirt Road Party, he played with the same reckless abandon I remembered from 25 years ago. He laughed and joked with the bands, content to sing backup, playing cover tunes.

Joe was a natural entertainer who shined even brighter when he shared the spotlight with others. This was what he was born to do, I realized. I felt my heart swell with pride and love, even as I wondered how I could possibly fit in with his lifestyle.

I made my way to the backstage area as the Dirt Road Party set wound down, hoping to catch Joe before his set started. He met me at the edge of the roped off area and pulled me into his arms. I buried my face in his neck and breathed in deeply, wanting to commit this moment to memory.

"You did it!" he said, loosening his hold on me just enough to look me in the eyes.

"We did it! None of this would have been possible without you."

"You underestimate yourself, Julie." He took my chin in his hand. "You are an amazing woman. You always have been." We managed a quick kiss before a crowd surge threw me off balance.

"The earth moves when you kiss me." I laughed as we drifted apart.

"Julie, there's something . . . ."

The band had just finished their set and the crowd went wild. I couldn't hear Joe.

"What?"

"We need . . . ."

The noise grew as Miss Irene and Vanessa announced the amount raised so far.

"What?" Now I couldn't even hear myself.

Miss Irene announced Joe.

"We need . . . ." I tried to read his lips. He looked so intense, so serious.

The crowd pushed us apart.

"Later," I mouthed. Then I kissed my fingertips and held them out to him.

His lips said "I love you." He reached for me, but our fingers missed. I saw Sophia pulling him toward the stage. Gary was pulling me back toward the VIP area, to the right of the main stage.

There was something uncomfortably familiar about the situation, but I shook it off. All that mattered was that Joe loved me, and soon we would be back in the solitude of my apartment and I could hear him whisper those same words to me over and over.

I turned to glare at Gary, but he was smiling over my head. His bosses and his bosses' bosses were waiting for us. They were congratulating us on Gary's promotion. They were telling me how much I would love Des Moines, and warning me not to get too used to it, as they expected Gary would be moving on soon. The bosses' wives were gushing about the Gala and how they needed me to organize their volunteer efforts. I realized that we *had* been selected as a team.

Someone handed me a glass of champagne for a toast. Gary's arm was still around my waist. He pulled me close and kissed me, his lips cold and tingling. I pushed him away, then turned to blush modestly at the bosses.

They were looking at us expectantly. Someone had asked something. They were waiting on my reply. I smiled, giggled, and looked to Gary for an answer.

"The movers will be here Monday," he told them. Then he pulled me in for another hug and kissed my hair. I choked on my champagne.

"But I, the Gala, the wrap up . . ." I stammered. This had gone on long enough. I had to put a stop to this charade. I had to say something.

Another roar went up from the crowd.

Sophia's voice – breathy and coquettish – cut through it all.

"I'd like to thank Mrs. Gary Westbrook for inviting us here tonight."

I tried to turn toward the stage, but Gary was holding me. The bosses were clapping and congratulating me, pouring more champagne.

"Mrs. Westbrook did a wonderful job bringing all these talented musicians together." I struggled against Gary's embrace, but there were more hugs, more toasts.

"Joe and I are so grateful to Mrs. Westbrook. You folks know Pleasant

Glen has a special place in Joe's heart. Twenty-five years ago Joe Davenport left Pleasant Glen, headed for the Big Apple."

I finally broke free and spun to face the stage. Across the sea of faces, Sophia caught my eye. She grinned smugly.

"Tonight history repeats itself! We will be leaving for New York right after the show. I'm pleased to announce Joe will be one of the headliners at the Skyscraper Music Festival."

I struggled to catch my breath. I felt lightheaded. My knees buckled. Gary caught me before I collapsed. I looked around, tunnel vision recording luridly detailed images in my brain.

Sophia's face, her emerald green eyes gleaming under fake eyelashes. Her lips curled in a winner's sneer, bleached white teeth framed by Cheap Tart Red lipstick.

Joe's face, his jaw clenched tightly. His eyes on Sophia. This is what he had been trying to tell me.

Gary's face, his eyes saying "I told you so." His arms tightened around my waist.

Joe was leaving. Gary needed me.

I couldn't believe this was happening again.

I had lived a make-believe life before. I survived.

I wouldn't believe it.

I pushed against Gary's arms, pivoting past him like a turnstile. I waded through the VIP crowd, toward the exit. I reached the edge of the parking lot. Hidden in the shadows, I doubled over, taking great, gasping breaths.

The crowd was still cheering.

I didn't believe it.

The band started playing.

Joe joined them, a beat late. He pounded on the piano, his voice shaking. He regained his composure. Ever the entertainer.

This is what he was born for.

This is what he tried to tell me.

He would leave after the show. I would not be here.

We would not say goodbye.

I unlocked my Mini Cooper and collapsed into the driver's seat. I pulled out of the parking lot, and headed home.

Alone.

31

I parked in the driveway and entered the garage through the side door. Miss Irene and Big George had taken her car to the Gala, leaving The Scout alone in the big space. Moonlight spilled in through the window and pooled around her, setting her aglow. I approached her reverently. She was as beautiful and mysterious as the first time I saw her. My life had changed so much since then. I had changed so much since then.

"How could I have been so wrong?" My voice echoed in the emptiness.

I walked around The Scout, doing my pre-ride check. I threw my leg over the seat and eased down onto the saddle. My hips ached from standing all day. I was exhausted. It was all I could do to hold The Scout upright. I knew there was no way I could ride her, but that was alright.

I just needed to hear her voice.

I leaned down to set the choke and rested my head on her tank. The Scout was hard and cold against my cheek. Not at all like Joe's shoulder, I thought.

I drew in a ragged breath, squeezing my eyes tightly closed to hold back tears.

"There you are, dear." Big George stood in the doorway, his face lost in shadow. "You left before Joseph . . . ."

"I listened long enough. I couldn't . . . ." My voice gave out.

"You know better than to ride when you're upset, Julie."

"I know. I just needed to hear her."

"You just needed what, dear?" Big George tilted his head and slowly walked over to me.

"You told Miss Irene that everyone hears something different, hears what they need to, when they listen to The Scout."

Big George was standing in front of me now, resting a hand on The Scout's headlight. He grinned sheepishly and looked at the floor.

"I may have laid it on a little thick," he said. "She told you all about The Scout's history, I'm sure. Told you how I brought The Scout back to her after . . . what happened." I sniffed and nodded.

"I didn't know what to expect when I pulled up in the driveway that day. I didn't know Irene well, just that she was a very determined lady. I half expected her to take a swing at me." He chuckled, and I had to smile.

"But when she met me at the door, her face was so sad, Julie. So sad. I realized I had misread her completely. She blamed herself for what happened. I couldn't stand to see her like that.

"You see, I blamed myself, too. I could tell right away what kind of man Frank was. And Doris, well, she tried, but . . ." Big George shrugged and sighed.

"Then Irene caught a glimpse of The Scout, sitting there in the back of my truck. Her whole face changed. She set her jaw just so. Got that determined gleam in her eyes. I braced myself for the worst.

"'Can you teach me to ride?' she asked, just like it was the most natural thing in the world. I figured she was going to ride whether I taught her or not, so she might as well learn the right way. I owed her that much.

"I think at first she kept The Scout as a penance, maybe. But she's always been a tough girl. Independent. Maybe too independent. Learning to ride restored her confidence. Gave her back a sense of control. Along the way she found freedom and adventure. I'm not so sure she didn't enjoy shocking people just as much or more than the rest of it.

"The Scout gave her something to focus on while her heart healed. Maybe that's what she meant by The Scout talking to her. But she did it all herself."

"You helped," I said.

"Maybe," Big George shrugged. "After Doris left, Irene took us in. She helped me raise Junior. I know motors, not babies. She saved him. She helped me start the shop. That saved me.

"We fell in love. I think that saved us both.

"I've always been a little afraid that if she got rid of the Scout she wouldn't need me anymore. So I've done everything I could do to customize The Scout for her. I set the suspension for her light weight, adjusted the controls to match her style. She tends to be a little heavy on the accelerator, a little quick on the brakes. I'm trying to get all that switched over for you. You two are alike in some ways, but it's a work in progress."

I thought of how similar Frank and Gary were. I had been certain that Joe was my Big George.

"The timing advance, though," Big George sighed, and shook his head. "That's where you two give me fits." I frowned, not sure what he meant. Learning to adjust the manual timing advance on The Scout had been one of the most challenging things about riding her. I knew Big George had done what he could to make it easier for me.

"Do you remember what I taught you about top dead center?"

"Well, you said I need to set the timing so the spark energizes right *before* the piston reaches top dead center. That way the fuel will ignite right *after* the piston reaches top dead center, pushing the piston down the cylinder more efficiently. Ish." I understood what he told me, more or less, I just wasn't confident in my explanation.

Big George chuckled. "That's close enough. I've watched you ride. You're . . . catching on. Sometimes you still set it a little early. You're getting that explosion while the piston is still moving up. That's what causes your pinging." Big George illustrated this by making a fist with one hand and bringing it up toward the palm of his other hand, then pulling it back down before it touched. "You're a little anxious. You anticipate too much. You rush things. You need to relax, let things happen.

"Irene, on the other hand, is too cautious." I raised an eyebrow. Miss Irene? Cautious? "I know she can appear reckless, but she's actually very deliberate," Big George continued. "It's hard for the rest of us to see her reasoning sometimes. Anyway, Irene hesitates. She doesn't set the spark until the piston has already reached top dead center. By the time the fuel ignites, the piston is already on its way down again. She's wasting energy, missing the full benefit of the spark. Missing out on opportunities. Then again, sometimes I think she's just being contrary."

"I heard that." Miss Irene was leaning against the doorframe, hiding in the dark.

"I know," Big George said without looking over at her. "Do you understand what I'm trying to say?" He was still looking at me, but I thought he was asking us both.

Miss Irene sighed and walked over. "He's more than just eye candy, Julie. He's the best mechanic I know. The best man I know, too." She reached out and took his hand.

"Does your offer still stand?" she asked him.

"Same as always," he said.

"I'm not wearing white."

"I think that's for the best."

Big George pulled her close and put his arms around her. They shared a gentle kiss. Then Big George jumped a little as Miss Irene goosed him.

"How's that for cautious?" She laughed and hugged him.

"Nearly 50 years, Irene. Fifty years. You're lucky I'm a patient man." He kissed the tip of her nose.

"Speaking of patient men . . . ." Miss Irene turned to face me. "You know, cell phones are a lot more effective when you don't leave them behind the bar."

I patted my pockets, feeling for my cell phone, just as Miss Irene held it out towards me.

"I would imagine Joseph is getting a little anxious," Big George said.

"But Sophia said they were leaving for New York right after the show."

"I guess that's something the two of you should discuss."

Joanne Salemink

32

Maybe Big George was right. Maybe my timing was off. The least I could do was give Joe a chance to explain. I hugged Big George and Miss Irene and ran to my car. I figured if I hurried, there was a chance I could still catch Joe before he left the Gala. Phones had failed us before. I needed to talk to Joe face to face. Or at least try.

We roll the sidewalks up in Pleasant Glen by 11 p.m., even on a summer Saturday night, but I met a steady line of cars leaving the park. Still, quite a few stragglers remained – gathering their folding chairs, rehashing the day's events, and helping with the clean up.

On stage, The Average Joes were packing up, or trying to, anyway. A mixed group of musicians – including all of The No Talent Slugs – had stuck around for a late-night jam session. The stage lights had been turned off and the sound boards were being disassembled, but they continued to play an acoustic set under the glow of the security lights.

Bob's piano – he had loaned it to Joe for the night – was being loaded into the back of a truck.

No one had seen Joe – or Sophia – since his set ended.

His last text had been sent at 11:20, soon after he finished. *Need to talk. Where r u?* I had glanced at it while driving and nearly sideswiped a Pontiac. I texted back: *On my way. Plz wait!*

I was too late. Maybe I could catch him at the airport before his plane

335

left.

My phone vibrated in my pocket.

I love you.

Love you too. Send.

I realized I didn't even know which airport he was flying out of. What if they were leaving from O'Hare?

Still waiting on that lingerie.

That would be at least a five hour drive.

Hope it's that thong.

Even if I did make it to Chicago, how far could I go without a boarding pass?

It'll keep till you get back. Send.

Why not now?

What? I scanned the crowd of musicians again, then looked out over the groups in the park.

Where r u? Send.

I couldn't *see* him, but I could *feel* him walking up behind me. The skin on my neck tingled. I closed my eyes, blew out the breath I hadn't realized I was holding, and relaxed back into his waiting arms. Even though we were hidden in the shadows, Joe kissed the upstage side of my neck – away from the remaining crowd.

"About that lingerie," Joe whispered, his lips tickling my ear.

A shout went up as the musicians launched into the chorus of one of Joe's big hits. They started calling for him to join them. "We need to make a quick getaway," Joe said. "These guys will go all night."

I took Joe's hand and we ran through the darkness, down a short pathway to the football field. We didn't stop until we got to the far end of the bleachers, lit only by the moon. Joe pulled me into his arms and kissed me until I was breathless.

"I started to worry when I couldn't find you after the show," Joe said when we came up for air. "You know, cell phones only work when you answer them."

"So I've been told. Miss Irene properly scolded me. As did Big George."

"I knew I'd win them over eventually."

"Oh, Joe! When Sophia made that announcement, I . . . ." I dropped my head onto Joe's chest and choked back tears. Joe held me close and rubbed my back, giving me time to recover. "I didn't think I could go through that again."

"Yes, well, apparently Gary and Sophia had been comparing notes. And Sophia has a flair for the dramatic." Joe eased me back and looked me in the eyes. "Julie, I would never leave you without saying goodbye. I didn't mean to do it then, and I wouldn't – couldn't – do it now. When I think about what Gary did . . . and all those years you thought I . . . . You must have hated me!"

Joe looked out over the football field and swallowed hard. His features softened and his shoulders relaxed as his anger at Gary melted into sadness. I turned his face back to me and kissed him gently.

"I could never hate you, Joe Davenport. I love you! I knew there had to be an explanation." While I wanted to blame this whole mess on Gary, I knew Joe and I both shared some responsibility as well. "I tried to find you, but . . . ." I shook my head, "I didn't want to hold you back."

"Hmmm, that wasn't your decision to make, now was it?" Joe arched one eyebrow and grinned at me as he repeated my earlier admonition back to me. "Promise me we'll make those kind of decisions together from now on."

"After New York?"

"*Before* New York. Sophia forgot that I can read a contract, too. I don't have to be there until Wednesday. I was hoping you would . . . that is, if you want to . . . ."

"I want to! I want *you*, Joe Davenport. You're all I've ever wanted."

"Just keep that in mind during sound checks, and the waiting. And the . . . did I mention the waiting? Backstage isn't always the most exciting place to be, but I promise I'll make it up to you."

"I'm looking forward to that. I've waited this long for you, I can wait a little longer. As long as it isn't another 25 years."

"Promise."

Over in the park, the band was playing "Brown Eyed Girl." Joe and I sank down onto the green grass behind the stadium, and were just about to *sha la la - la la dee dah*, when we found ourselves caught in the bright beam of a flashlight wielded by PGHS football coach Butch Frieh.

"All right kids, let's move it along. Oh fer Pete's sake! Julie Robberson?" A lot had changed since I was in Coach's PE class – heck, a lot had changed in the last two months – but I still had a healthy respect for authority figures. Especially if that authority figure could – at least at one time – make me run wind sprints. Joe and I stood there as awkwardly as any two guilty high school students while Coach looked us over, frowning and shaking his head.

"Hmph. I've been running gasser drills all night, roustin' a bunch a' middle-aged lotharios, tryin' ta' live out some adolescent fantasy behind the bleachers." Then he scowled at Joe and winked at me, much like he had done when he "didn't" find Vanessa and me putting a for sale sign in front of the high school at the end of our senior year.

"Keep an eye out for troublemakers, will ya? I gotta make a swing by the baseball field. Dunno what genius decided to use baseball as a metaphor for sex, but I'd like ta' . . . ." Coach headed off across the field, muttering under his breath. "Whatever happened to parkin' on a dirt road? Whatever happened to watchin' submarine races?"

As soon as Coach was out of our sight, Joe pulled me close again and began to sing playfully. This time I recognized a line from "Zanzibar" about stealing second base if the girl would give the sign.

"You know, Billy Joel is my *second* favorite piano man," I said, kissing that spot on his neck, just below his ear.

"Dare I ask who is your favorite?"

"Why don't we go back to my place, and I'll show you." I hooked a finger in the waistband of his jeans, just above his zipper, and tugged him with me as I backed down the path toward the parking lot.

Joe stopped abruptly.

"Is this going to involve that red thong?" he asked.

"Yes. Yes it is."

"Are you trying to seduce me?"

"Yes. Yes I am."

"Then why are we standing around here talking?" Joe took my hand and we hurried to his truck. The park had finally cleared out. The only music we heard was the chirping of crickets. Joe opened the passenger-side door of his truck for me, and I slid to the center of the seat. I snuggled next to him as we drove away, leaving my car alone in the parking lot.

When we got back to my apartment, one of the garage doors was open. The Scout sat inside, still bathed in moonlight. But now the sidecar sat next to her – Miss Irene and Big George's way of welcoming Joe to the family. How did they know so quickly, I wondered. Or, had they known all along?

Before we headed upstairs, I convinced Joe to leave our cell phones in the truck.

"There've been quite enough interruptions for one night, Joe Davenport. I'm not letting you get away, and I'm not letting anyone else come between us, either!"

"Hmmm, I think I like this 'take charge' attitude you've developed," Joe said, flashing his rock-star, half-grin.

I took the statue hiding the spare key into the apartment with us, and locked the door. Turns out I didn't even need the red thong to convince Joe that we had waited long enough to make love. After a very enthusiastic and satisfying reunion, we lay spooned together on my bed, watching the stars outside my window twinkle.

"It took millions of years for the light from those stars to get here," I said, drowsy and content.

"I know how they feel." Joe's hand slipped over my hip, and he began gently stroking the inside of my thigh.

"Was it worth the wait?" I rolled over to face him, bringing my leg up and around his, pulling our hips together.

"Do I need to prove it to you again?" he asked, gently rolling me over onto my back, his kisses trailing down my neck and heading south.

"Yes. Yes you do." And we went back to making up for lost time.

As the sun was beginning to rise, I heard Big George singing.

Irene, good night

Irene, good night

Good night, Irene

Good night, Irene

Joe joined quietly, his tenor husky with sleep.

I'll see you in my dreams.

Scout's Honor

Made in the USA
Middletown, DE
06 April 2018